The Path to Dark Love

Karina Vega

Karina Vega

Book Cover by [AI designed and generated by Karina Vega]

To Doru,

I love you more than words can explain.

Thank you for pushing me into writing my thoughts, and thank you for teaching me the depth a man can love a woman.

Author Note

Hello dear reader,

Welcome to my universe.

I write dark romance in Australian English, exploring intense emotional bonds, moral ambiguity, and love that is obsessive, consuming, and unapologetically extreme. My stories are not for the faint of heart, and this book is no exception.

The Path to Dark Love is written using dual points of view for key scenes. This is intentional. Certain moments are presented through both Angela's and Dominic's perspectives to allow you deeper access to their inner worlds, emotional turmoil, and the unspoken motivations behind their choices. Reading the same event through both lenses is designed to offer contrast, tension, and clarity rather than repetition.

Please be mindful of your personal boundaries before continuing. This book contains content that may be distressing for some readers, including:

- Graphic violence and torture (detailed descriptions)

- Explicit sexual content and mature language

- Obsessive, possessive behaviour and dark relationship dynamics

- Physical and psychological abuse (not committed by the MMC)
- Underage sexual assault (off-page)
- Eating disorders and disordered eating behaviours
- Depression and self-destructive thought patterns
- Suicidal ideation and attempts (off-page)
- Kidnapping, restraint, and non-consensual situations (contextual, not sexual)

Your mental health matters. If any of these topics are triggering for you, I encourage you to proceed with care or step away if needed.

This book is intended for **18+ readers only**.

The Path to Dark Love is part of a series, but it can also be enjoyed as a standalone as its the first book in the series.

If you would like to stay connected, visit www.karinavega.com

From my heart to yours,

Karina V.

Blurbs

Angela:

One more day.

One more fight with the person in the mirror.

I see them come and go — beautiful, elegant, exquisite women — and then there is me. No matter what I do, no matter how hard I try, the woman staring back at me is never good enough.

It's hard to accept that, regardless of how much I try to improve.

Accepting the person in the mirror is the hardest battle in front of me.

Wanting more feels pointless — catastrophically stupid, even.

Then I met a man.

Not a boy. Not a guy.

A man.

When I looked into his ocean-blue eyes, it was as if two souls found each other in the midst of millions of souls, recognised one another, and bonded for eternity.

There is an unimaginable pull towards him, unlike anything I have ever felt before.

It drags at me relentlessly, ignoring logic, fear, and every internal battle I fight to stay in control.

But there is something there.

I can't quite name it, but I feel it — an edge to him. A darkness just beneath the surface.

And even so...

I don't think I can let go.

Dominic:

How can I ever be enough when I am always too much.

Too intense. Too honest. Too direct.

How can I be enough when my own parents did not want me.

Then I met an angel, and somehow, somewhere in this universe, everything went quiet.

With her, there is only silence.

All the noise in my head — every racing thought, every brutal edge — is silenced in an instant.

I know my life and my actions make me unworthy of this woman.

But none of that matters now, because she is mine.

I knew it the moment I saw her.

Soon, she will know it as well.

I will not stop until she gives herself to me willingly.

Angela is everything I have ever wanted and more. Her strength. Her vulnerability. Her fire.

All of it completes me in ways I never thought possible.

Maybe one day she will learn to love my darkness too.

But until that day, I will make her love me more than reality itself.

Contents

1. Dominic 1
2. Angela 14
3. Dominic 23
4. Angela 34
5. Dominic 43
6. Dominic 52
7. Angela 59
8. Dominic 69
9. Angela 85
10. Dominic 101
11. Angela 123
12. Dominic 142
13. Angela 164
14. Dominic 186
15. Angela 207

16. Dominic 234
17. Angela 261
18. Dominic 281
19. Angela 305
20. Dominic 327
21. Angela 357
Epilogue Angela 380
Epilogue Dominic 396
Afterword 397
Background story 399
Also by 401
Stay Connected 429

Chapter One

Dominic

It's one of those days where you start questioning all your decisions, not just for the day but for the past month, maybe even the entire year. We just finished a "session," and instead of breaking, the idiot decided to keep his mouth shut for two solid hours. What the hell is wrong with these people? I mean, if we captured you and started torturing you, it isn't rocket science. You talk. You tell us what we want to know. Who in their right mind thinks it's a good idea to hold out just to piss me off, knowing full well it was going to end with their death anyway?

Seriously, who takes that route? Like I said, absolute idiots.

Now I'm in the car, on my way to Barrow, and all I can think about is how I want to bring the bastard back to life just so I can kill him again. But slower this time, much slower, for wasting my precious time. I almost feel like drafting an email, a critical email, to these idiots, outlining some basic ground rules for torture. You know, just common sense stuff. That thought actually makes me chuckle, and I can feel the darkness in my mind easing a little. Hell, it might even be funny. Imagine sending that out: a *Guide to Torture Etiquette* for all the mafias.

"*Dear idiots,*

Please be so kind as to stop wasting my time when I have you in for "questioning".

You are already mine to do as I please, so you could save yourself some pain and me some time by spilling your guts and answering my questions quickly.

It is entirely up to you if you need me to be kind/not so kind/mental on your ass.

See you soon,

Dominic."

"Right! What is it this time? Package, letter, something else?" Elijah said with a straight face. He is my boss and like a father to me. Elijah's presence commands attention the moment you see him. His features are chiseled, giving him an air of stoic elegance. His eyes seem to hold untold depths of wisdom and experience, their mere existence enough to send a shiver down your spine.

An undeniable aura of intimidation surrounds him, an unspoken power that seems to emanate from his very being. Even without uttering a word, Elijah exudes a quiet confidence that demands respect. His closed eyes, rather than hindering his perception, seem to heighten his awareness as if he sees more with them shut than most do with their eyes wide open. *Did he know I made another joke with his eyes closed?*

"Email," I replied with one word. It might be a storm in my mind, but outside, I always joke. Elijah enjoys my company because I am quieter about the negative, and when I do speak, it's funny most of the time, or at least I think it's funny. In my 12 years working for him, I have never seen Elijah laughing out loud, he seems incapable of emotions like the rest of us. Yet, despite his apparent emotional detachment, Elijah has a depth that belies his stoic exterior. His silence speaks volumes, each unspoken word pregnant with meaning. It is as if he exists on a plane beyond the reach of mortal emotions, his very presence a reminder of the transient nature of human feeling.

"I just think they're idiots", I say with amusement on my lips. "How stupid can someone be to make us skin him alive? What the fuck is wrong with these idiots? We've already got him. Where did Bogdan hire this person? How can someone be this stupid?"

"Ah! That's a lot of questions for little result". Elijah says, not even bothering to open his eyes to acknowledge the storm of annoyance in me, signalling the discussion is over.

I get it, I do! There is nothing I would not do for Elijah and my brothers, but if I were captured, I'd annoy my captors with my jokes until they killed me faster.

Loyalty and respect! Under Elijah's guidance, I have become who I am today. Throughout our journey together, he's consistently shown me unwavering loyalty and treated me with the utmost respect. I would give my life for him and my brothers without a second hesitation. For Elijah, we are not merely dismissed as insignificant beings, soldiers that can be disposed of and replaced at any moment. Instead, he embraces us as his own, nurturing us and training us to become the best version of ourselves.

Loyalty and respect, till death!

I stare out of the tinted window of our SUV as we stop at the light, and next to us, a little green Volkswagen Beetle pulls up. It’s blasting “Can’t Stop the Feeling!” loud enough to rattle the frame, and inside, there's a girl singing completely off-key, dancing like her life depends on it. *What the actual fuck?*

And just like that, I forget how to breathe.

I sit there, stunned, staring at this ugly-ass green Beetle, covered in ugly-ass purple flowers, blasting an ugly-ass pop song... and yet inside is an angel who just knocked the wind out of me. My mind goes dead quiet. Completely silent.

What the hell just happened?

"Do you want to follow her?" Elijah's voice cuts through the silence. I didn't even notice him open his eyes. Silence. Complete and utter silence.

"Right," he says knowingly, as if fully aware that my mind has short-circuited and I've forgotten how to breathe, let alone communicate.

"Vasile, follow the Beetle with the terrible music," Elijah instructs our driver, his tone as calm as ever. "And please, let's not scare the poor girl. We're just observing, right, Dominic?"

I can't respond. I've lost all connection to reality, to my surroundings, everything is consumed by the girl and her ugly car. So I just nod, barely acknowledging his words, signalling I won't engage.

She stopped in front of a flower shop with green and purple flowers in its design and logo. Right, that makes more sense now, maybe the girl doesn't have ugly-as-fuck taste in things, maybe her boss is a moron with zero taste, and she is suffering in silence like me. *Yes, I'll accept this option as I look at my angel.*

I reach for the car door, and the air inside shifts immediately. I can feel it, the tension, the silent disapproval from Elijah. His deep voice slices through the haze in my mind like a whip. "I think we should leave the girl alone. She's not from our world, Dominic. She wouldn't understand what we do."

His words hit me hard, cutting through the intensity of my desire and making me feel as though my very will to live has been stripped away. I can't breathe. I need to see her, to talk to her, even if just for a moment.

"Yes, boss," I manage to say, my voice strained, fighting the desperation in my chest. "But I was thinking... the Barrow could use some more flowers to brighten up the place."

The moment the words leave my mouth, I realise how utterly ridiculous I sound. *Flowers? Really?* It's the stupidest thing I've ever said. But before my mind can scramble to recover with a joke or something to defuse the awkwardness, my body moves on instinct, drawn to her like a magnet. I'm out of the car, pulled by an invisible force, every fibre of my being screams to get to that flower shop, to get to her.

The next thing I realise is that I am in the shop, not even knowing if I closed the car door with the speed I ran out of there, and this smell of green things and flowers hits me. My next hit is an overwhelming variety of colours and textures, like what the fuck, it's like information overload!

"Hi, can I help you with anything?" An woman in her mid-40s smiles at me from behind the counter. Her face radiates calmness, and now that I take her in she's an older version of my angel.

"Thank you. I'm browsing for a bit and will let you know." My sentence is cut short as my angel comes in from the back room, shivering, and an immense urge to go and comfort her overwhelms me. What the actual fuck! *Since when is it "MY" angel and for me to "COMFORT" someone?* What the actual fuck is happening to my mind and body? Less than 30 minutes ago, I was skinning someone alive, and now I feel like I can't breathe because of *MY angel.* I think I am losing my mind. *I must be losing my mind.* Am I imagining things? I turn and look at the SUV where Elijah is, and I take comfort in knowing that this is real, even if my mind is in absolute panic and I feel overwhelmed by the floods of emotions.

"The delivery went well, mum. They loved the colour scheme I used this week, and they asked if I could make an arrangement for his home and deliver it later today." *What the fuck? Who is he that is about to die, and where is his home so I can burn it down?* I am pretending to look at some ugly, hell-long flowers that I think I could use as a whip if I am short on other torture tools while listening to their discussion. This man will die today, and his home will be in ashes by tomorrow morning. *How dare he ask for my angel to deliver flowers to his home?*

"I'm sure he loved the arrangement last time you delivered" the older lady says. "Did he give you a budget or theme?"

"Not really. He said to just make something that I am happy with."

Fuck, that is a good line! "Excuse me, could you help me, please?" I turn and make a point to look at my angel so I don't end up speaking to the older lady. The moment our eyes connect, my mind goes silent again. *Silence!*

My angel has this otherworldly grace, something I can't quite put into words. When she's around, it's like everything slows down, like the whole world holds its breath. Just being around her, there's this calm that seems to pull everything in, making the world go quiet.

Her features, sculpted as if by divine hands, exude an otherworldly beauty that could captivate anyone and bring any man to his knees. Even her movements are graceful, as every gesture has a purpose, meant to enchant me. Her words, spoken with a voice like the gentle whisper of the wind, penetrate my mind and soul as if they've found their home there.

Even without wings, there's something about her that feels... angelic, like she's a bright light cutting through the shadows in my life. It's like she was made to fit into a part of me I didn't even know was empty. But then it hits me Elijah was right. *She wouldn't understand.* She's too pure for someone like me.

"How can I help you?" She looks straight into my eyes, and I realise that her eyes are almost black, and I can feel my body being pulled by hers. I instinctively think I might hurt her or taint her with my darkness if I get too close. When she smiles, I'm scared I'll jump on her and pound, but then I hear my phone ping and know Elijah just texted me to leave. *Just this one time!* Fuck me I deserve this one time to be this close to an angel! *Just once!*

"Angela, I will arrange these flowers outside if you need me." The older woman looked at me while speaking to my angel. *How unusual.*

Angela, what a name.

"I am not the best with flowers, so I will need all your assistance and guidance with this," I say, returning her smile. She looks taken aback but quickly recovers and smiles again, keeping her tone friendly but professional. She continues, "I noticed you looking at Gladiolus. Would you like something along those lines?" The mere thought of it makes me laugh inside, imagining whipping someone to death with a fucking long flower. My brothers would forever laugh at me.

"Not quite, but thank you for noticing. I am a blank canvas, feel free to suggest anything that comes to mind." I say, trying fucking hard to sound casual like her. At least I am speaking, the words are fucking coming out. I look over my shoulder, and the old lady is arranges some flowers outside. The next moment, Elijah rolls down his window, and she looks at him and smiles. His face is blank as usual, but his eyes. *What was that?* It disappeared as fast as it was there, and he rolled the window back, giving him his much-loved privacy.

"Can you give me some information about who these flowers might be for? Or a type of flower that she likes or that you like? Or any information?" I am pulled back to Angela as if she were my gravity. *How is she doing this?* Is she "MY GRAVITY" now? I need to leave! Fuck me, this might truly have been the most stupid thing I've ever done in my life!

I think of the only fucking flower I actually know to name as I take my phone out of my pocket, trying to seem calm and collected. "I like roses." Gladiolus, what a shit name for a shit flower. Maybe we should track down who named this awful flower and whip them with it.

"Great! Any preference with the colour?"

"What flowers do you like?" I realise I am saying it out loud as I see her surprised face. "If it is something that you can share, of course."

She takes a deep breath and cleanses her hands on the apron, and that's when I realise she is nervous. *Interesting!* I might be making a fucking life mistake here, but at least I am not alone in it. She is nervous! She is with me in this fucked up situation. *I got you, my angel!*

"I love these yellow and orange roses. They are named Monica, the colour is a bit strange for some, if I am honest, but what is amazing about this rose is its perfume," she says with a shy smile, picking up some ugly-looking roses and shoving them in my face to smell.

"I like it! How many should we put in an arrangement if I am trying to impress someone?" I say, lifting the corner of my mouth with a seductive smile. As she starts to blush, I realise she picked up on my vibe, and I am most definitely not the only one in this situation.

"Perhaps around 30. How about I start the arrangement and see how we go? Can you let me know a budget that I can't exceed?" she says with a melodic voice, carefully avoiding eye contact. Her voice, her presence, her everything, her entire being is messing with my head. As I glance down and notice her more than generous breasts, I suddenly feel like a teenager again, getting hard at the speed of light.

Alright! Alright! Calm the fuck down, boy, we might scare her, and we might lose our angel. The thought takes me by surprise because until this moment, I was sure I wouldn't see this girl again, and I am just indulging in a bit of harmless fun.

"No limit, please have fun with it and make it as beautiful as you can," I say with a full smile on my face. It might be blood money, but it is still money, and she does not need to know it's blood money. I am paying with a card, for fuck's sake, so there is most definitely no traces of blood. Let her have fun with it. I started reading the text from Elijah and almost burst out laughing.

Elijah

Hey, Romeo. Make sure you keep your cool and be discreet about asking for her number. All the death threats flooding your mind, calm them the fuck down. She is not yours yet; don't scare her if you are into her. Make sure you are into her before you do something stupid.

I quickly type a reply to mess with him a little. Shit, this is the most he's spoken to me in one go in a very long time. This might be serious, after all.

Dominic

I need Hunter to come with me later to deliver an "arrangement" to some fucker that thinks my angel needs to do home delivery.

Elijah

My angel?

Well, shit!

Dominic, don't start something that can only end one way.

Get back in the car.

Dominic

She is making an arrangement for me, and then we will leave and not come back. I will be there in a few minutes.

I look again at the car and can feel his presence and forceful gaze. I notice the older woman is still outside, and then I look at the car again, and I can feel that the gaze is not on me but on her.

I turn to look at Angela, memorising every movement of her beautiful body. The way her delicate hands cradle the flowers, the precise concentration in her eyes, and the deliberate way she avoids looking at me all captivates me. The silence between us grows heavy, thick with unspoken tension. She finally breaks it, her voice curious yet professional, attempting to make small talk.

"Do you work around here? I've never seen you before... or am I mistaken?" She asks, her eyes flickering up for just a moment before quickly returning to the flowers in her hands.

"No, I can't recall being in this shop before. It is a cute place you have here. Is it yours?" I say, patting myself on the back for sounding all kind and professional.

"It's my mum's shop," she says, her voice soft but steady. "The lady outside. I just help with deliveries and sometimes in the shop. I'm still studying, and this helps with the bills."

Before I can fully process her words, an unfamiliar feeling stirs deep inside me. It's like a dormant force has awoken, an instinctual need to unravel every mystery that surrounds her. I crave to know more, to understand everything that makes her who she is. And more than that, a fierce urge rises within me, a need to protect her, to shelter her with strength so relentless it could rival a thousand tsunamis.

"What do you study? If you don't mind telling me." I play the innocent as I pretend to be on my phone.

"Criminal law. I absolutely love it. The psychology of it fascinates me, especially the cause-and-effect element." I feel sucker punched! *Fuck me!* Out of all the women in the world and all the professions in the fucking world, she fucking had to be into criminal law? Wait, she did not say she loves it because of putting bad guys away, she said she loved the psychology of it. *What the fuck does that mean?*

"Interesting," I say with a smile. "What made you study this?" I look at the car and can feel Elijah's fury coming to life and radiating toward me. *I'm fucked!*

"I think we are all different in our own way. I believe, as I said, in the cause-and-effect element of life. Also, I take a lot of comfort in law, knowing where the limit is. What do you think?" She gives me the biggest smile I have ever received in my entire life, and the response is clear as I look into her eyes. "Beautiful!" She blushes a deep shade of red and looks away for a moment, breaking our connection. *Silence! Just fucking silence!*

"Do you need a vase, or are you happy to take them as is?" it's then that I look at the flowers and notice they are actually not that bad. My brothers would still laugh their asses off to see me with flowers, but they are actually nice, except for the ugly-as-fuck colour.

"I think I will take the vase as well, thank you," I say, trying to figure out how to pass the flowers to her without coming across as a creepy imbecile. Maybe I should email myself a highly important email on how not to be a creepy imbecile because, clearly, I might need some strong pointers.

"I'm just going to the back to clean up the fridge, Angela. Could you please come and help me once you are done with the gentlemen?" the old lady says as she walks past me toward the back.

"Sure, Mum, I am almost done. It comes to $480, thank you. Would that be card or cash today?" my angel says, giving me a very cold and professional smile. I don't care for it! I want the smile with the blush and the melody of her symphonic warm voice.

Blood money! Blood money! She is an angel, and you are touching her with your blood money.

What the fuck?! Is that my conscience? I thought I killed that fucker long ago, why would my insides scream at me that my money is bloody? *Is a fucking card!* There is no fucking blood on the card! I don't care for this conscience or this fucking voice in my head. *She is mine now! My angel! My fucking angel!* Ping, I hear my phone go off.

Elijah

She is not yours! Calm down, Dominic.

I hate how well he knows to read me. *She is mine!* She and he just don't know it yet!

"Card, thank you."

"Do you have one of those little cards to write a message?"

"Yes, of course. They are behind you. Please take whatever you like, it's on the house." She says with a shy smile again, now that her mum is out of sight. *Oh! So the old lady is the problem?* She can be removed very easily. Death by flowers! I almost burst into laughter at that thought! Where was that fucking long and awful flower again?

"That won't be necessary. Please charge me $600 and include a card as well. No need to wait while I think of something to write. Feel free to join your mum. Thank you, Angela." The moment her name leaves my mouth, she physically recoils as if I'd struck her. My voice had been calm, professional, hadn't it? *Did I mess it up that fast?*

I search her eyes, looking for the truth, and that's when I notice it, a faint blush creeping down her neck. *She likes me back.* I can sense it now, simmering just beneath the surface. The tension breaks as she lets out a soft laugh, an angelic sound that feels like it shouldn't even exist in this world. That sound, combined with her graceful movements, completely washes over me, leaving my body numb in the best possible way.

Elijah

Get in the car. I can feel you are making bad decisions by the second.

"Thank you again, Angela. You were very helpful," I say with a smile on my face.

"Not a problem at all! See you next time," she says, turning and walking toward the back door, giving me a perfect view of her ass. My brain short-circuits instantly. Okay, she's not allowed to wear clothes. *Wait, what? That doesn't even make sense!* In a matter of seconds, my thoughts spiral into chaos at the sight of her.

Oh, fuck! I want to bite that ass, mark it all over until she can't sit for days. I want to trail my mouth over her legs, her ass, bite, lick, suck, and claim her until she smells and tastes like me. What is it about this woman that makes me lose my mind without her even trying? I've never been on my knees for anyone, yet here I am, undone. *Calm down, Dominic. Calm the hell down.* If Elijah steps out of the car, all hell will break loose, and you won't get the girl.

No! Not a girl. She is not a girl. She is an angel.

What should I put on the fucking card? What should I say and not sound like an idiot? Fuck! Perhaps the silence that she makes in my mind may not be the best because I cannot write two sentences while I am looking at the card. *I'll just settle on honesty when all else fades away.*

"Thank you for existing, Angela."

Chapter Two

Angela

"I'm just going to the back to clean up the fridge, Angela. Could you please come and help me once you are done with the gentlemen?" Mum says as she passes us by.

"Sure, Mum, I am almost done. It comes to $480 today. Thank you. Would that be card or cash today?" I say, giving him a courteous and professional smile.

"Card, thank you. Do you have one of those little cards to write a message?"

"Yes, of course. The cards are right behind you. Please take whichever you like, it's on the house," I say, smiling widely, desperately trying to seem calm while internally freaking out now that Mum's out of sight. This is my chance to turn on the charm. God, I hope what I'm putting out is sexy vibes and not some weird "*stay away from me*" vibe. Who am I kidding? Mum always calls me the "*serial killer of hot vibes.*" I bet this hot-as-hell, mesmerising, mysterious man is going to walk out of here thinking I'm a total moron who can't handle a simple smile. I mean, I did get all hot and bothered, but he doesn't need to know that!

"That won't be necessary. Please charge me $600 and include a card as well. No need to wait while I figure out what to write. Feel free to join your mum. Thank you, Angela." Oh, my God. Did I just hear him say my name like that? It wasn't just a name, it felt like a silent prayer, spoken with so much depth it nearly knocked the breath out of me. My legs almost gave out beneath me. My heart races, my body reacts in ways I can't even describe, and the heat between my thighs betrays me. The sudden realisation makes me laugh, all these inappropriate thoughts flooding my mind while I stand there mortified. Without thinking, I turn and bolt toward the fridge, my cheeks burning, heart pounding, wondering what the hell just happened.

"What the fuck is wrong with me?" I mumble to myself, leaning against the fridge door, closing my eyes, and sinking onto a bucket conveniently placed to commemorate my misery apparently.

"I don't know, darling. Do you mean besides not getting any for months?" Mum's voice comes from behind, her attempt at humour poorly masking her amusement. "Or how you flawlessly self-sabotage whenever a nice man shows up?"

"Mum, please don't. If you laugh at me again, I swear I'll cry." I try to hold it together but end up blurting out everything. "Did you see him? My eyes were practically melting. Did you see that body? Those broad shoulders? Oh my goodness, his eyes! I nearly fainted when I walked in and saw him!" My words spill out, but my mind is still swimming in inappropriate thoughts.

I open my eyes to find Mum staring at the cameras with a strange intensity, her expression completely different from her usual warmth. Her eyes hold something unsettling. *What happened?* I think, alarmed by the shift in her demeanour. The moment she notices me watching her, her face softens, and she becomes the sweet, calm version of herself again.

"What happened?" I ask, unable to hide the concern in my voice. "Is something wrong?"

"No! No! Everything is fine. He just left the shop. It's safe for us to come out of the fridge now." Mum's voice is calm, but the sudden tightness in my chest tells me something's off. Before I can question it, she turns to me with a small smile. "My darling, before we head out, I just have to ask... did you like him?"

"Noooo, what? Where's this coming from?" I try to sound casual, but the panic rises in my throat. "I'm so busy with Uni and the bar exam prep, not to mention the mock trial that's already driving me insane. I was actually going to ask you for a few days off just to focus on my studies. I'm absolutely and utterly not interested," I say, pushing out every word with as much fake conviction as I can manage, despite my mind being flooded with thoughts of him and regretting my now-wet underwear. "I sounded like a complete idiot the entire time, babbling on about yellow and orange roses, shoving flowers in his face. What kind of lunatic did you raise, seriously, Mum?" I exaggerate my facial expressions, throwing my hands up in mock exasperation. "Honestly, I blame you! Why didn't you teach me how to be sexy and flirty, or literally anything other than this awkward mess?"

"Ah, so you want to be something else, do you?" Mum's face shifts into a look of pure amusement, confident, knowing. "Come with me, you serial killer of hot vibes." She motions me out of the fridge with a teasing grin, and I groan, knowing she's about to make me face whatever ridiculous lesson she has up her sleeve.

We walk together out of the fridge. I hate that fridge, and if Mum asks me to finish cleaning it today, I'll cry and call Dad to tell her off. I am allowed to self-pity and cry and feel sorry for myself. I did not get any in months, and I can't even fucking remember the last time I orgasmed as, apparently, it is too much to ask for guys to actually fucking please a woman. Nowadays, they shove their dicks in you a few times and then they're out, looking at you with those damn puppy-dog eyes, like you enjoyed it. *No, I didn't fucking like it!* How fucking hard is it to learn about a woman's anatomy and her erogenous zones? If you ask one of these fuckers about cars, they will eat your ears away with the most boring shit that ever existed under the sun, but to put in the effort to learn how to please a woman, nope, nothing, never!

The moment I look at the counter, I notice the vase with the flowers is still there. With trembling hands, I trace the delicate lines of the intricate design, marvelling at the craftsmanship and thoughtfulness behind each detail as if it was made by different hands and not my own. In this moment, time seemed to stand still as I drank in the beauty of the unexpected gesture, and I can feel my heart overflowing with gratitude and wonder.

"Why?" the word is barely a whisper as I fight with all I have not to cry. Why would this man do this?

"Open the card, Angela. Read his reason why he left the flowers behind." Mum says with a calmness I don't possess.

"Thank you for existing, Angela."

My knees feel weak like they might give out beneath me as if every part of me is suddenly alight with warmth and recognition. It's more than just gratitude it's a deep, overwhelming sensation that floods my body with every beat of my heart. Right now, words feel inadequate to express how much this simple gesture means to me. I'm completely enveloped in its significance, realising how something so small can have such a profound impact. It's humbling, a reminder of the power of kindness and how it can touch someone's life in a way that leaves a mark forever.

"What is happening? Am I imagining this?" I look at Mum for reassurance, to confirm I am not dreaming and making her my anchor to reality.

"Yes, that absolutely amazing and beautiful man left the absolutely amazing arrangement for you. How sweet and kind is that?" Mum says with a kind word and a smile on her face. I am in my own bubble of gratitude, and it takes me a second to realise Mum's smile did not reach her eyes.

"Are you okay with this?" I am starting to come back to reality. What if this guy is just like Jake, and this is going to go very badly, very fast for me?

"Why wouldn't I be?" my mum says, her tone peaceful and filled with warmth. "Young love is always sweet and lovely. You should definitely enjoy your life. I raised a beautiful, strong, and intelligent woman who, let's face it, couldn't flirt to save her life. But you don't need to, my darling. The right man would chase you forever until he wins your heart. If it's not this guy, someone else will be. Never sell yourself short, know your value, and always know your worth. Clearly, this guy didn't hesitate for a second to find you and pull off this silly, sweet gesture just to get your attention."

I smile through my tears as she continues, "Tell you what? Let's mess with Jake and then dump their contract. How about we create a ridiculous $1,000 arrangement, something crazy and over-the-top for his sorry ass. We'll deliver it together, then you can keep the money, take those weeks off, and focus on your exams. Sound good?"

I can't hold it in any longer. I burst into tears and wrap my arms around her. Each sob is a flood of pent-up emotions: frustration, longing, and relief, all spilling out at once. In her embrace, I find the comfort and strength I've been craving. Her presence, as always, is a refuge of unconditional love, guiding me through my hardest moments and giving me the space to let go of everything I've been holding inside.

"Absolutely! Please tell me we can drop them off tonight?" I give her my best puppy eyes, hoping with everything in me that she'll say yes, that we'll do it right away.

She looks at me, her face softening. "Yes, my darling! You are the most precious thing in my life. I should've stopped this the moment you told me he was making you uncomfortable. I honestly thought it was just harmless flirting and that maybe you weren't catching on. But if you're feeling repulsed by him and his comments, then this ends now."

Her warm smile reaches her eyes and settles in my heart.

For the next few hours, we hustle through all the online orders, filling up both our delivery van and the backup car. The massive, ridiculous arrangement for Jake takes up most of the space, but we're on the road soon enough, belting out our favourite songs and laughing at the absurdity of the night. It feels good, light, even until Jake's mansion comes into view, and a wave of nausea hits me hard.

I hate everything about this man the way he moves, the way he talks, even the way he stands there like he owns the world. There's just something about him that makes my skin crawl. To most people, he's the picture-perfect catch: a successful lawyer, partner at his firm, probably raking in seven figures a year, with a flawless face, body, and a mansion straight out of a magazine. What more could a woman ask for, right? Well, this woman? I dry heave every time he's near. His "beauty" makes me sick, and his voice? It's like nails on a chalkboard. I pity any poor soul who ends up with a sorry piece of shit like him.

"You don't need to say anything. Not even hello. Clearly, he saw you earlier today." Mum says looking intensely at me, assessing the correct level of panic I am in.

"Is ok, Mum, it's not like he will try something while you are here."

"Angela Josephine Puscasu! I am your mother, and I gave birth to you. If anyone even thinks of coming after you, they'll face my full fury!" Mum's voice is fierce, but then, just as quickly, she bursts into laughter. Something's off. She's laughing hard, but her eyes... they missed the memo to join in on the joke. Instead, they burn with a silent rage. All this laughter is for my benefit, I know. She's trying to keep me calm, but the intensity radiating off her is impossible to miss.

We pull up to Jake's mansion and step out of the car at the same time. As I approach the towering doors, a cold wave of unease washes over me, curling its icy fingers around my chest. What kind of miseries hide behind these lavish walls? What twisted secrets are masked by all this luxury? With each hesitant step toward the entrance, my heart races faster, and I brace myself for the inevitable moment of facing Jake again.

We ring the bell since, for once, the butler hasn't magically appear to open the door. From inside, we can hear Jake shouting that he's on his way. Mum and I are both hauling this massive, hideous arrangement because the beauty in Jake's eyes is size, not design. To him, $1000 equals big, and that's all that matters.

The moment the door swings open, I feel like I've just detached from reality, as if my body is floating into some parallel universe. Because this, *this could not possibly be happening.* The entrance hall is dimly lit by smokeless candles, and there's this weird smell in the air that I can't quite place. To top it all off, John Legend's "All of Me" is blaring in the background, and I'm mentally screaming at full volume. *This cannot be happening.* And then I see Jake, shirtless, wearing only grey sweatpants that hang so low it's criminal. Very little is left to the imagination, especially with the raging hard-on he's practically pointing at us.

"Good evening, Jake," Mum says in a perfectly professional tone as if this is just another day at the office. "Where would you like us to place the arrangement?" I'm speechless, standing there like an idiot, completely floored by the fact that my mum is still managing to form coherent sentences.

"Monica! What a pleasant surprise. I wasn't expecting you. Are you staying for dinner?" Jake says, completely unfazed by his indecency.

Dinner? I'd rather eat dog shit than sit through a meal with him, even at a Michelin-star restaurant.

"How kind of you to offer. Such a kind *boy*, as usual." My mum's condescending tone drips with icy sweetness, the word *boy* landing like a slap. "Unfortunately, we'll have to decline. We're extremely busy moving forward. In fact, that brings me to an important point about our services." Her voice remains calm and professional, but I can feel the quiet storm brewing inside her. "We've signed several new contracts, which will require all of our resources for the foreseeable future. Regrettably, we'll need to cut some of our smaller contracts to manage those resources more sustainably. I'll make it official tonight when I email your brother and you, but since I'm here, I wanted to mention it personally."

I feel numb. Blown away by my mum's strength. She's so calm, so composed, yet I can feel her fury burning beneath the surface. It's chilling.

"Is that so?" Jake's tone shifts, condescending and mocking. His eyes narrow, his body language full of hostility. "Monica, I cannot believe how ungrateful and unprofessional you are. You were nothing before we took you on board! Drop us because we're a 'small company'? How *dare* you! We turned over 100 million in revenue last year, and your shiny little shop considers us small. I cleaned up, ordered dinner, and was about to give your daughter the privilege of my time, and now you stand here in my home and drop us as a client?" His voice rises with each word, fury radiating off him. "Get the fuck out! Now!" Jake spits out with venom, his voice trembling slightly. He clearly didn't expect this.

Mum just smiles. That terrifying smile that never reaches her eyes. The kind that sends chills down your spine.

"That will not be a problem. We will just leave the arrangement here on the floor and will invoice you tonight as well," she finishes with another professional smile. "As for your attention to my daughter, please be kind to yourself and pack away that joke of a dick you're pointing around. With that, you can only tickle a woman, not satisfy her, and you'll probably hurt yourself in the process. So, as I said, be kind to yourself."

As we turn to leave, I glance back and notice Jake's face, flushed with a mix of fury and embarrassment, his mouth opening and closing like a fish gasping for air.

Once we are out the gate and driving towards my apartment, I turn around to Mum and say, "I cannot believe that just happened. You were out of this world, amazing! Mum, that tongue of yours!"

"Shhhh, my darling," Mum says softly, her voice unsettlingly calm. "I need a minute to think and calm down. I might turn this car around and skin him alive. Give me until we reach your apartment, please."

I freeze, not from the words themselves but from the eerie calmness with which she delivered them. When I glance over at her, something in her eyes confirms my fear. Something deeper than the cool exterior she projects. *I'm scared!* Scared of Jake retaliating, bad-mouthing us, dragging our business through the mud. Scared of him ruining my reputation as a lawyer before I've even begun. But mostly, I'm terrified of the look in Mum's eyes, the calmness masking a storm, and the weight her words might truly carry.

Chapter Three

Dominic

I step out of the shop, and with every step I take away from her, I can feel my heart sinking deeper into some abyss I didn't even know existed. This unexpected, visceral pain gnaws at the core of my being, leaving me shaken. *What is this?* I ask myself. *What's going on with me?*

My mind and body, particularly the part below my belt, are finally in agreement, both screaming at me to go back to Angela. But the conversation is over. *It's done,* I tell myself. What more can I do? This whole thing is irrational, right? I try to push it aside, thinking maybe the "session" earlier messed with my head. Maybe I'm cracking, and this is my breakdown.

Yes, that has to be it. I discreetly adjust myself so it's not obvious I'm dealing with a raging hard-on and slip into the car. As the silence begins to fade, my mind starts to race again, spinning faster. "*Thank you for existing, Angela.*"

Fucking hell! What would she even think of that? Was it too much? Too strange? Or did it mean something to her?

"Monica is off-limits," Elijah's voice cuts through the air like a blade, cold, deep, and dripping with threat, as I sit next to him in the backseat.

"Monica? Who, the old..." I barely get the words out before Elijah lunges at me, faster and more vicious than I thought humanly possible. His hand clamps around my throat, fingers digging into my Adam's apple like he's ready to tear it out with his bare hands. My instincts scream, my pulse races.

"This is the only time I will repeat myself on the matter." His voice is calm, dangerously quiet just above a whisper. "Monica is absolutely off-limits for everyone," he says, each word deliberate, his eyes locking onto mine with an intensity that sends a chill down my spine. He tightens his grip for emphasis, forcing my airway to constrict. "You do not make a move against her, on her, or even think of her. Monica is absolutely off-limits for everyone." He holds me there for a few agonising seconds, the primal fury in his eyes sending every nerve in my body into overdrive. And then, just as swiftly, he releases me, calm and composed as if nothing had happened.

Oh, fuck. The old lady is doomed! She's caught his eye, and there's no turning back for her now.

"Boss, I didn't mean any disrespect," I manage to rasp, carefully choosing my words, making sure not to say *her* name again. "I understand where I stand now regarding the matter." I tread lightly, knowing another slip-up might be the last mistake I ever make.

"The discussion is over," Elijah responds in a dry, clipped tone before closing his eyes, dismissing me as if nothing had just happened.

"Have a look at your device. I asked Sofia to send you everything she can find on Angela Josephine Puscasu," Elijah's calm, calculative tone slices through the tension in the car like a scalpel.

My breath stops for a second, dread filling my lungs. *This was inevitable.* He had asked me to return to the car a few times, but I stubbornly stayed behind, wanting more time with her. And now Angela is on their radar. *Fucking perfect.* I didn't even get a chance to stalk her in peace, to soak in every detail of her being, and now they already know more than I do about her. Each breath becomes a battle against the rising tide of panic. My instincts scream at me to find a way out of this, to stop her from being consumed by this world, but my desperate, irrational need for Angela pulls me under, and before I realise it, I'm opening the laptop.

The screen lights up, and there it is a detailed dossier on Angela, waiting to unravel her life before my eyes. *Everything.* From the basics like her name, age, and address to her deepest layers, her likes, dislikes, beliefs, and interactions. Every trace of her digital presence, every connection she's ever made, mapped out with chilling precision. Every person in her orbit, every detail of her life, is exposed to me. Sofia never misses anything. In an era where our lives are encoded in data, they have it all on her. There are no secrets left untouched.

"Thank you," I manage to mutter, my voice hollow, lost in the flood of information.

"Be careful," Elijah warns, still in that unnerving calm. "It's all in or nothing. Don't make contact if you're not sure. I don't want to clean up after you." His eyes remain closed, lost in thought or meditation, but the weight of his words sits heavy in the air.

I was surprised Elijah spoke at all. This encounter left both of us unsettled in a way we hadn't experienced before. Something unspoken, something significant had happened, and it wasn't the type of moment where a joke or casual words would fit. It felt almost sacred, fragile in its weight, and we both recognised it. The usual urge to speak or break the tension felt out of place, even vulgar, as if acknowledging it out loud might shatter the gravity of what had just transpired.

The rest of the car ride to the Barrow was enveloped in heavy silence. Elijah didn't say another word, retreating into his usual, unreadable self, and I kept my eyes on the screen in front of me, meticulously studying Angela's information. I memorised her schedule and her habits, trying to piece together a plan. *I needed to know*, to stalk her every move until I could understand what exactly was happening inside me, inside this inexplicable connection we seemed to share. Whatever this was, I couldn't leave it to chance, I needed to know more.

In my world, Elijah's word is law, above anything else, loyalty and respect. If he said I was not to make contact if I was not all in, it meant I would probably be killed at worst or heavily tortured at best if I didn't follow instructions. Given my position in the Unity Bridge Team, I would think it's going to be torture. I just hope they would not go for extremities or, even worse, my dick or my balls, we definitely need those. So, I need to plan my strategy very carefully with Angela and ensure no stone is left unturned.

Nestled amidst a landscape of modernity and innovation, the Barrow stands as a beacon of effortless power, an architectural marvel that embodies the spirit of progress. Rising majestically against the skyline, its sleek glass facade reflects the ever-changing hues of the sky, mirroring the dynamic nature of the industry it represents. As visitors approach, they are greeted by a grand entrance flanked by meticulously manicured gardens that offer a serene oasis amidst the bustling urban landscape. The exterior, adorned with geometric patterns of steel and glass, exudes an aura of sophistication and cutting-edge design.

Upon stepping through the threshold, guests are enveloped in an atmosphere of refined elegance and technological sophistication. The expansive lobby, bathed in natural light streaming through floor-to-ceiling windows, boasts minimalist decor accented with vibrant splashes of colour. A mesmerising art installation in a peculiar shape that art lovers would call a masterpiece sits in a bright red to the side of the lobby. The building hosts 30 levels, of which none are free, and all are owned by Elijah's various business ventures. His Unity Bridge Team is made up of Sofia, Buddy, Hunter, Vasile, Alec, Kirill, Stefan, Alexandra, Liam and I. All floors have different types of businesses and are run by the UBT.

Bogdan was part of our organisation until 3 months ago; then, he thought that the best way to fuck up his life was to take something from Elijah and think he could get away with it. Well, I say fuck up his life, he probably said, "*Best plan of my life*". Regardless he's a dick for breaking his principles, or perhaps he never had them in the first place, and we all lost respect for him; in other words, we will hunt him down until we find the hole he is hiding in. Even rats come out for some sun sometimes, so he will surface one way or another. The facial recognition software will get him.

Today's unfortunate encounter was with one of Bogdan's associates that annoyed the fuck out of me, and in the end, we still got our information. Again, perhaps I should send that email out, these fuckers need to know where they stand. Clearly, common sense is not common, so we need to write it down for some of these people. I chuckle to myself softly.

"You are *not* sending the email, Dominic." *How the fuck does Elijah do that? How can he read minds like that?*

"Hi, flower boy!" Sofia bursts laughing at me as we step out of the elevator. *Great, here we go!*

"Really? That's the best you got?"

"No! No! Actually, I have a few, *lover boy*," she says with a wink and then starts laughing even harder at my disgusted face.

"Fuck you! You evil witch with your shitty attitude and terrifying vibes."

"Oh, I love you too, lover boy!" She can barely breathe from laughing so hard. Fucking Sofia! What does she know, anyway? Probably nothing. In all my time here, I've never seen her with anyone, so either she's got one hell of a vibrator, or she's fooling all of us, pretending to be single. Either way, screw her! No one's dumb enough to mess with Elijah's daughter.

"Play nice," Elijah mutters as he walks into his office, completely unfazed by the chaos.

"Did you find everything you need, lover boy?"

"Did I tell you today, fuck you?!" I fire back.

"Oh, don't be like that, lover boy! You're practically glowing with love," she says, laughing so hard she's nearly doubled over.

"Oh, fuck off! The day will come, witch, when I'll destroy you for this. It'll be sweeter than honey on my tongue."

"Or maybe sweeter than your flower girl's juices on your tongue?" she quips, and at that point, she's bending over, gasping between bouts of hysterical laughter.

Fucking Sofia. I can't even come up with a decent comeback.

Well, that'll have to do for now. I can't hurt Sofia, so I'm getting out of her venomous orbit. I turn around, heading straight for the Security Centre while texting Hunter and Buddy on the way. We still need to go over the data I extracted from Bogdan's associate, but damn it, now that witch mentioned Angela's juices, and my cock went steel hard in seconds. *Fuck me!*

How would she taste? My thoughts are racing, and if I don't get control, I'll be walking around with a boner like some horny teenager. *I need to calm the fuck down.* Her taste, her scent, the way she'd melt under my touch... *Focus!*

Yes, a plan! That'll cool me down. When I finally have her, I'll take my time, tasting every inch of her, devouring her until she begs me to fuck her raw. That's the plan.

Down, boy. You'll get your fill of her, every inch, every moan. There's no need to rush this. You'll have her in every way possible soon enough.

"Hi, lover boy!" Hunter greets me with that stupid grin plastered on his face.

"Fuck you," I growl, not in the mood for any of his nonsense.

"Come on, don't be like that. You know you can come to me if you need pointers on how to satisfy a woman, right?"

"What the fuck is this? Kindergarten, where everyone thinks they need to touch or talk about my toys?" My patience snaps. "Fucking leave me alone, or I'll knock you out."

"Lover boy got sensi..."

I don't let him finish. I grab a keyboard and smack him across the face with it, cutting off whatever dumb comment he was about to make. Silence, finally. That'll shut them up about me and Angela for a while.

"Fuck you, man!" Hunter grumbles, rubbing his cheek. "Not cool or necessary. I only had like ten more jokes lined up, and you had to ruin the vibe. Fucking idiot."

"Can we start working, or are you still playing around?" Buddy's deep voice silences the atmosphere and demands attention.

Buddy is Elijah's right-hand man, and if anyone can claim the title of Elijah's friend, it's him. In our organisation, nobody else comes close to having that kind of relationship with Elijah. I don't know much about their history, just that it runs deep. You can see it in how they move and communicate, understanding each other's questions and next steps without a word. Buddy's African. He mentioned once he was born in Zimbabwe, or maybe it was somewhere in South Africa. Like Elijah, he's got that same powerful presence, carrying this quiet, unshakable wisdom. But Buddy's got scars, literal ones, on his arms and hands. They speak of an unspoken pain, something he's lived with, that none of us really understand.

Then there's Hunter. A motherfucker from Australia though, weirdly, he doesn't have one of those heavy accents. We used to mess with him when he first joined, calling him "fake Aussie." He found his way to Elijah after leaving SASR, and it didn't take long for him to work his way up into UBT. The guy's built like a damn mountain and blond as the Australian sun. When I asked him why he was both a fire expert and a cybersecurity whiz, he just laughed, called me a dick, and said, "Fire consumes everything. Always gives you a fresh start. Cybersecurity is just for fun." He's laid-back, always up to no good, a constant joker. Well, if I'm being honest, so am I, but this "lover boy" crap needs to stop.

"Bogdan's man was an idiot, made me skin him, and then he started to sing. Regardless, he said Bogdan is still having issues with part of the coding in the software and that he is somewhere in Eastern Europe at the moment, but he did not know where, as all communication was via a video game. We got the game name and his user profile details, so we are good to go for the next step."

"Very well, Dominic," Buddy says with a cold tone. "Give all the information to Hunter and Sofia and let them take the lead. If they need backup, you will take point on the ground." The finality in his voice puts an end to the meeting, and he leaves the Security Centre without another word. One of the best things about working for Elijah and Buddy is the meetings are always under 20 minutes. Short, sweet and to the point. No pampering of egos, no nonsense, straight to the point and clear directions. *You've got to love that!* It's like their words and time are precious, and they are not willing to spend it on stupid shit, and if a topic is a waste of time, then they will not come anywhere near it. *I guess this is the key to success, clarity, straight to the point, respect and loyalty.*

"See, you're not completely useless, just chasing skirts all day," Hunter says, backing away with a grin and taking a defensive stance.

"You really can't help yourself, can you?" I respond, rolling my eyes.

"No, mate," he laughs. "I was digging through some data extraction from our last op when Elijah texted Sofia to run a full background on the shop owner and her family. It was so unexpected, Sofia and I couldn't stop laughing for five minutes. We never dig into civilians, ever."

Wait, shop owner? So it wasn't Angela that Elijah wanted the information on. He's got his eye on the old lady, not my angel. A wave of relief washes over me. If Angela's not the target, that means she's still under the radar, for now. Monica, though, she's probably screwed. Elijah doesn't request background checks unless someone's life is about to get really complicated.

That's a problem for another day. Right now, I've got an angel to stalk, and I can practically hear choirs of angels singing my happiness. I'll learn everything there is to know about her, and then... I'll stalk her. Then, decide how to approach her. Maybe take her out on a nice date because, after all, I'm not a complete animal. But after that? Oh, I'll taste every inch of her until I'm sated. Then I'll bury myself so deep inside her pussy that she will forget that we were ever apart as two people, and she'll see us as one joined person from that point onwards. *Yes! Perfect plan!*

"You started fucking her in your mind, didn't you? You perv," Hunter interrupts, shaking his head with a smirk.

"What are you on about?" I say, grinning like the Cheshire cat. "I'm as innocent as a monk," I add, readjusting my pants because, well, just thinking about my angel sends my mind into overdrive, and my cock turns to steel. Definitely need to handle that later when I'm alone, or these balls of mine are in real danger of turning blue. And that just won't do.

"You had a damn look on your face," Hunter snorts while flicking through screens, not missing a beat.

Sofia is the head of Cyber Security at UBT and Elijah's daughter. Though she isn't his biological child, he always introduces her as his daughter, and few people know she is a daughter by choice. Elijah found her in Africa when she was just a little girl, and since then, the two have been inseparable. Every time Elijah looks at Sofia, there's this unmistakable glow of parental pride and love radiating from him. It's as if the bond they share is something deeper than blood, something forged by loyalty and trust.

Hunter, on the other hand, is UBT's fire expert and head of Security. The guy's probably a genius, considering all of Elijah's companies and subsidiaries, spread across multiple continents, are run from this single building, and Hunter is the mastermind behind its security. His laid-back demeanour hides the fact that he's likely one of the sharpest minds in the organisation.

“Hi, cupcake. Did you miss me?” Hunter grins, flashing a smile as wide as the Grand Canyon, as Sofia walks in and takes a seat beside him.

“Drop dead, you stupid fuck,” she snaps back without missing a beat.

Hunter just bursts out laughing, leaning back in his chair, clearly enjoying himself. “I'll take that as a yes. Dominic's got some new toys for us to play with. Are you excited?”

Sofia's smile is pure sweetness, but her words cut like a knife. “You can take that as a yes if I get to cut your balls off first. And if you keep up with these stupid jokes, I'll drain your accounts and drop Interpol right on your ass.”

The glowing smile on her face is in stark contrast to the sharp edge in her voice, a clear reminder of just how dangerous she can be when pushed.

"Okay, you two love birds, I will leave you be," I say pressing send on the email containing all the details I extracted today. I walk out as they start bickering again. They hate each other, but it is fun to watch, especially when Sofia has enough and lunges at him. She might be a small woman, but she can hold her own in close combat, and the number of times she ended up with her legs around Hunter's neck you would think he does it on purpose.

Elijah is the head of the modern mafia, as I call it. Yes, he deals in drugs, but that makes up less than 10% of his income. We deal with information sales, exchanges, and extractions. More than 70% of his work is around cyber security and cybercrime. The remaining roughly 20% is divided into various "clean" businesses that make our outside image impeccable making us seem like the most outstanding citizens you would ever meet.

I am Elijah's enforcer, or more precisely, the negotiator. The guy who gets the job done no matter the cost. I oversee all the boots-on-the-ground operations and handle the interrogations. Honestly, I think it's my sense of humour under pressure that made Elijah move me up the chain so fast. Who wouldn't appreciate a clever remark or a joke in the middle of torturing someone? Despite the title, when Elijah found me and gave me this life, I grabbed it with both hands and feet and never looked back. Twelve years have passed, and I'd take a bullet for any of my brothers, loyalty and respect above all else.

I take the elevator to the garage, heading toward my car while skimming through Angela's file again. She lives alone and had two serious relationships in the past. Side note, I need to track down those fuckers and kill them, but I'll store that for later. Law school, working, charity work with kids with ASD, and countless photos of her. A warmth spreads through my chest the more I know about her. She is an exceptional creature.

"I think I'm fucked."

Chapter Four

Angela

I wake up the next day, replaying the events from yesterday over and over in my head. My goodness! How tall was that man? He must've been 6'5", maybe 6'6". Does a man like that even exist? He was a giant! How had I not noticed him before? You'd think a man that tall, walking like he owns the whole world with those piercing blue eyes, would have been the talk of the town. People should be saying, "Have you seen that giant? He walks like everyone belongs to him, and his eyes look like the clearest blue sea." The thought makes me chuckle. I sound like a horny teenager. Who even is this person I'm obsessing over?

"Angela, calm down. Get your mind out of the gutter and focus! You've got a bar exam to pass, or you'll forever be embarrassed by your failure." I say out loud, trying to pump myself up. Right, let's start the day on the right foot: a deep breath in, slow release. "I am strong, I am capable, I am intelligent." My daily mantra. But my eyes drift back to the card again: *"Thank you for existing, Angela."*

Seriously, what does that even mean? He actually left me a card with those words. Why didn't he ask for my number? Am I reading too much into this? Was he just being polite, playing some kind of game? Did I scare him off by saying I'm about to be a lawyer? Does he not like intelligent, educated women? He didn't seem like the type who'd be intimidated by a woman's success. Ugh, I'm going to give myself a headache thinking about this.

"Angela, get out of bed and stop overthinking!" I grumble, but at least I allow myself one last thought: *Well, he was hot as hell, so I think I've earned the right to be a little star-struck.*

I get out of bed and put the coffee machine on, then put some bread to toast and get the butter and jam out of the fridge. I lean on the kitchen island and remember my Mum's words: "*That will not be a problem. We will just leave the arrangement here on the floor and will invoice you tonight as well. As for your attention to my daughter, please be kind to yourself and pack away that joke of a dick you are pointing around, as with that, you can only tickle a woman and never satisfy. You will probably hurt yourself in the process, so as I said, be kind to yourself.*" The astonished look on Jake's face as we walked out of his home, his eyes widened in disbelief, his jaw slackened, leaving him momentarily speechless.

The worst part was my Mum's look and reaction, how her emotions flickered across her face, each fleeting expression a testament to the tumult of thoughts racing through her mind. "*Shhhh, my darling. I need a minute to think and calm down. I might turn around the car and skin him alive. Give me until your apartment to calm down, please.*" She had never spoken such harsh words in front of me, and I had never seen that expression on her face, as if she would actually skin someone or hurt them beyond repair.

I start drinking my coffee and having my toast while I prepare my work on my tablet and organise my notes. I bring out my whiteboard and examine the notes and map for the defence strategy I've developed so far.

State vs. James Thompson

Opening Statement:

Your Honor, members of the jury, I ask you to consider the facts impartially as we embark on this trial. While the prosecution paints my client as a criminal, we will demonstrate that there is reasonable doubt regarding Mr. Thompson's involvement in the alleged burglary. We will present evidence that casts doubt on the reliability of the eyewitness testimony and raises questions about the integrity of the forensic analysis. It is our contention that Mr. Thompson is innocent until proven guilty, and we trust that you will weigh the evidence carefully and reach a just verdict.

I jot down notes meticulously, going over every witness the prosecution plans to call. I review my cross-examination questions, focusing on the weak spots in their testimonies. I know where I can apply pressure and find the cracks in their version of events. Special attention goes to the lab results. Physical evidence is a hard thing to fight, but I can cast doubt on the credibility of the lab technician, the chain of custody, or the conditions under which the samples were taken. The goal isn't to erase the evidence, just to plant enough doubt, to make the jury question and let their emotions fill the gaps.

Satisfied with my notes, I check the clock. 6 p.m. Already. I hate how my life is sometimes, but I can't help it. Whether it's OCD or just an obsessive need for perfection, I can't walk into an exam unprepared. The idea of embarrassing myself publicly sends me into a panic. So here I am, alone in my apartment, spending the entire day preparing for a make-believe trial. *Fuck my life!*

And to make things worse, I haven't even checked in with Mum all day. Guilt weighs heavy on me, so I pick up the phone and call her. She answers on the second ring, and the familiar warmth in her voice immediately lightens the load just a little.

"Hi, my darling. How are you? How is the study going?" Mum answers with her bubbly voice larger than life. I thought she would be mad or at least still upset after what happened last night.

"Hi, Mum. I'm well. I am as prepared as I'll ever be. Mr. Thompson is still a dick, but he will hopefully be a free dick soon." I say, bursting into laughter.

"There you go, my darling. I knew you had it in you. I love you so much, my precious girl," Mum says in that sweet, calm voice that always soothes me. "About last night, I'm sorry I got so upset. I just wanted you to know we dropped them as clients, like we talked about. The invoice was paid, and I've already transferred the amount to your account. You'll deal with your fair share of nasty men in law, both to defend and defend yourself from. But remember, you'll never be alone, Angela. I will always protect and support you, no matter what. Just tell me when something doesn't feel right."

Her words wrap around me like a warm blanket. Mum has always been my rock, her love, care, and devotion an unspoken bond that has carried me through every trial. It's not just what she says, it's the unwavering presence, the constant support that has never made me feel alone. And now, hearing her put that love into words, it deepens my gratitude in ways I can't fully express.

"Thank you, Mum. I know I am who I am today because I've always had you to rely on. From the bottom of my heart, thank you," I say, my voice thick with emotion as I try hard not to cry. I know she doesn't do well with tearful moments, but this one hit both of us deeper than usual. I take a deep breath and decide to lighten the mood, steering the conversation towards my giant mystery man.

"Mum, what did you do with the flowers from that guy?" I ask, trying to keep the casual tone, though I feel the excitement bubbling up again.

"What guy, my darling?" she replies, feigning innocence.

"You *know* what guy! The one I was about to pass out from just talking to," I say, bursting into laughter like a schoolgirl with a crush.

"Angela, don't be silly. No man should make you feel like that by simply speaking to you," she says, her voice taking on that familiar, firm tone. "Come on now, remember who you are and what you're capable of."

"The problem isn't that I don't remember who I am, Mum. The actual problem is that I've never met anyone like him. I don't know what it is... I can't quite put my finger on it, but I've never felt like this for a man before," I confess, my voice barely above a whisper.

Silence. A rare pause from my mum that stretches long enough for me to feel awkward. "Mum?" I prompt.

"Yes, my darling. I've never heard you speak like this before. I just need a minute to process it."

"Why would you need to think about it?" I ask, feeling a bit defensive now. "There was nothing wrong with him. If anything, I'm the one who needs to think this through. He was the perfect gentleman, and, Mum, he's probably the most beautiful man I've ever seen. Sure, there are a lot of good-looking guys out there, but he was... different. I felt the air in the shop change when he walked in. And when I started talking to him and heard his voice? My knees went numb. I don't think I've ever felt like this before," I finish, my words tumbling out in a rush, almost like a confession.

"Yes, you're right. You're the one who needs to process this," she says softly, but there's an unusual weight in her tone. "It's just that you're my only daughter, and you're the centre of my world. I can't help but feel a bit... aware of the situation."

I let out a soft laugh, trying to ease the tension. "Mum, you don't need to worry so much. I'm not a child anymore. I'm going to be a lawyer soon, remember? You raised me to be a strong, independent woman. You should feel proud of yourself," I say, hoping to calm her motherly concerns enough so I can savour the excitement of whatever this feeling is.

"Very well. I will go finish dinner. Make sure you eat, and best of luck tomorrow for the mock trial. I love you, my darling."

"I love you too, Mum. I will come to the shop after school. Bye."

I hang up the phone and head to the kitchen, deciding that a sandwich is exactly what I need while my mind continues to spin in circles about him, *my giant*. As I start gathering the ingredients, I can't help but let the fantasy take over.

"He was beautiful," I say to myself, smirking. "Let's say until you're six feet tall, you're handsome, but beyond that, you're beautiful. That seems reasonable," I declare as if I need to convince someone.

Those ocean-blue eyes of his were mesmerising, deep and endless, like the sea on a perfect summer day. They weren't just blue, they held flecks of azure and turquoise that shimmered in the light like sunlight playing on the waves. There was something about them, a depth and mystery that seemed to hold stories untold. I remember the way they locked onto mine as if he could see straight through every wall I had built and into the very core of who I am. It wasn't unnerving, though. It was comforting like he was offering a silent strength without needing to say a word.

And that smile. It wasn't fully there, but it was always playing at the corner of his mouth, teasing the promise of something more, something deliciously mysterious.

"He's beautiful," I whisper to myself again, laughing softly. A man like that, handsome wouldn't do him justice. To call him anything less than beautiful would be a crime against the universe.

"And I am nothing if not fair, right?" I chuckle out loud, shaking my head at how ridiculous I sound, but for some reason, it feels so good to indulge in the fantasy.

I feel like he awakened this hidden world within me, a realm where my deepest desire dwells. In these moments, I feel consumed by a hunger that defies reason and a need for passion and ecstasy that sets me ablaze with longing. It is a craving for connection forged in the heat of desire, for the intoxicating rush of pleasure that sweeps me away on a tidal wave of sensation. Without a second thought, the food is forgotten as I make my way to my bedroom, lay on the bed and reach for my lube. I start slowly massaging my breasts and then pinching my nipple hard and pulling. My back arched, and I can feel that my pussy is getting hotter by the second. I start replaying in my mind the moment I saw him in the shop, how tall and broad his shoulders were. I imagine him engulfing me in a hug and wrapping me in those strong arms. I can feel my body getting hotter as I keep massaging my breasts and imagining him, the hug, his smell, his voice, imagining how his touch would feel on my skin and my breasts.

I add a generous amount of lube to my hand. I'll have fun today and get all this stress out of me. I trace my right hand down my stomach exploring and caressing my soft skin, and stop on my pussy. I start circular motions on my pussy with my entire hand to create more pressure and tease myself more sweetly. I keep playing gently without slipping any fingers in until I can feel my pleasure building up and my core getting hotter and wetter by the second. I move my left hand from my breast to the entry of my pussy, and I can feel the stickiness and slick juices awaiting me, and I press a finger in, creating pressure on the wall of my pussy as I slowly pull it out. "Oh, fuck!" the words just escape me as my desire and need intensify, and I know this is going to be an amazing masturbation session. My mind wanders back to all the beautiful things about my giant. I remember his crystal blue eyes, the gaze in his eyes, the smile on the corner of his lips that promised sinful things. I start building layers of pleasure and add another finger and press and slowly pull out while continuously massaging my clit with my right hand. The tumult of my desire is reaching unexplored depths, and my entire body feels stimulated and on fire from the constant teasing.

I move in front of the wardrobe mirror and start imagining that he is looking at me while I please myself. I replay our dialogue and remember how his body moved and how his presence dominated the room. I start stimulating the layers of skin surrounding my clit, tapping around the clit on the side and then on the top of her without drawing back the skin, and I can feel my left side being more sensitive. The tempting teasing is a delicious song that plays a melody perfect for my body, soul and mind. I enjoy sharing this moment with him, my beautiful stranger, *my beautiful giant.* I start drowning small circles on both sides of the clit with very delicate pressure, then start increasing it as I get closer to her. I can feel my movements creating a memory, a feeling, a desire unimaginable within me. I take my left hand out of my opening and gently pull back the skin of my clit, exposing the bundle of nerves. I can see her in all her glory in the mirror, and I can feel how my pussy is starting to weep with arousal. I can see how the surrounding areas and my clit are so swollen, ready for more attention, while my pussy is drenching the floor. I start circling the area closer to my clit with my thumb and forefinger. I can feel how I reached the point of no return, as my body is screaming at me for a release. I move onto up and down motions of my thumb and forefinger with gentle strokes, exposing and hiding my clit in the process. I start increasing the pressure with every stroke of my joined fingers and insert three fingers in my pussy and start scissoring them inside, adding pressure to the walls and pulling out with force and plunging back in. When I start curving the middle finger while scissoring the others on the walls and thrusting with all my might, a pressure like nothing before explodes within me, and I scream at the top of my mouth, a scream of pure unimaginable ecstasy. I start squirting as I keep massaging my clit up and down, and the release is splashed on the floor, and the mirror which gives me the most delicious primal view of myself, my pleasure, my core, my soul. Waves of pleasure pass through me from the memory of him, from the view, from me loving myself. I had never squirted before, and the glistening juices were evidence of my love for myself, of my desire to please myself as much as is proof that this man, whoever he is, claimed a part of me somehow. My soul is calling for him, and my mind and body realised that this connection was something special that I could not just ignore or walk away from without fracturing my soul.

"My beautiful giant, I don't even know your name."

Chapter Five

Dominic

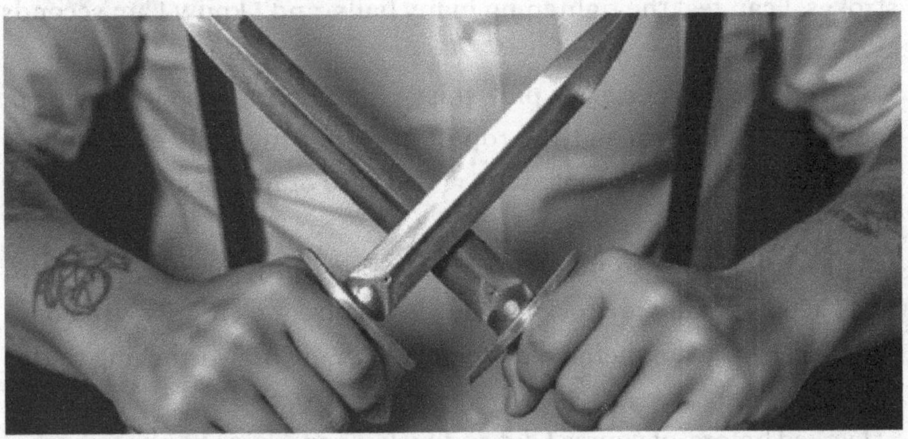

"I'm happy! Oh, so happy! Today, I'm going to stalk the hell out of a perfect angel!" After my workout, I sing to myself in the shower early in the morning. "I'm happy, oh, so happy!" I glance down at my half-hard cock and grin. "It's okay. Soon enough, you'll be buried deep inside an angel." As the words leave my mouth, he stands at attention like he's got a mind of his own. "Right! One more for good luck?" I burst out laughing, gripping my cock and stroking it hard.

The water cascades on my back, and my imagination starts running at the same speed as my mind, and I can vividly see how I would make out with her under the rain against a wall. I would press my body against her and run my tongue against her lips, demanding entry, pleading and praying for her not to push me away.

The moment she would open those full lips, I would devour her, fighting with her and savouring all of her taste. I am angrily pumping my cock as if punishing him, with every stroke imagining my tongue deeper into Angela's mouth.

The image of me lifting her legs to wrap them around my middle so I could grind against her is so clear in my mind as the image of the angry veins on my cock screaming at me for a release. Through the imagined droplets of rain, I can almost hear a soft moan from my angel. My hand is in perfect rhythm with my mind, pumping even more agitated strokes. I can feel the tightening in my balls, and I know I am seconds away from losing my mind.

Once I see her perfectly pink pussy in my mind, as clear as I can see the precum beads at the top of my cock, my balls explode in a symphony of pleasure that starts at the base of my cock travels to my heart and finishes in my mind.

The explosion is so powerful I cease breathing for a few seconds, and I keep stroking my cock for the aftershock and empty myself onto the tiles. I am overwhelmed by the reaction my body is having to this woman.

I jerked before, of course I did and fucked tons, but I don't remember having something like this, it just feels different. Even the mere memory of her feels different. Watching the water wash away my cum, a new plan forms in my mind, "Soon, all the cum will be on her and in her." I quickly finish showering and plan for the rest of the day in my mind.

It's a new day full of possibilities and endless resources at my disposal to stalk the woman of my dreams. How can I not be happy?

It would be blasphemous and ungrateful. So the only logical thing to do is to use all my resources to gather all the possible information and address any doubts, install cameras around her place, confront a few soon-to-be-dead exes, and threaten some professors for her and most importantly, stalk the shit out of this beautiful, intoxicating, divine angel!

I need to talk with Elijah or Buddy. I've had wonderful, great plans lately, and I think I deserve a pay raise. At this rate, I'll be a millionaire in no time. Actually, I am already a millionaire. Never mind that I'll set a new goal for all my grand ideas to pitch to the boss. Or... are all these plans really just circling around Angela? I can literally feel my brain racing at full speed. *Calm down,* I whisper to myself and start breathing exercises, trying to rein in the buzz of thoughts before I head to the office.

The moment I step out of the elevator, I notice the open plan of my office floor buzzing with energy. It's just past 8 a.m., and everyone's running around like little ants, looking or pretending to be busy. I make my way to my corner office, offering a quick "good morning" on the way. As far as my team knows, this is a legitimate business operating in pharmaceuticals. That's all they need to know, and they need to do a good job at it. Do I care about their performance? No. Profitable? Maybe a little. If we are not, then it looks bad on paper, and red flags might come up, and we don't want that. So I dedicate some part of my day here, just for appearances, but I have a strong executive team, and I don't need to babysit any of them. Once I'm in the office, I check my emails and find a notification from my clean-up team from yesterday. They informed me that they had disposed of the body and the warehouse is now functional. There's nothing new there, but it's good to know.

Where most mafias hide in abandoned warehouses for their "sessions," "interrogations," or whatever euphemism fits the day, we hide in plain sight. Our operations are embedded within legitimate companies, hardware, timber, or pharmaceuticals, all of which come with warehouses perfect for when business needs a little more... discretion. When we built these warehouses, we incorporated soundproof sections accessible only by UBT members via facial recognition. We even run a Foodbank, which ironically serves to fortify our legitimacy. We're not the mafia of old, with old iron fists or blood ruling. It's more efficient these days to drain someone's bank accounts and ruin their life than to skin them alive. And yes, *I'm still bitter about that stupid fuck.*

The front businesses run flawlessly, and we've never had a raid. Nothing suspicious would ever show up; even if they scanned the building, it would only register as a storage room.

As I work through my morning plans, my mind inevitably drifts back to Angela. I open her folder, staring at the photos, and that familiar, overwhelming sense of obsession takes over. Her deep black hair falls in silky waves, framing her face like an inked halo against her fair skin. Those intense, hypnotic eyes seem to penetrate the soul of anyone who meets them, as if she can read their very essence. Her soft, delicate features give her an almost ethereal grace, a kindness that contrasts with the hold she has over me. And those full, plump lips... God, they're intoxicating. Her smile is a weapon, capable of dismantling me if she ever chose to wield it. She's pure enchantment, and there's no turning back now.

I feel myself hardening as I look at her photos, each glance pulling me deeper into this spiral of obsession. "You're so beautiful, my angel," I murmur into the empty room. "How the hell am I supposed to convince you to stay with me?" A bitter taste invades my mouth at the thought that she might not even want me. *She might not like me.* That possibility gnaws at my mind, but then I remember the way she stood defensively yesterday when she mentioned some other guy. *Who the hell is stupid enough to mess with you, my angel?*

I dive deeper into the folder, looking for clues. Then I see it: an order from the day I first saw her, a large invoice to some law firm called Jake and Jack. My body tenses. "Sofia, you might be a witch, but you're damn good at your job. Who the fuck are Jake and Jack?" A quick search shows that it's a law firm where Angela is supposed to intern. "Like fuck you are! Over my dead body!" Pure fury explodes in my mind. *Calm, Dominic! Calm!* I start my breathing exercises and try to stop my Ferrari brain from speeding uncontrollably.

I dig deeper into the Jake and Jack firm's data, uncovering a series of sexual harassment complaints made against Jake over the years. *What. The. Fuck.* Every instinct inside me screams that something happened to her, that this lowlife hurt my angel, and my blood boils. I want to tear him apart. *I want to see him bleed.*

Breathe, Dominic! In, one, two, three, four. Hold, one, two, three, four. Out, one, two, three, four. Hold, one, two, three, four. And again. My eyes open, and standing right in front of me is Buddy, staring at me dead in the eyes, his presence steady and knowing.

A rush of panic shoots through me as Buddy's calm yet firm words hit me like a freight train. He's been in my office for fifteen minutes. He watched the entire breakdown? *Fuck.* My mind is racing, my breath spiraling out of control, and my obsessive thoughts are consuming me.

"I might be mistaken," Buddy says, his tone controlled and authoritative, "but did you just have an episode?"

I try to pull myself together, brushing off the intensity of what just happened. "I'm fine. I got it under control. My last episode was over a year ago."

He doesn't flinch, not buying my attempt at playing it down. "That's good, except you just had one right now. You zoned out so completely that you didn't notice me walk in, stop right in front of you, or stare at you for fifteen minutes while you lost it." His words hit with such precision that it's impossible to ignore. "So, you've got two choices.

One, come clean and let me help you, or two, keep lying, and I'll get Elijah involved. Pick."

When Elijah found me in the Vatican following my priest, I was in my early teens, and I was broken as broken can be, both mentally and physically broken. The pain that I was carrying around was so immense that I tried to end my life on several occasions, but every time, one of the other priests or one of the other ministrants found me in time and pulled me back. The pain, the shame, the confinement and the fact that I knew there was no other future in my life brought me to my knees, and I was a living corpse completely detached from reality. When Elijah walked past me, I did not even notice him, I was so lost in space that day that I did not lift my eyes from the floor. The next thing, this exceptionally tall man was pinning the priest to the wall and looking straight into my eyes, then he asked me, "Hey, are you ok?" he gave me a warm look, not a smile. I knew he was a bad man on the spot. I could feel his darkness emanating from him, and I could hear the pleading screams from the priest like he was far, far away, but I felt nothing. I returned his stare and just shook my head. The next thing, this larger-than-life man just pressed harder on the priest's neck, and a cracking sound enveloped the hallway. It took me several moments to realise it was over, the priest was gone, just like that. "Do you have where to go?" I shook my head again, "That's fine. You can come with me for now if you want. Nothing will happen to you. Stay next to me and I will protect you with my life. You are safe!" I never thought that a feeling like this would ever bloom within me, but hearing his words, '*You are safe!*', a sense of peace and gratitude envelops my entire existence, and I realise I am crying. The words play and replay in my mind, *I am safe! I am safe! I am safe!* I can hear him speaking on the phone rapidly with someone called Buddy as he navigates us through the corridor way as fast as we can. The moment I breathe the fresh air for the first time on my own and I know that slimy fucker is gone, I turn to my saviour and with tears in my eyes, I say, "Thank you! Thank you for getting me out of there."

Words cannot express the depth of my gratitude towards Elijah and Buddy for everything they have done for me. Their unwavering support and kindness have made an immeasurable difference in my life, and I am profoundly thankful for their presence in my life. Not only did I have a new beginning, but they embraced every side of my fucked up existence and never pushed the darkness away from my life, but they utilised it and taught me how to make the most of my skills and aptitudes, to see myself as a strength, not a weakness. There is nothing I would not do for this man at any hour of the day. Elijah saved me in every way that mattered. So now, as Buddy waits for me to answer, I know I can't keep hiding the truth. Not from him or the people who saved me.

"I met an angel," I say, my voice barely more than a whisper, as if admitting it too loudly might take the magic away.

"Yes, I've heard," Buddy replies, settling into the chair across from me. "And?"

"She's the most beautiful woman I've ever seen in my entire life. There's nothing about her I don't like. It's like her very being is calling to mine without saying a word. How strange is that?"

"It's not strange. It's called being smitten with someone. You didn't think it'd happen to you at some point?"

"Not really. But the strangest thing was the silence. There was silence in my mind when I was near her. How fucking strange is that?" I lean forward, still baffled by the experience.

"Right. Was that from the beginning, or did it take a while?"

"From the start. She was singing off-key, completely butchering a song, and the moment I saw her, it felt like gravity shifted. Like she was the one pulling me in. And when I got closer, my mind just... shut up. It was quiet."

Buddy listens intently, his expression neutral but focused. "And why did you have an episode?"

I sigh, trying to explain the jumble of thoughts. "I picked up on something she said about a customer, some lawyer. I looked him up, and the bastard has multiple sexual harassment complaints against him. So, my mind just started racing, thinking something might've happened to her because of him. This pressure to hurt built inside me. I wanted to make him suffer, to make them all suffer, and then... kill them. And that's when I spiralled."

I pause, collecting myself before continuing, my voice more resigned. "I know with everything going on, I should stay focused, but I thought... maybe I'd take a few days. Indulge myself with some harmless stalking, install a few cameras, threaten a couple of people in her life, and come back ready to focus on Bogdan."

My plan, laid bare, hangs in the air between us. Buddy doesn't react immediately. He's weighing my words, silently dissecting every detail. He knows I'm putting it all on the line here, trusting him to judge what's next. There's no hiding anymore.

"You know how Elijah and I feel about relationships. We don't get involved," he says finally, his voice measured. "I'm sure Elijah already told you not to make contact unless you're absolutely sure." He pauses, reaching for his phone, then locks eyes with me, searching for something beneath the surface of my words. "With your condition, though, I'm going to have to assign Hunter to go with you for now. You know we consider your ADHD a gift, but given all the emotions running through you right now, your ability to regulate them safely is... compromised."

He continues, his tone firm but not unkind. "It's not that I don't trust you, Dominic. It's that if someone triggers you and you start killing, we need to make sure you come back in one piece and even more so, ensure that nothing traces back to you or us. So, for now, Hunter goes with you."

I hate the guy. Well, *hate* is a strong word, but I definitely don't like him. I know I don't really have a say in this, it's a take-it-or-leave-it situation but still, I don't want a babysitter with a damn smartass mouth. Hunter is going to give me indigestion with all his stupid jokes, always pushing my buttons.

"I understand, and I appreciate your support with this matter," I say, slipping easily into my professional tone. My posture straightens, my features harden into a mask of confidence, no room for doubt or argument.

Buddy studies me for a moment, his expression unreadable. "I hope this works out for you, Dominic. It sounds like you found something special."

"I found an angel. I'm sure of it," I respond, conviction lacing my words. *This much is true.*

Chapter Six

Dominic

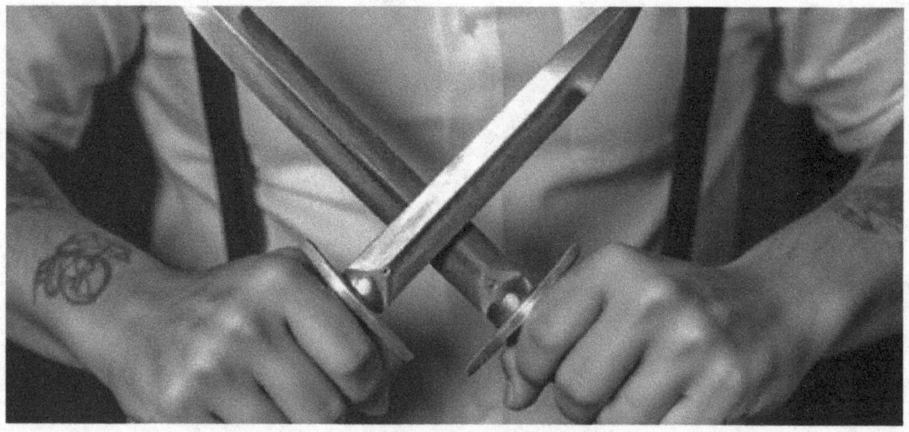

I step into my apartment, and the first thing that hits me is the smell. Something off, unfamiliar, and unsettling. Instinct kicks in immediately. "What the fuck?" I mutter under my breath as I reach for my gun, moving slowly, deliberately, toward the open living area.

And there he is. The fucker, spread out on my couch like it's his place, eating, watching AFL like he's king of the world.

"You want me to shoot you?" I say, my voice flat, completely void of amusement.

Hunter barely glances up, stuffing his face with food. "Shoot me? Then who'd babysit your ass, lover boy?" He smirks, talking with a mouthful of food like a child.

I stare at him, unimpressed. "Are you serious right now? What the fuck is wrong with you? And what are you eating? I hope you saved me some, because that smell's been noticeable since I walked in."

He looks at the takeout containers, shrugging casually. "Some Indonesian stuff I can't pronounce, so don't worry about the name, just eat. It tastes like chicken, but I wouldn't bet on it." He laughs like it's the funniest thing in the world.

"Fucker," I mutter, shaking my head.

We eat in silence for a while, and the tension between us is thick. My eyes drift to the screen showing the AFL game. It's strange how this sport can seem so thrilling yet so dull simultaneously, an enigma much like the man sitting beside me. The Aussies sure have a unique way of entertaining themselves. The players move with a certain grace and brutality that should be captivating, but instead, it feels monotonous. It could be the company that's clouding my perception. This man, with his inscrutable gaze and infuriating presence, is a pain and a blessing. A blessing because it means I can follow my angel to the ends of the earth, and pain because I need to carry his sorry ass with me all the way there. *Fucker!*

"Listen here, fucker..." I don't get to finish my sentence. In a swift, almost imperceptible motion, Hunter pulls a knife and presses the cold blade against my neck. The sharp edge bites into my skin just enough to draw a thin line of blood. "Easy there, Dominic," he growls, his voice a low, menacing rumble. "I am not here to hurt you. I'm here to help, but listen carefully, motherfucker. You'll tell me the truth right now because I am not going to babysit a sorry fuck that just wants to get his dick wet. Is this for real, or are you just fucking around?" His eyes bore into mine, dark and unwavering, promising violence if I lie.

The threat in his tone is palpable, dominating, and it would have made any lesser man piss himself in fear. But I am not like most men. I've been in far darker moments than this, and I know this is his way of testing me, of seeing if I'm worth his time. If Hunter wanted to kill me, he would have shot me the moment I stepped into the apartment, not brought me dinner and engaged in these theatrical shenanigans. This is a dance, a dangerous waltz of power and trust, and I need to show him that I'm not just playing games.

"Well, isn't this lovely?" I say, nudging his dick against the barrel of my gun. The cold metal presses against his trousers, a stark reminder of the precarious balance of power between us. "You might kill me, that's true, but you'll live without a dick, of course," I taunt, laughing right in his face. "They'll probably call you '*Hunter the ball chaser*.' Well, that's what I would have called you anyway if I survived the scratch." I burst out laughing, nudging him again for emphasis.

To no one's surprise, he starts laughing too. Despite being clever as fuck and stronger than most, Hunter's sense of humour is up there with the best of them. "That is a clever way of pushing a knife away," he admits, his voice amused. "There's no way I'm compromising my cock and balls for the likes of you, fucker." He eases the pressure of the blade against my neck, a subtle acknowledgment that we've reached a mutual understanding. We both know we are at the same level of strength.

"But you still didn't answer my question," he continues, his tone serious once more. "Is this for real, or are you fucking around?" His eyes narrow, the laughter gone, replaced by a steely determination. This is a man who demands the truth, and damn it, I need him if I am to chase Angela to the extent that my soul is screaming for her. I let the gun fall on the floor as a sign of resignation and move away my hands as a sign of surrender.

"I found an angel, brother," I confess, my voice thick with sincerity and a vulnerability I have never felt before. "I just cannot quite explain it. I've never felt like this before about anything in my entire life. The only thing I know without a doubt is that I will chase this woman to the ends of the earth if I must. I won't fucking give her a centimetre of space, and I will suffocate her with my love until she accepts me as well."

Wait, what? My love? What the fuck is happening to me? My mind is already sprinting ten steps ahead, building futures, catastrophes, absolutes — but even I know this feeling needs boundaries if it's going to survive. The realisation hits me like a freight train, but it's too late. *Fucking, shit, fuck!* The words are already out of my mouth, hanging in the air between us. I feel exposed and raw, but there's no taking them back now. Hunter can do whatever he wants with them. His expression shifts, a flicker of something unreadable crossing his face. Maybe he'll mock me, maybe he'll understand. Either way, I've laid my heart bare, and for better or worse, he knows the truth now.

"Alright then," he says, removing the blade and sitting down next to me. "Let's get your girl, and let's hope to fuck she likes your sorry arse too. Otherwise, it's a painful existence for you, brother." As he speaks, that flicker of emotion appears again in his gaze, just for a split second, before vanishing as if it were never there. It's so fleeting that if I didn't know any better, I'd swear he likes someone. But no, *no fucking way*. Hunter, with his dismissive clown laid-back attitude, feeling something as human as affection? The thought seems absurd, yet the flicker of emotion is not something I ever saw before on him.

"I brought a few toys for us to play with, and I brought some more info and a proposed plan on how to do this." He smiles at me with the confidence of an arrogant ass, as he knows he got this. He's the man if you need to find someone and the bastard knows it.

"We can plant the cameras in her apartment tomorrow when she is out to Uni. We can put some in her car and her mum's shop. With the phone, do you want to go old school and put a tracker or hack into it? Please say old school! Pretty please?" he gives me the best puppy dog eyes that he can master.

I would have laughed at his childish enthusiasm, but the idea of shop cameras killed the vibe for me. Like fuck, Elijah would kill both of us without a second thought. Hunter needs to hold his horses with that old lady if he plans to live this adventure with me.

"No shop cameras, Hunter," I say firmly. "That old lady in the shop is off limits, like for real. Elijah made it abundantly clear that she is not to be touched or even mentioned by any of us."

"Well, damn! That woman is in a world of trouble," he says, his tone a mix of surprise and hesitation. For a moment, I see a flicker of doubt in his eyes, but it quickly vanishes. Hunter's usual bravado returns, but I know the gravity of the situation has sunk in. We're treading dangerous waters, and the last thing we need is to provoke Elijah's wrath by crossing lines that shouldn't be crossed.

"Never mind then. Let's keep our heads where they belong," he says and starts laughing. "Yes, both heads fucker, because you might lose your top head, but I think I am more valuable than you and would probably lose my cock head because of your stupidity. So let's not do that and stay as far, far away from that shop woman as possible. Shall we?"

"Now, where was I? Oh, yes! There is this piece of shit, Jake, that I am a bit concerned about because I think there is some bad blood there, but I am still monitoring the situation. Do you think we are allowed to hack the shop? Please say yes," then he gives me the eyes again.

"Stop that shit right now! What am I, your fucking whore? Stop giving me the puppy eyes, for fuck's sake!" I punch him in the chest. "You hacked into the shop's data? Well, I promise you I won't piss on your grave when Elijah ends you. That is as good as it will get from me" I start laughing at his panicked face.

"You sorry excuse for a man! I did my homework to help you, but now you don't have my back? I will delete the data right now!" he screams in my face.

"Fine! I will not tell if you don't. But put some more firewall rules to make sure others will not make the same fucking mistake and die at a young age."

Hunter nods, understanding the gravity of the situation, and gets to work. For the next fifteen minutes, he's methodical and efficient, his focus unwavering as he sets up the shop's firewall system. Meanwhile, I inspect the goodies he brought with me, marvelling at the sheer sophistication of the equipment. Hunter is a good man, resourceful and thorough.

There's everything from PTZ cameras that can be remotely tilted, panned, and zoomed to small hidden cameras that are virtually undetectable without specialised gadgets. He even brought a network video recorder that will allow us to view the footage on any device we need. There are also sensors for her doors and windows, ensuring no point of entry goes unwatched.

I sift through the additional information he brought, noting that it isn't much more than what I found today anyway. Still, it's comforting to have all our bases covered. As Hunter works, I can't help but feel a strange mix of excitement and dread.

"Right, lover boy, the shop is all done. Let's never bring it up again."

"Agreed!"

"We can go and install it all tomorrow when your girl is out. We'll ensure it's all working as expected. You can have fun stalking her at Uni, and once I'm done, I'll let you know and confirm you can see all the alerts. You happy, motherfucker?"

"Fuck yes, I am!" I exclaim, a sincere, warm smile spreading across my face. It's strange, this feeling, almost like a sense of accomplishment. If my brain was messed up before, now it's on a new level of confusion around my emotions. *What is this feeling I'm experiencing? What is happening to me?*

"You look like an idiot!" Hunter bursts out laughing. "You sorry fuck, you've got it bad."

I punch him lightly on the shoulder. "Laugh all you want, Hunter. The day will come when you like someone, and I'll be there to laugh at you." My words cut his laughter short, like a machete slicing through butter, and that look is back in his eyes. *Oh, interesting!*

"Lover boy, lover boy! Who said I would ever fall for someone?" he retorts, but there's a hint of something deeper in his tone.

The room falls silent for a moment, the air thick with unspoken emotions. Hunter's usual bravado falters, just for an instant, revealing a vulnerability he rarely shows. It's as if my words have struck a nerve, hinting at a hidden part of him he's not ready to confront. The moment feels like it's bonding us closer somehow, as neither of us has ever said a true, honest feeling before to each other.

"Well, we'll see about that," I say, trying to lighten the mood. "As long as you don't go after a witch, I will back you up when the time comes, brother."

Chapter Seven

Angela

It's happy hour at the Saint George bar, just down from the Uni, and we're all celebrating the end of the semester and the final of that god-forsaken mock trial. We're at least on our second drink, chatting away happily as if we just had our first actual trial. I feel exhausted but know how important networking is for my future career. Despite my disdain for some of my colleagues and my strong preference for being at home and enjoying peace, I need to sit here, save face, and pretend I like them.

Well, *pretend* might be a strong word. After all, I wouldn't be a good lawyer if I didn't bite back from time to time. The look on that fucking bitch Sarah's face when the "jury" ruled "Not Guilty" was priceless. I genuinely thought she might pop a vein in her head. She had been so sure of her airtight case, her confidence bordering on arrogance, and seeing her deflate was a small victory I savoured quietly.

As the evening wears on, the conversations flow more freely, lubricated by the alcohol. I catch snippets of plans, gossip about professors, and the occasional boast about upcoming internships. My mind drifts, a part of me still buzzing with the adrenaline of the mock trial's conclusion.

But I can't shake the nagging feeling that I would rather be anywhere else. I remind myself of the forced camaraderie and the feigned smiles, it's all part of the game. Networking is crucial, and these people, for better or worse, are my future colleagues. I take another sip of my drink, letting the perfume of the expensive wine envelop me as tightly as the alcohol does, and I start to relax and allow myself to enjoy this moment.

I won! I actually won! I fucking attacked that forensic analyst in cross-examination, and I intimidated him. And that, ladies and gentlemen, none of these idiots can take from me. If anything, they know how I can bite and I can crush, so they will be wary of me moving forward.

I glance around the room, taking in the faces of my peers. Some are genuinely celebrating, others are pretending just like I am, but they all have one thing in common: they witnessed my victory. As our professor mentioned, I smirked, feeling a dark satisfaction in knowing that my performance today had set a new benchmark for them to follow. I've marked my territory in this competitive world of future lawyers, and my reputation is starting to take shape.

The exhaustion starts to ebb away, replaced by a heady mix of pride and confidence. The future may be uncertain, but I have proven my mettle tonight. I lean back in my chair, savouring the taste of victory as much as the wine. This moment is mine, and I plan to enjoy every second of it.

"If it's not the unbelievably talented lawyer in the making, Angela Puscasu," Sarah says mockingly, her voice dripping with sarcasm. "Oh, you were so fearless today," she yells over the music, loud enough to attract people's attention at the following bar table. "You were unbelievable! You almost made Steve cry with the speed and ferocity of your cross-examination."

She smiles, the most fake, exaggeratedly big smile I have ever seen. She flicks her hair and looks over her shoulder to ensure she has everyone's attention. The exaggerated theatrics are meant to belittle me, turn my moment of triumph into a public spectacle, and ensure others are paying attention to how she looks down on me.

I feel a surge of irritation but keep my composure. Her jealousy is palpable, and her need for validation from the onlookers only highlights her insecurity. I slowly sip my wine, allowing a small, confident smile to play on my lips.

"Thank you, Sarah. You did very well representing the State," I respond smoothly, my voice calm and measured. "Your acknowledgment means a lot coming from someone as experienced as you in courtroom theatrics. It seems my performance made quite an impression. I look forward to our next trial together."

The subtle barb hits its mark, and I see a flicker of annoyance cross her face before she masks it with another overly bright smile. The people around us chuckle, some giving me nods of approval. I can tell they see through her charade, which further bolsters my confidence.

"Of course, I will need to ensure I wear clothes more revealing to distract and corrupt jurors' attention," Sarah sneers, her voice dripping with venom. "But you know what they say: justice is blind. Perhaps it's blind because it's easier to follow someone's short skirt instead of paying attention to the facts."

She takes a step closer to me, her eyes narrowing to slits, ensuring I can see the poison dripping from her murderous gaze. The music and chatter around us seem to fade, leaving only the tension between us.

I meet her gaze steadily, refusing to be intimidated by her blatant attempt to provoke me. "Interesting strategy, Sarah," I reply coolly. "But some of us prefer to rely on our skills and intellect rather than cheap theatrics. Maybe you should give it a try, given that you were dressed in a tiny red skirt the entire week, and your breasts were barely contained under your bra." I stare her dead in the eyes and return her gaze with my best '*you're a piece of shit*' look. "Perhaps then, you would rival me for real as this type of play in the real courtroom would have send you to jail by the judge if you did not read that far into the code of conduct."

Her face contorted with barely suppressed rage, and for a moment, I wondered if she would lash out physically. She did not expect me to call her out on her bullshit and put her in her place. For sure, she thought she had me. But then she laughs, a high, brittle sound that grates on my nerves. "Oh, Angela," she says, her voice mockingly sweet. "You really think you're better than everyone else. But mark my words, darling, one day you'll realise that all your integrity won't get you as far as my *cheap theatrics*."

I can see the onlookers exchanging glances, some whispering behind their hands. Sarah's outburst has drawn even more attention, and not in the way she intended. I can feel the tide turning in my favour.

"Maybe, Sarah," I say, leaning in slightly, my voice low and steady. "But I'd rather fail with integrity than succeed through deceit. And from where I'm standing, it looks like your theatrics are already starting to backfire."

Her eyes flash with fury, and she takes a step back, clearly realising she's lost this round. She turns on her heel, storming off to another part of the bar, leaving me with a sense of triumph and a room full of witnesses to our exchange.

As I watch her retreat, I feel a surge of pride. This battle of words is just as crucial as any courtroom drama, and tonight, I've proven that I can hold my own against even the most vicious opponents. I take another sip of my wine, savouring the victory, however small, and the knowledge that I've made a formidable enemy think twice about underestimating me again.

"Nicely done!" Steve's voice takes me by surprise.

"You are as fearless in a bar as in a courtroom. Look at you go!" He leans closer, pretending to peer into my glass as if it isn't see-through. "Oh! You're almost out of wine. Can I buy you another one?"

"I appreciate the offer, but this was my last drink. Thank you," I say, smiling politely and trying to discreetly move back. I don't know what's wrong with me that I attract all the shittiest guys in the world. Steve looks like an alright guy from the outside, but there's something about him I can't put my finger on, which screams at me to stay away.

A feeling of unease starts to creep in, a sense of being violated by his proximity, as if his presence is scraping at my skin. I gently get off the bar stool and step back to ease this feeling while holding his gaze. The worst thing you can do when you're in front of someone who makes you uncomfortable is to show any signs of weakness. My mom taught me a lot about how to read people and stand my ground, no matter what. Worse comes to worse. What is he going to do in a room full of people?

Steve's eyes narrow slightly, and I see a flicker of frustration cross his face. He wasn't expecting me to refuse his offer. "Come on, Angela, just one more drink. After the way you smashed me today in cross-examination, I think we could celebrate your victory together", he insists, his tone masked in politeness and professionalism, but I pick up the undertone that is a bit too forceful.

"Maybe some other time, Steve," I reply, my voice firm. "I'm done for the night, unfortunately." I take another step back, putting more distance between us.

His smile falters, but he quickly masks it with a laugh. "Alright, alright. There's no need to crush my dreams so savagely," Steve says, raising his hands in mock surrender. "Just thought I'd offer."

I maintain my polite smile, but inside, a sense of relief washes over me. His attempt to guilt-trip me doesn't go unnoticed, but I refuse to let it affect me. "I appreciate it, really," I say, keeping my tone light but firm. "But I have an early start tomorrow."

I nod, maintaining my polite facade, but the unease lingers. Walking away, I can feel his eyes on me, sending a chill down my spine. I weave through the crowd, searching for a familiar face, someone I can latch onto to shake off this uncomfortable encounter. I will stay for another half an hour and then leave. I cannot leave now and make it obvious that I am trying to get away from him, but I most definitely need to get away from a situation that is just me and him.

For the past week, I have had this strange feeling that wherever I go, I am watched. It is the weirdest thing to feel that someone's eyes are on you, but I cannot spot anything out of the ordinary. The amount of time I stopped on the street to "fix my makeup" so that I could check in the mirror if someone was actually behind me is ridiculous. Of course, no creepy man was stalking me or following me. Everything was normal, and I was sleep-deprived and slowly losing my mind, clearly.

I gently move through the crowd toward the bar, saying my hellos and thanking my colleagues for the occasional compliment. After I sit at the bar, I try to get the bartender's attention to ask for water. As I'm waiting, I glance across the bar and freeze. There, amidst the crowd, is the man from the shop.

A strange pressure builds around me as if I'm underwater, and the water's soft caress envelops both of us as if we are calling for each other without words, and this man is the last breath of air I need to survive. It feels like the world has slowed down, the bar noise fading into the background. My breath catches in my throat, and an inexplicable connection tugs at me, drawing me toward him. *"Thank you for existing, Angela!"*

His presence is overwhelming, a magnetic force that pulls me in despite the distance between us. His eyes meet mine, and in that instant, a silent understanding passes between us. It feels like he's been waiting for me, just as I've unknowingly been waiting for him, like we understand something we didn't even realize we knew.

The bartender finally notices me and comes over, but I barely register his presence. "Water, please," I manage to say, barely above a whisper. My focus moved away from the man across the bar for a split second to give me a moment to compose myself and find my strength and courage, and I couldn't shake the feeling that he was just as aware of me as I was of him. *I'm not imagine him, right?*

I look across the bar again, and he doesn't move; he just watches me with an intensity that makes my heart race. I take a deep breath, trying to steady myself, but his predatory look is making me feel unsteady. This encounter feels like fate, a moment charged with significance that I can't fully grasp yet. I need to know more to understand why this man, out of everyone in the crowded bar, has such a profound effect on me.

The bartender returns with my water, and I take a sip, the cool liquid grounding me momentarily. But my eyes never leave him, and I know I have to find a way to speak to him. The pressure around me intensifies, and the need to connect with him grows stronger with each passing second.

With a deep breath, I muster the courage to stand and make my way toward him. Each step feels like a lifetime, but I know this is something

I can't ignore. Whatever lies ahead, this man holds a key to a part of my soul I didn't even know was locked.

"Hi," my voice sounds weaker than I would like, and there is no trace of the so-called confidence that I thought I possessed. "You probably do not remember me, but..."

"I remember you, Angela," he says, his voice smooth and confident, sending a shiver down my spine. Then he smiles, a smile so breathtaking that my knees threaten to give out beneath me. It's not just any smile. No, this one comes with a dimple, and that dimple, on full display, is more than I can handle. My heart, my mind, my very sanity, it's all under attack, crumbling under the sheer force of his presence.

It feels like he's sucker-punched me, knocking the breath from my lungs. I physically take a step back, unable to tear my eyes away from that devastating smile, my gaze locked on the dimple that's doing its best to undo me completely.

A man should not be allowed to be this attractive! It should be illegal in some states, and I definitely think this state should be one of them. *Oh, shit! What do I say now?* All thoughts and rationality have left the building, and the wine flowing in my veins does not help because the only thing that is coming to my mind is, what would he do if I jumped on him and kissed the living shit out of him.

I try to steady my breath, my mind racing to find something coherent. "I... I remember you too," I manage to stammer, my voice barely above a whisper. His gaze is unwavering, and I feel a flush rising up my neck, betraying my internal turmoil.

He leans closer to regain the proximity lost by my step back, and the space between us seems to shrink into nothingness. The air is charged with an electric tension, and I feel like I'm standing on the edge of a precipice. His presence is overwhelming and intoxicating, making it hard to think straight.

"So, what brings you here tonight?" he asks, his voice low and inviting. Every word seems to wrap around me, pulling me deeper into his orbit.

I swallow hard, trying to regain some semblance of control. "Celebrating the end of the semester," I reply, hoping my voice sounds steadier than I feel. "And you?"

He shrugs casually, but his eyes never leave mine. "Just happened to be in the area. Thought I'd check out the local scene."

His smile widens, and I can see a flicker of amusement in his eyes as if he's fully aware of his effect on me. My heart pounds in my chest, and I struggle to find something, anything, to say that doesn't sound ridiculous.

"It's a nice place," I say lamely, inwardly cringing at my lack of wit. But he just chuckles, the sound sending shivers down my spine. We both know this is just the foreplay in anticipation of what is to come.

"It is," he agrees, his gaze intense. "But it just got a lot nicer."

The compliment catches me off guard, and my cheeks heat up even more. Desperately, I search for a way to keep the conversation going despite the chaotic swirl of emotions inside me.

"I'm glad you think so," I say, trying to match his cool demeanour.

His words hang in the air, heavy with implication. My mind races with possibilities, but all I can think about is how close he is and how much I want to close the gap between us even more.

Summoning every ounce of courage, I decided to take a chance. "Would you like to join me for a drink outside on the terrace?" I ask, my voice steady despite the turmoil inside.

His smile widens, and he nods. "I'd like that."

We make our way out to the terrace, and as he moves to sit beside me, I feel a thrill of anticipation. This man, with his devastating smile and hypnotic eyes, has turned my world upside down as a matter of fact. And I can't wait to see where this night will lead. One thing is for sure, I might not be able to pick up on sex vibes from guys, but I'm acutely aware of my own desire. At this moment, I am barely restraining myself from jumping on his lap and having my way with him.

The thought pulls a chuckle from me, and I blush, feeling as if I were a teenager all over again. He raises an eyebrow, clearly amused by my reaction. "Something funny?" he asks, his tone light but his eyes probing.

I shake my head, trying to rein in my wandering thoughts. "Just... something silly," I say, waving it off. "It's nothing."

He leans in closer. His intoxicating cologne overwhelms me with its luxurious complexity of bergamot, musk, and leathery notes, which are so clearly defined now that our location is more intimate. "Care to share?" he teases, his voice a low murmur that sends shivers down my spine.

I swallow hard, my pulse quickening. "Just... I was admiring your dimple," I reply, hoping he can't see right through me. "Is not every day you see a man with dimples." I can feel my face heating up, and I think perhaps he will regret now leaving me that lovely note.

He smiles, that dimple flashing again, and I feel my resolve weakening. "Life does have a way of surprising us," he agrees, his gaze never leaving mine.

The next thing I realise, he leans, takes my hand, and places it in his hand as if it were nothing. I find myself drawn deeper into his orbit, the initial awkwardness giving way to a comfortable, almost electric connection. Every word, every glance, feels charged with possibility, and I can't help but wonder where this will all lead. I never went out with guys I did not thoroughly know, but here I am with this man whose name I don't even know, completely absorbed by his presence as if something within him is calling my soul to go to him.

I lean back slightly, sipping my water to steady myself. The night stretches out before us, full of potential and promise.

Chapter Eight

Dominic

The past week has been nothing but unbearable. Watching Angela from afar, unable to touch her or even speak to her. *Hell,* that kind of torture should be forbidden. I swear, *fuck my life!* But what choice do I have? I had to endure it because, one, it's the right thing to do, and two, Elijah would have my balls. And, let's be honest, we need those, so losing them isn't an option.

So here I am, once again, watching her from a distance in some bar filled with drunk or semi-drunk Uni students, playing the part of the in-love stalker. Some might call it creepy, but I'd call it dedicated. And if they had a problem with it? Well, they could fuck off. Seriously, though, she's a sight to behold, like a dark angel, powerful and breathtaking. She doesn't need to say a word to command the room, every head turns to her, drawn in like moths to a flame. Her midnight-black hair cascades down her shoulders, framing a face so perfect it's as if it were carved by the hands of the gods themselves. High cheekbones, eyes that pierce through people as if she can read their very souls and, *oh, those lips*, promising untold secrets, passions, and sinful things. Her body? Let's just say every curve and dip is designed to break my heart over and over again.

Her beauty isn't just in her appearance, it's in how she carries herself, with a grace and confidence that leaves everyone in her wake. She's not just beautiful. *She's mesmerising*, a force of nature that captivates every corner of my soul, commands my thoughts and actions and has been since the moment I met her.

When she moves, it's like watching professional dance in motion, each step deliberate, each gesture elegant. She radiates a strength that is both intimidating and awe-inspiring, a reminder that she is not to be trifled with.

Yet beneath that powerful exterior, I can feel how her being is calling out to me, and tonight, if she comes to me, will be the day I make contact, and I will never let her go after that. But I will not initiate it. *I will let her decide her own fate,* and if she does choose me, she will be mine forever. Whether she wants it or not, there will not be any getting rid of me.

I can't help but be drawn to her, this dark angel who has completely upended my world, as if she was born with the right to claim power over me. Her beauty isn't just something to admire from afar; it's a beacon, pulling me closer, making resistance feel impossible. And whatever happens next, one thing is painfully clear: she's left an indelible mark on my soul. The world, as I once knew it, will never be the same again because now it revolves around her.

In the past week, I've dissected every detail of her life, every moment, and every trace of her existence, and all I've learned is how utterly perfect she is. There's not a single aspect of her that doesn't call to me. Her looks, her spirit, the determination that fuels her, the fire that blazes in everything she does. Every part of her sings to me, and I'm completely and hopelessly lost in it.

The first time I saw her waking naked in her apartment, I jerked off so hard I thought I might hurt my cock by the end of it. Her beautiful round hips and ass, her big breasts and beautiful pussy were all it took for me to tattoo that image forever in my mind and for her to seal her fate with mine.

She was drying her hair with a towel, and the movement made her breasts bounce with a rhythm that drove me wild. Every sway, every curve of her body, was an invitation to fantasies that left me breathless. I imagined how she would look, bouncing on my cock with all her strength, the vision so vivid it felt almost real.

When I came, it was so powerful I lost the ability to breathe, and my vision went white. The sheer intensity of my orgasm left me shaking, my body overwhelmed by the force of my desire for her. She had become an obsession, a dark angel whose presence could completely unravel me.

Every detail of that moment is etched into my memory, a reminder of the uncontrollable lust she ignites in me. Her image is a permanent fixture in my mind, driving me to the edge of sanity with an insatiable need to possess her. She has become the centre of my world, the one desire I cannot escape.

I had to save all the recordings on my cloud, delete the recordings from the UBT cloud, and threaten Hunter to pull his eyes out if he restored them and take a glimpse at my angel. The fucker just laughed, called me names and told me I had it bad. Fucking genius! *Fucking Sherlock over here, ladies and gentlemen!* Now, he knows that this woman is more important to me than my next breath. But who gives a fuck? He is here to "*help*" me, so help he shall provide, or he will do all his hacking without eyes.

The night carries on as, one after another, women approach me as if it's their given right to walk up to a strange man in a bar and talk to him.

"Hi, handsome. Why are you drinking alone?"

"Hi, cutie. Want some company?"

"Hi, mate. Got a smoke?"

"Hi, love. We could not help but notice how handsome you are. Care to join me and my friend for a threesome tonight?"

What a fucking joke! Why are they all over me, and the woman I want is speaking with some beach-face cunt instead of coming to me? Wait! Is this how women feel whenever a strange man comes to talk to them, and they are not interested? *What the fuck?!!!! That is shit!*

I burst out laughing, the situation's absurdity hitting me in full force. I turn to the slimy girls who have been hinting at a threesome and say, "I'm not interested."

It's like my reply doesn't register. One of them, undeterred, starts rubbing her breasts against the side of my shoulder, grinding on my last nerve. Her touch is invasive, her persistence irritating beyond measure.

I force a polite smile, trying to pull away subtly. "Really, I'm flattered, but no thanks," I say, my voice strained with the effort to remain civil.

She pouts, her lips forming a mock frown as if genuinely puzzled by my rejection. Her friend giggles, clearly amused by my refusal. I can't help but think about how surreal this all is. The attention, the lack of boundaries, *it's suffocating.*

My eyes dart back to my angel, still engrossed in conversation with the beach-face idiot. A pang of frustration and jealousy shoots through me. This whole scenario is maddening. All I want is her, yet I'm trapped here with these persistent intruders in my personal space.

Taking a deep breath, I look them dead in the eyes. "Sorry ladies, I just got my test results today, and I have STDs" I stop trying to put space between us as I know they will run for the hills in a moment. "I am happy to have a threesome but only bare. I don't like anything between my cock and pussy juices."

The look of utter horror on their faces says it all. I am barely able to contain my laughter, which gets a thousand times more amplified when one of them squeals in horror.

Well, that was fun! That should teach them not to go and ask for a threesome from strangers. How fucking stupid can they be?

Anyway, I look back at my angel and fuck me, these stupid girls distracted me, and now my angel is speaking to some guy? What are the chances of me being able to slice his throat and still leave with Angela willingly tonight? I take a second to weigh my outcomes, but no, there is no chance for her to want me if she sees the messed up shit I am capable of.

I will not approach her, I will stick to my plan and let her decide her own fate. I feel a mix of anticipation and defiance. Tonight, I'm not letting anything or anyone stand between me and what I want, except for my angel. She will be the one who will make contact, and when she does, I will be the one who will seal our lives forever.

Patience, Dominic! Patience.

I take a deep breath, trying to steady the storm raging inside me. My eyes remain locked on her, tracking every move, every gesture. Her smile is professional, cold, and her body is rigid. Everything about her is captivating, but it's clear, she doesn't like this guy. Still, I know I can't rush it. She has to come to me willingly.

As the minutes tick by, the room seems to blur around the edges, leaving only her in sharp focus. The unwanted attention from others fades into the background as I hone in on my goal. I remind myself that this is a delicate game of strategy, where patience is my greatest ally. *Why did I make this plan again instead of just taking her, consequences be damned? Oh, yes! I wanted to give her a choice.*

I order another drink, my fingers drumming lightly on the bar counter. The anticipation is almost unbearable, but I force myself to stay calm. I've waited this long, a little more time won't kill me. Blue balls might, though. Can a man actually die from blue balls? I should probably Google that and make sure I get a release tonight. No way am I going out like that. Hunter would laugh his ass off at my funeral.

Everything will be ok! She will feel the pull and the undeniable connection between us, and she will come to me. *She had to come to me. She just has to.*

I catch glimpses of her walking in my direction, and each step sends a jolt of electricity through me. It's working. She'll notice me soon, sensing the invisible thread that ties us together. I lean back, projecting confidence and nonchalance, hoping to lure her in.

The moment our eyes meet, I see recognition, surprise, and lust flicker in hers. *Oh my! Well, hello, beautiful angel. Just come to me, and I'll fulfil all your desires and then some. Just come to me, my beautiful, sinful angel.*

Finally, after what feels like an eternity, she makes her move. My heart pounds in my chest, a drumbeat of victory and anticipation. I keep my expression composed, but inside, I'm a whirlwind of emotions.

As she approaches, her gaze never leaves mine, but I notice the blush rising on her neck. And I know, just know, she's as nervous as I am. *This is it!* This is the moment I've been waiting for. I can already see the future unfolding before us, a tapestry of intertwined destinies.

"Hi," her voice is a melody to my soul, and that complete silence covers my mind again like a warm blanket in the dead of winter. "You probably do not remember me, but..."

"I remember you, Angela," my voice came across as smooth and confident. I am so overwhelmed with happiness at the realisation that she came to me. *She picked me! She came to me, and all my dreams will come true.* A full smile spreads over my face, my joy explodes out of me like a steaming volcano unable to contain itself.

Her presence is like a dream made real, and every second she stands before me feels like a victory. I can't help but let my emotions show, the joy bubbling up uncontrollably.

"I... I remember you, too."

Angela's lips curve into a soft smile, and for a moment, everything else fades away. The bar's noise, the people milling about, all of it becomes a distant hum as I focus solely on her. My mind is inundated with images of her nakedness and the possibilities of what this night could bring, and I can hardly contain my excitement. *I need to calm down. I cannot scare her away!* I need her to fall for me before I inform her that she is mine from tonight onwards and that she will never escape me, even if she tries.

I lean in closer, making sure I don't give her any more space than absolutely necessary. I could inhale her, absorb her, devour her for the rest of my life. Her entire being is mouthwatering to me.

Calm, Dominic. Calm!

"So, what brings you here tonight?" I ask, keeping my voice steady.

"Celebrating the end of the semester," she replies, a touch more composed now. "And you?"

"Just happened to be in the area. Thought I'd check out the local scene." I lie through my teeth like a pro.

Well, I can't exactly say, Hey, beautiful angel, I've been stalking the shit out of you for the past week. I've seen you naked a couple of times, know your life inside and out, and if I don't fuck you soon, at least one of my balls, if not both, might explode from the fucked-up desire you stir in me. So how about it, sweetheart? Take some responsibility for being the hottest creature on the planet and either drop to your knees or spread those legs wide because I'm going to park my cock in your sweet pussy for the rest of my days.

Wait, what? How is this her responsibility? What is happening to me? What kind of powerful *Jade* shit is she pulling on me, making me question myself like this?

The thought makes me smile because, damn, that would be hilarious. Nope! I definitely need to suppress that kind of brutal honesty, or she'll run from me *like I'm a problem. And I'm not. I know I'm not. I just... get a little passionate.* That's all.

"It's a nice place."

"It is," I say with confidence and ease. "But it just got a lot nicer."

Her eyes widen slightly, and a blush creeps up her cheeks. The sight sends another wave of happiness through me, deepening the connection I feel between us. I held her gaze for what feels like a lifetime, where the world fades and it's just the two of us, completely lost in each other.

"I'm glad you think so. Would you like to join me for a drink outside on the terrace?" Her sweet, sinful voice echoes my lustful thoughts, strengthening the pull I have over her.

"I'd like that," I say, unable to hide the happiness that this woman brings me by mere existing.

As we make our way out to the terrace, I sit in the chair right next to her, close enough that there's no room for her to pull back, no space for her to think this isn't inevitable. Tonight, we begin the dance, and by the end of the night, she will know *she belongs to me.*

When she started laughing, I raised a brow at her, scared that my features gave away my inside beast and the nasty things he wanted to do to her. "Something funny?"

She shakes her head. "Just... something silly," she continues, trying to wave it off. "It's nothing."

This is my moment, and I am going to make the most of it. I lean closer as if to envelop her in my presence, and her perfume wafts around me, dragging me down a path of no return. The freshness of it and the flowery notes are like a whip to my heart, making it race at twenty thousand miles per hour. My cock goes rock hard, and the speed of things makes me feel lightheaded. I shake my head slightly, trying to recompose myself and smile at her.

"Care to share?"

"Just... I was admiring your dimple," she looks at me like she is still holding back. "It is not every day you see a man with dimples." That blush that never fully left her face and neck is on full display again, and I feel more encouraged to make my move and touch her. *I need to touch her!* I need to feel her skin on mine, and I need it more than my next breath.

I smile again at her having the courage to be so blunt and make a point of looking straight into her mesmerising eyes. "Life does have a way of surprising us."

Enough is enough! She is mine, and she needs to learn it!

I lean in, gently take her hand, and place it face-up in my palm. Slowly, I begin tracing lines from the centre of her palm to the tips of her fingers. Her body responds, a soft tremble, a quiet gasp, and then she leans back as if needing the support. *I'll be your only support from now on, my beautiful angel.*

I lower my gaze, studying the details of her palm, committing each line to memory. For now, this is how I'll love her, softly, patiently, with every stroke.

"Angela," I say softly, my voice laced with the intensity of my emotions. "You have no idea how happy I am that you came over."

She smiles back, her eyes sparkling with curiosity and perhaps a hint of something more. The world around us seems to fade away, leaving just the two of us in this charged moment. I can feel the heat between us, a palpable connection transcending mere attraction.

"I couldn't resist," she replies, her voice barely above a whisper. "That note was quite something..."

Her words trail off, but the meaning is clear. The attraction is mutual, and it's drawing us together like magnets. I reach out, my hand lightly brushing her arm, and the contact sends a jolt of electricity through me. Her skin is soft and warm, and I can feel the shiver that runs through her at my touch.

I need to kiss her! I need to kiss her! I will fucking lose my mind if I don't feel her seductive lips on mine. This is it. This is the moment I've been waiting for, and I'm not going to let anything ruin it.

The intensity of my desire is overwhelming, a force of nature that I can't resist. I lean in closer, my heart pounding in my chest, and I can see the anticipation in her eyes. Her lips part slightly, and it's all the encouragement I need.

Without another thought, I close the distance between us, capturing her lips with mine. The world around us ceases to exist as I lose myself in the taste and feel of her. Her lips are soft, warm, and more intoxicating than I could have imagined. The kiss is everything I hoped for and more, a perfect blend of passion and tenderness.

Her response is immediate, her arms wrapping around my neck as she presses closer. I can feel her heartbeat racing in time with mine, the electricity between us crackling in the air. Our kiss deepens, a dance of tongues and breath leaves me dizzy with desire.

Every sensation is heightened, every touch sending waves of pleasure through my body. Her fingers tangle in my hair, pulling me closer, and I respond by tightening my hold on her waist, anchoring us in this shared moment of bliss.

As we finally break apart for air, I rest my forehead against hers, both of us breathing heavily. Her eyes are half-closed, her cheeks flushed, and I know without a doubt that this is just the beginning of something incredible.

My phone rang for a while, I yank it out, throw it to the floor, and stamp on it. The finality of the action brings a strange sense of relief. I know exactly who's responsible for interrupting the most perfect moment of my life. Tonight, Hunter's getting stabbed in the nuts for this.

"Well, clearly, you don't need a phone," she says with amusement in her voice.

"Nothing is more important than this moment with you, Vita Mia." The sincerity in my voice is clear, and the finality of my declaration is the promise of a beginning between us.

"I've wanted to do that since the moment I saw you," I whisper, my voice rough with emotion.

"Me too," she replies, her voice breathless and filled with the same longing I feel.

I lean in again, tilting her head back to deepen the kiss, and all reality vanishes around me. This woman consumes me, subdues me, devours me somehow because there is nothing else but her. Every thought and every sensation is centred on her, and I am lost in the moment.

When she moves her leg on top of mine and starts grinding her knee against my cock, a surge of raw desire courses through me. Her touch sends shivers down my spine, and I feel like she is not only my life now but my beginning and end. There is nothing without her.

My hands roam over her back, pulling her closer, needing to feel every inch of her against me. The intensity of our connection is overwhelming, and I am drowning in the sensation of her warmth, her softness, her presence. Each movement she makes, each gasp and moan, pulls me deeper into the abyss of desire.

She is everything, my world, my reality. In this moment, nothing else matters. The noise of the bar and the people around us all fade into complete oblivion. It's just her and me, lost in our own universe.

Her grinding becomes more insistent, her body moving against mine with a rhythm that matches the pounding of my heart. I can feel her need, her desire, and it mirrors my own. We are two halves of a whole, brought together by an irresistible force.

I break the kiss to catch my breath, my forehead resting against hers. "You have no idea what you do to me," I whisper, my voice husky with longing.

She smiles, her eyes dark with passion. "I think I have an idea," she murmurs against my lips, her voice a seductive purr that sends another jolt of desire through me.

With a renewed sense of urgency, I kiss her again, pouring all my emotion into it. She responds with equal fervour, and I know that I am completely, irrevocably hers. She is my addiction, my obsession, and I will never be the same again.

This woman is mine! She is my life! My beginning! My end!

I feel so lightheaded from all the pulsing blood to my cock that when I break the kiss again, I take a few seconds to breathe properly and shake my head in an effort to regain some clarity over myself.

"Vita Mia, if you don't stop grinding your knee on me, I'm going to lose my mind right here in this bar and we can't have that."

She smiles, deliberately pressing harder with her next rub, and a groan escapes me before I can hold it back. What is this woman doing to me? I'm going to come in my pants like a damn teenager and embarrass myself.

"Vita Mia, what does that mean?" she asks, a wicked smile lighting up her beautiful face, as her hand moves to rest on my other knee, all while keeping the pressure on my cock.

"My life."

Her hand inches slowly toward my cock, and I know the battle is lost. I can't stop her *I won't stop her.* I need to feel her on me, and I need it now.

"Vita Mia, please stop," I whisper, leaning in, resting my forehead against hers. "You have no idea how much I want this, how much I want to do every filthy, nasty thing to you... and more." My lips brush her chin, trailing soft kisses upward, along her eyelids, her eyebrows, until I finally kiss her forehead.

"Angela," I murmur, my voice barely audible, reflecting the storm of emotions inside me. "I need you to know this isn't just a moment for me. This is the start of something real."

I search her eyes, desperate for a sign, an answer to what I'm feeling. "So please, have mercy on me, Vita Mia, and stop grinding on me, because I will come and I will embarrass myself. I can't stop without your help because every part of me is screaming for you, and my cock... it's already yours. There's no stopping it if you don't stop now."

Her eyes widen, searching mine, and she whispers, her voice full of sincerity, "I feel the same way."

I start kissing her again, deepening the kiss and savouring her warmth and the sweetness of her taste while slowly moving her hand from my leg to my chest, as I cannot bear not having her touch me and move her other leg off mine.

"Fucking hell! That physically hurts not having you that close." I said with surprise and pain in my voice, and I mean it. Half of my brain is calling for me to *be respectful* and make sure our first time is beautiful and precious for her, and the other half is calling me a *stupid fuck* and saying that I should start fingering her under the table and then go and fuck the living hell out of her in the bathroom.

"Vita Mia, the things you do to me!" I envelop her in a hug while pulling her on my lap and resting my head on her shoulder.

All of these extreme emotions are invading my being, and I feel genuinely overwhelmed with them all. But there is still silence in my mind, and even if I am scared of these feelings, the call to own her very existence is so strong that I need to have her at all costs.

She is mine!

Mine to have!

Mine to keep!

Mine to devour!

"I am battling a losing fight in my mind, little angel," I say into her neck. "Part of me wants to fuck you raw, and part of me wants to be respectful and take this one step at a time."

A shiver passes through her at my sincere words, and she hugs me tighter and slowly rubs the side of her ass on my rock-hard cock.

I groan in her neck and start again, begging for mercy. "Vita Mia, please! I want to touch you so much my muscles hurt. Grinding your sweet ass on my cock is not merciful, it's the opposite. Please, let me do this right by you," my voice, a pleading, longing whisper in her ear.

When she softly chuckles, I grab her hips and start rocking her on my cock harder. The attraction, the need, the desire, the passion that this woman awakens in me is something that I did not know was within me. My actions are complete opposites to my pleading for mercy, but my beast is so unbalanced that if I don't feed him a bit and get some pleasure from her, I will lose my mind until the next time I see her.

She starts moving in sync with me and lets her entire weight press on me. After a few rubs, the urge to move my hand between her legs and finger her to find her own pleasure is so suffocating that I growl, stop moving, and look into her beautiful abyssal eyes.

“Vita Mia, I'm going to move you off my lap because I can't take it anymore. Both of my brains are in perfect agreement right now to take you to the bathroom and fuck you raw, but you deserve better than that for our first time.” I wink at her, gently lifting her off me and setting her down beside me.

I take her hand in mine again, pressing soft kisses along the inside of her arm and across her palm. The gesture feels so intimate that I can't stop, continuing until I gently bite her skin, followed by a soft lick to soothe the sting. The taste of her is all-consuming.

"Fucking hell, Vita Mia! You're like my personal brand of heroine," I say with pained desire in my voice.

"And you are like custom-made for me. Are you playing me? How is it possible for you to anticipate what I want like this?" The worry in her eyes is like a knife to my insides that she is twisting with every passing second.

"Baby! What is this?" I pull her closer to me and hug her as tightly as possible without actually hurting her.

"Vita Mia, never doubt me again. Please have mercy on my heart." My body starts trembling at the thought of losing her because she is doubting me. *You know what? Fuck it!* Cards on the table and let her choose me again. Either way, I am not going to give her a way out, but at least like this, I know where I stand with her and the level of work I might need to fight through to make her mine.

"I was enchanted with you the moment I heard you singing your heart out, off-key, may I add. You are so mesmerising and divine that my entire being called after you, and I had to follow you to the shop." I search her gaze for any signs of panic or concern, but what I find is surprise and attraction, so my heart keeps spilling at her feet for her to do with it as she pleases.

"I felt like an idiot in the shop, talking to you," I lower my eyes to where I am holding her hand and lift it to my lips for another soft kiss.

"I cannot explain it because I've never felt this before, and it scares the shit out of me. But what scares me more is not having you," I say, my voice trembling with raw honesty. "What I am certain of is that I want this! I want this more than I've ever wanted anything in my life!"

I kiss her hand again and rest it on my cheek, feeling the warmth of her skin against mine. "I want this, and I will not stop until I have you. My entire being gravitates to you, and I am sure you can feel it, too."

Her eyes soften, and I see a flicker of understanding and emotion in them. The connection between us is undeniable, a magnetic pull that neither can resist. "I feel it too," she whispers, her voice barely audible but filled with conviction.

My heart swells at her words. I press her hand more firmly against my cheek, savoring the contact. "This is real, Angela. This feeling, this connection, it's something extraordinary. And I don't want to let it go."

She nods slowly, her eyes never leaving mine. "I've never felt this way before either," she admits, her voice tinged with awe. "It's terrifying and exhilarating all at once. But I am scared shitless that you will break my heart. If I let go, this feeling within me will grow and consume me to no end, and I will be lost in you. You will own me, and that terrifies me."

I lean in, my forehead resting against hers. "Then let's embrace it together because I know I'm already on my way to losing myself in you," I say softly. "Let's face the fear and uncertainty together because I believe what we have is worth it. You are worth it."

She smiles, a radiant expression that lights up her face. "Okay," she murmurs, her breath mingling with mine. "Let's do this."

The moment is charged with emotion, a silent promise passing between us. I pull her closer, our bodies pressed together, and I kiss her deeply. It's a kiss filled with all the unspoken words, the fears, and the hopes we share. It's a kiss that seals our commitment to this journey.

As we part, I look into her eyes, seeing my own feelings reflected back at me. "I won't let anything come between us," I vow, my voice steady and determined. "We'll take this one step at a time and make it work."

She nods, her expression resolute.

"Go out on a date with me, Vita Mia."

Chapter Nine

Angela

When I got home, I was buzzing with so much adrenaline that I ran up the stairs to my apartment. Me running, *an abomination.* The moment I closed the door, I collapsed to the floor, not from the four flights of stairs I had just run up, but from the burning feeling in my heart.

I kissed him. He kissed me. Well, he devoured me because that was not just a kiss. Every time his lips met mine, my mind went blank. His cologne, his presence, his smile, the dimple, those unbelievable ocean blue eyes, they overwhelmed me completely.

"Oh! How are you real?" I call out to the empty apartment, my voice echoing slightly off the walls.

I lean back against the door, my heart still racing. The memory of his touch, his kisses, plays over and over in my mind, each recollection sending a fresh wave of heat through me. It felt like a dream, one too vivid and perfect to be real.

I can still feel the ghost of his hands on my skin, the way he held me as if I were the most precious thing in the world. A smile spreads across my face, and I let out a breathless laugh. "This is insane," I mutter to myself, shaking my head in disbelief.

Getting to my feet, I head to the kitchen for a glass of water, hoping to calm my racing heart. As I pour the water, my hands are still trembling slightly from the intensity of the night. I take a long sip, the cool liquid grounding me, bringing me back to reality.

But even as I stand there, a sense of euphoria bubbles up inside me. His words echo in my mind, as do his promises and his passion. There was something so genuine, so raw about the way he spoke to me as if he could see right into my soul. And I knew, in that moment, that this was just the beginning.

"This is real," I whisper to myself, a determined smile forming on my lips. "And I'm going to embrace every moment of it."

With renewed energy, I push away from the counter and head to my bedroom. Tonight, I will dream of him, of us, and tomorrow, I will face the world with the knowledge that something extraordinary has begun.

It's then that I realise I don't even know his name.

"What the fuck is wrong with you, Angela?" my disbelieving voice echoes through the empty apartment. "Who does that? You made out with a complete stranger and didn't even ask his name? What the fuck is wrong with me?"

The ice-cold bucket of reality crashes over me. *This isn't me. This isn't me at all.* I should cancel the date, forget about it. I need to focus on my bar exam and move on with my life.

But an unfamiliar pain creeps through my chest, something I didn't even know I was capable of feeling. I pull out my phone, panic starting to rise, when it hits me again: *I never asked him his name.*

A sense of shame and confusion is taking over my happiness, and then I remember that *he saved his number in my phone when he dropped me off.*

I know his name! See, I know his name. I'm okay!

With a mixture of relief and curiosity, I open my phone and look at the last entry. When I see how he saved himself in my contacts, I burst out laughing. He saved his name as "*The love of my life."*

"What a cocky guy! The love of my life, my ass," I mutter, shaking my head in amusement. "I just met you and let you kiss me a bit. Well, a bit more than a bit, but still."

The absurdity of the situation makes me laugh even harder. *Did anyone ever call him out on his cocky humour?* I wonder. Probably not, with those ocean-blue eyes and that devastating smile.

I stare at the contact name for a moment longer, a grin still on my face. His boldness is both infuriating and endearing, a combination that makes my heart flutter. I tap on the contact, considering whether to text him or wait. The anticipation is thrilling, and I know I won't be able to resist for long.

Finally, I type out a message:

Angela

Hey, 'Love of my life,' this is 'The girl who let you kiss her a bit.' Did anyone ever call you out on your cocky humour? Because you totally deserve it.

I hit send and lean back against the bed, the adrenaline from the night still buzzing in my veins. As I wait for his reply, I think about how unexpected this evening turned out to be. Meeting someone who could make me feel so much in such a short time it's both exhilarating and terrifying.

My phone buzzes almost immediately with his reply:

Dominic

Hey, beautiful! Glad you found the humour in that.
And no, not many have called me out, until now.
Can't wait to see you again.

My heart skips a beat, and I can't help but smile at his response. The flirtation, the promise in his words, it all makes me feel alive in a way I haven't in a long time. This is just the beginning, and I can't wait to see where this journey will take us.

When I woke up the next morning, I was a mess. I fell asleep without changing or taking any makeup off. Well, I don't wear a lot of makeup, but still, my eyes are completely black, my breath is awful, and my clothes look like rubbish. I definitely drank too much last night as this migraine starts building in my head, squishing my thoughts out. I walk into the shower, letting the water cascade over my body and enveloping me in its warmth. By the time I'm done, I feel a bit better, especially now that my face is not black from the mascara and dried drool is in the corner of my mouth.

"I look sexy as hell when I wake up. Clearly, that is the perfect way to charm a man." I giggle while staring at myself in the mirror.

I notice the fullness of my breasts and remember when one of my exes made a remark that they were too heavy. *What a fucker!* It's shit, I know, but the memory still stings. I glance down at the stretch marks on the side of my abdomen and flinch at the thought of what *"The love of my life"* will think of them.

"I cannot go out with a man like him. He will break me beyond repair! He is far too handsome for someone like me," I whisper to myself, the doubt gnawing at my confidence. "If he were just intelligent but not so good-looking, I could deal with that. But he is the most beautiful, handsome, extraordinarily attractive man I have ever seen in my life."

The thought overwhelms me, and I decide to text him and cancel our date tonight. Suffocating pain mixed with doubt envelops my mind, and my migraine intensifies tenfold in mere seconds.

I pick up my phone, my hands trembling slightly as I open our message thread. The anticipation and excitement from earlier feel like a distant memory, replaced by a crushing sense of inadequacy. I start typing:

Angela

Hey, I'm really sorry, but I don't think tonight is going to work for me. Something came up. I hope you understand.

I stare at the message, my finger hovering over the send button. A part of me screams to hit send to save myself from the potential heartache and rejection. But another part of me, a quieter yet stronger voice, urges me to pause.

Taking a deep breath, I close my eyes and try to calm the storm inside my head. I think about the way he looked at me, the way he made me feel cherished and desired in such a short time. *Was I really going to let my insecurities ruin something that could be amazing?*

With a surge of determination, I delete the message and instead type:

Angela

Hey, I'm looking forward to tonight. Can't wait to see you again.

I hit send before I can second-guess myself, and then I toss my phone onto the couch, feeling a mix of fear and relief. The decision to push through my doubts feels like a small victory, a step toward embracing the possibility of happiness.

I stand up, taking a moment to stretch and shake off the lingering anxiety. *I can do this,* I tell myself. *I deserve to be happy, and I deserve to be with someone who makes me feel this way.*

The door to my apartment opens, and my mum walks in with a big smile on her face and carrying a box of my favourite pancakes.

"Good morning, my darling! I missed you so very much this past week, and I am so happy this semester is over. So I thought I would surprise you with breakfast in bed." She leans over, kisses the top of my head, and hugs me.

"Good morning, Mum. I missed you too. I smashed it in court, and they all know it now," I say with full confidence to the woman who taught me more about people than anyone professor could from a book.

Her eyes light up with pride, a warm smile spreading across her face. "That's my girl," she says, pulling me into a tight embrace. "I never doubted for a second that you'd show them what you're made of."

Her words fill me with a sense of accomplishment and validation. Mum has always been my rock, the person who believed in me even when I doubted myself. She taught me to read people, to understand their motivations, and to navigate the complexities of human interactions.

"Thanks, Mum," I reply, pulling back slightly to look at her.

We sit down at the kitchen table, and I recount the highlights of the trial, her eyes never leaving mine as she listens intently.

"And you should have seen their faces, Mum," I say, excitement bubbling up as I describe the reactions of my opponents. "They didn't know what hit them when I went on my attack cross-examination!"

She chuckles, her eyes twinkling with amusement. "I can just imagine. You must have been a force to be reckoned with."

"We went out for drinks celebrating afterwards," I say shyly, looking at the leftover pancakes on my plate. "And I met someone." I still avoid her eyes as I am not sure how she will react when I tell her who it is.

"There you go, my sex vibes, serial killer," she says and bursts out laughing. "Tell me everything!" she wiggles her eyebrows at me.

"Oh, Mum! You are so silly sometimes!"

"Little bit!" she says with humour in her voice, "Now spill it, Angela." She leans her head on her hands and focuses on me, as if every word coming out of me is the most valuable thing there is for her.

"You actually know him," I say, barely above a whisper. "You remember the guy from the shop with the note?"

My mom's face goes completely blank, void of any visible emotion. *Well, this can't be good.*

"Is that so? And how did you bump into each other?" she asks, her tone too even, too controlled.

"Oh, you remember Steve, my colleague? The one who kept asking me out? He was making a move on me again, so I went to the bar to get some water, and there he was."

"Just like that," she says, her features shifting back to calm, confident, radiating her usual warmth. She pulls out her phone and starts typing furiously, faster than I ever thought she could type.

She looks up at me, a warm smile spreading across her face, but her fingers don't stop, still attacking the screen as if locked in a battle.

"Are you texting dad? Please, Mum, this is not a big deal. I don't want people to know what's going on with me. You know privacy is important to me, and this has not even actually started for me to say anything to anyone. The only reason I am telling you is because you were there when he left that amazing note for me."

"No, No," she brushes me off, "I am emailing myself a list of things I need to finish this weekend that just popped into my mind. Your dad does not know anything and will not know until you are good and ready." She smiles at me and winks again.

"Just be careful, my darling. Okay? I want you to promise me that you will tell me everything. I might be getting old, but I still know a thing or two about man, and if this one is for you, then I want to make sure he is the right one for you."

I reach across the table and squeeze her hand, appreciating the depth of her worry and the wisdom behind her words. After I promised I would be as honest as possible with her and we chatted about the shop and the latest gossip, she left, saying she needed to sort out some things today.

I am left all alone in my apartment with hours to kill until *The love of my life* will come to pick me up for our date. He refused to tell me anything about where we were going or what his plans were. The anticipation and excitement are like a pulse of adrenaline running through my body, consuming all in its path.

I checked my phone, and there was no text reply from him. It's ok, the man has a life, of course, he does not need to text me the second he reads a text. Well, actually, he did not even read it. Did he smash his phone again? "What a lunatic, going around smashing phones left, right and centre."

After a day of wasting time in my apartment, I start getting ready for the date a few hours before. I take a quick shower and shave off any new regrowth, making sure my skin is as smooth as possible. As I step out of the shower and towel off, I feel a mix of anticipation and anxiety building inside me.

I start putting lotion on my arms, massaging it in and enjoying the relaxed moment. The scent of the lotion is calming, a subtle reminder to take things one step at a time. But the moment I start massaging my abdomen and notice the stretch marks, doubt and shame start poisoning my mind and heart again.

I've never been one of those skinny women with a perfect body that would stop a man in his tracks, but I think I am beautiful in my own way. Or at least, I try to believe that. As I work the lotion into my skin, I can't help but trace the lines of the stretch marks, each one a silent testament to my body's journey.

By the time I start putting lotion on my legs and massage my inner thighs, I see white marks there as well. My heart sinks, and I'm seconds away from crying. The insecurity is overwhelming, a crushing weight on my chest that threatens to suffocate me.

I sit down on the edge of my bed, taking deep breaths to steady myself. "It's just skin," I whisper to myself, trying to shake off the negative thoughts. "It's just a part of who I am."

But the pep talk doesn't help much. The doubt lingers, gnawing at my confidence. I close my eyes and try to think of his smile, the way he looked at me, the connection we felt. I remind myself that he seemed genuine, that he wanted to see me again.

I stand up and force myself to keep going. I finish applying the lotion and move on to my hair, styling it with extra care. Each step in my routine is a small victory, a reminder that I am capable of pushing through my insecurities.

As I put on my makeup, I focus on accentuating the features I love about myself, my eyes, my lips. The process is therapeutic, a way to reclaim a bit of my confidence. By the time I'm done, I look at myself in the mirror and force a smile.

"You're beautiful," I tell my reflection, even if I don't fully believe it at the moment. "You deserve to be happy."

I slip into my dress, the fabric hugging my curves in all the right places. It's a bold choice, one that makes me feel both powerful and vulnerable. As I add the finishing touches, earrings, a spritz of my favourite perfume and try to channel the strength and determination that brought me this far.

I check the time and it's still half an hour to go. I check my phone and a text from *The love of my life* is on unread.

Dominic

I'm downstairs, Vita Mia.

Come when you are ready. I will wait for you all the days of my life.

This man and his words! Taking one last look in the mirror, I take a deep breath and head out the door. Tonight is a chance to embrace the possibilities, to let go of the doubt and enjoy the moment. No matter what happens, I am determined to face it with my head held high.

As I step out of the apartment building, I see him leaning casually against his car, a gorgeous, deep ocean blue Aston Martin. He looks so incredibly attractive that I pause for a moment, taking a deep breath to steady myself before walking over. Honestly, it should be illegal for a man to be this handsome.

"Hi," I say, my voice a little shaky but filled with genuine warmth.

"Hi," he replies, his eyes locking onto mine. "Ready for our date?"

"More than ever," I answer, stepping closer to him. He reaches out for my hand and places it on his chest, then he cups the back of my neck and rests his forehead against mine. The warmth of his touch and the steady beat of his heart beneath my palm make my own heart race.

"You are so beautiful, Vita Mia. My chest hurts at seeing you," he murmurs, his voice filled with raw emotion. His words send a shiver down my spine, and I feel my breath hitch in my throat.

He leans in and presses a feather-soft kiss on my lips. The contact is gentle yet electrifying, sending waves of warmth and desire through me. It's as if the world around us fades away, leaving just the two of us suspended in this perfect, intimate moment.

His fingers lightly trace the back of my neck, and I melt into his touch, my body responding to the tenderness and passion in his kiss. I can feel his heart pounding under my hand, mirroring the intensity of my own feelings.

When he pulls back slightly, his eyes search mine, filled with a mixture of adoration and longing. "I can't believe you're here with me," he whispers, his voice trembling with sincerity. "You make everything else seem insignificant."

He pulls me closer, wrapping his arms around me in a protective embrace. I rest my head against his chest, listening to the steady rhythm of his heartbeat. In his arms, I feel safe, cherished, and completely loved.

For a moment, we stand there, lost in the comfort and warmth of each other's presence. The doubts and insecurities that plagued me earlier fade into the background, replaced by the certainty of his affection.

"Let's make tonight unforgettable," he says, his voice filled with determination. "Just you and me, embracing every moment. I want all of you, Vita Mia, give me all of you as you already have all of me."

I don't get a chance to make a remark or show my surprise as he starts kissing me with a desperation and intensity that catches me off guard. I let myself go and enjoy the moment, savouring the feel of his embrace, the starving way he kisses me, his intoxicating and addictive cologne, and his hands caressing my back.

We stay there, exploring and enjoying each other, losing ourselves in the other's existence. His lips move against mine with a fierce hunger, each kiss deepening the connection between us. His hands trace the contours of my back, sending shivers of pleasure through me. I respond with equal fervour, my fingers tangling in his hair, pulling him closer.

Every touch, every breath we share feels electric, a current of passion that binds us together with each passing second. I feel as if I'm losing control, swept away by the sheer intensity of our desire, and we haven't even gotten in the car yet.

He pulls back slightly, his forehead resting against mine, both of us breathing heavily. "You drive me crazy," he whispers, his voice a mix of awe and urgency.

"You do the same to me," I reply breathlessly, my heart pounding in my chest. "I never imagined it could be like this."

He smiles, his eyes dark with longing. "There's so much more, Vita Mia. So much more I want to show you, to share with you."

I nod, unable to find the words to express the whirlwind of emotions inside me. Instead, I pull him closer again, capturing his lips in another searing kiss. His response is immediate, his arms tightening around me as if he can't bear to let go.

Minutes or hours could have passed, time seems to lose all meaning as we stand there, wrapped in each other's arms. The world outside ceases to exist, leaving only the two of us bound by an undeniable connection. *How does everything always fade away when I'm with him? What kind of power does this man wield?*

Finally, he pulls away, his eyes searching mine. "Let's go," he says softly, his voice filled with promise. "Let's make this night truly unforgettable."

He opens the car door for me and leads me in. Once he is seated and starts the roaring car, speeding through traffic, all the doubt vanished from my mind.

This man wants me. Out of all the women in the world, he wants ME.

There is no doubt that he could have any woman he desires, and yet, for some reason, he has chosen me. The thought sends a thrill through me, but it also brings a wave of panic.

If I weighed the gravity of the situation through an emotional lens, the intensity of it all is overwhelming. The idea of being the object of his desire, of him choosing me above all others, makes my heart race and my mind spin with doubt and fear. *Am I enough for him? Can I live up to his expectations?*

But if I look at it from a practical, realistic point of view and weigh his actions and the actual words he has spoken, I am flooded with a sense of security. This man actually wants me. He has shown me through his tenderness, his words, and his actions that his feelings are genuine.

Regardless of who he can or cannot have, *HE CHOSE ME!*

That realisation brings a sense of peace and reassurance that cuts through the panic. I take a deep breath, letting the certainty of his choice wash over me. He has made it clear that I am the one he desires and that knowledge is so powerful.

He has seen something in me that draws him, something that makes him want to be with me. And as I stay here, feeling the warmth and intensity of his presence, I realise that maybe, just maybe, I am worthy of his affection.

With that thought, I let go of my insecurities and allow myself to fully embrace the moment. *He chose me, and I will not let my fears ruin what could be something beautiful.* I look over at him, a smile spreading across my face, and I see his eyes light up in response. I lean over, place my hand on his thigh, and gently squeeze.

He places his hand on top of mine, and I notice a slight tremble in his touch. I lift his hand and kiss the back of it, then rest my cheek on it for a few seconds before placing my hand back on his thigh.

We arrive at an Italian restaurant, and as we make our way out on the terrace, I notice it is completely empty, except for the hostess and a waiter. The moment we step out and the fresh night air hits me, I am left speechless at the beauty of the place.

There is a set-up table in the middle of the terrace, overlooking the astonishing city nightlights. The scene is complemented by beautiful overhead lights and box arrangements at every pillar, which are entwined with lush greenery. It's something straight out of a dream.

The terrace is an oasis of beauty and tranquillity amidst the bustling city below. The overhead lights cast a warm, inviting glow, creating an ambience of intimacy and charm. The box arrangements at the base of each pillar are filled with vibrant flowers, their colours vivid even in the soft evening light. The pillars, wrapped in cascading vines and leaves, add a touch of natural elegance to the setting.

The table itself is elegantly set, with fine china, sparkling glassware, and flickering candles adding to the romantic atmosphere. The city lights twinkle in the distance, creating a mesmerising backdrop that seems almost magical.

As I take in the scene, I feel a sense of awe and wonder. This place, this moment, feels almost surreal. It's as if we've stepped into a world where beauty and romance reign supreme, a world where anything is possible.

He guides me to the table, pulling out a chair for me with a gallant flourish. I sit down, my heart still racing from the whirlwind of emotions that have defined our evening. He moves the chair from across the table and takes the seat next to me as if he cannot comprehend putting distance between us, his eyes never leaving mine.

"This is incredible," I say, my voice filled with genuine admiration. "It's like something out of a fairy tale."

He smiles, reaching for my hand and placing it on his cheek. "I wanted to create a night you'll never forget," he replies, his voice soft and sincere. "You deserve nothing less." He leans in and places a soft kiss, barely touching my lips, before resting his forehead on mine. "The things you do to me, Vita Mia. You deserve it all, and I am here to deliver it."

This man and his words! In moments like this, I feel like my insides will liquefy, and I would become transparent for him to see all these emotions overwhelming me.

As we sit there, surrounded by the breathtaking beauty of the terrace and the city lights beyond, I feel a deep sense of contentment. This is more than I could have ever imagined, and I am grateful for every moment.

We place our order, and when the food arrives, it's a feast for the senses. I went for the gnocchi with truffle sauce, because if exceptional gnocchi is on the menu, there's no stopping me. *The love of my life* ordered the tagliatelle with beef ragu, which looks and smells absolutely mouthwatering.

"*Love of my life*", I say with a mocking tone and a big smile on my face. "Can I know your name now?" I lean my head on the palm of my hand and give him my best puppy dog eyes.

He burst out laughing, and that majestic smile with the dimple is on full display, taking my breath away with it.

"Dominic DeLuca, Vita Mia," he says, staring into my eyes, searching for a reaction as if that name would mean something to me. "But you can still call me *The love of my life*. That suits me better than my name when it comes out of your lips."

"Oh, my! Dominic DeLuca! Cocky much?" I burst out laughing at his surprised face as I called him out on it.

"Vita Mia, one day you will wear the DeLuca surname, but for now, I'm happy for you to call me *The love of my life*," he replies, his words filled with confidence and sincerity.

My body freezes, my mind goes blank at his words, and I can feel a blush creeping up my cheeks. *Did I imagine it, or did he just say that one day I will have the DeLuca surname? Surely not!*

"Did you really just say that?" I ask, my voice barely above a whisper, still processing his declaration.

He nods, his gaze unwavering. "I did," he confirms, his voice steady and sure. "I know it's soon, but when I look at you, I see my future. I see the woman I want by my side for the rest of my life."

The sincerity in his eyes, the conviction in his voice, overwhelms me. This isn't just a line, it's a window into his heart. A rush of emotions floods through me, a blend of fear, excitement, and hope. Part of me feels like I should run from words like these, but another part is screaming to stay, to be with him. It's as if, without him, I wouldn't be whole and losing him would mean losing a piece of myself.

"Dominic, this is... a lot to take in," I admit, my voice shaking slightly. "But I can't deny the connection I feel with you. It's intense and real, and it's scaring me just as much as it's thrilling me."

He reaches across the table, takes my hand, places a kiss on my palm, and sets it again on his chest as if he wants me to feel how erratic his heart is beating for me. His touch is warm and grounding, and it helps steady my racing thoughts. "I understand, Vita Mia. I'm not asking for everything all at once. I just want you to know how serious I am about you, about us."

I look into his eyes, seeing the earnestness there. The doubts that plagued me earlier feel like a distant nightmare, completely forgotten, replaced by a growing sense of certainty. This man, with his overwhelming charm and confidence, has chosen me. And despite the whirlwind of emotions, I can't help but feel that maybe, just maybe, this is where I'm meant to be.

"Okay," I say softly, squeezing his hand. "Let's take it one step at a time."

A radiant smile spreads across his face, and he leans in to kiss me gently. "That's all I need, Vita Mia. One step at a time, together."

Chapter Ten

Dominic

"Oh, my! Dominic DeLuca! Cocky much?" she exclaims, her eyes sparkling with mischief.

The bravery in this woman knows no limits, and a surprised expression escapes me before I can mask it away. But the moment she starts laughing, a carefree, genuine sound that lights up her face, I feel like I could fall to my knees right here, right now, and beg her to love me if that is what it takes.

Her laughter is infectious, and I find myself chuckling along with her. There's something incredibly freeing about her confidence, her ability to call me out and still make it feel like a shared joke. It makes me want her even more, this fearless woman who stands before me.

"Vita Mia, one day you will wear the DeLuca surname, but for now, I'm happy for you to call me *The love of my life*."

What the fuck did I say? Way to go, dumbass! There is no way in the world she will not run for the hills now. Fuck that shit! I will chase you for the rest of my days, Vita Mia, if I have to.

I look into her eyes to see the gravity of the catastrophe of my words spoken prematurely, and that adorable blush is on full display. There is an internal battle of fight or flight within her, but I think the shock of it is dimming some of the intensity of my words. *There you go!* That is the perfect dumbass comment to make on a first date with a woman that you would do anything to have. I need to keep to the speech I planned in my mind if I am to get her. *Keep to the plan, Dominic! Keep to the plan!*

"Did you really just say that?" Angela asks weakly.

Well, this is it, ladies and gentlemen! I either go all in, or I make excuses that I will need to recover from later on because there is no fucking way I will give her any room to escape me and this need to come out sooner or later.

"I did," I say with a clear and confident voice. "I know it's soon, but when I look at you, I see my future. I see the woman I want by my side for the rest of my life."

There! It's all out in the open now. I feel vulnerable, like someone opened my chest and pulled out my deepest secrets. *It's fucking terrifying!*

Angela's eyes widen, and for a moment, I see a mix of emotions flicker across her face, shock, uncertainty, and something that looks like hope. The silence stretches, and my heart pounds in my chest, each beat echoing the vulnerability I feel.

"Dominic, this is... a lot to take in," she admits, her voice shaking slightly. "But I can't deny the connection I feel with you. It's intense and real, and it's scaring me just as much as it's thrilling me."

I reach across the table, take her hand, place a kiss on her palm, and set it again on my chest. The feel of her palm on my chest is like she is touching my heart and my soul at the same time. It is like my being is calling to somehow absorb her into me, and this gesture is bringing me so much comfort that I can touch her, I can feel her. *She is mine to do as I please.*

"I understand, Vita Mia. I'm not asking for everything all at once. I just want you to know how serious I am about you, about us." I need to comfort her so she does not pull away. *She cannot pull away! It would break me to pieces and create a monster out of me.*

Just keep to the plan, Dominic!

A few moments pass where my internal turmoil is fighting a raging war, at which the end is a complete snap. *Fuck the plan!* I am going to show her as much as possible of myself and what she awakens within me. I cannot tell her that I'm in a mafia, but I can tell her how much I want her and how much I need her in my life. I can let my emotion show on my face, and I can start loving her as I need to: powerful, passionate, intense, obsessive, dangerous. She is mine, and she needs to realise this as well. *She is mine and forever will be mine!*

"Okay," she says softly, squeezing my hand. "Let's take it one step at a time."

The relief that floods through me is like a hug to my soul. I lean in and press a gentle kiss to her lips, savouring the closeness. "That's all I need, Vita Mia. One step at a time, together," I whisper.

She looks up at me, her eyes filled with a mix of emotions. "Thank you for being honest with me, Dominic. It means a lot."

As we stand there, the city lights twinkling around us, I feel a newfound sense of hope and determination. *This woman is fantastic!* I cannot believe I am this lucky to find someone this strong and vulnerable at the same time who is crazy enough to give me a chance and embark on a life with me. Well, in all fairness, she does not have a choice, but she does not know this, so the victory is oh so much sweeter.

"Right, before I make a bigger ass of myself speaking out too much, I have a game for you," I say, giving her the biggest smile I can muster and winking at her. "Are you up for a game, Vita Mia?"

She starts laughing, a mischievous smile playing at the corner of her mouth. "No strip poker, I hope," she says, giggling. "I am not going to get naked in a public place. Even more so in a classy place like this." She winks at me and laughs again, the sound light and infectious.

"Abso-fuckin-lutely not! I would take out any man's eyes that could see you like that! I will be the only one who sees you naked moving forward," I declare, my voice filled with possessive intensity.

Before she can respond, I lunge at her and start kissing her passionately, sealing my dominant words with dominant actions. My lips crash against hers, and I pour all my desire and determination into the kiss. She is mine, and she better start learning this if she doesn't want to see dead bodies dropping left, right, and centre around her.

Her initial surprise melts into reciprocation, her hands gripping my shoulders as she kisses me back with equal fervour. The world around us fades away, leaving only the heat and intensity of our embrace. My hands slide down her back, pulling her closer, needing to feel every inch of her against me.

When we finally break apart, both of us breathing heavily, I rest my forehead against hers, keeping my gaze locked with hers. "You're mine, Angela," I whisper fiercely. "And I'm yours. No one else matters."

She gazes up at me, her eyes a mix of passion and amusement. "Dominic, you are something else," she murmurs, her voice tinged with affection. "But I have to admit, I like the idea of you all possessive as much as I like the idea of being yours."

I smile, feeling a surge of triumph and love. "Good. Because I'm not letting you go."

We stand there for a moment, wrapped in each other's arms, the connection between us growing stronger with every heartbeat. The game, the playful banter, all of it fades in the face of the deeper bond we share.

"Alright, what's this game of yours?" she asks, her eyes twinkling with curiosity. She laughs, the sound filling me with joy. "Okay, I'm in. Let's see what you've got, Dominic DeLuca."

"I will ask you three questions, and you have to answer truthfully, then you can ask me the same question back or you can ask me something you want," I reply, my tone teasing. "But I promise you'll enjoy it, even if you don't expect to."

She starts laughing again, and the easygoing attitude and light banter are making my heart swell with anticipation and my mind more dizzy than if I were half drunk. Clearly, I am drunk on this beautiful and intoxicating creature. *Fuck me! She is so beautiful!*

"Let me see what you got, Dominic DeLuca," she says and winks at me.

Fuck me, this woman! Calm Dominic! Calm! You cannot fuck her in a restaurant. You will have to murder too many people after that. *Calm!*

"What is your biggest regret?" I ask calmly and confidently, anticipation dripping from my words.

"Not being braver." Her smile falters, and a darker note appears on her face.

"By the way, you need to elaborate. You can't just give a one-word answer," I say, trying to lighten the mood again.

"What? This is renegotiating the verbal contract! I did not agree to that, and pushing for renegotiation so early on in our relationship seems unethical," she says with a playful tone, catching onto my attempt to shift the energy.

"Relationship? Also, don't think I didn't notice how you're teasing me by calling me by my name, Vita Mia. I suggest you call me by my love name if you don't want me to start kissing you until I literally take your breath away."

Her eyes widen slightly, a mix of amusement and challenge lighting them up. "Oh, so we're playing by those rules now, are we?"

I lean in closer, my voice dropping to a husky whisper. "Yes, we are. And I take my rules very seriously."

She laughs softly, the tension easing as she relaxes back into her playful self. "Alright, *The love of my life*, I'll play along. But you still owe me an answer about this verbal contract."

I smile, feeling the lightness return. "Deal. Now, back to your biggest regret."

She takes a deep breath, her eyes thoughtful. "I regret not being braver when I felt hurt. Looking back, there were a lot of times when my pain muted my fighting spirit, and I let people get away with things that I should not have. As I told you, I believe in cause and effect. If you get pushed, you must push back. It pains me to have these memories that I was not stronger and pushed back harder in moments that really matter to me."

I nod, absorbing her words. "Fear can be paralysing, but recognising it is the first step to overcoming it. And you have a chance to be brave now, to take those risks."

She looks at me, her eyes softening. "You make it sound so simple. But if I think about it, perhaps this was one of the reasons I wanted to become a lawyer. To be strong, to be brave and to fight for what I want with everything I've got."

"It's not simple," I admit. "But it's worth it. *You're worth it.*" I smile with admiration and adoration at the woman who is pulsing through my veins as she belongs there, running through me and keeping me alive.

"You are going to be an amazing lawyer, Vita Mia. You are absolutely amazing!"

She smiles, a genuine warmth in her eyes. "Thank you, Dominic."

I wink at her. "Anytime, Vita Mia."

We sit in comfortable silence for a moment, the city lights twinkling around us. The intimacy of the conversation, the connection we share, grows deeper with every passing second. After the revelation she just shared, I sense she needs a few moments to process, to let go of any lingering feelings or at least start analysing them from a different angle.

"Now it's your turn," she says, breaking the silence. "What's your biggest regret?"

I take a deep breath, thinking about her question. *I cannot tell her the full truth because she would run screaming away from me.* "My biggest regret is not finding you sooner."

She reaches out and takes my hand, squeezing it gently. "Sounds like we've both learned some valuable lessons. Me that I should be brave always and push back, and you that you're full of shit."

The conviction and serious tone with which she said those words made me laugh so hard that tears form in my eyes.

"You're beautiful, clever, amazing woman! What the fuck are you doing to me? You are an extraordinary woman, Angela, fully deserving of calling you *Vita Mia* because that is what you are becoming. I gravitate toward you and inhale every gesture and word coming out of you." I start peppering kisses on her inner arm, working my way up to her palm, then finishing on her fingers, then placing the hand on my knee.

"Stop trying to distract me, Love of my life. I see you!" she gives me her best suspicious look. "Fine, shoot your next question."

"What is your biggest fear?" I ask, my voice soft yet filled with curiosity.

I see her scared face for a split second, panic changing her features, and I regret the question as fast as it came out of my mouth. My angel, my life, my desire. *If only she knew how much I wanted to protect her, to take away all her fears.*

"My biggest fear?" she repeats, her voice trembling slightly. She looks down, avoiding my gaze, and I can see the internal battle she's waging.

I reach out and gently lift her chin, making her look at me. "You don't have to answer if you don't want to," I say softly, my thumb brushing her cheek. "But I want you to know, whatever it is, I'm here. I will carry all your fears for you, and I will fight all your battles. Just let me in, just let me carry them with you. Please, Vita Mia."

Her eyes well up with tears, and she blinks them away quickly, trying to maintain her composure. "I'm afraid you will think less of me," she finally admits, her voice barely above a whisper. "I'm afraid if I am honest, you might not understand."

My heart aches at her confession, and I pull her into a gentle embrace. "There is nothing that would make me think less of you", I whisper into her hair. "I am here, and I'm not going anywhere. *You are everything, Vita Mia.*"

She clings to me, her body trembling with the effort to hold back her tears. I stroke her back, comforting her as best as I can, wishing I could take away all her pain.

"Okay, I will tell you," she murmurs against my chest. "My biggest fear is to be poor, not having enough money for food or ending up on the streets alone."

Her eyes are full of tears now, and she tries to study me and read my reaction as best as she can while controlling her emotions. I can see the vulnerability in her gaze, the raw fear that she's kept hidden for so long.

I study her for a while longer, giving her time to regulate her emotions before I ask more. I need to understand where this fear is coming from, to know how to help her overcome it.

Gently, I brush a tear from her cheek and look into her eyes. "Thank you for sharing that with me, Vita Mia," I say softly. "I want to understand where this fear comes from. Was there something that triggered it?"

She takes a deep breath, her eyes flickering with uncertainty before she begins to speak. "I am half Romanian, and when I was little, my mum used to take me back from time to time so I would know that part of my heritage." She starts to pull back from me, and I hug her tighter, preventing such an abomination as putting space between us.

She smiles at my reaction, takes a deep breath to steady herself and looks at me with a longing mirrored in my eyes.

"You don't think I'm superficial? That I want money to be rich and to look down on others?" A tremble starts to rock through her body at the admission of her fear.

"Baby! Oh my goodness, Vita Mia." I hug her tighter again, kiss the top of her head, and nuzzle my face in the crook of her neck. "You are going to be a lawyer. Therefore, you are a fighter, Amore Mio. You are going to be rich through your own hands and strength. There is nothing superficial about that. It's admirable and a testimony to your strength."

"But I still cannot quite picture the trigger. So what, you are half Romanian?" I ask, trying to understand the root of her fear.

"Well, I was probably around five years old when I went with my mum to the markets," she begins, her voice trembling slightly. "We were enjoying our day when I saw a little boy, probably my age, begging for money. He was beaten up, dirty, and visibly hurt. Even at that age, I could understand that something was terribly wrong for this boy."

Tears start pouring down her cheeks now, cascading sorrow for that little boy. I feel an excruciating pain in my chest and pull her closer, wishing I could take away her pain.

"I asked my mum why the boy was begging, and she said that there are a lot of gypsies in Romania and that some of their tribes do not treat their kids very well. They force them to beg and steal and do all sorts of things, and if they don't listen, they get beaten up, tortured, or killed." She is visibly shaking now in my arms, and the only thing I can do is hold her, kiss her hair, and brush my hands along her back in an effort to comfort her and encourage her to let it all out.

"It was then that I swore to myself I would never be poor, and I would never end up on the streets," she continues, her voice trembling with emotion. "Seeing that boy, knowing what he went through, terrified me. It made me realise that could've been me if my mum and dad weren't around, and that thought scared me to death."

I hold her tighter, my heart aching for the pain and fear she has carried with her for so long. "I'm so sorry you had to see that," I whisper, my voice filled with empathy. "But I want you to know, Vita Mia, that you will never face that fear alone. I am here for you, and I will do everything in my power to make sure you always have everything you need and want."

She bursts out laughing and pulls out of my arms to wipe her face. "There you go! The most stupid, ridiculous statement of the day. Enough to pull a crying woman out of her darkest moment."

She nods, her eyes shining with tears but also with gratitude. "Thank you, Dominic. It means a lot to hear you say that, but I cannot accept anything from you." She looks at me dead in the eyes with so much confidence. "And just so we are clear, Romanians are not gypsies, and it's an insult to call a Romanian a gypsy. Furthermore, gypsies that people imagine in their mind are nothing like the real rich people that are where my mum comes from. There are tribes that are awful, but the rest of them are quite intelligent, kind and lovely."

"Wow! A front-row seat to the amazing lawyer in the making." I smile, making sure she sees my dimple, she did say she loved it, after all. *What kind of cruel man would I be to deny her that pleasure?* I laugh at my own ridiculous comment while she gives me that determined look, sticking to her guns.

I pull her closer, my arms wrapping around her protectively. "I promise you, Vita Mia, I will do everything in my power to make sure you never have to face that fear again. You are safe with me."

She buries her face in my chest, and I can feel her body slowly relaxing as the weight of her fear starts to lift.

"What is your biggest fear, Love of my life?" she asks after sitting back in her seat fully.

"Going back to Italy," I say, not meeting her eyes.

"I don't get it," she says with curiosity in her voice. "Please elaborate."

"Going back to Italy and facing a family that did not want me."

I cannot look at her. I never said those words to anyone, not even Elijah, not even Buddy. *How fucked up can you be to abandon your child just because he's different.* I know I am a lot, and I know I am intense, passionate and out of control sometimes, but I needed them, I wanted them, and they just abandoned me in that hellhole.

"Oh!" she gasps and hugs me.

I am not sure if she ever initiated a hug before, but fuck me, it feels like I am melting at her feet, and all that pain is slowly been dissolved by this beautiful creature. *She truly is my life now.*

We sit in silence for a while, the only sound being the soft hum of the city around us. I gently stroke her hair, offering her the comfort and reassurance she needs as she hugs me tightly and comforts my pain in return.

She pulls back, looks me dead in the eyes with what she probably thinks is a suspicious look and stares me up and down a few times.

"You are so adorable, Vita Mia, and I could eat you all up!" I say, then burst out laughing.

"How are you doing this? Where are these questions coming from? There is something suspicious here because I have been on dates before, but they never felt like this. So what the hell are you doing, playing, or is it the wine? How are you doing this?" she asks, her eyes narrowing playfully as she studies me.

"I hope to all that is precious that you never had a date like this before because, fucking hell, I put a lot of thought into this." I take a sip of the beautiful wine and smile at her again. It fucking hurts in my chest to look straight at her. *She is fucking gorgeous!*

"The wine is good, but the company is what is making this unforgettable." I lean in and place a soft kiss on her lips, savouring the brief but electric contact.

"Are you ready, Vita Mia? The last question..." I ask, my voice dropping to a low, intimate tone.

"Dominic DeLuca, I tell you right now, if you make me cry again tonight, there will be severe consequences," she laughs, taking a mouthful of her dessert. The sound of her laughter is like music, and it lifts my spirits even higher.

"Consequences. I like that! I do want anything and everything with you, so let me have them all," I say, my eyes locked onto hers, conveying the depth of my sincerity.

She laughs again, shaking her head in amusement. "Alright, what's this final question then?"

I take a deep breath, gathering my thoughts and the courage to ask the question that has been lingering in my mind.

"What is your biggest wish?"

She looks at me, her eyes softening as she contemplates the question. "That's a tough one," she admits, setting her fork down. "I hope you'll understand this too. I crave something authentic in my life. Someone truly honest, with both the good and the bad." She studies me for a moment before continuing. "Since I was little, I've felt this pull to something dark. No, not just a pull, *a need*. I know life is made up of light and shadow, and when someone only shows the best side of themselves, it feels fake. Like they're hiding behind lies. I hate liars, and all I want is for someone to be real with me, to show me everything, no matter how messy or dark."

Holy fucking shit. Did she just say she craves the dark as much as the light? What the actual fuck? Is it possible she'd understand if I told her who I really am? My mind starts racing at breakneck speed, and for the first time since I met her, I feel unbalanced, completely thrown by her presence and her words.

This is too much! Can I really tell her that I can fucking ruin some life without a second thought or hunt, torture, and kill someone? Surely she would think I am a psychopath and run for her life. *No!!! I most definitely cannot tell her that part of myself.*

Deep breaths, Dominic! Deep breaths! Calm down! Calm!

Her answer touches me deeply, and I reach across the table, taking her hand in mine. "You are an amazing woman, Vita Mia. *I will share all of me with you.*"

A mischievous smile plays at her lips. "Your turn, Love of my life. Spill!"

I take a deep breath, feeling the weight of my words before I speak them. "My biggest wish is for you to accept me as I am," I say just above a whisper. "*All of me.*"

Her eyes widened slightly, and I could see the surprise and curiosity there. "Accept you as you are?" she repeats, her voice soft and questioning.

I nod, my heart pounding in my chest. "Yes. I have my flaws, my past, and my insecurities. I want you to see me for who I truly am and still choose to be with me. That's my biggest wish."

She squeezes my hand, her eyes searching mine. "Dominic, you have my word that as long as you are truthful with me and don't give me a reason to leave, I will not look for a reason to leave." She lifts my hand and kisses the back of it, then looks into my eyes with the longing I feel for her.

"Whatever it is, there will be a time when you feel comfortable telling me. Just don't lie to me. And in return, I will try to understand. You have my word, Love of my life."

A wave of relief and gratitude washes over me, and I can't help but smile. "Thank you, Vita Mia. That means more to me than you could ever know."

She leans in, her eyes filled with warmth and affection. "We're in this together, Dominic. No matter what."

I lean forward, closing the distance between us, and kiss her gently. The kiss is tender and filled with promise, sealing our commitment to each other.

As we pull back, I rest my forehead against hers, feeling a sense of peace and fulfilment. "You are my greatest wish come true," I whisper.

"Ok! Ok! My turn!" she squeals excitedly, jumping out of my arms.

"Are you ready, Mr. DeLuca?" Excitement and something else is bubbling in her voice, her eyes sparkling with mischief.

"By your reaction, I'm a bit scared, I admit," I reply, faking reservation and letting a mock panic show on my face.

She laughs, and a delightful sound fills the air with joy that goes straight to my heart. "Don't worry, it's nothing too scary... or maybe it is," she teases, her grin widening.

I raise an eyebrow, leaning back slightly. "Alright, hit me with your best shot. What have you got for me?"

She steps closer, her expression turning serious for a moment as she tries her best to make a serious, analysing face that might intimidate me. *She is very funny!*

My goodness, me, this woman! Fucking hell, since I picked her up, I've tried my best to control myself and not fucking get a hard-on the entire time we are at dinner, but the more I learn about her, how she moves, how she talks, how charming she is, how intelligent, funny, and strong she is, the more I feel all my self-restraints fading away as if they were never there in the first place.

She tilts her head slightly, her eyes narrowing in mock concentration. "Alright, Mr. DeLuca, are you ready for me?" she asks, her voice dripping with playful seriousness.

"Bring it on!" I join the little teasing play.

"We will need two pieces of paper and pens for this game. I have neither, so we are not off to a great start." She says, then bursts out laughing, tilting to the side, laughing so hard.

Fucking hell. Seeing her like this mischievous, playful, joking around with me, I just know, with every fibre of my being, this woman was made for me. A fierce sense of ownership floods my heart, mind, and cock. *She's mine. She's mine. She will always be mine, and she'll learn that soon enough, there's no escaping it.*

I'm so fucking hard it's becoming painful, but I know she needs this. She needs this banter, this honesty, this time with me. I know she's the one custom-made for me. But I'm giving her all the time she needs to process her feelings. *She'll learn. She will learn. She has to.*

I fake a face of pure shock, slide my hand into my suit jacket, and pull out a Montegrappa pen, waiting for her reaction.

She starts laughing hard, and for a moment, I am confused about what exactly happened because this should impress someone, not make them laugh.

In between laughter, she points to my pen, and I can barely understand her. "You come here with this BIC imitation and pull it out of your jacket as if it was a Montblanc made out of gold." She is physically tilting in her chair, laughing so hard.

Fuck me sideways! This woman! She is so funny when she is carefree, so eclectic, so enticing. I feel I am losing connection with reality, and all that exists is her.

Her laughter is infectious, and I find myself chuckling along with her, unable to resist the joy radiating from her. "I had no idea my choice of pen would be such a source of entertainment," I say, my own laughter bubbling up.

She wipes away tears of mirth, her eyes sparkling. "You really thought you were going to impress me with that pen, didn't you?" she teases, her voice still trembling with laughter.

"Well, I thought it had a certain charm," I reply, grinning. "But clearly, I underestimated your keen eye for luxury stationery."

She leans forward, still giggling, and takes my hand. "Dominic, you don't need a fancy pen to impress me. But for the purpose of this game, hand it over."

Her words make my heart skip a beat, and I feel a warmth spread through my chest. I learned early on that no one cares about me at all. I learned that if I want to laugh and have any resemblance of happiness, I need to make myself laugh. Sitting next to this creature that is larger than life itself, I realise that *she does care* and is already making me happy. *She is my life! She is my everything!*

She laughs again, the sound like music to my ears. "Now we just need some paper and another pen."

The way she looks at me, her eyes filled with genuine affection, makes me feel like the luckiest man in the world. Her laughter, her carefree spirit, it's all so intoxicating, and I find myself more captivated by her with each passing moment.

I get up from my seat, find some paper napkins and return triumphant at the table.

The moment I lock eyes with her again, I pull a Montblanc pen engraved with gold letters from the other side of my suit jacket. I wink and smile at her, registering her surprised and amused face.

"You naughty boy!" she says. She starts laughing and reaches for the pen.

"Hey. You said we both need a pen. Hands off the precious Montblanc pen engraved with a gold letter." I tease her back with a mischievous tone.

"Right! At least let me hold it for like one minute and smell it for two minutes," she says with a straight face.

"What? That is hilarious! You are so weird! I have never smelled a pen in my entire life. What should it smell like?" I reply, chuckling at her strange but endearing request.

When I tilt the pen to smell it, she places her hand on my knee again, this time for support, laughing so hard that her face looks a bit funny, and no sound is coming out. She's just shaking her head, silently saying no, while her whole body trembles with laughter. The moment the sounds explode outside is a mixture of laughter and crying all at the same time while she is trying to say something that is impossible to understand.

I've never seen anyone laugh this hard, this genuinely. A rush of joy and affection washes over me as I watch her lose herself in the moment. Her laughter is intoxicating, and I can't help but join in, feeling lighter and happier than I've ever been.

"You little minx! You're messing with me!" I pull her close and kiss the living hell out of her, deepening the kiss as my hands caress her back, drawing her in as much as I can.

"Was this the game?" I murmur, absorbing every reaction from her. When she shakes her head, I release her with a grin and set the second pen on the table. I make some space to see her napkin, joy and anticipation coursing through me.

She is funny, like really funny!

"What's next, Amore Mio?" I can barely recognise my own voice, it just sounds hopeful and happy. I don't think I have ever sounded hopeful before.

"Right! Stop making up Italian words and focus." She looks me dead in the eyes with a stern look that is more adorable than anything else.

"You need to answer three questions and explain why as a deep, complex answer. Makes sense?"

I am so amused at her tone and the stern words coming out of her mouth that I want to devour her mouth again. "Yes, Vita Mia. I can handle that." I smile my sweetest, subdued, shy smile.

"Questions 1: What is your favourite colour and why?"

"Questions 2: What is your favourite animal and why?"

"Questions 3: What is your favourite mess of water and why?"

"When you're done," she continues, "we can swap the napkins and find out the result of the game." She looks into my eyes, a sincere and hopeful smile playing on her face. "Just, please be honest no matter what, okay?"

"Yes, Vita Mia. I will be honest no matter what." I don't get it, but it seems by her reaction that this is important to her. Perhaps it is some sort of psychological test that I cannot clearly see yet. *Fucking hell, I hope not! I hated it in my childhood, and I still hate it.*

When we both look up from our napkins, she has this wicked smile playing on her face. There is definitely more to the game than this question.

"Are you ready?" she teases again.

"I was born ready," I say with confidence and authority. "But I am scared because I think you are going to pull something funny on mine." I continue to pretend I am genuinely scared.

"Don't be ridiculous! We want the night to be unforgettable, right?" she says, giving me the most sexy fuck me eyes I have ever seen in my life.

"Now, we are going to exchange napkins and read them out loud. The key to the game is this:

1. The colour represents how we see ourselves.

2. The animal represents our ideal partner, and

3. The water mass represents our desired sex life."

Fucking hell, this woman! I fucking knew it! I fucking knew it would be some deep look into my soul of some sort that would expose me for who I really am.

Before I can pull the napkin away from her, she grabs it and hugs it to her chest.

"I was honest, Dominic DeLuca," the look in her eyes is pure vulnerability, "I hope you did not mess with me."

"I did not." For once in my life, I don't have a comeback because I am fucking terrified that she would see something that would make her run.

"Well, don't give me that look," she says, smiling at me. "This is supposed to be fun. I got it from a psychologist, and you will see it's actually really fun and true."

Fucking hell! I know it!

If you run, I will chase you for the rest of my days. You and your crazy psychological games! *Oh, she will run.* Panic rushes over me, followed by an unimaginable fury. *She'll fucking run.*

I reach for my wine, take a long sip, and try my breathing exercises, hoping she doesn't notice, at least not make a comment about it.

"Love of my life, look at me," she says, placing her palms on my cheeks and lifting my gaze to hers. "I would prefer a hard truth to a sweet lie. It can't be that bad," she laughs. "I told you, don't give me a reason to leave, and I will never do." She places a soft kiss on my lips.

"I'll go first if you want. You can read mine first."

I look at the napkin in front of me, my heart pounding. Her words and the warmth of her touch bring a small measure of comfort, but the fear still lingers.

"Alright," I say, my voice steadier now. "Let's do this." I take the napkin from her and look at her neat handwriting, then begin "translating" the abomination.

Angela

"Questions 1: What is your favourite colour and why?"

Purple – because it has depth, is unique, elegant, and classy.

"Questions 2: What is your favourite animal and why?"

Otters – because they are strong, intelligent, cute as hell, and always stay together as a family.

"Questions 3: What is your favourite body of water and why?"

Waterfalls – because they are strong, wild, and unstoppable.

I try to sound confident and comfortable when I start with the first 'answer'.

"You are unique, elegant, classy, and have a lot of depth. Vita Mia, that is 100% correct! I couldn't have described it better myself." I take her hand and kiss her inner palm. The gesture grounds me a bit more. She is all of that and more, perfect in every way. "Well, you are also very intelligent and hilarious, but I don't see how purple can represent all of that. So, I can add to it, right?" I say, kissing her palm again.

"You look for a partner who is strong, intelligent, cute as hell, and values staying together as a family," I say, starting to pepper kisses all over her palm and arm, kissing, biting, and licking to get my fill of her.

"Vita Mia, please give me this credit. I am cute as hell! You said it yourself, you like my dimple," I say, laughing at her reaction. Her cheeks flush, and she tries to hold back a smile, but it's clear she's amused.

"I can swear on anything you want. I am fucking intelligent as hell, and you will see it in time," I continue, leaning over to kiss her cheek. "And I am strong," I add, winking at her and kissing the tip of her fingers one by one. "And one day, you will have my name because you will be mine, only mine, from tonight onward."

She looks at me, her eyes wide with a mix of surprise and affection. "Dominic," she whispers, her voice trembling slightly. "Don't mess with me! You can't say something like that and not mean it."

"I mean it with all my heart," I reply, my voice steady and sincere. "I want you, Angela. All of you. And I want to give you all of me."

I hold her close, feeling the warmth of her body against mine, the steady beat of her heart echoing in my own chest. "One more question, Vita Mia," I say, pulling away slightly from her.

"You like your sex strong, wild, and unstoppable." As the words come out of my mouth, I feel all the blood rush from my body straight to my cock.

What the fuck?

"Vita Mia, do you want to kill me?" I say, trying to breathe through the dizziness.

I close the distance between us, capturing her lips in a kiss that is anything but gentle. It's fierce, hungry, and demanding, a reflection of the storm of emotions and desire raging inside me. She responds with equal enthusiasm, her hands tangling in my hair, pulling me closer.

As the kiss deepens, I can feel the heat between us building, an unstoppable force threatening to consume us both. My hands roam over her body, feeling every curve, every inch of her that I can reach. I gently lift the edge of her dress and touch her pussy. *Fucking hell!* She is hot and wet and ready for me, and as I start to massage her over her laced panties, she moans into my mouth, and the sound sends a jolt of pleasure straight to my cock.

When we finally break apart, both of us are breathing heavily, our foreheads resting against each other. "You're driving me crazy," I whisper, my voice ragged with need.

She smiles, her eyes dark with desire. "Good," she replies, her voice equally breathless. "Because you're doing the same to me."

I take a deep breath, trying to steady myself. "Let's get out of here," I say, my voice filled with urgency. "My apartment is in the building."

She nods, her smile turning wicked. "A little bit presumptuous, Mr. DeLuca."

"Not at all, Vita Mia." I offer her my hand as I stand up. "You already were mine since the shop. I just needed to teach you that you're mine." She rewards me with an audible gasp at my confession.

As she stands, I pull her close, and once we're in the elevator, I press the penthouse button. The moment the doors close, I'm on her like a starved man.

Her skin is soft, her curves full and sweet beneath my hands. I kiss, bite, and lick everywhere I can reach, her taste is intoxicating, sweet and perfumed, like a drug. The more I take in, the more I need, an all-consuming desire pulling at my very core.

With Angela, everything is more intense, more vibrant, more alive. And I can't wait to show her just how strong, wild, and unstoppable our connection can be.

The moment we are in the apartment, I slam her against the first wall and kneel before her. I lift her dress to her waist, and the image of her pussy through the laced panties is a sight to behold. She is wearing one of those, what the fuck are they called, garters or something? That is just tipping me over the edge.

"Fucking hell!" I growl from the floor in front of her. "You think I'm presumptuous, and you come dressed with something like that?" I place my face against her soaked pussy and inhale deeply.

"I am going to devour you!"

Chapter Eleven

Angela

"You are unique, elegant, classy and have a lot of depth. Vita Mia, that is 100% correct! I could not have described it better myself." He leans over, takes my hand, and kisses my inner palm. The tender and gentle gesture sends a shiver down my spine. *Does he really think that?* "You are also very intelligent and hilarious, but I don't see how purple can be those, so I can add to them, right?" *Well, there you go! Maybe he does think these things of me.*

"You look for a partner to be strong, intelligent, cute as hell, and to stay together as a family," he starts licking, kissing and biting my inner arm and palm. The sensation of his lips on my skin and the occasional bite followed by a lick and kiss is all it takes to push me so close to the edge of losing control that I am afraid it is written all over my face, how unbelievably attractive and devastatingly handsome I find him.

"Vita Mia, please give me this credit. I am cute as hell! You said it yourself, you like my dimple," he says with a teasing grin.

My face warms, my blush is betraying my desires for this man. His playful confidence only makes him more irresistible, and I struggle to keep my composure.

"I can swear on anything you want. I am fucking intelligent as hell, and you will see it in time," he leans over to kiss my cheek. "And I am strong," he adds, winking at me and kissing the tips of my fingers one by one. "And one day, you will have my name because from tonight on, you'll be mine."

The sincerity and determination in his voice make my heart race. His kisses, soft and deliberate, are the start of the volcano building within me, but his declaration is what makes my heart and mind skip a beat, grounding me in the here and now. *This cannot be! Does he really feel this way about me?* The anticipation makes my skin tingle, and I can feel a warmth that is both thrilling and terrifying spreading through me.

I look at him, unable to hide my true feeling of surprise and desire. "Dominic," I say just above a whisper, my voice trembling slightly. "Don't mess with me! You cannot say something like that and not mean it."

"I mean it with all my heart," his response instant and firm. "I want you, Angela. *All of you.* And I want to *give you all of me.*" He hugs me tightly in his arms, and I could feel all my restraints falling at his feet like they were not there in the first place. I am so overwhelmed by this man, by how beautiful he is as a person and how unbelievably handsome he is. The fact that he chose me is mind-blowing, but the fact that he actually wants me, every part of me, is the chain that shackles me to him and drags me to the deepest parts of losing complete control and falling hard for this man. I am falling for him, and there is no turning back if I let go, it will be all of me trapped in his orbit.

"One more question, Vita Mia," he says, pulling away slightly from me.

"You like your sex strong, wild, and unstoppable," he says, his voice low and intense. He pauses for a second, taking a deep breath as if trying to steady himself through whatever is going on in his mind.

"Vita Mia, do you want to kill me?" he asks, his eyes darkening with a mix of desire and torment.

I can see the struggle in his eyes and the effort it takes for him to maintain control. The raw honesty of his reaction sends a thrill through me, making my heart race even faster.

This is it! This is the moment I make my decision. *Do I pull away, or do I lose myself in Dominic DeLuca?*

The option is taken away from me when Dominic launches at me with all his might, capturing my lips in a fierce, hungry, and demanding kiss that is anything but gentle, a reflection of the storm of emotions and desire raging inside us. The last of my boundaries vanishes as my desire takes over, and my body moulds against his, pulling him closer.

His hands roam over my back, gripping and exploring with an urgency that matches my own. I can feel his heartbeat against my chest, a wild rhythm that syncs with my own. Every touch, every kiss, feeds the fire within me that burns hotter and fiercer with each passing second.

I respond with equal fervour, my hands tangling in his hair, pulling him closer as our lips move in a desperate dance. His kisses trail from my lips to my neck, each one leaving a trail of heat that makes me shiver with anticipation.

As his hands explore my body and his mouth devours my neck, I can feel the volcano within me erupt, and my mind is completely in the moment, savouring this man. The moment he touches my core, a deep growl escapes him, discovering the dampness of my panties, and when he starts teasing me over the lace, a moan escapes me at the pleasure that consumes me at his every touch.

"You're driving me crazy," he whispers, his voice ragged with need.

"Good," I reply, smiling, my voice equally breathless. "Because you're doing the same to me."

The predatory look in his eyes says it all. I truly am in for an unforgettable night. "Let's get out of here," he says, his voice filled with urgency. "My apartment is in the building."

I smile at his direct comment as if he already knows that the night would lead in this direction. "A little bit presumptuous, Mr. DeLuca."

"Not at all, Vita Mia," he says, offering me his hand as he stands up. "You were already mine since the shop. I just needed to teach you that you're mine."

The remark takes my breath away. *What? How?* My mind races to comprehend the depth of his words, but the intensity in his gaze tells me he means every word.

I can feel my body and mind completely letting go for once in my life. There are no boundaries I can't overcome with him. I'm all in, and I completely let go. This man can do whatever he wants to me and my body because I am truly and utterly lost in him.

I take his hand, feeling the strength and warmth in his grip. As he pulls me to my feet, our bodies press together, and the electricity between us is undeniable. He cups my face with his other hand, his thumb brushing gently across my cheek.

"Angela," he whispers, his voice low and filled with emotion. "You have no idea how much you mean to me and how much I need you."

I lean into his touch, my heart swelling with love and desire.

His eyes darken with intensity, and he leans in, capturing my lips in a kiss that is both tender and possessive. It's a kiss that speaks of promises and desires, of a future together that neither of us can deny.

Once the doors of the elevator close, our kiss deepens, and I feel the last remnants of my reservations melt away. This fire is inevitable. My hands move to his shoulders, gripping him tightly as if anchoring myself to him. His hands roam over my back, pulling me closer and moulding our bodies together.

When we finally pull apart, we're both breathing heavily, our foreheads resting against each other. "You're mine," he repeats, his voice a raw declaration.

"I'm yours," I reply, my voice trembling with the weight of my emotions. "Completely."

The bond between us feels unbreakable, a connection that goes beyond words. At this moment, I know that I am exactly where I am meant to be, with the man who has claimed my heart and soul.

"Vita Mia," he says softly, his eyes searching mine. "I promise to always protect you, to cherish you, to make you feel loved every single day." His words are like a soothing balm to broken parts of my soul I didn't even know existed. I feel complete somehow as if I don't need to carry all of my burdens on my own any more. I feel he cares enough for me to see things within me that I don't even notice and can mend my broken parts with such ease, as if I were perfect all along.

This man!

The moment we step into the apartment, he throws me against the nearest wall and drops to his knees before me.

"Fucking hell!" he growls from the floor, lifting my dress and looking up at me. "You think I'm presumptuous, and you wear something like this?" He presses his face against my soaked pussy, inhaling deeply.

"I'm going to devour you," he declares, his words clear and final, sending shockwaves through me. I'm already on the edge of ecstasy.

The way he kneels before me, breathing me in, it's the sexiest thing anyone has ever done to me. My whole body feels like it's on fire, and though he's the one on his knees, I'm the one melting away.

"Dominic, oh, baby, you don't need to do this," I say, playing with his hair.

He starts licking at my pussy over the panties and grabbing my ass to push me more towards his face.

"Vita Mia, I told you, my name shouldn't come out of your mouth." He says in a husky voice and starts pushing the panties aside with his tongue.

"I am going to devour you all tonight." He licks my folds and inhales deeply, savoring me. "I am going to fuck you raw until you are not able to walk." He gives me two more licks on my folds.

He looks up at me, lifting one of my legs and placing it over his shoulder. He starts kissing, biting, and licking my inner thigh while rubbing slow, circular motions over my pussy.

My body takes over, and delirious moans escape me as I respond instinctively to the overwhelming sensations evoked by the sight of this remarkably handsome man kneeling before me.

"Love of my life, what are you doing to me?" I say in a pleading, trembling voice. *I want more! I want so much more from him!*

The kisses are travelling closer and closer to my core, and I can feel the buildup of pleasure starting to consume me. The heat, the pleasure, the sensation of his lips on my skin, the occasional bites and licks are almost enough to push me over the edge.

When he is licking at my folds again, and his tongue sends long strokes of pleasure through me, the sensation and deep desire of needing him inside me is so consuming I start to tremble softly.

"Love of my life, please." I moan again and push his head into my pussy, starting to move my hips. I start rubbing on his face as he licks and softly bites my folds, sending jolts of electrifying pleasure through me.

"Please, what, Vita Mia?" he says with a wicked smile on his face.

Please, I need to feel you inside me," I plead, my voice thick with need.

"Amore Mio, this is just the beginning. I'm not stopping until you come all over my face."

He starts licking more aggressively than softly, parting my folds with his tongue. The moment he maneuvers my leg to give himself more access and starts long licks from my entry to the tip of my clit a few times, then starts sucking hard on my clit, I'm a goner.

A guttural scream escapes me as I grind on his face while he sucks on my clit hard, and I come on his beautiful face. My mind blanks, my vision whites out, and my ears buzz.

"Fuck, my love! Oh, I'm so sensitive. My love, please." I say in a pleading voice, trying to pull away.

"Fucking take it, Vita Mia," he says, pulling me back to him. "I am not done yet! Let me do my job." He starts again with the long licking strokes, avoiding the clit directly as if he knows my body, and this is an everyday thing, somehow as if he knows my body better than I do.

He tilts my hips up slightly, his tongue teasing the entrance in soft, deliberate strokes, not yet penetrating. A moan escapes me as my hips rock involuntarily, moving as if they have a mind of their own and they've known Dominic since the beginning of time.

"My love, please!" I plead with him. "I need you, love of my life!" I stroke his hair and try to pull at him. "I need you inside me, please."

His wicked tongue is inside me now, exploring, rubbing, and demolishing my reality. The sensation is overwhelming, sending shockwaves of pleasure through my body. The moment his thumb starts rubbing my clit hard in up-down motions while fucking me with his tongue, I feel my control slipping away. An unbelievably powerful volcano ready to erupt from within.

The intensity builds quickly, a tidal wave of ecstasy rising within me. My breaths come in ragged gasps, and my fingers grip his hair tightly.

The combination of his skilful tongue and the expert pressure on my clit drives me to the edge in minutes.

I come with a cry I did not know I was capable of, a primal sound that echoes through the room. My body convulses with the force of my orgasm, and I feel a rush of liquid release squirting onto his face. The sensation is both liberating and intoxicating, an expression of pure, unrestrained pleasure.

I try to pull away, but he starts lapping everything up, moaning into my pussy like a starved man. I try to move my hips back, but he moves both hands on my ass and buries his face in my pussy, lapping and moaning and swallowing me whole.

"You taste like fucking sin, Vita Mia," he growls into my pussy. "Fucking hell! If I did not want to let you go before, you have no chance now. *You are all mine!*" He growls, then licks me clean and swallows.

He doesn't stop, continuing to lick and suck, drawing out every last tremor of my climax. The waves of pleasure are endless, each crashing over me with renewed intensity. My mind is a haze of ecstasy, my body completely surrendered to the sensations he's creating.

"I need better access! I need more of you." He lifts my other leg on his shoulder and stands, supporting my back with his arms.

"Love of my life, I can walk," I say in a gasp, surprised by his strength. *How is he so strong?* "I'm scared you'll drop me." I grip his hair tightly, anchoring myself.

He gently lays me on his bed, and the last remaining tremors pass through me as my chest heaves and I struggle to catch my breath, my body tingling from the aftershocks of my orgasm. Dominic looks up at me, his face glistening with my release, a satisfied and almost feral grin on his lips.

"You are incredible," he murmurs, crawling up to kiss me, letting me taste myself on his lips. The kiss is gentle but deep, a stark contrast to the intensity we just shared, and it makes my heart swell with affection.

I smile weakly, still trying to recover. "That was... unbelievable," I manage to say, my voice hoarse. "I've never experienced anything like that before."

He brushes a strand of hair from my face, his eyes filled with adoration. "You have no idea how beautiful you are when you let go like that," he whispers.

His words send a shiver through me, and I pull him closer, needing to feel his warmth against me. "You make it easy to let go," I admit, my voice soft but filled with emotion.

"I need you, Vita Mia. I need all of you," he murmurs, his voice thick with desire as he starts pulling at my clothes, desperate to get me naked before him.

Panic surges through me. Oh, no! *He will see all of me.* He will see all my white marks, all my extra curves, all my defects, and it will put him off. He'll realise I'm not what he expected beneath the clothes and run off for someone perfect, someone smaller.

"Wait," I say, my voice trembling as I grasp his hands to stop him. "Dominic, please, I..."

He pauses, his eyes searching mine with concern. "Vita Mia, what's wrong?" he asks softly, his hands gentle on my arms.

"I... I don't know if I can do this," I confess, feeling the tears welling up in my eyes. "I don't look like all the other women you've been with," I continue in a shallow voice. "I don't want you to be disappointed, and I want to set your expectations correctly," I conclude, faking confidence I don't feel in the slightest.

His expression softens, and he cups my face in his hands, his touch tender and reassuring. "Vita Mia, listen to me," he says, his voice calm and soothing. "You are beautiful to me. Every part of you, every mark, every curve. I want all of you, just as you are."

"But... the white marks, the extra curves..." I trail off, my insecurities laid bare before him.

He shakes his head, his eyes filled with love and determination. "Those marks, those curves, they're a part of you. *And I want all of you.* Nothing about you could ever put me off. You're perfect to me, Angela."

"Also, what other women? There are no other women, Vita Mia. The moment I met you, everything was erased, and there were no women before you in my mind. You are the beginning and the end. I mean it with all my heart." He leans in to kiss me softly. "Trust me, Vita Mia. If you don't believe my words, let me show you how beautiful you are with my actions, and let me fuck you to my heart's content."

Taking a deep breath, I nod, feeling the panic slowly recede. I let him continue to undress me, his movements slow and reverent, as if he's unwrapping the most precious gift.

When I am finally bare before him, I close my eyes, bracing myself for his reaction. But instead of rejection, I feel his hands gently caressing my skin, his lips trailing kisses all over my face and neck.

"You're stunning," he whispers, his voice filled with awe. "Absolutely stunning."

The sincerity in his words and the tenderness of his touch make my insecurities melt away. I open my eyes and see the love and desire in his gaze, and it fills me with a newfound confidence.

"I don’t think I’ve ever seen more beautiful, full breasts in my life." He lowers his head and starts kissing one and exploring the other one. When he starts licking around the nipple and softly bites under the breast, he lets out a growl of pleasure that sends a jolt straight to my pussy.

"Amore Mio, all of you is sinful!" he says in a guttural voice, his eyes dark with desire. "Your breasts are so full and soft I could sit with them in my mouth for days! What the hell are you doing to me, Vita Mia?"

His words send a shiver down my spine, and before I can respond, he starts kissing more aggressively, sucking, biting, and licking at both my breasts with an almost feral intensity. The intensity of his actions makes me gasp, a mix of pleasure and surprise flooding my senses.

My back arches instinctively, pushing my chest closer to him, needing more of his touch. My legs part, driven by a primal need, and my hands travel to his hair, pulling and tugging as I lose myself in the sensations he's creating.

"Dominic," I moan, the sound escaping my lips unbidden. "Yes, just like that."

He growls in response, the sound vibrating against my skin as he continues his assault on my abdomen, tracing the white marks as if they were erotic pathways. His hands roam over my body, exploring every curve, every inch of me, with a reverence that makes my heart race.

"You taste so good," he murmurs against my skin, his voice filled with awe. "I can't get enough of you."

The combination of his words and actions sends waves of pleasure coursing through me. My hips start to move of their own accord, seeking friction, craving more of him.

His hand trails down my body, his fingers teasing the sensitive skin of my inner thighs before finding my wetness. He groans as he feels how ready I am for him, and his finger slips inside me, curling and thrusting in perfect rhythm as his mouth finds one of my breasts again.

I cry out, my body trembling with the intensity of the sensations. "Dominic, please," I beg, not even sure what I'm asking for, only knowing that I need him more than anything.

"Tell me what you want, Vita Mia," he says, his voice a low growl. "Tell me, and I'll give it to you, whatever you want, it's yours."

"I need you inside me," I gasp, my voice barely a whisper. "Please, love of my life, I need you."

He pulls back slightly, his eyes locking onto mine, filled with raw, unfiltered desire. "Anything for you, Vita Mia," he says, his voice thick with emotion.

He starts undressing, and once the shirt is off, I can see why he could carry me with so much ease. Seriously, the man is hiding some serious muscles under those clothes.

"You are so beautiful, love of my life," the words just explode out of me before I can come up with a better way of telling him that he is fucking hot as hell. A blush starts at the base of my neck and travels to my cheeks. *Come on, Angela, you could've been a bit sexier just now.*

The honest smile that he rewards me with for my remark says it all. *He liked it!* Oh, maybe honesty is best, after all.

He removes his belt and throws it on the bed beside me. "I need that for later," he says, winking at me.

What the fuck?

I get up and reach for his pants and boxers to pull them down, as I seriously cannot wait to see him in all his naked beauty.

"Cannot wait, Amore Mio?" he teases me and starts laughing.

I slowly pull his clothes down, and his cock springs free, and all reality ceases. *What the actual hell?* I have no words as I stare at his cock.

I can feel my cheeks are now a very bright shade of red, and I probably look like an idiot staring at his cock.

"Vita Mia, it is all yours. You don't need to look at it like that," he adds for good measures to tease me some more.

"Dominic, I don't understand. I've seen cocks before in my life, and I've seen porn, but this is some scary stuff," I look up at him in disbelief. "There is no way that immense cock would fit in me Or maybe today's the day I start internal bleeding for fun, clearly." I say and burst out in laughter.

I take his shaft in my hand and align his cock to his abdomen.

"Fucking hell, Angela," he lets out a groan at my touch. "If you touch it like that, you might as well suck on it."

I feel my face getting even more hot. I've never given head. I've only had one guy go down on me, and it was more uncomfortable than exciting. I only slept with two other guys, none of whom made me orgasm for real, so I had to fake it so they would leave me alone. I am so embarrassed at the lack of skills in front of this sexy as fuck man. *Distract him!* That's what I'm going to do.

I smile mischievously up at him and continue, "Look at it, this would not fit Dominic. The tip of your cock is at your belly button. That translates to internal bleeding for me, love of my life." I lean over and kiss his abdomen. "Are you packing any other sizes by any chance?" I bat my lashes at him and start laughing.

He joins in, his laughter so deep and full that his cock starts moving up and down in my hand with the motion. He stifles a moan, and then he starts jerking in my hand a few times and looks at where my hand is gripping him.

"You little minx! You are so funny, Amore Mio. Everything about you is perfect," he leans over and kisses the top of my head.

"It's okay if you've never sucked a cock before, Vita Mia. If anything, it makes it even more perfect," he thrusts a few more times in my hand.

How did he know? Are my movements that amateurish?

"Amore Mio, nothing you do could ever be less than perfect. I want this so much, I'm on the edge of losing my mind," he says, lifting my gaze to meet his.

"If you want, you can take it in your mouth, but you don't have to. Either way, we won't be able to do it for long because I need to be inside your pussy as soon as possible. We can explore every kind of sex together. You have no idea how happy it makes me to share your firsts."

The look of adoration in his eyes, mixed with the sincerity in his voice and the kind, reassuring words coming out of him, is like a blanket around my heart. Before I can second guess myself, I am lowering my mouth to the head of his cock and shyly lick the tip.

Dominic lets out a loud growl that reverberates through his body, and I stop for a second. "Don't stop, baby, you're doing an amazing job," he brushes my hair for reassurance. "Your lips feel unbelievably hot on my cock, Vita Mia. Let your instincts take control."

I feel a wave of confidence wash over me at his reaction and at his words. I move my other hand to his shaft, jerking him with both hands as I lick the tip of his cock. A full-body tremble starts over him, and when I grow bolder, licking around the head in circular motions while continuing the up and down, rotating motion with my hands, he lets out a deep animalistic growl and gently pulls away.

"Amore Mio! Come on, you are a natural!" he leans over and kisses me, dominating and forceful, that takes my breath away. When he pulls away, he looks into my eyes, and the deep desire in them is both an aphrodisiac and a promise of pleasure and pain.

"We can explore going down on each other later because I will come in your mouth if we don't stop now," he kisses my lips again. "You give amazing head, Amore Mio. Just remember that and let your instincts take over, Vita Mia. You drove me to the edge in mere seconds, and I wanted to empty myself down your throat."

"Dominic!" is a scream of embarrassment. "You cannot say things like that!"

He starts laughing hard at my reaction and tilts me back in the bed. "And why not, Vita Mia? Isn't it the truth? Someone put me to promise that I will always tell her the truth," he teases me.

"You cannot be so direct, Dominic. It's making me feel embarrassed."

"I love that! I love everything about you, Amore Mio."

Stop changing the subject, Dominic," I say, giving him my best stern look under the circumstances. "And I am still scared of you monster cock, just so we are clear."

"My monster cock, huh?" he replies with a mischievous grin. He leans over and starts peppering kisses on my neck, then my breasts, and then my abdomen. He looks up at me with so much love and desire, as if he is the missing part of my existence. "Well, my monster cock and I are here to serve you, Vita Mia."

He starts licking my belly button and gently maneuvering my legs to open wider. "Let go, Vita Mia," he murmurs, his voice a seductive promise. He moves to the side of my abdomen, to my stretch marks, and starts kissing, licking, and biting them tenderly. His hand traces long, teasing strokes along my folds, sending shivers through me. "Just let go, Vita Mia. Let me love you like I want to love you."

With that, he slides a finger inside me, curving it up and fucking me with so much desire that my back arches and a moan escapes before I can even take a breath. He lowers his head below my belly button, just above my pussy, and starts this rhythmic dance with his tongue, adding a second finger.

"Love of my life, please!" My voice is desperately needy, on the verge of crying for more.

He responds by increasing the intensity, his fingers moving faster, scissoring inside me, stretching me in the most deliciously intense way, hitting that perfect spot inside me as his tongue works magic on my clit. My body responds instantly, hips bucking against his mouth, seeking more of the incredible pleasure he's giving me.

"That's it, Angela," he murmurs against my skin, his voice vibrating through me. "Let go for me. I want to hear you."

The sensations are overwhelming, each stroke of his fingers and flick of his tongue pushing me closer to the edge. I grip the sheets, my knuckles white as I feel the tension building, coiling tight within me.

"Dominic, I'm so close," I gasp, my voice trembling with anticipation.

"Come for me, Vita Mia," he commands softly, his voice full of love and desire. "Let me taste you."

His words push me over the edge, and I cry out his name as my orgasm crashes over me, waves of pleasure radiating through my body. My muscles tighten and pulse around his fingers, and I can feel the gush of my release, but he doesn't stop, drawing out every second of my ecstasy.

As I come down from the high, he gently withdraws his fingers and moves up my body, kissing his way back to my lips. I taste myself on him, and it's the most intoxicating, sexiest taste I've ever experienced. Our mingled scent is overwhelming. *Us, together.*

"You're incredible," he whispers, his forehead resting against mine. "And I love everything about you."

"I have no words, Dominic," I reply, my voice filled with emotion. "Thank you for making me feel this way... so cherished."

He smiles, his eyes shining with adoration. "Always, Vita Mia. Always."

He stands and positions himself between my legs, his hands gripping my hips as he slowly, torturously pushes the tip of his cock inside me. The feeling of him stretching me is almost too much to bear, and a long, low moan escapes me.

"Is okay, Vita Mia. I got you," he says in a sweet reassuring voice. "We are going to take it easy, so the pain is minimal, Amore Mio." He allows a few seconds for my walls to adapt to the intrusion as his hands start working the areas around my clit for added pleasure.

"That's it, Vita Mia. Look how you are opening up for me and welcoming me home," he says in a guttural ecstasy-filled voice, his gaze fixed where our bodies are joined.

"You are so beautiful, Amore Mio." He leans down to kiss me with all his might while sliding another inch inside me.

He moves his hips slowly, taking his time, careful not to hurt me, while sending wave after wave of pleasure through my body. The pain is there, his cock is as thick as it is long, stretching me to my limits in the most deliciously intense way possible. But his touch, his caresses, his kisses, his warmth, and his love are all palpable, surrounding me.

My entire being is in this moment with him, moaning, touching, exploring, kissing, reacting, initiating.

This is not just fucking. This is the thread that connects soul to soul in this life and the next.

When he is almost fully in me, filling me completely in the most exquisite way, I let out a deep, loud moan from a mix of pain and pleasure. "You're mine," he whispers, his voice fierce and possessive. "Only mine."

"Yes," I breathe, wrapping my legs around him, pulling him deeper. "Only yours, love of my life."

He jerks his hips, leaving only the tip of his cock inside me. Then, with a forceful, brutal thrust, he buries himself fully, and we both gasp at the overwhelming sensation. Our movements become a dance, a rhythm as old as time, as we move together, completely lost in each other and the connection that binds us.

As the intensity builds, I can feel the edge approaching, the wave of pleasure building, ready to crash over me. "Dominic," I cry out, my nails digging into his back. "I'm going to..." my voice trails off.

"Come for me, Vita Mia," he commands, his voice rough with his own impending release. "Come for me now."

With his words, I tumble over the edge, my body convulsing with the force of my orgasm as gushes of warmth wash over where we are joined. He keeps thrusting in me, letting me ride my orgasm to its fullest. He lowers his mouth to my breasts, sucking on a nipple with the desperation of a madman, as his thrusts grow more agitated, rougher, almost animalistic.

"You are exquisite, Vita Mia," he says into my chest. "Everything about you is driving me insane with pleasure and desire. I want your all, Vita Mia, so please let go with me," he looks up into my gaze with pleading eyes. "Please, Amore Mio." The sincerity in his words and the begging tone in his voice make it clear where our future stands. "Be mine!"

Erratic moans escape me, as if my body has merged with his, and I am a spectator enjoying the deliciously savage things he's doing to me. "Yes, love of my life. I'm yours, because there could never be another answer."

He pulls up on his knees while still buried deep in me, moves both of my legs over his arms and lifts me, suspending me halfway in the air, completely at his mercy. He moves off the bed and pulls me with him, and this new angle, with only my upper back touching the bed, gives him a depth I never thought possible..

"Dominic, too deep, baby," I say in a pleading voice.

"Vita Mia, trust me, please," he says, looking at where we are joined. "Please let go with me." He lifts his gaze and looks into my eyes with a pleading expression. "Amore Mio, I just want to love you," he thrusts gently. "Let me love you like my soul is screaming at me to," another thrust. "All I want is to please you," another thrust. "And bind your existence to mine." This time, he thrusts so deep that I can literally feel it in my abdomen.

"Dominic!" I scream his name in a moan so loud that it ricochets on the walls. "Fuck, baby! That is so good, love of my life! Fuck!" My voice rises, caught in the pure, unfiltered pleasure of his touch.

"Just let go with me, Vita Mia," he adds and then starts thrusting faster, more aggressive, rough, and animalistic. Our moans envelop us in a symphony of pleasure and pain.

"Amore Mio, I'm going to come in you. I need to mark you! I need to mark you as mine!"

"Yes, love of my life. I want it all inside me, please!" I can barely speak between thrusts and the indescribable pleasure that this man is creating within me.

He leans over, pulling me into an animalistic, rough kiss, hugging me tightly to his chest. I feel his muscles tense beneath my hands, and I let go, allowing the primal part of me to rise to the surface. I kiss him back with the same passion and desire he's pouring into me. I match his desperation, meeting him thrust for thrust as his soul calls to mine.

"Vita Mia, I'm coming!" he says, burying his face in the crook of my neck. He deepens his thrusts, and as his muscles stiffen even more, he finds his own release shuddering through him as he calls out my name.

The brutal thrusts, the sweetness in his touches, the declaration in his words, and the intensity of the moment are tipping me over the edge with him. With a loud cry, I come all over his cock, finding my release again.

We collapse together, breathless and spent, our bodies still intertwined. I gently stroke his hair, my touch tender and loving.

There are no words to describe what just happened between us. It is as if two souls found each other in the midst of millions of souls, recognised one another, and bonded for eternity.

As we lie there, wrapped in the afterglow of our connection, I feel a sense of peace and fulfilment that I have never known before. "Thank you for tonight," I whisper, my fingers tracing the lines of his face. "For showing me what it truly feels like to be loved."

He leans in and kisses me softly, his lips warm and tender against mine. "I'll spend the rest of my life making sure you always feel that way," he promises, his voice filled with sincerity. "You are my everything, Vita Mia."

Chapter Twelve

Dominic

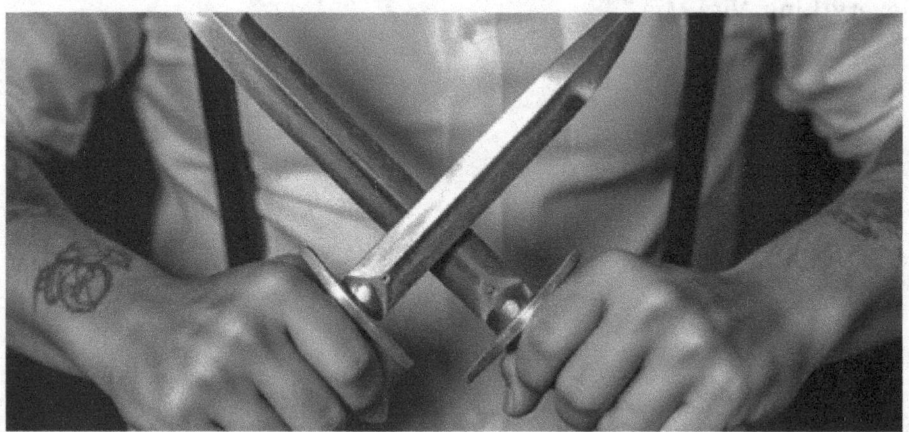

"You are exquisite, Vita Mia," I murmur into her beautiful, full breasts, my voice a mix of reverence and desperation. "Everything about you is driving me insane with pleasure and desire. I want your all, Vita Mia, so please let go with me."

I'm begging like the most pathetic man, but I don't care. I need to convince her to let go with me, to make her understand that I cannot live without her after this. "Please, Amore Mio." My voice pleads for mercy, like a man about to die, because if she says no, I know part of me will die, and the rest will haunt her to the ends of the earth.

There is no future without Angela. Thrust! *There is no tomorrow in which we are not together.* Thrust! *There's nothing I wouldn't do for this woman.* Thrust! *She is mine, and I'll worship her until she understands that truth.* Thrust! *She is mine!* Thrust! *Only mine!* Thrust! *And anyone that says otherwise will die by my hands.* Thrust!

"Be mine!" I beg, pleading for my life. That is what she is... *my life.*

I feel her body uniting with mine, trembling in my arms. I hear her singing the most erotic melody my ears have ever heard. But she is no ordinary creature. I need to conquer her body, mind, and soul. And I am ready to fight with all I've got to make her mine. *She is mine!* She'll take her place beside me, or I'll fucking die trying.

"Be mine," I whisper fiercely, my lips brushing against her ear. "Let go. Trust me. Be mine."

She moans, her body arching against mine, and I can feel that she is close to surrendering. "Please, Angela," I plead again, my thrusts becoming more desperate, more insistent. "I need you. I need all of you."

Her hands clutch at my back, her nails digging into my skin as she finally gives in. "Yes, love of my life," she cries out, her voice breaking with emotion. "I am yours. Completely yours."

The words are like a lifeline, pulling me back from the edge of despair. *She is mine!* She knows she's mine! She admitted it, *she's mine*!

You are done for, Vita Mia. There is no stopping me anymore. You've given yourself to me, and now I'm going to devour you whole!

I am going to show her what fucking is actually all about, and all those desires of hers will be forever satisfied moving forward. I pull back onto my knees while still buried balls deep in her wet, sweet pussy, and I maneuver her legs over my arms, lifting her. The new position brings a gasp out of her, and a sinful moan escapes her lips, the look in her eyes is pure, delirious ecstasy. She probably never tried this position before, but as I said, my monster cock and I are here to serve her and serve well. I will ensure she is not able to walk by the time I finish with her.

When I am off the bed, supporting her weight with my arms, I lean forward to completely bury myself deep in her hot pussy. Her walls stretch so well for me, enveloping me in her heat, and I can feel how her scent, her moans, and the softness of her skin are permanently tattooed in my mind and my subconscious.

I give her a few moments to adjust to the new depth and catch her breath. *Fuck, this woman is hot!* The look of despair from the pain, mingled with her pleading for more, is a cry to my beast to pound into her with all his might. Everything she did and said tonight fed the beast, and now he's coming out in full force to dominate her. *Fuck, this woman is just unbelievable!*

"Angela," I growl, my voice thick with raw need. "You have no idea what you do to me."

Her eyes flutter open, glazed with pleasure, as she nods weakly, gripping my arms for support. "Dominic... please..."

I can't hold back any longer. With a primal roar, I begin to thrust into her with a relentless rhythm, each stroke pushing us closer to the edge. Her moans grow louder, matching the intensity of my movements, and I can feel her body responding to every touch, every thrust.

"Dominic, too deep, baby," she says in a pleading voice.

"Vita Mia, trust me, please," I say, looking at where my cock is pounding in her sinful pussy that is devouring me as much as I am devouring her. "Please let go with me." I lift my gaze at her beautiful face, ready to beg until the end of time if that is what it takes because tonight, I am going to have all of her.

"Amore Mio, I just want to love you," I start to thrust more gently. "Let me love you like my soul is screaming at me to," another thrust. "All I want is to please you," another thrust. "And bind your existence to mine." I thrust so deep this time that the only thing stopping me from going deeper is my balls. *Fuck!* The sensation of her heat wrapped around me is unreal, deliciously sinful.

"Dominic!!!" she screams my name in a moan so loud that it ricochets off the walls.. "Fuck, baby!!! That is so good, love of my life! Fuck!!!"

"That's it, Vita Mia," I whisper, my voice rough with desire. "Take all of me," I say, starting to pound into her like a madman.

"Just let go with me, Vita Mia." My beast is on full display as I add my last plea for mercy, and then I start thrusting faster, more aggressive, rough, and animalistic. Our moans envelop us in a symphony of pleasure and pain.

Her body arches, her nails digging into my skin as she surrenders completely to the pleasure. The sensation of her tight, wet heat around me drives me wild, and I increase my pace, determined to make her unravel under my rough touch.

Her ragged gasps match the ecstasy building in her eyes. "Dominic, I'm so close," she whimpers, her voice trembling.

"Come for me, Angela," I command, my thrusts becoming even more forceful. "Let go."

My muscles ache, and my balls throb from the effort of restraining my release. Her intoxicating scent is everywhere on my body, and the taste of her release is still lingering in my mouth. I know I am moments away from losing all control and exploding into a million pieces. But the beast within me needs to own, dominate, and mark her as mine.

"Amore Mio, I'm going to come in you. I need to mark you! I need to mark you as mine!" The desperation in my voice is palpable, and when I look into her eyes, she melts under my touch, pure ecstasy written all over her beautiful face.

"Yes, love of my life. I want it all in mine, please!" An animalistic growl comes out of me at her words, and my thrusts are deep and urgent, ready to fulfill any desires she might have.

I need to feel her closer! I need her entire body against mine! I need her warmth enveloping my body as I seal our lives together forever. I lean over and wrap my arms around her tightly while I start devouring her mouth in a rough kiss that sends bolts of electricity through my body.

She's amazing! She's perfect! She's mine!

The love, affection, and desire that she has shown me, mixed with the rough passion at every touch, is all the confirmation I need to know her true intentions. *She let go with me!*

"Vita Mia, I'm coming!" I say, burying my face in the crook of her neck.

My thrusts are long and deep, completely overwhelmed by the sensations she's pulling out of me. Her warmth, her touch, her taste, her scent, *everything about her*, —her love, passion, desire, intelligence, and wickedness—condemns me to a life *utterly intoxicated by her*.

With each powerful thrust, my mind lets go, and I scream her name. Each stroke is more intense than the last, driving me closer to the brink. My balls tighten as the pressure builds, ready to release.

"Angela!" I roar, my voice raw with passion and need.

With one final, powerful thrust, I reach the peak, and my body convulses with the force of my orgasm. I thrust a few more times, each movement pushing me deeper into the euphoria. My balls tighten, releasing long streams of cum that fill her completely. The sensation is overwhelming, a rush of ecstasy that wipes everything else from my mind.

My vision blurs, my ears ring, and for a moment, it feels like I've forgotten how to breathe. The world narrows to this single point of connection, the intensity of our shared release binding us closer than ever.

As the last of my orgasm pulses through me, I can feel her walls still spasming around my cock. I keep thrusting into her, prolonging her release as the intense pleasure washes over us, sealing our bodies and souls for eternity.

We collapse together, breathless and spent, our bodies still entwined. She gently strokes my hair, her touch tender and loving. *Fuck, this woman is everything!*

I lift my head, looking into her eyes, which are still glazed with the remnants of her own climax. "Vita Mia," I whisper, my voice hoarse but filled with love. "You are everything to me."

I can feel the emotions behind the look in her eyes, her happiness says it all. There's no going back. We are one from this point on.

She smiles weakly at me. "Thank you for tonight," she whispers, her fingers tracing the lines of my face. "For showing me what it feels like to be truly loved."

I lean in and kiss her softly, pouring all the warmth and tenderness I have into it, showing her what she means to me. "I will spend the rest of my life making sure you feel this way," I swear more to myself, as she is now the centre of my life, and it's my responsibility to fulfil this promise. "You are my everything, Vita Mia."

I start peppering kisses on her beautiful face. "Thank you, Vita Mia," I say softly. "Thank you for existing."

The look of pure adoration in her eyes says it all. Now she understands that I've known she was my soulmate since the shop, and this connection between us is as inevitable as the sun rising in the sky every day. She is mine, and I am hers, and nothing could ever break the unshakable bond between our souls.

We lie there in silence, our bodies still connected, our breaths slowly returning to normal. As I shift us onto our sides, keeping myself deep inside her, I know that the bond between us feels stronger than ever. Now that she's fully aware of it, I know she'll guard it with all her strength, just as I will.

Eventually, sleep takes us, and when I wake to light filtering through the floor-to-ceiling windows, casting a soft glow over the room, the first thing I notice is the warmth, I'm hotter than usual. Something presses against my chest, and when I look down, *I see her*.

Fuck. She's keeping me warm. I can literally feel my soul rejoicing in the fact that she's the one holding me close.

What an incredible sensation to be able to hold your life in your arms and for her to warm your body as your own personal blanket of love against the world. Her presence is soothing, perfectly fitting against me, and the gentle rise and fall of her breathing is a comforting rhythm that syncs with my own heartbeat.

Her hair is splayed across my chest, soft and fragrant, and I can't resist running my fingers through it gently, careful not to wake her. She murmurs softly in her sleep, snuggling closer to me, and the simple act makes my heart swell with a profound sense of obsession and protectiveness.

As I gaze at her peaceful face, I know that my life and actions make me unworthy of her. But I don't give a fuck because she is mine. I knew it the moment I heard her awful singing. Now she knows it as well, and she gave herself to me willingly, so there is no stopping this. *She is mine!* The woman in my arms is everything I have ever wanted and more. Her love, her strength, her vulnerability, all of it completes me in ways I never thought possible. Maybe one day she will learn to love my darkness as well, but until that day, I will make her love me more than reality itself.

I brush a soft kiss on her forehead, my lips lingering on her skin. She stirs slightly but doesn't wake, her body instinctively seeking mine. I tighten my hold on her, feeling the warmth of her skin against mine, and I know that I would do anything to keep her mine.

"Love of my life..." she lets out a soft moan. "You are poking at my leg with your monster cock," she starts laughing with her eyes still shut.

"It's your fault, Vita Mia," I say, hugging her as close as possible to me. I want to pull her so close, it's as if I could absorb her into me, carry her with me always. "It's your fault for being so fucking sexy that my mind just goes to the gutters all the time." I start peppering kisses on her face and neck. "If anything, I think you should kiss him good morning for the inconvenience of making him hard as fuck first thing in the morning," I add for good measure, just to test the waters. *Maybe, just maybe, I'll get lucky and get head first thing in the morning.* I burst out laughing because there's no way she would do it, that would actually blow my mind.

"Kiss him good morning?" she says in a suspicious voice, continuing to laugh. "Nice try, big boy, but I know what morning wood is," she laughs harder, pinching my chest and sides. "Better luck next time."

She moves on top of me, straddling me, looking down at me. She lets out a wince from the movement, and my heart stops beating for a moment.

"Am...Amore Mio?" I jump slightly, and she makes another wince. "Fuck! Let me look."

I roll her onto her back and move between her legs to take a closer look at her pussy. "Baby, you look thoroughly fucked," I say and burst out laughing. "Vita Mia, on a scale of 1 to 10, how much does it hurt?"

"You and your fucking monster cock!" she says, trying hard to give me a mean, evil look, but the corner of her mouth betrays her with a smile. "It's 100, Dominic, and I'm not sure why I let you put that thing in me," she teases, trying to kick me with her leg.

Fuck me, this woman is delicious! The feistiness in her is driving me crazy! I can feel my cock getting even harder and my beast coming out to play again. *Stop being so adorable, or I'll fuck you again right now, and you might actually be scared of me. No, we cannot have that!* I belong inside her as much as oxygen belongs in my lungs. *Calm down, Dominic! Calm!* I take a few long breaths, but our mixed scent invades my nostrils, and a loud growl escapes with my breath out, knowing I'm seconds away from pounding into her. My beast is screaming at me to act, to claim her again, so he can claim her and cement any lingering doubts about my ownership. *She is mine! All mine! Now and forever!*

"Amore Mio, you smell mouth-watering. I am really trying not to fuck you raw right now, so please have mercy and stop being adorable, or I will jump on you, and what happened last night will happen even harder now, as I'm learning your body and you'll squirt all over me again."

I look up at her beautiful face, and a completely blushed and shocked expression awaits me. Before I can stop myself and mask my true self, I burst out laughing.

It takes me a few moments to realise she hasn't joined in the laughter and she stares at me, gently trying to pull away

"Oh! No, you don't," I say abruptly once I catch on to her plan and pull her legs back beneath my arms. "What just happened?" I don't know what I did, and *I don't know how to fix it.*

All my previous sex partners were a one-night stand. No connection, no meaning, no purpose well, except to empty myself. I'm good-looking, so women come to me without me even asking. I just need to look at them and smile, and for some reason, they think it's okay to approach a complete stranger and suck him off. I am not complaining it's just I can not imagine a reality in which I am a woman, and I would ever suck a stranger's cock. But again, no judging.

Relationship skills? Define relationships...

If you count the UBT, I'd call it camaraderie. We know our place, our strengths and weaknesses, and we work as a team or we're out.. Simple! Efficient.

The only other relationships I have are with my 'subjects'. I am very efficient at that if it counts. I can read someone's pain tolerance in the first two minutes of working on them. Perhaps those could be considered people-reading skills, if we stretch our imagination.

But I don't see how my intrapersonal skills are of any use at reading this creature before me that is still fucking trying to pull away. *Never! You hear me?!* my beast growls in my mind. *You will never escape us*, he continues with confident aggression.

Even I know I shouldn't say that out loud right now, *so what the fuck am I supposed to say*? I start crawling up until my face is above her beautiful breasts, and my arms on either side of her, supporting my weight

"Dominic," she starts, her voice shaky, "I just need a moment."

"A moment for what?" I ask, my tone softening as I look into her eyes, trying to understand her sudden shift.

"It's just... it's a lot to take in. You and everything that just happened," she admits, her eyes avoiding mine. "I need to know that it's real, that it's not just a dream or a fleeting moment. We've known each other for such a short time, and we're already having sex. You're saying things so directly, and this is so intense, the things we said to each other, this feeling within me, and..." I can see she is spiralling out of control.

Her words hit me hard, and I realised that my intensity might have overwhelmed her. I take a deep breath, releasing her legs gently and cupping her face in my hands. "Angela, I promise you, this is real. You are my everything, and I want to build a future with you. I'm here, and I'm not going anywhere."

I move to her side completely, take her hand, and start kissing her inner palm, then work my way to the tips of her fingers.

She looks up at me, her eyes glistening with unshed tears. "Promise?"

"Promise," I say, kissing her softly, hoping to reassure her. "I know it might take you some time to realise how things really are, and I know I can be intense sometimes, but I will prove to you every single day that you are my everything, and that this is our future."

Her lips tremble as she smiles, a mix of relief and love in her eyes. "Okay, love of my life." The sweetness in her gaze is all it takes for me to know she is back, she believes me, and she knows I'm hers as much as she is mine.

I lean in and begin kissing her with all the warmth and tenderness I can muster to convey my connection with her without accidentally being too rough. I reach for one of her breasts and start massaging it, and when I take the nipple between my thumb and forefinger and pull and twist while deepening my kiss, I can feel myself losing control faster than a tornado ripping through.

"Dominic..." she breaks the kiss and moans loudly into my mouth. "Don't start something that you cannot finish." She looks into my eyes and smiles.

"Fuck, Vita Mia. What is with me when I am around you? This is something else," I say and pull at the nipple again. *I need to control myself! I need to control myself!*

Her reward is another moan as her back arches off the bed, and her chest rubs against my palm, trying to feed my beast more.

"Amore Mio, we need to stop, and you need to let me look at you to check if you're okay," I say, kissing her shoulder before biting hard enough to leave a mark. "You need to have something of mine with you at all times, so I will be leaving little souvenirs on your body from now on." I start kissing and licking the spot to make it better.

"You dick!" she kicks me with her knee, a mix of annoyance and amusement in her eyes.

I laugh, catching her knee and holding it gently. "I mean it, Angela, I need to mark your beautiful skin. Now, let me look, I need to make sure you're not hurt."

She sighs, her playful resistance fading as she looks at me with genuine affection. "Okay, fine. But be gentle."

I nod, my expression turning serious as I carefully move her into a more comfortable position. I inspect her body, tracing my fingers lightly over her skin for any signs of discomfort or pain.

When I am next to her legs, I just look up at her with adoration and concern. I'm so scared she is actually hurting because of me. "Show me what's mine, Vita Mia," I ask softly, my concern evident.

She smiles shyly as she gently opens up for me to let me look at her perfect pussy that is now all swollen and red. I trace my fingers gently over the folds, and she releases a deep breath.

"Does it hurt badly, Vita Mia?" A mixture of pain, pride, desire, and need is confusing the hell out of my mind. I would endure any torture for her not to be in pain. I'm also so proud that she is this deliciously sore from my actions. Our combined scent is hitting me again, and my need to make her squirt all over my face is almost unbearable, not to mention that my cock is screaming at me to let him pleasure her.

She shakes her head. "Just a bit sore, but it's a good kind of sore," she says with a small smile.

I return her smile, relief flooding through me. "Good. I never want to hurt you, Angela. You mean too much to me."

She reaches down, brushing her fingers through my hair. "I know, love of my life. And I trust you."

Her words warm my heart, and I lean down to kiss her pussy gently. "You are my everything," I whisper against her folds. "And I will always take care of you." Another kiss." "But I won't promise not to make you sore again, because that would be a lie. I want nothing more than to take you and fuck the shit out of you!" I breathe out all my truth in one go, then lick her folds, parting them slightly.

I pull back, knowing she can't take even oral right now, and glance up into her eyes, searching for any hesitation. She looks mouthwateringly beautiful in the morning, and the desire in her gaze makes me certain, there's nothing under this sky I wouldn't do for this woman, including... *drawing her a spa bath.*

I've never done that before, I realise, feeling a bit deflated. *But I think I read somewhere it's good for sore pussies.* Am I an idiot for not checking first? *Should I have googled this? Should I have bought some cream or something? Fuck.* What do I do now?

"Dominic?" she asks softly, her voice pulling me out of my consuming thoughts.

"Yeah?" I reply, trying to mask my uncertainty.

"What are you thinking about?" she asks, her eyes filled with curiosity and amusement.

I take a deep breath, deciding to be honest. “I was thinking about drawing you a spa bath. I read somewhere it’s good for... you know, soreness.” *Fuck, this is so embarrassing*, but I want, no, *need to take care of her*. *Yes, I should have googled this and been prepared.* The guilt is starting to suffocate me, tightening in my chest as I feel myself losing control. I try to discreetly do some breathing exercises, hoping to slow my racing thoughts before she notices anything’s off.

She smiles, her eyes lighting up with amusement. "You are too sweet, you know that?"

Wait what? I look at her beautiful face and the adorable smile she’s wearing, and silence envelops my mind again. *Fuck! This woman and her power over me!* I don't think she realises that she has so much power over me, or she would be more careful about how she wields her smiles around me. Life and death do not measure the power she has, more like if she would ask me to take my heart out and lay it at her feet, I would do it without a second hesitation.

I shrug, feeling a bit sheepish. "I just want to make sure you're comfortable. I don't want you to be in any pain."

Her smile widens, and she reaches out to cup my face. "Thank you, Dominic. That sounds wonderful. And don't worry, I'm not in pain. Just a little sore, but it's nothing I can't handle."

Relief floods through me, and I lean down to kiss her gently. "I'll go start the bath," I say, pulling away reluctantly.

She nods, watching me with a look of pure adoration. "Okay. I'll be right here."

I get up and head to the bathroom, my mind racing with thoughts of how to make this as perfect as possible. I turn on the water, adjust the temperature until it's just right, and then start adding some bath salts I found in one of the cabinets. They smell like vanilla, lavender, roses, or something nice, and I hope they will help her relax. *I’m not sure if this stuff is helpful or even still in date, but it smells good, so let’s hope for the best.*

I dash to the kitchen, grab her some water, and frantically search for candles. *Candles! She'd like candles, right? Don't all girls like candles? Fuck me! You moron! You should've been more prepared! Presumptuous, my ass, you look like a fucking amateur at your best.*

Still, I can't help but grin. Last night... fuck, last night was unbelievable, unreal, unexpected, unquestionably and hands down, the best night of my life.

Panic like nothing else explodes in my chest at the thought she might leave me if everything is not perfect. *Like fuck you are!* My beast screams in my mind. *You will NEVER escape us! I will hunt you for eternity!* My body starts to tremble slightly at the overwhelming force of my feelings, and as I squat to take a few deep breaths, I spot some candles in one of the cupboards.

Thank God! I grab a handful of them and a lighter I found nearby and rush back to the bathroom. Setting the candles around the tub, I light each one, hoping the soft glow will create a relaxing atmosphere. The flickering light casts a warm, inviting glow over the room, and I feel a bit more at ease. *Is okay! This does look good, right?*

When everything is ready, I go back to the bedroom and scoop her up in my arms. She lets out a surprised giggle, wrapping her arms around my neck.

"Love of my life, you didn't have to do all of this," she says, her voice filled with gratitude.

"I wanted to," I reply, carrying her into the bathroom and gently setting her down by the tub. "You deserve to be pampered."

She looks around, taking in the warm glow of the candles and the inviting scent of the bath salts. "This is perfect," she says, her eyes shining with appreciation.

I help her into the tub, making sure she is comfortable before sitting behind her to keep her company. "How does it feel?" I ask, hugging her from behind.

She closes her eyes, a contented sigh escaping her lips. "Amazing. Thank you, my love. This is exactly what I needed."

I can feel her relaxing against me, and I smile with a sense of accomplishment and relief. "I'm glad. Just relax and let me take care of you."

She opens her eyes and reaches out to take my hand. "I never had anyone take care of me," she says just above a whisper. "Well, no one except my parents." Her voice is so small with the confession that my chest squeezes with an unfamiliar feeling. I'm not sure what it is but I don't care for it. I feel like stabbing someone for making her feel this small, and it's quite the conflict in feelings because half of me wants to convince her to let me fuck her, and the other half wants to hunt down whoever made her feel so small. *Shit, man!* This woman is just too much!

When she kisses my inner palm, mirroring my gesture of affection, I melt away next to her, and my mind goes silent again. *Oh, my heart!* I might have a fucking heart attack at this rate.

"Are you ok, love of my life?" she says, taking one of my fingers into her mouth, sucking on it.

"Vita Mia, please!" I lean over and, kiss the top of her head and wrap my legs around her. "If you don't want my monster cock as you call him, to accidentally, on purpose, take a sneak peek at your delicious pussy I suggest you stop that sucking right now."

I wrap my arms around her tighter, cupping her breasts in my hands and squeezing them gently. She's completely cocooned in me, and I've never felt this protective, this sweet sense of adoration before. It's more than a feeling, it almost has a taste. As I bury my face in the crook of her neck, I realise I can actually taste that sweetness, and a calmness washes over me.

For the first time in my life, *my mind is at peace.* I feel complete as if I've found what I was missing all along.

I try to move back and give her some space, but I just cannot find the strength in me to let go of this feeling. *I cannot remember ever feeling at peace before.* I have always been the strange one in the mix—the one who speaks too much, explodes too quickly, is too loud, too intense, too in-your-face. And now, this creature has brought me peace like nothing else, as if the feeling is a given in her presence, as if she has every right to take complete control over my existence.

Her scent, her warmth, the rhythm of her breathing, all of it envelops me, grounding me in a way I never thought possible. I kiss the soft skin of her neck, tasting the salt of the water mingled with her sweet fragrance. Each kiss is a silent promise, a vow to protect her, to cherish her, to keep her close always.

"Vita Mia," I whisper, my voice thick with emotion. "You make me feel whole. You bring me a peace I've never known."

She turns her head slightly, her eyes meeting mine with a look of pure love and understanding. "You are wonderful, you know that?" she says, wrapping one hand around my neck and one hand on top of my own, trying to hug me back.

Wonderful?! Well, I've been called many things in my life. Wonderful has never once come out of someone's mouth.

Her words touch something deep within me, and I hold her even tighter, afraid to let go of this newfound sense of tranquillity. "I never want to lose this feeling," I admit, my voice barely above a whisper. "I never want to lose you." My voice cracks at my raw confession, but you know what? *Fuck it!* I would rather look like a desperate fool and have the woman of my dreams than play it cool and lose her. There, now it's all in the open!

"You won't," she reassures me, her voice steady and calm. "We have each other, and that's all we need."

I nod, burying my face deeper into her neck, inhaling her scent, letting it fill my lungs and soothe my soul. "Thank you," I murmur. "For being everything I didn't know I needed."

She turns to face me completely, straddling me and placing her hands around my neck. She lowers her lips to mine and places the lightest, gentlest kiss known to men. With a deep intake of her air and scent, she settles deep within my heart, mind and soul. *This is it! I'm forever lost!* Not even Elijah can separate me from this woman! I would rather lose it all and be with her, than keep my life and have one day without her.

She places her head on my chest and moves her hands around my back in a bear hug. Now, I am the one completely cocooned. "You know," she says after a while, her voice thoughtful, "I never imagined I could feel this way about someone. That anyone could make me feel so cherished."

I smile, my heart swelling with emotion. "Neither did I. But with you, it feels like everything finally makes sense."

She snuggles closer, relaxing in my embrace again. "I'm glad we found each other, love of my life."

"Me too, Amore Mio. Thank you for giving us a chance."

As the water cools, I know we need to get out, but I still can't believe my luck, that this incredible creature accepted me as I am. She could have run, and I would've chased her. She could have screamed, and I would've silenced her. She could have said no, and I would've died. But she said yes. *She said she's mine.*

She wants to hear again and again that I'm serious about her. She wants me as much as I want her. This is unreal.

A tremor passes through her, and I know, I pushed this as far as it will go, we need to get out of the water. "Let's dry up, Vita Mia," I say, standing up with her in my arms.

We get out of the spa, and I reach for the towels to dry her off, and she takes a step back. *What the actual fuck? What did I do now?* my mind screams at me. *Fuck! I am awful at this.* How did I fuck it up now?

"Baby?" I look at her with pleading eyes, concerned that I don't even know how to fix whatever it is I did.

"Talk to me, Vita Mia. Please, don't push me away," my voice tremoring with emotions. It doesn't sound like my voice; it doesn't feel like me either. It is as if she brings this other hidden person out of me that was created just for her.

"I... I am just embarrassed a bit for you to look at me straight now in broad daylight," she says, looking at the floor. "If you dry me, you'll be able to see all my defects clearly, and it's just making me uncomfortable," she finishes off barely above a whisper.

I feel like someone kicked me in my gut. *Where is this coming from?* Because she's so beautiful, it's hard to look directly at her, with or without clothes on. I am trying like hell to keep my beast in check and not scare her with my monster cock, as she calls him. *Hey!* That nickname is starting to grow on me. *Focus Dominic! Leave your cock alone and go and hug her, she needs comforting*. I can hear my brain talking to itself, and I know I am losing it again. *Breathe Dominic! Breathe!*

"Did I say something wrong?"

She shakes her head, her gaze still on the floor, her hands crossed in front of her as if trying to hide her core from me.

"Did I do something wrong?"

She just shakes her head again.

I take a step closer.

You know what? *Fuck it!* I've already laid it on thick and spoken my mind, and she didn't run. *So screw it!* I am just going to tell her exactly how I feel and do damage control afterwards.

"Vita Mia, look at me." I take a step closer again. "Please, look at me." I reach out, lifting her gaze to mine and taking one of her hands in mine. "Vita Mia, listen to my words and hold onto them whenever you feel this doubt in your heart." I move her hand to my cock and squeeze it around my girth. "See what you do to me. Look at how my body reacts to you." I take a step closer, and now I am in her space, breathing her air. "This," I gently squeeze her hand again, "is yours, to do with it as you please." I lean down and kiss her forehead. "You are everything to me." I move to kiss her cheek. "And you are so fucking beautiful, it hurts my heart to look directly at you." I find her lips and kiss her so fiercely that I forget that I should be gentle with her.

Her breath hitches, and she looks up at me with those wide, expressive eyes that always see right through to my soul. "Dominic," she whispers, her voice trembling with emotion.

"Yes, Vita Mia."

"This is the sweetest thing anyone has ever said to me," she says, her hand tightening around my cock, making my breath catch. "Just please be patient with me on this. It will take me some time to feel relaxed being naked in front of you."

I lean my head to hers and say firmly, my voice unwavering. "You deserve everything and more. Take all the time you need, Vita Mia."

I reach for the towel again, and this time, she waits for me, letting me touch and explore her body as much as I want. *Fuck me, this woman is intoxicating!* Everything about her screams at me to fuck her raw. *Breathe Dominic! Breathe!*

"You alright there, love of my life?" she teases with a mischievous tone in her voice. "It looks like your mind is permanently in the gutter." She rolls her head back in a full-on blast of laughter.

"You little minx! I will fuck you raw if you don't stop being adorable," I say, jumping up, kissing and hugging the hell out of her.

"Stop! You're still wet," she laughs, trying to push me off. "Let me dry you off."

I freeze at her words. Oh, shit. I completely forgot the scars on my back. My first instinct is to pull away and hide from her, but if I do that, then she will never open up to me about her insecurities. I reach for the dry towel and hand it to her, looking deep into her eyes and letting go. *Be it as it may, I will not hide from her.*

"What is that look for?" she says with a mischievous smile. "I already saw your ding-ding-dong," she starts laughing, working her way to my front. The moment she moves to my back and sees my scars, her laughter dies a thousand deaths.

"Baby..." her voice is small, trailing off. "What happened?" she reaches to touch me, her movements feather-like. "Oh my god! What happened?" She hugs me from behind, pressing her cheek to my back and squeezing tightly.

"Italy." One word is all it takes to explain the magnitude of my scars.

Time stays still as she hugs me as if trying to push the scars away from my body. Then I feel her lips on my back, and it seems like she's crying.

"Vita Mia, no!" I try to pull her to my front.

She is crying, I know for sure! The soft tremble in her lips break my heart into a million pieces. "Vita Mia, please don't." I try to reason with her.

"Let me, Dominic!" she says in a shattered voice, licking one of the whip marks. "Let me carry this with you."

Her words and actions pierce through my defenses, and I feel the raw vulnerability of the moment and allow her to do as she pleases. Once she stops, I turn to face her, taking her tear-streaked face in my hands. "Angela, you don't have to carry this burden," I say softly, my voice breaking. "It's mine to bear."

She shakes her head fiercely, her eyes blazing with determination through the tears. "No, Dominic. We're in this together. Your pain is my pain. Let me share it with you."

Her words resonate deep within me, and I realise just how much she truly cares for me. She wants to be a part of every aspect of my life, even the darkest parts. I pull her into a tight embrace, feeling her warmth against me, and I let the walls around my heart crumble. Maybe one day she will accept my darkness as well, accept that I'm part of the mafia, that I am capable of hurting people if asked of me.

"One of my exes called me names while we were having sex," she says quietly with her face buried in my chest. "He called me fat and said that my breasts are too heavy, and he couldn't have me on top because

I was suffocating him." She is full-on shaking uncontrollably now. "As you probably noticed, all the stretch marks and my curves, I was bigger than this not long ago. He actually dumped me a few weeks later after that incident."

She is squeezing me so tightly now that I can feel her muscles tense, and my sides start to ache, but I don't stop her. She needs to let it all out. She needs to let this poison out of her, or it will eat her alive.

"I fell into depression after that, and I felt like no one would ever accept me for who I am, let alone love me for the person inside." She is quietly crying in my chest, and I am just rubbing my hands on her back, hoping like hell that it's comforting her in some way. "So I started dieting, and when that didn't make me lose weight, I started forcing myself to vomit after every meal." She is sobbing like a child, crying in her protector's arms.

I am numb. I am shocked. I feel broken for her.

"Angela, please look at me," I try to pull her away from me so I can look her in the eyes and she can see my sincerity and love. She just squeezes me tighter and shakes her head in my chest. "Baby, please! I adore you, please! Look at me. I need you to read my heart as I speak to you. Please, look at me," my voice is weak and vulnerable, and I am seconds away from crying my eyes out for her. *For my love.*

Slowly, she loosens her grip and looks up at me, her eyes red and puffy from crying. "Dominic, I don't know if I can believe that someone like you could really love someone like me."

"Vita Mia," I say, my voice filled with emotion. "You are so beautiful my chest hurts when I look at you. Your past, your scars, your insecurities, they don't change how I feel about you. If anything, they make me fall more for you because they are a part of you, and I love everything about you." I rest my forehead on hers and try to steady myself. "Maybe my words are not enough for this moment, but you will learn that I will always tell you the truth." I kiss her forehead and hug her again. "But remember what you do to my body, remember how I loved you last night, remember how my entire being was alive at your touch." I pull back and let her see in my soul that I am telling her the truth. "Amore Mio, it does not matter what some fucking idiot said to you, you are beautiful to me. I feel like I exist because of you. I feel like my soul has been singing since the moment I heard you sing. I feel like I breathe the air that comes out of you. Fucking believe me, please!" The desperation in my voice is so clear I cannot recognise myself.

She searches my eyes, looking for any sign of doubt or insincerity. Finding none, she lets out a shaky breath and nods. "I believe you..." she trails off.

"And I will be here to remind you every day," I promise, leaning in to kiss her forehead. "You are my everything, Angela, and nothing will ever change that."

As we hold each other, the weight of our shared confessions and vulnerabilities starts to lift. We are two broken souls finding healing in each other's arms, and I know that, as long as we have each other, we can face anything.

"I promise to always be here for you," I whisper, my lips brushing against her ear. "You are mine to protect, and you are mine to love. No one will touch or offend you from now on if they value their life." I softly kiss her cheek.

She nods, her tears slowly subsiding as she takes comfort in my words. "Thank you, Dominic. For everything."

"Thank you, Vita Mia. For trusting me with your heart."

Chapter Thirteen

Angela

I feel so at peace in his arms, as if all my decisions led me to this moment. He was so sweet to draw me a bath. I melted in his arms as he opened the door, and I saw how much effort he put into the gesture. In saying that, he should take care of me because he destroyed my pussy and take some responsibility. The thought brings a soft laugh as I hug him tighter, trying my best to laugh only in my head.

Well, him destroying my pussy is neither here nor there because I did let him, and truth be told, I would have begged him if he hadn't been the one begging first.

As I nestle closer to him, the warmth of his body envelops me, and I feel a profound sense of security and love. Every touch, every whisper from him reassures me that I made the right choice and that he is what I truly want.

I can feel the water getting colder, but I cannot bring myself to let go of him. Maybe a few more minutes, and I will get up. As the thought passes through my mind, a tremor passes through my body, and I feel him stiffen against me.

"Let's dry up, Vita Mia," he says, standing up with me in his arms. *Damn! He is strong!* He's carrying me around like I weigh nothing. Haha, the joke's on him because I weighed myself yesterday. *I know I'm still big-ish.*

But as he effortlessly lifts me out of the tub, all those thoughts about my weight and insecurities fade away. His strength isn't just physical, it's emotional, a steady rock that makes me feel secure and cherished. I wrap my arms around his neck, burying my face in his shoulder, feeling the warmth of his skin against mine.

He gently sets me down on the soft bath mat, grabs a large towel, and reaches for me. I instinctively take a step back and look at him, and he has this horrified look in his eyes. I take another step back and try to cover my worst parts from him. *Oh, no! This is so embarrassing.* I just want to grab the towel, cover myself, pretend nothing happened, and run out of here. I look up at him again, and I am just ashamed, embarrassed, and scared! *Fuck! I didn't think this through when I said yes to the spa.*

"Baby?" his voice is soft, full of concern. "Talk to me, Vita Mia. Please, don't push me away." His voice trembles with emotion.

His reaction is blowing me away because he is so strong. He didn't let go of me last night until I gave myself to him, and now, well, now, he just seems small, somehow having that much worry in his eyes. His concern is so palpable that it just takes my breath away, and a new type of concern blooms within me, a concern for him.

"I… I'm just a bit embarrassed for you to look at me directly now in broad daylight," I say, not lifting my gaze from the floor. "If you dry me, then you will be able to see all my defects with a clear mind, and it's just making me uncomfortable…" I trail off at the end because this is the worst sitting here naked and wet, may I add, in front of the world's sexiest, most mind-blowingly hot man to ever walk the earth.

"Did I say something wrong?" he says just above a whisper with so much concern and vulnerability in his voice that I am moments away from crying. *This is so fucking embarrassing!* And I am just making it a thousand times worse now because I actually said something about it. Why could I not just play it cool, and if he did make a remark about my extras, then I could have made a joke, or I could have kicked him in his nuts or something! Well, not the nuts because they're too close to that majestic cock of his, and the world needs some happiness, after all. *Fuck!!!*

I'm an idiot, and that is that! I try to move my hands to cover more of me, just shaking my head. No intelligent words are coming to me at the moment. My brain has left the building with my dignity. End of story!

"Did I do something wrong?" he asks, his voice filled with concern.

I shake my head again, unable to form a coherent response.

He takes a step toward me. *Fuck, no!!!*

"Vita Mia, look at me," he says, taking another step closer. "Please, look at me." He lifts my chin and takes one of my hands in his. "Vita Mia, please listen to my words and hold onto them every time you feel this in your heart."

I feel like I'm going to be sick, maybe even faint. How much worse can I possibly embarrass myself? *This is not happening!*

He moves my hand to his cock and squeezes it around his girth. "See what you do to me. Look at how my body reacts to you." He gets closer. He is in my space now, and I cannot breathe! "This," he squeezes my hand again, "is yours, to do with it as you please," he continues, his voice steady and full of emotion, kissing the top of my head. "You are everything to me," he moves to kiss my cheek. "And you are so fucking beautiful, it hurts my heart to look directly at you." He finds my lips, and the kiss can only be described as an attack on my senses because he is devouring me, trying to conquer me or remind me of something he is scared I forgot.

My heart aches with the sincerity in his voice, and I feel tears building up in my eyes. *For fuck sake, Angela, don't make it worse by crying!* Count your blessing that the man clearly is short-sighted and cannot see very well. So leave it at that and be happy he is fucking attracted as hell to you because, damn, this monster cock looks even better in the daylight. I still cannot believe what he did to me last night. I will probably be sore for the next week, but I will say yes to him every single time.

I pull away gently and search his eyes, looking for any hint of insincerity, but all I see is love and acceptance. Slowly, I start to relax, my fear giving way to a tentative trust. "Okay," I whisper, barely audible. "Okay."

I gather all the courage that is still within me and whisper his name, "Dominic..."

"Yes, Vita Mia."

"That is the sweetest thing anyone has ever said to me," I say, my hand tightening around his cock, and a shiver runs through him. "Just please be patient with me on this. It will take me some time to feel relaxed being naked in front of you."

"You deserve everything and more. Take all the time you need, Vita Mia," he said, then he leans his forehead to mine again. *What is with him kissing my inner palm and this forehead thing?* Every time he does it, I feel like my heart melts away, and this flood of wetness starts in my core.

Seriously, everything about him makes me feel at ease, like he knows my body how to sing it, my mind how to challenge it, and my soul how to conquer it.

I cling to him, my heart pounding in my chest. The warmth of his body, the steadiness of his presence, all of it reassures me as I try to understand what is happening to me.

As we stand there, wrapped in each other's arms, I know these feelings are too complex to analyse now, so I hit pause on it and enjoy the moment. I feel a sense of peace start to settle over me. Maybe this isn't the end of the world. Maybe, just maybe, I can let go of my fears and trust him completely.

"Shh, Vita Mia. Just listen," he says as if he can hear my mind racing with thoughts. He presses my hand harder against his cock. "This is yours. I am yours. Every part of me belongs to you. Okay?"

Well, a girl can get used to this! A gorgeous man in front of her, a monster cock in her hand, wetness between her legs. What more can a girl ask? Clearly, I am losing control again because I feel like shoving this cock back where it belongs if I am the one who can do whatever she wants with it. *Should I risk internal bleeding?*

Focus, Angela! I take a deep breath and try to regulate my voice to sound at least a bit confident and professional. A small smile tugs at my lips, and I nod. "Okay."

He grins, a look of relief washing over his face. *Oh, that dimple!* How can I focus on anything decent when he's so fucking hot? Seriously, if this does not work, I should start a petition to exile men who are this hot out of here!

He takes the towel and begins to gently dry me off, his touch careful and loving. As he works, I feel my insecurities start to melt away, replaced by a growing sense of trust and acceptance. As I look at him, taking his time caring for me. I notice his erection is now on full display, with a bit of cum forming at the tip. This man is really into me, all of me, and I am finally beginning to believe it.

"You alright there, love of my life?" I tease, unable to hide my amused, cheeky tone. "It looks like your mind is permanently in the gutter," I add quickly and burst out laughing my ass off.

"You little minx! I will fuck you raw if you don't stop being adorable," he says, jumping on me and attacking me.

"Stop! You're still wet," I say between laughter, trying to push him off. "Let me dry you off."

He freezes for a second in my arms. Okay...

"What is that look for?" I ask, reading a strange look in his eyes. "I already saw your ding-ding-dong," I start laughing again, continuing the banter and starting to dry off his front. I am still trying to come up with another cheeky remark when I move to his back, and I feel like someone reached into my chest, pulled my heart out and is currently stomping on it with all its might.

His back is full of scars. I think they're whip scars. *But how? Why?* They look old and deep, and the more I look at them, the more I feel like crying. This is just too much! Who would do such a thing?

"Baby..." I whisper, my voice breaking as I trace a scar with my fingers. "What happened?" I fight with everything in me, not to cry, not to let go. I need to be strong for him, but I also need to know, *I just need to know.* "Oh my God! What happened?" I reach for him and hug him from behind, pressing my cheek to his back and squeezing tightly.

"Italy."

Time stays still as I hug him, trying to process the single, pain-filled word. I have so many questions, I have so much concern about his pain and his memories. I want to take it away and make it mine as well, so he knows he is not alone anymore. We can share this pain, but as I asked for time, I think he deserves the same. This is not something easy, and he needs to process what is happening between us as well before he can share something like this.

Regardless, I will make it abundantly clear to him that he is not alone and that he cannot push me away. This is our pain from now on, regardless of the story, regardless of the scars, regardless of the memories. The realisation of my feelings is the final blow to my heart, and tears run down my cheeks as I cry a silent, heartbreaking cry. I start kissing his scars slowly as if they were fresh wounds and I could actually hurt him, but the desperate desire to make it better somehow is overtaking my rational mind.

"Vita Mia, no," his voice is alarming, full of concern.

"Vita Mia, please don't," the vulnerability in his voice is too much for me to handle now, and a sob escapes my lips.

"Let me, Dominic!" I say, my voice shattered, as I lick one of the whip marks. "Let me carry this with you." He tenses at my touch, his breath hitching.

I swallow hard, my heart aching for him and continue kissing every single scar on his back with all the love and care I can muster. My tears are so overwhelming now, cascading down my cheeks as if washing his scars away, and as I touch him and try to wipe them, I trace the scars and try to steal them away from his back and his memory.

When I slow my motions and lean my head on his back, trying to compose myself. He reaches back and hugs me as much as he can in this position. The warmth of his touch is comforting, but the scars beneath my cheek are a painful reminder of his past.

He turns slowly, facing me with a mixture of pain and vulnerability in his eyes. "Vita Mia, you don't have to carry this burden," his voice breaking. "It's mine to bear."

Fresh tears well up in my eyes as I reach up to cup his face. *Absolutely not! He will learn that this is ours, never again, just his*! "No, Dominic. We're in this together. Your pain is my pain. Let me share it with you."

His eyes close briefly, and when he opens them, I can see the depth of his emotions. It is longing, adoration, acceptance, and something else, something that tells me he finally understands.

He pulls me into a tight embrace, holding me as if afraid I might disappear. "Thank you," he murmurs into my hair.

I hold him just as tightly, feeling the strength of our bond.

I've never felt this close to anyone before, and as the realisation hits me with full force, I feel all my barriers crumbling to the ground. There's nothing left separating me from this man.

"One of my exes called me names while we were having sex," I whisper, my face buried in his chest. "He called me fat, said my breasts were too heavy, and that he couldn't have me on top because I was suffocating him." The words pour out of me like they have a life of their own, unstoppable. My body trembles uncontrollably as the memories surge forward. "As you've probably noticed, all the stretch marks and curves, I was even bigger not too long ago. He dumped me a few weeks after that incident."

The pressure of everything that happened in such a short time and all the amazing and horrible things we shared is making something in me break free to share my darkest secrets as if it were something normal and *natural with him*.

"I fell into depression after that, and I felt like no one would ever accept me for who I am, let alone love me for the person inside." I think I am squeezing him hard because my arms hurt, but I might be wrong because all I can consciously realise are these words that are coming out of me, spilling my darkest pain and my lowest moments in life. "So I started dieting, and when that didn't make me lose weight, I started forcing myself to vomit after every meal."

This is it! The moment of no return! I confess I was bulimic, and all my good looks are because I did that to myself. My sobbing is so fearful that I would be so embarrassed right now if I weren't mortified by how I let loose and just told him everything. *Fuck, Angela!* You are the world's most stupid woman that exists! This is the most handsome, perfect man who ever looked in your direction, and for some reason, he actually likes you back, and you go and say something that messed up after your first date!

My brain screams that I'm a complete idiot, that I've ruined any chance with this man. But my heart... my heart tells me this was inevitable. My soul is his match, and all my darkness belongs to him, just as his darkness is mine. This connection isn't built only by the light, it's forged in the darkness too. It's the path we both had to walk to find each other.

Dominic's arms tighten around me, and he gently lifts my chin, forcing me to look into his eyes. "Angela, please look at me." I hesitate because all in me is starting to crash back down, and whatever I find in his gaze, it will confirm that we are one or crash me beyond repair.

"Baby, please! I adore you, please! Look at me, I need you to read my heart as I speak to you. Please, look at me," his voice is weak and sounds vulnerable.

That pain in his voice is what makes me look up, and his gaze is intense and filled with compassion and sorrow. "Dominic, I don't know if I can believe that someone like you could really love someone like me."

"Vita Mia," he says, his voice filled with emotion. "You are so beautiful that my chest hurts when I look at you. Your past, your scars, your insecurities, they don't change how I feel about you. If anything, they make me fall more for you because they are a part of you, and I love everything about you." He rests his forehead on mine, and a shiver runs through his body. "Perhaps, my words are not enough for the moment, but you will learn that I will forever tell you the truth." He kisses my forehead and hugs me again. "But remember what you do to my body, remember how I loved you last night, remember how my entire being was alive at your touch."

He pulls back, and he lets me see the truth about his feelings in his eyes. The sincerity in his voice and the warmth in his eyes are all the reassurance I need. My soul is calling to his, and she knows that his words speak the truth, that we are safe, protected, accepted and loved by him.

"Amore Mio, it does not matter what some fucking idiot said to you, you are beautiful to me. I feel like I exist because of you. I feel like my soul has been singing since the moment I heard you sing. I feel like I breathe the air that comes out of you. Fucking believe me, please!" His voice sounds so desperate, broken, and panicked, like his next breath won't count, and he might suffocate if I don't accept his truth.

I search his eyes again for any signs of hesitation or doubt, but the only thing staring back at me is the other half of my soul, screaming at me in pain to believe him. I take a deep breath and nod. "I believe you..." I say weakly.

"And I will be here to remind you every day," he kisses my forehead again. "You are my everything, Angela. And nothing will ever change that."

We hold each other as if not just our bodies are connecting but our minds, souls, and futures. I had never thought that telling a man my darkest and most shameful secrets would bring us closer, but it did. In saying that, I never would have thought I would tell anyone, but how he shared his darkness with me. I know that in that darkness, there is something calling to me, that it is as much a part of him as his light is, and for some reason, I want it all from him.

As we stand there, the warmth of his embrace and the steady rhythm of his heartbeat against mine, I feel a profound sense of connection and completeness. It's as if the act of sharing our deepest pains and fears has woven our souls together, creating a bond that is unbreakable and true.

"I promise to always be here for you," he whispers into my ear. "You are mine to protect, and you are mine to love. No one will touch or offend you from now on if they value their lives."

I nod, as I can hear the sincerity in his voice, even if what he said is intense and scary. Maybe he meant it, and my battles will no longer be a one-woman job. "Thank you, Dominic. For everything."

He looks down at me, his eyes soft and filled with understanding. "Thank you, Vita Mia. For trusting me with your heart."

He is right. I am trusting him with my heart. "Don't fucking make me regret this, Dominic." I look straight into his eyes, searching for any hesitation.

He leans his forehead against mine again and holds me tighter. "You are mine now, Vita Mia. No matter what, you are mine, and I take care of what's mine. As long as I live, you will never be alone." A shiver runs through his body, making my heart jump with happiness. *I think he means it!* Well, based on that comment and the fact that his cock is getting hard again, I think he is telling the truth. *Men cannot fake body reactions, right?*

"You are mine, Amore Mio, and I will never let you go. So prepare yourself because you are stuck with me forever." His voice is a mix of love and determination, a promise that resonates deep within me.

He leans in and starts kissing me with a force I did not know was possible. It's a battle of passion and desire, each of us pouring all our emotions into this kiss. His lips are demanding, moving against mine with a fervour that leaves me breathless. I respond with equal intensity, my hands tangling in his hair, pulling him closer as if I could fuse our souls together.

I know I should be scared of how fast this is going. I know I should be scared of his words, of him owning my existence. I know I should not have shared so much. But the thing is, my consciousness, my subconscious, and my soul all agree that this is where all the steps of my life brought me toward *the arms of this amazing man*.

Even the logical part of my mind agrees now with my heart, which in its very essence knows that this is right. Every moment, every decision, and every hardship has led me to this point *to him*. It feels like fate, like destiny, like every piece of the puzzle finally falling into place.

"Love of my life," I whisper, my voice trembling with the weight of my realisation. "I... I know this is fast, but I can't help feeling like this is exactly where I'm meant to be. But that is just crazy."

He looks at me, his eyes filled with a mixture of longing and understanding. "Vita Mia, I have never felt like this before. Do you think your feelings are fast? Is this thing between us fast?" He holds my gaze for a few seconds measuring his words, and I can see the moment he says *Fuck it,* and then continues. "Amore Mio, you provoke this feeling within me where I want to chain you to me, to devour you, to imprison you, and to worship you for all the days of our lives. This is not a relationship, this is uniting with the person you were created for." He says with the raw possessiveness of a madman.

"Put it deep into your mind, Vita Mia. There is no escaping me, there is no you and me, there are no others. It's just us since the moment you said yes to me!" The finality in his voice brings a shiver through my body. No one has ever spoken to me in this way before.

His words, fierce and passionate, resonate deep within me. They ignite a fire in my soul, a fire that is both exhilarating and terrifying. "Dominic," I whisper, my voice trembling with the intensity of my emotions, "I have never experienced anything like this either. It's as if my entire existence has been leading me to you."

He pulls me closer, his grip firm yet tender. "Then trust in this, in us. Because what we have is beyond anything I've ever imagined. It's destiny, fate, whatever you want to call it. We are meant to be together, and I am never letting you go."

I nod, my heart pounding in my chest and, as he finishes his words, he lifts me up and places me on the basin counter, his gaze wicked with intent. "You might be sore from my monster cock, as you like to call him, but I need you more than I've ever needed anything in my life." The next moment, he lowers himself to the floor and looks up at me.

There will not be a day when this view of him looking up at me is not going to be hot as fuck, especially with that wicked smile of his and the clear intent in his eyes. "Love of my life..." I trail off because I want this so very much that I am willing to endure any discomfort, but on the other hand, he is the one on his knees again.

"Shh, Vita Mia, show me what's mine," he murmurs, his hands caressing my thighs, spreading them gently. "Let me take care of you. Let me show you how much I need you."

My breath catches as he leans forward, his lips brushing against my inner thigh, sending shivers through my body. "My love," I whisper, my voice trembling with desire and anticipation.

He looks up at me, his eyes dark with passion. "Amore Mio, you are everything to me. I want to worship you, to make you feel how much you mean to me."

His words send a thrill through me, and I can feel my resolve melting away. "I want you too, love of my life. So much," I confess, my voice barely above a whisper.

His smile deepens as he kisses his way up my thigh, his hands gently guiding me to the edge of the counter. "Then let me," he says softly, his breath warm against my skin. "Let me love you."

As he begins to pleasure me with his mouth, I am overwhelmed by the intensity of the sensations. His tongue is skilled and relentless, bringing me to the brink of ecstasy with each stroke. I grip the edge of the counter, my head falling back, lost in the pleasure he is giving me.

"My love," I moan, my voice filled with need. "Oh, yes!"

He hums against me, the vibration adding to the pleasure, and I can feel myself spiralling higher and higher. His hands hold my thighs firmly, keeping me in place as he devours me with an intensity that leaves me breathless.

The world fades away, and all that exists in this moment is this connection between us. I am completely at his mercy, and I wouldn't have it any other way. As the waves of pleasure crash over me, I cry out his name, my body trembling with release.

He doesn't stop, continuing to pleasure me until I am a quivering mess, barely able to keep myself upright. When he finally pulls back, his lips glistening with my essence, he looks up at me with a satisfied smile.

"Vita Mia," he says softly, his voice full with love. "I want one more where you squirt all over my face. I want all of you on me." He smiles up at my surprised face and starts licking around my clit to control the pressure on her after the first release. His mind is wicked, his skills are exceptional, and as he starts to work me, he is closer and closer to my clit and adds two fingers inside me, stroking gently and deeply, I can feel myself heading over the edge at lightning speed.

My breath is panting, my mind is foggy, and my ears are almost blocked. Reality fades away as I start to lose myself again in him. It is then I feel Dominic stop and freeze, and I realise there is a doorbell going off.

"I am going to kill him," Dominic says from between my legs, the words vibrating at my core.

Wait, what? My mind panics and runs in all directions with questions and alarm bells.

He gives me another long stroke of his tongue from my back to the tip of my clit and sucks hard on her. He growls into her when he realises the moment is ruined, and the only thing coursing through me is panic, and the only thing passing through me is panic.

"It's ok, Vita Mia," he says, kissing my inner thigh before getting up. "It's just one of my idiot colleagues that I will murder tonight." He leans over, his mouth glistening from my juices, and kisses me so deeply and passionately, but the moment is definitely ruined.

I try to relax, to not make a big deal out of this, but my mind starts racing at a hundred miles an hour. *What if he's married? You idiot, you didn't even ask him! What if this place isn't even his, and it was all a lie?* No, that can't be right, he carried me into his bed last night in the dark without hesitation, even in that awkward position. *But I don't even know what he does for a living!* That part's true. I was so blown away by his presence, his charm, I forgot all my usual safety checks. *What the fuck is wrong with me?*

It's like a bucket of cold water has been dumped over my head, jolting me awake.

"Vita Mia, relax," he says into my lips. "I can literally feel you tensing up. The idiot is not going anywhere. He can wait another two seconds if that is the problem." He pulls back, searching my eyes.

"Oh..." he trails off, trying to decipher whatever look I am having at the moment. I'm not sure how composed I look on the outside, but on the inside, I am losing my fucking marbles because I am a complete idiot and should have been more careful!

"Dominic, I..." I begin, my voice trembling with the weight of my fears and doubts. "I don't even know if you're married or if this place is really yours. I don't even know what you do for a living. I..."

His eyes widen with understanding, and he takes my hands in his, his touch firm and reassuring. "Vita Mia, breathe," he says softly. "I promise you, I am not married, and this place is mine. Ask me anything you need. I will never lie to you." He pulls back a bit more, and I can see his relaxed posture. I don't think he is lying. "I don't think you will always like my answers, but you can be sure I will never lie to you." He places his hands on my cheeks and kisses the top of my head. "Is that okay for now?" He searches my eyes again, and when he is happy with what he finds in my gaze, he pulls back again.

"Now let me get Hunter so you can meet him, and then I can kill him in peace. Does that work for you?" I am waiting for him to burst out laughing at the ridiculous comment, but he does not. He leaves the bathroom and heads to the closet, and he is out of the room in seconds.

I stand in the doorway of the bathroom, just staring at him, trying to process everything. My mind is racing, torn between getting the hell out of here ASAP or trusting this feeling, trusting him, and getting dressed to meet this Hunter guy. I take a deep breath, trying to steady my thoughts. "Okay then," I mutter to the empty room. "Let's meet Hunter."

I walk into his closet, and it's the size of half my apartment. *Wow!* I seriously need to ask him what he does for a living and maybe get some of that for myself. Everything looks elegant, classy, and expensive as hell. *Right... don't get intimidated. These are just things. Things can be replaced. If he's a good guy, none of this should matter.* I take a few more calming breaths and find a drawer with casual T-shirts and, conveniently, one above it with boxers.

"What would he think if I wore his boxers?" I say to the empty room and start laughing, feeling my body starting to relax. "Well, only one way to find out..." I take out a pair, my mind instantly remembering his monster cock. "That is one good-looking cock, and that's that," I start laughing again. "I think this could be pretty hot if the boxers fit my ass." I pull and pull, they are on, but they are not comfortable. "Well, the moment this guy is out of here, your devil's work of underwear will be off me," I start laughing again. "At least I have my sense of humour, the hell with the rest."

I hear them talking as I walk into the open living space. When I turn the corner and spot a big blonde guy standing next to Dominic, all my stress evaporates

The guy says something, and before I can process it, Dominic punches him in the chest so fast, I almost doubt it happened. The blond stumbles back, leaning against the wall, and that's when it hits me, it *did* happen.

What the actual fuck is going on?! Did Dominic really just punch that guy?

"Dominic..." my words trail off as a mixture of apprehension and fear settles within me. "Did you just punch him?"

They both start laughing hard, and I am so confused about what's happening. This is not normal, this is very much abnormal, so why are they laughing?

"Vita Mia, come," he extends his hand to me. "Come meet Hunter."

"Angela, yes, he did punch me. I am very much wounded," Hunter places his hands on his chest in a mocking gesture and pretends he is hurt. "Get him!" he adds for good measure.

Ah! Right! They're full of shit! I start laughing in my mind. I can play this game...

"He is always violent, this guy," he keeps going. "I would not trust him with a wild tiger." He continues in a dramatic gesture and then winks at me.

"Fucker! If you value your eyes, you will never wink at my woman again!" Dominic says, his posture changing, ready to strike another punch.

Wait, what? My woman? My mind races in all directions at those words, but when I see Dominic is not really impressed, I know I need to defuse this. *Quick! Quick! Make a sassy remark, Angela.*

"Well, it's a good thing I'm not an ordinary wild tiger," I say, locking eyes with Hunter, pouring every ounce of confidence and dominance I can muster into my gaze. I hold his stare, making sure he knows I'm not just any woman, and if he thinks he can intimidate me, he's got another think coming.

Satisfied that my point has sunk in, I take Dominic's arm and wrap it around me, guiding his hand to rest on my curves. "My love," I say, meeting his beautiful ocean-blue eyes. "If you'd like, I can help you take his eyes out." I give him my best puppy-dog eyes. "He's got two, after all, one for me, one for you. What do you think?" I finish the comment with a cheerful tone.

Dominic bursts out laughing, the sound is rich and hearty. The tension in his body melts away as he relaxes into my touch, his head rolling back with the intensity of my joke. His laughter is infectious, and I can't help but smile widely, feeling a surge of triumph at diffusing the situation.

Hunter, on the other hand, looks momentarily taken aback, then smirks and shakes his head in amusement. "You two are something else," he says, crossing his arms over his chest. "I think I've underestimated you, Angela."

Dominic pulls me closer, his laughter subsiding into a warm and affectionate gaze. "You see, Hunter," he says, still chuckling, "Angela is not someone you want to mess with. She's fierce, and she's mine."

I lean into Dominic, feeling his strength and warmth envelop me. "And don't you forget it," I add, my voice playful yet firm. "We're a team, and together, we will kick your ass."

They both start laughing again at my silly remark of kicking ass, and when the laughter starts to subside, I extend my hand to Hunter.

"Also... Hi, I'm Angela," I say with a polite smile, trying to ease any remaining tension.

I can feel Dominic pulling my other hand towards him as if not to lose a millimetre of my warmth. His grip is firm and protective, and it sends a reassuring message through our connection.

"Possessive much?" Hunter teases, his eyes twinkling with mischief. "Hi, beautiful." He gives me a sexy smile. "I am Hunter."

"Fucker..." Dominic takes a step toward him, his posture bristling with protectiveness.

Hunter just moves to the side, starting to laugh. "Oh, this is priceless!" he says, laughing so hard his entire body is shaking. "I am going to have so much fun with this, it's unreal," he adds, continuing to taunt Dominic.

I can't help but roll my eyes at Hunter's antics. "Hunter, you really know how to push his buttons, don't you?"

Hunter winks at me, still chuckling. "It's a gift. What can I say? But in all seriousness, it's nice to meet you, Angela. Anyone who can keep this guy in check is someone worth knowing."

Dominic pulls me closer, his arm around my waist now, and looks at Hunter with a mix of annoyance and amusement.

"Vita Mia, I need to go," he says, looking at me with pleading eyes. "I have an emergency at work, and I need to leave as soon as possible," he says, lowering his hands on my hips." He says, lowering his hands on my hips, pulling me closer to him. He lowers his mouth to my ear, and I can feel the air changing as his whisper runs through me. "Are you wearing my underwear?"

My breath catches, and that's all the answer he needs as he tightens his grip on my hips, pulls me closer to him and kisses my ear and neck.

"Hey! Hey!" Hunter's mocking voice booms in the room again. "No funny business in front of company."

Dominic kisses my neck again and inhales me deeply before lifting his gaze to Hunter. "We did not ask for company. So the company can fuck off if they have any complaints to make."

"Hey, you ungrateful ass! The boss will be at work soon, and I have been banging on your door for a while. So how about you show some appreciation?" The finality of his words is the reality check that we both needed.

"What do you do for a job, Dominic?" My voice is small with fear and anticipation. *You idiot woman, this is a question you ask on your date or before the date, not after he fucked your brains out!*

"I'm the CEO of BioQuest International," Dominic says matter-of-factly as I try to recover my jaw from the floor. *What?!*

I blink, trying to process his words. "You're... you're the CEO of BioQuest International?" I repeat, my voice barely above a whisper.

He nods, a small smile playing at the corners of his lips. "Yes, that's correct. We're an international pharmaceutical company."

I shake my head, still in shock. "So, in other words, you are a modern-day drug dealer."

As the words leave my mouth, it is like time has stopped, and reality is in shock as I realise that I truly am a complete idiot. Why in the ever-living hell would I say something that stupid in front of company to an unbelievably hot guy who is a fucking CEO as well?

I am just speechless at my own stupidity.

I prepare myself for the reaction to my comment, but they both burst out laughing hard, and Dominic reaches over and hugs me tightly to his chest.

"Sorry. I meant it as a joke." I look into his eyes. "That's huge, Dominic. Congratulations."

He chuckles softly, his eyes twinkling with amusement. "I guess it is, but it's just a job, Vita Mia. And yes, I am a drug dealer, among other things." He squeezes me in an embrace again and then pulls away.

"Amore Mio, I really need to run. But I will be back as soon as I can." The look on his face says it all. The last thing he wants is to leave with Hunter. "Please stay, hang around, make yourself at home, and we can continue when I get back." He takes my hand and kisses my inner palm again. *Oh, fuck! How can I say no now?*

He leans over and whispers in my ear, "Make sure you still have my boxers on when I am back." He takes my ear in his mouth and sucks on it hard.

Well! I want to tell him, *Don't start something you can't finish, but again, we have company, so I just take a deep breath and try to settle the warmth in my core.*

"Sure, my love," I say, placing my other palm on his solid chest. "Go do your thing, and if worst comes to worst, we can catch up this week."

"No! I want to spend the day with you," he says quickly, his tone sharp and final, like he's already given this a lot of thought and Hunter being here feels like the world's most annoying inconvenience. "Please, wait for me," he adds, his pleading eyes pushing me over the edge.

"Okay, love of my life." I lean into him and give him a quick hug. "Go and come back to me."

Dominic's grip tightens around me for a moment before he reluctantly steps back, his eyes lingering on mine. "I'll be as quick as I can," he promises, his voice filled with determination. He runs to the bedroom, and five minutes later, he is in a suit, looking devastatingly handsome, more than any man should be allowed to.

"You sexy beast," Hunter teases from next to me.

"Oh, fucker! You know you'll be in a car with me, and things might happen. Body parts might go missing," Dominic says in a clear and steady voice.

"Oh, no! Angela, save me!" Hunter screams in a dramatic voice. *Seriously, what a joker this guy is! Is anything ever serious with him?*

Dominic leans down and kisses me softly, then rests his forehead on mine. "Wait for me, Vita Mia," he breathes deeply. "Please."

"It's okay, love of my life," I try to soothe him as I can hear the pain in his voice. "I will be here, waiting for you."

He kisses me again, deepening the kiss for a moment before Hunter clears his throat.

"I like that," Dominic adds as a whisper on my lips. "You waiting for me at home."

With one last kiss and some more bickering between them, they head out the door, and I collapse on the couch, trying to find my bearings. The silence of the apartment feels almost deafening after the whirlwind of emotions and interactions. I look around at the beautiful apartment for a few more minutes, taking in the modern decor, the large windows letting in natural light, and the personal touches that make it feel like Dominic's space. But then I realise how awkward this is. Like, really awkward! What am I going to do in his apartment for who knows how long?

The napkin!

Last night at the restaurant, he had read my note, but I had not read his! My heart races with curiosity and excitement. I jump up and run to my purse, digging through it until I find the napkin with his neat handwriting.

My hands tremble slightly as I unfold it, my eyes scanning the words eagerly:

Dominic

"Question 1: What is your favourite colour, and why?"

Green – because it is fresh, unique, brings life and joy, is versatile, and hopeful

"Question 2: What is your favourite animal, and why?"

Honey badgers – because they are extremely intelligent, resilient, family-oriented, and funny

"Question 3: What is your favourite mess of water, and why?"

Deep ocean – because of its strength, infinite depth, and intense pressure.

"Oh, my heart!"

Chapter Fourteen

Dominic

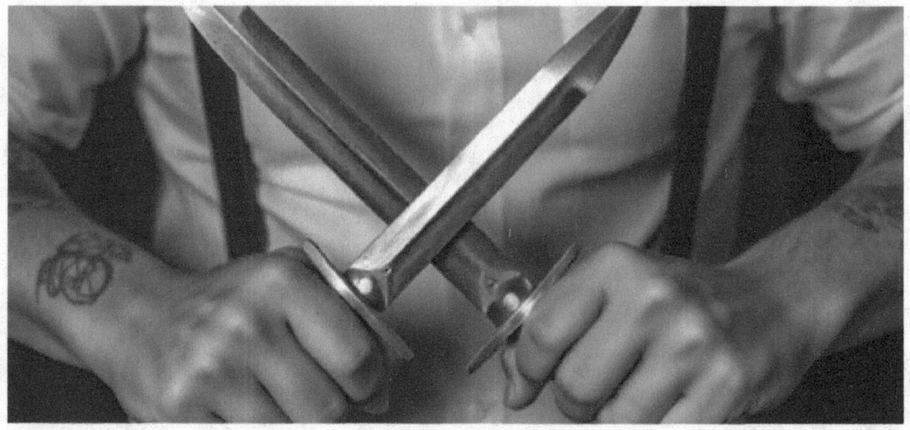

As the car almost flies down the road, I feel sick, like actually sick to my stomach, leaving Angela alone in my apartment. The feeling is so intense that I have to take deep breaths to steady myself. I know she is safe. She has been safe since the moment I met her. I've had two guys surveilling her since that first encounter at the shop, but this physical distance between us feels like it's pulling something vital out of me, and I might actually throw up.

Hunter glances over at me, his usual playful demeanour gone. "You alright, man?" he asks, concern evident in his voice.

I nod, but it's a weak gesture. "Yeah, just... It's hard leaving her. I know it sounds crazy, but I feel like I'm leaving a part of myself behind. I feel like I cannot breathe properly now."

Hunter chuckles softly. "You're in deep, Dominic. But I get it. She's something special. When you know, you know."

I grip the steering wheel tighter, my knuckles turning white. "She is. And it's not just about keeping her safe. It's about being with her, feeling her presence. This distance... it's unbearable."

Hunter leans back, watching me closely. "You're not used to feeling like this, are you?"

I shake my head. "No. I've never felt like this about anyone. It's like she's a part of me now, and being away from her is... it's physically painful."

Hunter smirks, but there's a hint of understanding in his eyes. "Well, you've got it bad, my friend. But that's a good thing. It means she's worth it." His tone calm and supportive. "Now that I've met her in person, I think you might be right about her. It feels like she completes you somehow..." he trails off. "But what do I know? I just hope it works out for you, brother."

I manage a small smile, my thoughts drifting back to Angela. Her smile, her laughter, and the way she looked at me with trust and love filled me with a warmth I couldn't describe. "She is worth it. More than anything."

Hunter claps me on the shoulder. "We'll be back soon. Just focus on getting this done, and then you can go back to her."

I nod, trying to push the gnawing anxiety to the back of my mind. "So what happened? Who did we get this time?"

"Is another Romanian known to work with Bogdan," Hunter says with a tone of annoyance in his voice. "Sofia and I have been playing that fucking game for more than a week now, but we aren't getting any useful responses, and we both have this feeling that we are missing something crucial. So when this guy was flagged by the facial recognition scan, we got him," he raises his eyebrows at me playfully.

"Alright. Elijah and Buddy are on their way?"

"They are flying back as we speak. And just to be clear, you owe me one for saving you and banging on your door," Hunter says, trying to sound annoyed at me, though I know he enjoys playing the role of my babysitter. I don't owe him a thing. "I don't think Elijah would have appreciated you playing hide the sausage and not focusing on these Romanian fuckers."

I punch his chest so fast and hard knocking the breath out of him.

"You ass! What's with all the punching today?" he says, trying to catch his breath.

"You think you're funny, Hunter, and you are, but when it comes to my woman, I'm not laughing. And if you don't want to find out how sharp my knives are on your neck or balls, I advise you to stop these remarks about how hot she looks in my clothes or anything about sausages because it'll get serious fast next time."

Hunter's eyes widen, and he raises his hands in mock surrender. "Alright, alright, I get it. No more jokes about Angela. I was just trying to lighten up the mood."

I glare at him, my jaw tight. "As I said, you are funny, but no jokes about Angela will be tolerated of any sort."

He nods, a hint of genuine concern in his eyes. "Understood, man. I'm sorry. I know how much she means to you." He knows he's in trouble, which is why he apologised.

I take a deep breath, trying to calm the storm of emotions inside me. *I cannot kill the bastard because Elijah would hunt me down within hours, so I am stuck with him.* I can still punch and hurt him if he crosses the line, but again, *life is sad, and I cannot kill him.*

As we near the warehouse, my phone buzzes with a message. I glance at it and see it's from Angela.

Angela

I read your note from last night.

Thinking of you. Can't wait for you to come back.

Her words bring a small measure of comfort, but the ache in my chest remains. I quickly type a response:

Dominic

Can't wait to be back.

I put the phone away and focus on the road ahead, determination coursing through me. I need to get this done as quickly as possible and return to her. She is my home now, and I can't stand being away from her for long.

Possessive? Maybe...

Obsessed? Probably...

Determined? Definitely!

Hunter notices my resolve and nods approvingly. "You have some moves, brother," his voice carrying a tone of surprise and admiration. "What note? Maybe someday you can share some of the moves with me..." his voice catches at the end as if he wants to say more, but he just cannot bring himself to admit it.

I chuckle, shaking my head. "I'm not sure what moves you think I have, but even if I did, my mind goes blank when I speak to her," my voice is soft with admission. "That's how I know she is my everything, there is silence in my mind when I'm around her."

Hunter's expression softens, a rare moment of genuine emotion flickering in his eyes. "Damn, Dominic. I never thought I'd hear you talk like that. She's really gotten under your skin, huh?"

I nod, a small smile tugging at my lips. "It's not that she got under my skin, it is that she calls to me. Her entire being inexplicably calls to me. It's as if she is the very breath in my lungs."

A few moments pass in silence, and when I look over at Hunter, he is in deep thought, his face blank. "She put me to play this game last night," I add to pull him out of whatever he was feeling just now. "It was a good game. It led me to know her better and broke the ice for us."

"You slept with her on the first date! You dog, you!" he says as I pull up in front of the warehouse. He does not wait for me to stop the car, and he jumps out, running.

"You better fucking run, you ass!" I yelled after him, surprised by his stupid remark and gesture.

I consider the shop our first date, the bar our second, and last night our official third. I would have fucked her at the shop if she had let me. But I know sshe might have thought I was a perv and refused to give me the time of day, so I waited until the third date. Truth be told, the game was great because when she said how she liked her sex, I was about to lose my mind and almost jumped on her at the restaurant. The fact that we made it to my apartment is a testament to my desire to make everything special for her. Otherwise, the restaurant would have been where it all happened for me.

I shake my head as I walk in to try to clear my mind. I need to extract this information quickly and return to her. The fucking idiot knows he's done for. He better not waste my time and make it worse. *Right?*

The large room is empty, just like all the other warehouses we use for these kinds of 'discussions'. In the far corner, there is a car, a chair with a tied-up guy, three of our guys, Hunter, and me. Logically, I should be out of here in 30 minutes or less. Let's see how fast the fucker sings, a wicked smile plays on my face as I approach the guy.

He is muscled, so he probably thinks he can take it, and he will not give us any information. The problem is, he's not getting out of this alive. He probably just hasn't realised it yet.

"Ce pula mea, mă țineți aici?" his voice booming with violence and attitude in the warehouse like a big drum. He probably thinks he is intimidating us and we will let him go.

"Credeți că sunteți mare sculă pe basculă?" he starts laughing in a mocking way, sizing us all. *Oh, he thinks he can take us all and make us fall at his feet.*

Oh! This is going to be fun!

I would love to take my time with your sorry ass and make you regret every day of your life, but unfortunately, I'm in a hurry, so you're going to sing fast.

"I'm sorry. Were you under the impression that we speak Romanian?" I say in an arrogant tone. "I don't need to speak Romanian to make you talk..." I trail off, letting my words sink in.

"Here is how this is going to go," I lower myself to look him in the eyes. "We know you work with Bogdan. We know about the way you guys communicate. There isn't much you can tell me that will actually be of value." I look him up and down in a sign of disgust. "So if you want to end your life quicker, you will sing all you know fast because I am in a hurry, and I really don't want to waste too much time on you."

My words are barely out of my mouth when he spits at me. The glob of saliva lands on my chest, right where Angela's hand usually rests.

For a second, my breath stops at the memory of her beautiful hand resting on my chest. In the next second, I realised this bastard actually spat at me, and rage bubbles up, hot and uncontrollable. Without thinking, I drive my boot into his chest with a solid kick that sends him flying backward, crashing to the ground a few metres away.

The impact of my kick reverberates through my leg, and the room goes silent, everyone momentarily stunned by the sudden violence. I take a deep breath, trying to steady myself, though the fury simmers just beneath the surface.

"You made a big mistake," I growl, stepping closer to the crumpled form on the floor. "You're going to tell me everything I need to know because now we're going to start playing. We're going to get to know each other very well, very quickly."

He groans, as he tries to regain his breath, his eyes wide with pain and fear. The defiance that was there moments ago has been replaced by sheer terror.

Hunter steps forward, placing a hand on my shoulder, a silent reminder to keep my cool. "Dominic, let's get the information we need before the boss arrives," he says calmly, his eyes flicking to the man on the ground. "The information is the most important thing."

I nod, forcing myself to draw another deep breath. "You're right," I say through gritted teeth. "But this piece of shit needs to understand that he's not in control here and that there is only one way out of this."

I lower myself down to his level and look him in the eyes as I pull out my knives and cut his hand restraints. The gesture draws a look of surprise from him, but before he can utter another stupid word, two of my guys are by my side. They know how this will work... he will scream, he will bleed, and he will talk. We just need to convince the fucker of these facts fast.

I stand, place my boot on his chest, glance at my guys, and smile. There is no hesitation from them. *We all know it. Loyalty and respect!* I am the senior, they will listen.

"Nail gun and gag," I command with a calm yet confident air.

"What?!" The sorry bastard beneath my boot tries to squirm and push me off. I press all my weight onto him and deliver a solid kick to his side with my other foot. The force sends him into a fit of coughing.

"Here's how it will go, fucker," I look down on him, my voice cold and devoid of any mercy. "You will tell us everything we need to know, or I will make sure you are suffering unimaginable pain."

One of my men retrieves the nail gun from the car, while the other secures the gag over his filthy mouth. Fear is evident in his eyes now, but it's still not enough. He needs to truly understand the gravity of his situation.

I nod at my guys, and they move in, they both hold him down. He attempts to scream through the gag, his eyes wild with terror.

"We're going to play a game I call 'Scream a little, talk a little,'" I say in a mocking tone, glancing over at Hunter. Remember that one, Hunter?" I say, winking at him as I take the nail gun from my guy and crouch closer to the bastard's face. "I'll bet you a grand, Hunter, that this bastard will start screaming and spilling in under three minutes. If it takes longer, you win," I say, giving Hunter a challenging look.

Before Hunter can respond, I fire the nail gun three times into the bastard's right hand. The muffled scream that escapes him is music to my ears.

"See what I mean, Hunter? I think this time the win is mine," I say, my tone dripping with challenge as I move to the other side.

The bastard is struggling against my men, yanking at his free arm and thrashing like a wild animal. Before I crouch again, I fire two nails into his left shoulder to quiet him down.

"Hey, fucker," I say, slapping his cheek a few times to get his attention. "Be polite to my guys." My glare pierces through him. "You brought this on yourself. Nobody told you to spit on me. Nobody told you to mouth off to us." I reach over and fire two more nails into his right shoulder. "Those two were just for symmetry, and because, honestly, you practically begged me to include the shoulders. Now, where was I..." I trail off, casually firing three nails into his left hand.

The agonised, muffled screams escaping him are music to my ears. His eyes are wide, bloodshot, and streaming tears, and I can hear his shallow, ragged breaths. *Did I break a rib? Maybe a few?* I aim a few sharp kicks at his ribs on my way down to his ankles, just to make sure he gets the message.

"So, what do you think, Hunter?" I say mockingly, as if we are just catching up over beers. My tone is casual, almost light, and I glance over with a grin.

Hunter chuckles, shaking his head as if this is just another day at the office. "You have always had a flair for the dramatic, Dominic. But hey, I would not mind taking your money, so it is on."

I smirk, feeling the adrenaline surge through me. "It's all about the show, Hunter. Keeps things interesting." The words are barely out of my mouth, and I shoot one nail into each ankle. Then, I stand to my full height and look down at the piece of shit at my feet, completely nailed to the floor. My guys and Hunter surround me, all of us looking down at him. He groans, his body trembling with pain. I squat down, looking him dead in the eyes.

"Now, are you ready to start talking, or do we need to continue this little game?" I pat his cheek to make sure he does not faint on me yet. I need him to start talking. I know he will not give me everything I need during the first break, but it will let him hope this might end soon. Then, I can become even more vicious.

He nods frantically, tears streaming down his face.

"The thing about hands, ankles, and feet is that they have a lot of bones and important muscles, and if you touch any of them the wrong way, it hurts like hell. That's what you're discovering firsthand." I smile at him and signal for one of my guys to remove the gag. That's when I notice some of the bastard's blood on my shirt.

Fuck!!!!! Fucking fucking fuck!!!!

I can feel my mind exploding with anger so vivid that for a second, I forget to breathe. *This fucking idiot got blood on me.* That means I need to change, that means I need to find identical clothes, that means I will be even later, and that means I will not see my angel for longer... *all just because this fucker bled on me!*

The rage is all-consuming. My vision narrows, and a red haze blurs the edges of my sight. I grip the nail gun tighter, my knuckles turning white. The sight of the blood on my clothes, where Angela's hands rest, only fuels my fury.

I crouch down, my face inches from his, my voice a low, dangerous growl. "You have no idea what you've just done," I hiss. "You've made this personal."

Hunter steps forward, a hint of concern in his eyes. "Dominic, we need to stay focused. Let's get this done and get out of here."

I take a deep breath, forcing myself to calm down. *He's right.* Angela is waiting for me, and I can't let this piece of shit delay me any longer. I close my eyes for a moment, visualising her face and her smile, and let it ground me.

"Alright," I say, my voice more controlled. "Kneecap it is," I shoot two nails into each knee faster than the guy can react.

"Fucker!!!" the idiot yells ricochets off the walls in an animalistic sound. My mind trails off to salt, *that would teach him some manners to not bleed on other people.* "You just ruined the fun, and now I want to hurt you," I say in a calm but menacing tone.

The look of confusion on his face is amusing, but at least he's smart enough not to contradict me.

I look down at the bleeding man, his eyes wide with terror. "Speak..."

"We talk through Eclipse Nexus, I swear to you," he says with pleading eyes to us. "I swear!" He is screaming it at us.

"Listen, fucker, as you are wasting more and more of my time, my mind is creating more and more interesting ways to make you shit yourself," I say, staring at him now with confidence and amusement in my tone. "So it can get very nasty bad for you very fast." I pick up the nail gun again and look him dead in the eyes. "I told you we already know a lot, so make yourself useful quickly." My tone is calm, as if I am asking him what beer he wants to have with me and Hunter.

"I swear I am telling the truth!" He involuntarily moves in panic, making the nails pull at his extremities, and a scream echoes in the warehouse.

I gesture for my guy to gag him again, cutting off his screams. "You really don't get it. I already have you. I already can do whatever I want with you. You are doing this to yourself."

As I notice the bleeding around the nails, I know what's next. *It's time for salt.*

"Let's see how you feel when your body fights against you," I say, my voice dripping with menace. I look at one of my guys and give a short, sweet, and accurate command "Salt."

My man nods and quickly fetches a bag of coarse salt from the car boot. The bound man's eyes widen with terror as he realises what's coming. His muffled protests are pitiful and desperate, but they fall on deaf ears.

I take the bag from my guy and approach the fucker. The anticipation of his reaction sends a cold thrill through me. "You see, pain can be a powerful motivator. It can bring out the truth in ways words never can."

I grab a handful of the coarse salt and hold it up so he can see. His eyes are filled with a mixture of pain and sheer terror. "This is going to hurt, but you brought it on yourself."

With deliberate slowness, I sprinkle the salt onto the wounds around the nails. His body convulses, and even through the gag, the scream that escapes him is gut-wrenching. He thrashes against his restraints, his eyes rolling back in agony.

"Look at you," I taunt, leaning closer. "Your body is betraying you. The salt is fighting its way into your wounds, tearing at your flesh. How long do you think you can endure this?"

His eyes are pleading now, desperate for mercy that will not come. I step back, letting him writhe in his torment. "We can do this all day," I say calmly. "But I suggest you start talking faster if you want the pain to stop because if you think this is pain, what comes next will make you pass out, then we have to bring you back, then you will pass out again, and so on and as I said I am in a bit of a hurry so I would appreciate some courtesy on your part." The guys start laughing at my crazy as fuck remark, but it is true. *I need to run, damn it!* I need to run to the office, change into my spare clean suit, and run to my angel. *Fucker and his blood!*

Hunter watches with an amused interest, his respect for my methods evident. "You really know how to make a point, Dominic."

I glance at Hunter, a small smile playing on my lips. "It's all about making sure they understand who's in control."

The man continues to struggle, the salt doing its work. I give him a moment, watching as the fight drains out of him, leaving only a broken shell. His eyes meet mine, and I see the surrender there.

I nod to my guy, who removes the gag. "Ready to talk now?" I ask, my voice icy.

"Yes, yes, please," he gasps, his voice hoarse with pain. "I'll tell you everything, just make it stop."

"Good," I say, satisfaction curling through me. "Start talking."

As he spills every detail he knows, I listen carefully, cataloguing the information. When he finally finishes, I step back, my mind already moving to the next step.

"Verify everything," I order my guys. "Make sure nothing is left out."

As they move to follow my instructions, I look down at the bleeding, trembling man, and in my peripheral vision, I notice Elijah and Buddy approaching us. They both take in the state of the team, ensuring we are all unharmed and then their gaze zeros in on the trash at my feet.

"Good?" says Elijah.

"Yes. They use Eclipse Nexus to communicate and Nebula Ascendants to confirm information." I tried to read their reaction, but there is nothing there, not even a flinch at the fact that we missed half of the information last time. *Either way, we got it now.* "We got the guy's loggings, and we are verifying everything now."

"When did the second video game piece come into play?" Elijah adds with an air of complete dominance over the situation.

I look at the guy and kick him to answer.

"Two days ago," he says between coughs. "Bogdan thought it would be safer to have an additional layer of security."

Elijah looks down at the man with a calmness that is both scary and admirable. "What is he building?" He asks the fucker as if speaking to an impertinent child.

"He is building a software to remote into people's devices without consent and access their bank details."

Elijah's demeanour changes, and for the first time since I have known him, I can see a reaction to someone's words. *Oh, fuck!* I am speechless. The silence in the warehouse is heavy as we all stare at the guy while Hunter is verifying everything with Sofia and the team.

Elijah's eyes narrow, his calm facade slipping slightly to reveal the storm brewing beneath. "Remote access to bank details," he repeats slowly, each word dripping with barely contained fury. "Do you have any idea what you've just admitted to?"

The man trembles under Elijah's gaze, coughing and trying to catch his breath. "I swear, that's all I know. Please, I don't want any more trouble."

Elijah's calmness is chilling as he steps closer to the man. "Trouble? That is amusing. Where is Bogdan, and what platform is he using for the code?"

"I swear on anything you want, I don't know anything else." The words are not even fully out of the man, and Buddy shuts him in the head, silencing him forever.

I can feel the tension in the air, thick and oppressive. Elijah's usually composed demeanour is cracking, revealing the intensity of his anger. I've never seen him like this, and it's both awe-inspiring and terrifying.

Hunter walks back over, his phone in hand. "Sofia confirmed it," he says, his voice steady. "Everything checks out."

Elijah nods slowly, processing the information. "Good," he says finally. "But this changes everything. We need to act fast and shut this down before it goes any further." We are all just processing the information for a few moments, not daring to say something, anything. The entire team is shocked at Elijah's reaction.

"What a weakling, praying on the vulnerable," Elijah adds while stroking his beard in deep thought. "We need to get to him before he finishes his code." He turns to Buddy, his facade all confident and dominant again. "Let's send some boots on the ground in Romania and be ready to get him."

"Done," Buddy's voice carries a finality as if he conjure magic and the request actually was completed.

"We need the team to start infiltrating all the platforms ASAP and track my code." The request is so calmly spoken as if it's not like looking for a penny at the bottom of the ocean.

"Done," Buddy confirms once again.

Well, I guess that is how progress is done. Boss speaks, everyone listens, and fucking does it.

Elijah turns, and Buddy follows, both with a calm demeanour, looking like they'd been discussing trivial matters and not about changing the way fraud is done.

"Dominic," Elijah's voice is like a reality call to my desperate need to get back to my angel.

"Yes," I jog to get in line with him.

"I understand you've made your choice." His words made me pause for a second, and then I nodded. *This was inevitable,* I knew it would come. Let's just hope I am not the next one nailed to the floor.

"I did, she is everything." As much as I want to come across as confident, the vulnerability in my voice is evident.

"As you know, we do not mingle in the team's love affairs. So normally, I would give you the option to stay or go, given that she is not from our world." His gaze on me is making my anxiety jump to rocker-high levels.

"However, given who she is, it was requested that you prove you're worthy of her." *What?*

"You need to take care of this Jake that keeps troubling her." Elijah continues as if we are speaking of groceries and not killing some guy. "I know you already looked into him, so I assume there won't be any problems?" I am speechless! Does this mean the old lady asked him to off the guy? *What the actual fuck?* Is it the old lady, or who would have a heavy voice with Elijah for him to ask this? *This is unreal!*

I nod again, hard for me to articulate words and just copy Buddy's lead. "Done."

"Good. One more thing, you'll transfer 50% of all your wealth to the girl." He didn't ask, he told me. "Women have expenses, and she should never have to ask for money, ever." He stares at me, daring me to contradict him.

"I just transferred a billion dollars for someone to ensure that." *What?!!!* His words offer a rare glimpse into a life I don't often see.

"I will transfer all if needed," I say, short and confident. There is no hesitation in my tone, I can make more money, but I cannot get another angel.

"75% it is," he places his palm on my shoulder and squeezes. "I'm happy for you, Dominic," his gaze pure fire. "Do not fuck it up, as this will not be forgiven." He stares at me for a few more moments, then a small smile appears at the corner of his mouth.

"Understood," I say and nod again.

Since the day he saved me, we have never had a discussion like this where he is the one going on and on, and I am the one with short replies. I feel shocked, relieved, happy, in love, obsessed... and ready to kill that fucker if it means my angel's mum will accept me.

Elijah's grip tightens slightly on my shoulder, a physical reminder of the weight of his words. "You have until the end of the week to take care of Jake. No delays, no excuses."

I swallow hard, feeling the weight of his words as my mind races. "Understood. He'll be gone by the end of the week."

Elijah's smile widens, but there's no warmth behind it. "Good. And make sure the transfer to her account is handled immediately. I don't want to hear of any financial issues."

"I'll handle it first thing," I assure him, trying to keep my voice steady. "Thank you, Elijah."

He releases his grip on my shoulder, his expression softening just a fraction. "Remember, this is more than just a test. It's a statement. You're showing commitment."

"I understand," I reply, my voice firm.

With that, he turns and walks away, leaving me standing there with a whirlwind of emotions. I take a deep breath, trying to steady myself. *This is it.* The ultimate test of my loyalty and love for Angela.

Hunter, who had been watching the exchange, steps closer. "You good?" he asks, his tone surprisingly gentle.

I nod, though my mind is still racing.

Hunter claps me on the back. "You'll be fine. Just do what you need to do."

"Thanks, Hunter," I say, appreciating the support.

We start walking towards the exit, and once we're outside, the cool air hits me, clearing my mind. Hunter walks beside me, a determined look on his face. "This is big, Dominic. We need to be ready for anything. I still cannot believe Bogdan was stupid enough to steal the code and run."

I nod absentmindedly as I pull out my phone and start making arrangements. The transfer of my wealth is the easy part. Taking care of Jake... that's going to require a different kind of planning. But I know I can do it. For Angela, for our future, I will do whatever it takes.

The weight of the conversation still lingers, but I push it aside, focusing on the tasks at hand. My fingers move quickly over the screen, sending messages and making calls.

First is the financial transfer. I contact my bank, ensuring that 75% of my wealth is transferred to Angela's account. The amount is staggering, but I don't hesitate. Elijah is right she should never have to worry about money.

"Transfer complete," the bank manager confirms over the phone.

"Thank you," I reply, ending the call. One task down. Next, the real estate agent. I know transferring international properties will be more complicated, so I emailed him a list of all the estates I want Angela to have moving forward. Whether she wants them or not, she'll be taken care of for the rest of her life. I followed up with a call to confirm he received the email and is starting the process ASAP.

"Mr. DeLuca, we are happy to assist you with this matter. However, it is a significant loss on your behalf, so I must insist. Are you sure you want to transfer this properties to Miss Puscasu?" the agent asks, his voice cautious.

"Yes, I'm sure," I reply firmly. "This isn't about loss, it's about ensuring she's taken care of. I want everything to be in her name as soon as possible."

There's a brief pause on the other end of the line before the agent speaks again. "Very well, Mr. DeLuca. We will expedite the process and keep you updated on the progress."

"Thank you," I say, ending the call.

With the financial and real estate matters handled, my focus shifts back to the more pressing issue, *Jake*.

"Drop me off at the office. I need to change," I say curtly as we step into the car. I need to get this blood off me, and I need to get to my angel.

After finishing the calls, setting everything in motion, a sense of calm determination settles over me. *This is my path, and I'm ready to walk it, no matter what it takes*. Angela is worth it, and I won't let anything stand in the way of our happiness.

"Tomorrow we come up with a plan how to take Jake out, we already have a lot on him so there should not be any issues." I take in a deep breath, trying to settle my racing mind. *I am doing this! If is the last thing I am doing under the sun, but I am doing this!*

Hunter just nods from behind the steering wheel. "You're really doing this." Amusement and shock creeping from his voice.

"She is my everything, brother," my reply is prompt and clear. "There is nothing under the sun that I would not do for this woman." The finality in my words, is evident as Hunter just nodes and speeds through traffic as if it were flies and not cars that we are passing.

My phone dings with an incoming message notification, and my heart jumps as all hopes bloom in my heart that it might be from her.

Angela

Clearly, you lost your way home, so I'm going to go now…

Dominic

Absolutely not!

Angela

Oh! That was quick… Did you miss me so much that you were holding the phone in your hand?

Dominic

I missed you more than you can imagine, Vita Mia.

Please wait for me.

I stare at the phone, and I feel like an idiot. *Fuck me!* I'm an idiot for wasting time with that piece of trash, I'm an idiot for falling so fast for Angela, I'm an idiot for having this desperation feeling within me, but I am not an idiot for begging. I would beg her until my last breath if need be, but she will never escape me.

Angela

Dominic is getting late, and I have a few things to sort out today.

As much as I want to see you again, I will leave now, and we can catch up this week.

I have never hated my name before. But a full-on pain settles in my chest at her calling me by my name as if we were strangers and not the closest thing to becoming one person. *The fucking blasphemy! Next time I am fucking that word out of her forever!*

Deep breaths, Dominic! Deep breaths!

Dominic

Vita Mia, I am probably another 30 minutes away. Please, let's at least have lunch together.

Also, you are forbidden from calling me by my name moving forward.

I will fuck it right out of you the next time I'm inside you, and you will not be able to walk for a week. Is that clear enough, Amore Mio?

Angela

Dominic!!!!!

Dominic

Fucking into oblivious it is, then! :)) XXX

My mind goes in complete silence....

Well, that shut her up, I think to myself, amused, looking at the phone as if she could reach out of it and touch my heart with her warm hands. Or is her mind drifting off to last night? Oh, my little minx and her adorable ways. I feel myself getting hard at the memories from last night, a sense of peace washing over me, like I've found my other half, my purpose in life, *my home.*

My home... what a strange concept, but with her, it feels right, it feels true.

I lean back in my chair, letting the memories of last night wash over me. Her laughter, her touch, the way she looked at me with those eyes that seemed to see right into my soul. It's all so vivid, so real. The way her body moved against mine, the soft gasps and moans that escaped her lips, everything about her is intoxicating.

I reach out and run my fingers over the screen as if I could somehow feel her warmth through it. *My angel.* She's everything I never knew I needed, everything I never thought I could have. *She's my home.*

The word echoes in my mind, filling me with a sense of calm and certainty. *Home.* For so long, I've wandered through life, never even considering I belong to someone. But with my angel, it's different. With her, I feel anchored, grounded. She's the missing piece that completes me.

A smile tugs at my lips as I think about the future. *Our future.* The plans I've set in motion today are just the beginning. I'll make sure she's always taken care of, always protected. She deserves nothing less.

"I will punch you in your balls if you get hard next to me, Dominic!" Hunter's aggravated voice comes from next to me. "Wipe that stupid look off your face, fucker! You look like a teenager in heat," he continues his assault on my ears.

"Who the fuck asked to look at me? And as long as I am not going to take him out for a breather next to you, you and my cock have no business being in the same sentence." I say and burst out laughing.

"Fucker, I was calling you for the past three minutes. We are at your office, and you were in Lala land dreaming about pussy so get your ass out and go change."

I zoomed out again! Oh, this woman!

Dominic

I'll be home in less than 30 minutes. Tell me, what would you like for lunch?

Angela

Italian, please.

I'm developing a taste for it.

Oh, fuck! Her double meaning is so evident and provoking any hopes of me not being hard to vanish like they were never there in the first place.

Dominic

Stop being adorable, or I'll have you for lunch instead of food.

The things you do to me!

We are in the elevator as I count the moments to run to my office and change.

Dominic

Same as last night?

It did work out quite well for us …

Angela

Same as last night. But if you are more than 27 minutes now, I am out of here, Dominic.

The blasphemy on her lips! It's on, Vita Mia! I will teach you how to speak to me from now on.

Chapter Fifteen

Angela

I am bored out of my mind! After they left, I snooped a bit through his things, like, *of course, I did.* As long as I did not accidentally leave some of Dominic's things in my purse on purpose, I think it's all fair game.

His apartment is a blend of sophistication and subtle luxury, with everything meticulously in its place. I can't help but smile, imagining him meticulously arranging everything. There's a sense of order here, a sense of control that mirrors Dominic's personality.

I wander through the rooms, taking in the details. His taste in art is impeccable, with bold, striking pieces that speak of confidence and strength. The bookshelves are filled with an eclectic mix of literature, philosophy, and strategy books, all hinting at the depths of his mind. *Okay! I like it! I like it a lot!*

As I move into his bedroom, I catch a glimpse of his cologne on the dresser and my mouth just waters. Unable to resist, I pick it up and spray a little on my wrist. The scent is intoxicating, reminding me of him. I close my eyes and breathe it in, feeling a shiver of pleasure run down my spine.

I go into the bathroom and take my time enjoying the beautiful shower with all the latest fancy gadgets. He probably thought these things were luxurious. I think they are useless, as it took me five minutes to figure out how to turn the shower from the top and not from the sides. *Who the fuck invented this shit?* It probably costs more than my rent per month, but it's completely and utterly useless since you still wash your body the same way. The moment I put his shower gel on my palm and inhaled his beautiful scent, all annoyance from my mind washed away.

"Oh, dear me!" I say in an erotic voice to the empty bathroom. "People should not be allowed to wear sex scents on them. Well, by people, I mean hotter-than-life people." I chuckle to myself at my absurd remark.

As I lather my body, I look up and notice the basin counter where Dominic ate me this morning. "Fuck!" A guttural sound escapes from me, the memory flooding back with vivid intensity.

I close my eyes, letting the water cascade over me, and replay the scene in my mind. The way he looked at me with those piercing eyes, the raw hunger in his touch, and the way his mouth moved over my body. It's almost too much to bear, and I can feel a familiar heat pooling in my core.

"Get it together, Angela," I murmur to myself, trying to shake off the lingering desire. But it's no use. The combination of his scent and the vivid memories is too intoxicating.

After a few more minutes of indulgent scrubbing, I finally rinse off and step out of the shower, feeling refreshed but still slightly dazed. I wrap myself in one of his plush towels, enjoying the softness against my skin. As I dry off, I catch sight of myself in the mirror, noticing the faint marks he left on my body. Little reminders of our passion, our connection.

I can't help but smile. Being with Dominic is like living in a dream, one that I never want to wake up from.

I open his wardrobe, running my fingers over the expensive suits and shirts. Everything is so him, sharp, stylish, and undeniably sexy. I pull out one of his shirts and slip it on, the fabric soft against my skin. It's way too big, but I love the way it feels, enveloping me in his scent and warmth.

As I continue my exploration, I find myself drawn to his home office. Papers are neatly stacked, a laptop sits closed, and a few personal items are arranged with military precision. I can't help but peek into a few drawers, finding nothing too surprising pens, notebooks, a few documents.

I wander back to the living room, still wearing his shirt, and plop down on the couch. The boredom is creeping back in, but there's also a sense of excitement. Being here, in his space, makes me feel closer to him, more connected.

I glance at the clock, wondering how much longer it will be before he comes back. I pick up my phone and send a few emails and messages to my friends and mum, and then I am completely bored and contemplating leaving.

"I feel awkward waiting for you," I say to the empty room with a sad tone. "Maybe I should leave and just write him a note like he did..." I trail off, unsure what to do.

I lean flat on the couch, my legs bent over the armrest, staring at my phone to magically tell me what to do.

"Text it is," I say out loud as if to challenge someone to stop me if this is a bad idea.

Angela

Clearly, you lost your way home, so I'm going to go now…

Almost immediately, he replies...

Dominic

Absolutely not!

Angela

Oh! That was quick… Did you miss me so much that you were holding the phone in your hand?

Dominic

I missed you more than you can imagine, Vita Mia.

Please wait for me.

Angela

Dominic is getting late, and I have a few things to sort out today.

As much as I want to see you again, I will leave now, and we can catch up this week.

I feel uncomfortable waiting any longer for him. I want to see him so much and to feel his skin on mine, but at the same time, this is going so fast and burning hot, and I've let things escalate so quickly. Perhaps this is a sign to put the brakes on a bit. *Yes, brakes.* Cars and relationships have this in common. *Brakes it is!*

I take a deep breath, trying to steady my racing heart. Maybe it's time to slow down, catch my breath and think things through. Dominic is intense, and being with him feels like a whirlwind. While that's exhilarating, it also scares me a little. *What if we crash and burn?*

I glance at my phone, half-expecting a message from him. *Nothing.* I sigh and decide to take a moment for myself. I wander back to the bedroom, the room where we've shared so much already, and sit on the edge of the bed. The sheets are still a bit rumpled from our moments together, a tangible reminder of the passion we shared.

Brakes. I need to find a way to slow this down without losing the connection we've built. I want him, but I also want to make sure we're moving at a pace that feels right for both of us.

Dominic

Vita Mia, I am probably another 30 minutes away. Please, let's at least have lunch together.

Also, you are forbidden from calling me by my name moving forward.

I will fuck it right out of you the next time I am inside you, and you will not be able to walk for a week. Is that clear enough, Amore Mio?

Angela

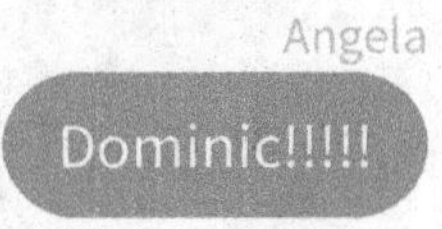

The word explodes in my text and in the room. The crudity of his words is something else!

Dominic

Fucking into oblivious it is, then! :)) XXX

I look at the sheets again and realise my misfortune to come into this room, and reading his raw, passionate words has shattered all my breaks like they were not there to begin with. "Oh, come on!" I say to the empty room as my core is throbbing now with a need for him while my mind is replaying all the filthy things he has done and said to me.

After a few moments of complete delirious need, my phone pings again with a text notification.

Dominic

I'll be home in less than 30 minutes. Tell me, what would you like for lunch?

I hesitate for a moment, my finger hovering over the send button. But then I press it, feeling a strange mix of anticipation and anxiety wash over me.

Angela

Italian, please.

I'm developing a taste for it.

I test the waters as I need to play with fire. His reply is instant, and I hit the mark.

Dominic

Stop being adorable if you don't want me to have you for lunch instead of food.

The things you do to me!

Same as last night?

It did work out quite well for us . . .

It did work out well last night... My mind drifts, flooded with the amazing feelings of how he loved, cared for, and cherished me. His pleading for us to lose ourselves together, to care and let go together, it's all still echoing in me.

I can feel the final traces of hesitation melting away. "Fuck it!" Maybe I'm wrong, maybe I am not, but there is only one way to find happiness, and that is if you risk it all.

Angela

Same as last night. But if you are more than 27 minutes from now, I am out of here, Dominic.

The provocation in my tone that it will be hell to pay if he does not keep his word brings a chuckle from me to the surface. This is so silly, but I cannot help it! Every time I speak to him, I feel like teasing him or pocking him somehow. It feeds this challenging side in me to see his reaction, to see how far I can push.

I smile, feeling a warm rush of happiness. Until he gets back, I'll just have to make do with his shirt and the lingering scent of his cologne. It's not the same, but it's enough to keep me content for now. I allow myself a few more moments in the messy bed wrapped in his shirt, lingering off to the memory of us last night.

I decide to freshen up, hoping to clear my mind and centre myself. I change into my clothes from last night, make the bed, take a few deep breaths, and remind myself it's okay to set boundaries, to take control of the pace of our relationship.

A little while later, I hear the door open, and my heart skips a beat. Before I can even think or rationalise my actions, I'm bolting to the front door. Dominic walks in, his presence filling the room with an intensity that's impossible to ignore. I leap into his arms like he's pulling me from underwater, and for the first time all day, I can finally breathe.

I have my arms wrapped around his neck, pressing and squeezing him to me as if I want to absorb his presence into mine.

"Welcome home," I say in a weak small voice.

What is with me? What is with this reaction? Shit! Shit! Shit! He will think I lost my mind jumping on him like this.

I try to pull gently away, but his broad hands press firmly against my back, holding me close. The way he is holding me like this, with his open palms covering almost all my back and his face nestled into the crook of my neck, inhaling my scent deeply, makes the gesture so intimate, so raw and vulnerable. It feels as if I am not the only one who has abandoned restraint, and we are truly lost in each other.

"Thank you for being my home," he whispers.

For a second, I wonder if I imagined it. Why would he call me his home? But then I feel a small shiver pass through his body, and I realise, if I think I'm losing myself in him, could it be that he's already lost in me? His words are a balm to my soul. *Does he really think I'm his home?*

We stay like that for a few more moments, both of us searching for balance again. When he finally pulls away, the look in his beautiful ocean-blue eyes is breathtaking, a mixture of longing, love, desperation, desire, and pain.

"Love of my life," I breathe, feeling overwhelmed by the intensity of his gaze. "Sorry to jump on you like this..." I trail off as I am so embarrassed at my reaction.

I reach up and cup his face in my hands, feeling the roughness of his stubble against my palms. "I want this, my love. I want us. But I also want to make sure we're building something that will last. Something solid."

He leans into my touch, briefly closing his eyes as if savouring the contact. When he opens his eyes several moments later and smiles, a genuine smile reaches his beautiful eyes and makes my heart skip a bit. I realise that I am still waiting for his comeback.

"Lead the way, Vita Mia." He takes my hand and kisses my inner palm. "And I will follow."

The sincerity, warmth, and love in his words are as real as him standing before me. *How can he be so confident in his feelings for me? Why is he not scared?* Before I can let panic take control of my mind, I feel his lips on mine in a soft touch, as if he were scared he could harm me with a mere kiss. He pulls away, rests his forehead on mine, and breathes deeply a few times as if seeking some inner strength that is failing to appear for him.

"Vita Mia, please do something." His voice is shaking, and a clear tone of pain escapes him. "Please, Amore Mio, do something." He starts peppering kisses all over my face and neck, growing every few seconds. "If leading will provide you the strength and confidence you need to let go with me, you have it all. Do as you please, Vita Mia, and I will follow."

He kisses my cheek with so much love and longing that its borderline obscene. "What I ask, please don't run from me. Please don't hide from me. Please know that I will chase you forever because I am not letting you go, not now, not ever. You are mine as much as I am yours, and if you need rules and boundaries or for you to have the lead in our relationship, that is perfectly fine as long as you understand that from last night, you are mine forever."

He leans his forehead on mine again, and the intimacy of his gesture mingled with his breath and his deep words brings a full-body shiver through me. I know I should panic. I know I should be scared. I know I should run. *But why is my heart at peace at his final words, at his confidence, at his full surrender to us?*

He is not scared. He is not in pain because he is scared. I think he is in pain because I am holding back.

Before I can second-guess myself, I lean in and kiss him. I wrap my arms around him and pull as hard as I can at him as if any distance between us would make me lose my mind.

Dominic responds immediately, his arms tightening around me, drawing me even closer. His kiss deepens, and I feel his desperation and need matching my own. It's as if we are both trying to reassure each other that this is real, that we are here, together, and that nothing can come between us.

"I will follow you to the ends of the earth, Vita Mia," he murmurs against my lips, his breath warm and intoxicating. "Just lead the way."

I pull back slightly to look into his eyes, seeing the raw emotion and unfiltered honesty there. "My love, I want this. I want us. But I need you to promise me that we will take things one step at a time. That we won't rush."

He nods, his eyes never leaving mine. "I promise, Amore Mio. We will go at your pace. Just know that my feelings for you are unwavering. I am yours, completely."

His words bring a sense of calm and certainty that I haven't felt in a long time. I smile, feeling the last of my doubts melt away. "Thank you, my love."

He kisses me again, this time slower, more tenderly. "Thank you for existing, Vita Mia."

My heart melts at his words again, just as it did the first time he said those words to me. My instincts kick in, and my hands start pulling at his clothes as if I were a feral animal in desperate need of food. I need to feel his skin on mine and feel him close to me.

As I pull his shirt up out of his pants without breaking the kiss, he grabs the edges of it and sends the buttons flying across the floor. I start exploring his chest and abs as if I were memorising every inch of his skin in my subconscious. His skin feels soft, his muscles strong, and as I move my hands around his body, exploring and teasing, I feel him starting to tremble under my palms. *Oh, damn! He is really into me! He is actually really into little old me!*

You know what? *Fuck it!* Only one way to happiness.

I start moving my hands down and start exploring his cock over his pants, teasing and squeezing now and then.

A deep growl comes out of him, exploding on my lips as he deepens the kiss in a war of passion and dominance. His hands are all over me, one moment tangled in my hair, the next sliding down my back, pulling me even closer. I can feel the heat radiating off him, and it's intoxicating.

"Vita Mia," he whispers against my mouth, his voice rough with desire. "You drive me insane."

I smile against his lips, loving the effect I have on him. "Good," I murmur. "Because you make me lose my mind."

In one swift motion, he lifts me up and carries me to the bed, never breaking the kiss. He lays me down gently, hovering over me, his eyes dark with need. I reach up and pull him down, needing to feel his weight on me, his warmth.

He presses against me, his body fitting perfectly with mine. "I need you, Amore Mio," he says, his voice a low rumble. "All of you, please."

"You have me," I whisper, wrapping my legs around his waist. "All of me."

He kisses me deeply, his hands roaming over my body, igniting every nerve ending. I arch into him, wanting more, needing more. His mouth moves to my neck, sucking and biting, leaving marks that I know will be there tomorrow. And I love it. I love knowing that I am his, that he is mine.

I slide my hands down his back, feeling the muscles tense and flex under my touch. I reach the waistband of his pants and start to unbutton them, my fingers trembling with anticipation. He helps me, quickly shedding the rest of his clothes until he is gloriously naked above me.

I take a moment to admire him, the way his body looks like it was sculpted from marble, every inch of him perfect. He is so handsome before me, almost making him unreal with that look of predatory desire in his gaze.

"Well, hello, monster cock," I look down at his cock and wink for good measure.

A deep, full laugh explodes out of him as if I had said the most hilarious thing in the world. "Did you just wink at my cock, Vita Mia?" He says in a playful tone.

"That I did," I start licking my lips and smile up at him. "So what? Did no one else ever winked at him before?" I continue just to torment him some more.

His cock twitches under my gaze, and I start laughing hard at his reaction. This is so funny and intimate and hot as fuck!

"Amore Mio, don't look at him like that because he will think that you might get all up close and personal with him and suck him off, and if you are not into that, you need to stop now because damn woman you are fucking killing me with your eyes right now."

"Dominic!!!" I burst out laughing so hard it takes me a few seconds to realise he is ripping my clothes off me to expose my breasts to him.

"Vita Mia, what did I say about you calling me by my name?" He takes one of my nipples into his mouth, sucks hard, and then bites on it. "It's blasphemy, that is what it is," he says into my breast. "And today, I will fuck that name out of your mind forever."

I come to my senses, and a deep moan comes out of me as my back arches, feeding him more of my breast, revelling in the sensation of his sinful tongue and skilful hands. He pulls back and looks deep into my eyes, questioning what I want to do next, giving me the the lead in our moment.

I would love to give his cock some licks to see that reaction out of him again. Maybe I am a natural at this, as he said. Well, there is only one way to know, but one thing is for sure, I want to see that look from last night and that reaction from him again.

A small, shy smile appears on my face, and that is all it takes for his face to bloom into a happy, playful, excited, cheeky expression.

"Don't get your hopes up," I add, trying to keep my voice steady and firm. "It might not be good, remember? Last night was the first time I licked a cock, and I was quite scared, as I am now at this, my love." I say as I try to lower myself before him.

He stops me halfway and brings me to his chest in a tight hug, a full-body shiver running through him. "Amore Mio, please, for all that is precious in this world, please understand that any touch from you is like fire to my skin and senses. You cannot do anything wrong to me, to put me off, so let yourself go and enjoy the moment. If you like it, if it brings you pleasure, let yourself go and enjoy it with me. If you don't feel it, that is perfectly fine as well, you are in control, Vita Mia, pull back, and we can explore other things together." He kisses my lips in a feather-like touch, taking all gentleness to a different level. "There is no pressure or expectation from me." He kisses the tip of my nose. "Don't get me wrong, I want to pound into this sweet mouth of yours as much as I need my next breath, but you are the one in control, and I will follow you."

I start laughing into his mouth and bite his lower lip hard, then I hold his gaze as I lower myself to my knees and wink at him.

His marvellous cock is right in my face, standing at attention as if it actually has a mind of its own. The size of him is quite intimidating, but I know I can take him. I am sore but in the most delicious kind of way. His head is shining, and a bead of precum is forming at his entrance. The veins along his shaft are swollen and angry, ready to pound into me as if I am his last breath.

I take a deep breath, my confidence growing with each passing second. I start by gently licking the tip, tasting the saltiness of his precum. He moans softly, his hands resting on my shoulders as if he is trying to keep himself grounded.

"Just like that, Amore Mio," he murmurs, his voice a mix of encouragement and raw desire.

I continue to explore him with my tongue, tracing the veins and the sensitive underside of his shaft. His reactions fuel my confidence, and I start to take him deeper into my mouth, inch by inch. His moans grow louder, his grip on my shoulders tightening as I work him into my mouth.

"You're doing amazing, Vita Mia," he praises, his voice strained with pleasure. "Just like that."

I look up at him, meeting his gaze, and the intensity in his eyes sends a shiver down my spine. I bob my head, taking him as deep as I can, my hand wrapping around the base to stroke up and down and twist my hand with what I can't fit into my mouth. His hips start to move in time with my rhythm, and I can feel him getting closer to the edge.

I feel him, his taste, his scent, his moans, *all my doing*, and I realise I am enjoying this with him, and it is hot as hell! I relax my jaw more and take him deeper into my throat, rubbing my tongue on the sensitive part of his shaft on the way out of my mouth. The new depth and rub bring an animalistic growl out of him. He moves his hands to the back of my head, and I relax into his touch and let him take control, moving us in perfect rhythm, seeking his release.

"Vita Mia," he groans, his voice filled with raw need and desperation. "So good. So fucking good!"

I can feel his hips thrusting gently, guiding me to the perfect pace. His fingers tangle in my hair, not pulling, but just enough to let me know he's there, that he's close. His breathing becomes ragged, and I know he's on the brink.

"Amore Mio," he pants, his voice strained. "I'm so close. Please, if you don't want me to come in your mouth, pull back."

Instead of pulling back, I relax even more, allowing him to go deeper, my throat contracting around him, and a moan of pleasure escapes around his girth. His moans turn into guttural growls, his body trembling with the effort to hold back. Then, with a final, deep thrust, he lets go, spilling into my mouth. I swallow as our desire overwhelms us, savouring the salty taste of him, the sensation of his release, the insane pleasure I brought to this man.

He stills, his grip on my hair loosening as he catches his breath. I pull back slightly, licking my lips and looking up at him. His expression is one of awe and satisfaction, his chest heaving as he tries to regain his composure.

"That was incredible," he says, his voice hoarse. He reaches down, pulling me up into his arms and kissing me deeply. "You are incredible."

I smile against his lips, feeling a sense of accomplishment and pride. "I guess I'm not so bad at this after all."

He chuckles, his eyes filled with warmth and love. "Not bad? You're perfect, Vita Mia. Absolutely perfect."

We hold each other for a while, and the connection between us is stronger than ever. This isn't just about physical pleasure. It's about trust, intimacy, and a bond that goes beyond anything I've ever known. And as we stand there, wrapped in each other's arms, I know that no matter what comes our way, we will face it together as one.

After a few moments, Dominic pulls back slightly, looking into my eyes. "You make me feel things I never thought possible, Amore Mio. You're everything to me." The tremor in his voice screams the truth to the universe, stating that he truly thinks I'm his everything.

I smile, my heart swelling with affection. "And you're everything to me, my love. You just simply came into my life and bulldozed your way into it," I say in a playful teasing tone. "No manners, ha?"

He chuckles, his eyes lighting up with amusement. "Manners are overrated when it comes to matters of the heart. I saw what I wanted, and I went for it."

"Well, I can't say I mind," I reply, leaning in to kiss him softly. "But maybe next time, a little warning would be nice."

"Noted," he says with a grin. "But something tells me you wouldn't have it any other way."

I laugh, knowing he's right. There's something thrilling about the way he's swept me off my feet, about the intensity and passion he brings to everything. "You might be right about that."

He pulls me close, resting his forehead against mine. "I promise to always be honest with you, Angela. To always fight for us, no matter what."

"Now," he continues in a playful tone. "How about you let me fuck that name out of you?" With the next breath, he throws me on the bed like I weigh nothing, and he is on top of me like a predatory animal.

"What do you mean?" I play the innocent. "Do you mean someone has called you by your real name? How dare they?" I lean in and kiss his shoulder. "Tell me who they are, and I will have a stern word with them." I bite his shoulder hard and then suck on it, bursting out laughing at his surprised face.

"You adorable little minx! You are going to be the death of me!" He lunges for a desperate, deep kiss that is more an attack on my senses than a gentle touch of our lips. "But even if I burn at the end of it, I will enjoy every moment with you for the rest of my days," he says breathlessly when he pulls back.

His strong arms rip the remainder of my clothes, and I am now fully naked in front of him. The pure look of desire in his eyes reminds me of all the care and love he has shown me so far, and all I need to do is *let go* with him.

Accept what is being given to me as *I am worthy.*

I am worthy of his attention.

I am worthy of his care.

I am worthy of his love.

With that in mind, I lean back, open my legs in a clear invitation, and smile at him, looking into his beautiful face. *He is so beautiful!* I look down, and his cock is at fully erect again, ready, angry for more, as if he did not just let me taste him a moment ago.

"That's right, Amore Mio, let me see what's mine." He traces his finger over my folds in a feather-like touch, more as a promise of things to come. "Let me see how you want me. Let me feel how wet you are for me." His touch becomes more daring, and he opens me up to look at my pussy in all her glory. "Fuck me, Amore Mio, you are so beautiful!" He looks up into my eyes to convey the truth he just spoke to my pussy. "Look at her glistening, pink invitation, as if she knows I own her now."

He slides one finger into me, twirling and wiggling, exploring like he is the actual owner and I am just the carrier of her. His touch sends waves of pleasure through my body, making me arch my back and moan softly.

"Do you like that, Vita Mia?" he asks, his voice low and filled with desire. "Do you like how I make you feel?"

"Yes," I breathe, my voice trembling with need. "I love it."

He adds another finger, stretching me, preparing me for him. His thumb finds my clit, rubbing gentle circles that drive me wild. My hands grip the sheets, and I can feel the heat building inside me, ready to explode.

"You're so wet for me, Amore Mio," he murmurs, his fingers moving faster. "So ready," he is rubbing my clit now like a madman eliciting moans from me like a song of pleasure to her lover. "But I need to taste you, I need to feel you on my tongue, and I need your scent on me, or I will die." And with that, he lowers himself at my opening and pulls my hips to the edge of the bed.

The first lick is so soft and careful I am almost surprised by him, but his deep growl makes it all too real. He moves back on my clit and starts circling her with his tongue while pumping his fingers in me in a savage rhythm.

"Baby, please," I moan, arching my back at the unbelievable sensations he is bringing to my body. "Please!" my words are cut short when he starts sucking on her so hard a guttural scream escapes me, and before I know it, I grab his hair and press his face more into my pussy for friction. "My Love! Oh, you are killing me!" I say, not recognising my own voice, my mind completely delirious with pleasure.

"You like that?" he taunts, licking around my clit again to tease me some more. "I am not getting up from here until I drink all your juices, Vita Mia." He gives me a long lick and slows his finger movements. "It's only fair since you drank me all up and made my wish come true."

He lunges at my clit again, completely taking it into his mouth and sucking on it like a man possessed. When he adds a third finger, arching them, pumping and rubbing my insides, the intensity builds, ready to detonate through me.

"Oh!" I gasp, my hands clutching the sheets as my body responds to his relentless assault. Every touch, every lick, every thrust of his fingers sends waves of ecstasy crashing over me. "Dominic, I can't... I'm going to..." My words trail off into a moan as the orgasm crashes over me with an unknown ferocity, momentarily blinding me, my body convulsing with the force of it.

He doesn't let up, his mouth and fingers continuing their assault, prolonging my pleasure until I am a trembling, breathless mess. I start squirting juices as if it's my purpose to coat him in my release. He moves quickly where his masterful fingers are and begins thrusting his tongue and fingers into me, lapping at my juices as if his life depends on it.

"That's it, Amore Mio," he murmurs against me, his voice vibrating through my core. "Let go for me. Give me everything."

His words are as cataclysmic for my sanity as his actions because, right now, I am not connected to reality anymore. I am somewhere floating in this universe of pure ecstasy where Dominic is eating me out and drinking me in and loving every molecule of my being as if it were the most natural thing to him.

"That's it, Vita Mia," he whispers, his voice full of satisfaction. "Let me feel you come for me."

As the waves of pleasure subside, he slowly withdraws his fingers, placing soft kisses along my inner thighs. I lie there, spent and satisfied, my body still trembling from the intensity of the experience.

He moves up and looks down at me, his eyes filled with love and adoration. "Fuck, you are incredible, Vita Mia," his words confident and full of satisfaction. "You are so fucking hot, Amore Mio," he lifts my leg up and bends it kissing my kneecap. "Please tell me I can keep going," his voice dripping with concern. "Please tell me if your sore?" The doubt and pain in his voice, a clear cry of his concern for me.

"I am deliciously sore," my voice is pure bliss, reflecting everything that just happened. "Please, my love," I beg, my voice breaking. "I need you. I need you in me now!" My truth is out there for him to do with as he pleases, but I do not care because it is true. My pussy is throbbing with the need for him to dominate, claim, and overwhelm her, and he better do something about it soon.

The feral look in his eyes at hearing my words makes me believe that he might be able to read my mind and that he knows exactly what I want from him. Without breaking eye contact, as if his cock instinctively knows the path to my pussy, he positions himself at my entrance and drives into me in a deep and delicious thrust. "You're mine, Vita Mia. Now and forever."

"Yes," I whisper, feeling him push inside me, filling me completely. The sensation is overwhelming, a mix of pleasure and intensity that takes my breath away.

We both moan at the sensation, the connection between us feeling almost electric. He allows a few moments for me to adjust to the exquisite fullness, then he moves slowly at first, savouring the moment, but it doesn't take long for the pace quickens, our bodies moving together in perfect harmony. His thrusts are deep and powerful, each one driving me closer to the edge.

He lifts my right leg over his shoulder, allowing him to reach deeper. The new position is mind-blowing, I can feel his length so deeply within me that we feel like a single entity, two souls merged as one.

He leans into me, creating more pressure with both his body and his cock, and rocks his hips, rubbing inside me, stretching me to a delirious, delicious delight.

"Dominic," I moan, my voice trembling with pleasure. "So deep... so good..."

"You're perfect, Amore Mio," he groans, his breath hot against my ear. "So tight, so wet! I can't get enough of you." His voice sounds so hot and desperate, I know, I just know he means every word and every thrust.

His words fuel the fire burning within me, and I arch my back, pushing myself even closer to him. The intensity of his thrusts increases, each one sending waves of ecstasy through my body. I can feel myself teetering on the edge of release, the tension building with every movement.

"Come for me, Vita Mia," he whispers, his voice filled with urgency and love. "I want to feel you come around me."

His words are my undoing, and I cry out his name as I shatter around him, my body convulsing with the force of my orgasm and my squirting coating us both, creating a symphony of obscene sounds. The world around me fades away, leaving only the sensation of him inside me, filling me completely and reducing me to nothing more than another piece of him.

"Fuck, baby! You are the most amazing creature to ever live," he says between deep thrusts, chasing his own release. "Ask me to come in you. Tell me you want my cum in you." The urgency of his thrusts is now animalistic, and his depth is borderline maddening. "Tell me you want me as much as I want you. Tell me you want my cum as much as I want yours release." The pleading vulnerability in his voice, combined with his words, is sparking a new orgasm within me, and I know I would agree to anything right now.

"Yes, love of my life." I arch my back again, meeting him thrust for thrust. "Come in me! Give me all you've got, and make me yours forever!" The words explode out of me in a shout, sealing our lives together.

Dominic's eyes darken with desire and relief as he registers my words. He quickens his pace, his hips driving into me with a force that takes my breath away. The sensation of his cock filling me so completely, the raw need in his movements pushes me to the edge once more.

"Oh, Amore Mio," he groans, his voice trembling with emotion. "I'm coming...I'm coming for you."

With a final, powerful thrust, he buries himself deep inside me, and I feel the hot rush of his release filling me. "Fuck, baby, you are amazing." He growls out his release with all his might. The sensation triggers my own climax, and I scream his name, my body convulsing around him as waves of pleasure wash over me. The potent aroma of our mixed release lingers in my bloodstream, and I just know this is something I will never get enough of.

We collapse together, breathless and spent, our bodies still entwined. I gently stroke his hair, my touch tender and loving.

We lie there, tangled together, our bodies slick with sweat, our breaths slowly returning to normal. He pulls me into his arms on top of him, holding me close, and I can feel the steady beat of his heart mirroring my own.

"You are mine, Vita Mia," he murmurs, his voice possessive and full of love. "Now and forever."

"And you are mine, my love," I reply, my voice filled with affection.

"You feel perfect in my arms, Vita Mia," he says, kissing the top of my head and hugging me tighter.

My stomach decides that this would be the perfect moment to growl so loud an actual yep comes out of me to top up my embarrassment. *Well, that is just perfect!*

Deep laughter explodes out of his chest, and this strong male sound envelops me like a blanket against the world. He wraps his arms and legs around me and starts rocking me from side to side while his beautiful laughter is like a lullaby to my soul.

"You are so adorable!" He screams at the top of his voice, squeezing me tight in his arms and legs. "I would fucking devour you if I could." He rolls me over, and he is on top now, then he starts peppering kisses everywhere on my face, neck, chest and breasts. "You are absolutely perfect, Vita Mia." He lowers his mouth on my nipple and starts playing.

My stomach makes another sound, and his head collapses on my abdomen, and he starts laughing again with this honest, deep laugh. His ear is on my stomach, and as he laughs hard, he is shaking me along with him.

"I think your stomach is officially a cock blocker," he taunts me with his silly words. "I think we need to have a word because such blasphemies should not exist." He turns his head and starts rubbing circles with his tongue in my belly button. "You are all mine, Vita Mia," he says, looking up at me. "And I will devour you daily from now on." The finality in his words brings another gasp out of me because the only thing I want to say right now is *You'd better deliver, you bastard, on that promise, or I will be all over you and your monster cock.* I burst out laughing at his comment and at my silly inner dialogue and take his face in my hands, stroking him gently.

"I'm hungry," I say, giving him my best puppy dog eyes. "Feed me!" I say, pretending to cry dramatically.

He starts laughing so hard that the bed shakes with its intensity. "I told you," he says between laughter. "You are absolutely adorable, and I want to devour you." He lowers his mouth to my hip, bites and sucks on it, and I know there will be a "souvenir" there later.

I try to kick him with my knee, but he knows my moves now and grabs it just in time. "Easy, Vita Mia. I need to taste you just a bit. It's not a big bite, just a little one." He lifts off me and gently strokes the spot. "I just have this urge to devour you, to possess you, to dominate and somehow absorb you. I don't know what's with me, all of this is new to me. But that's the truth," he looks into my eyes with a pleading, vulnerable gaze as if seeking forgiveness for his intensity. "But please, Vita Mia, please, please, a million times, please, just be honest with me. If it gets too intense, please tell me. Please lead the way, and I will follow. I don't want you to feel it's too much and run because there is no running. I will catch you and chain you to me."

I expect him to burst out laughing at his comment as if it's a joke, but when he doesn't and keeps that vulnerable, pained expression, I am a bit taken aback by this. *Surely, he is exaggerating, right?*

"Well, all terms and conditions of this engagement need to be clarified after you feed my tummy because, at the moment, I am starving," I say to lighten up the moment, as I pull him into a hug.

As I pull myself up into a sitting position, he is standing in front of me, hugs me with that open palm gesture as before. *Seriously, what is with this man and his soul-awakening gestures?*

"Feed me," I exclaim into his abdomen as I notice his cock getting hard. "And pack away your monster cock because there is no way I can take another round of what just happened." I look up and study his gaze. His body relaxed, so I continued. "You might have broken my pussy, so we need to add clauses in the contract about situations like this. And you, mister," I poke his chest, "need to learn some manners fast." I stop my teasing as he starts laughing again and squeezes me tightly.

"I adore you, Vita Mia."

What?!

He kisses my forehead, then my nose, and finally, my lips. "All right, food it is. But remember," he says, his eyes twinkling with mischief, "you're all mine. And I will be devouring you later, no contract needed."

I can hear him, and I can feel my face smiling at him, but my mind is screaming in all caps, in all languages that I know, at the full force of its lungs.

WHAT THE ACTUAL FUCK DID HE SAY?!!!!!!

I am in pure shock, and I am naked before this gorgeous man, and the only thing I want to do is RUN!

How can he say something like that on our first date?

How can he just blurt out something so heavy?

How can he... adore me?

Why would he adore me?

I get up and run to the bathroom to compose myself. I yell over my shoulder for him to feed me, as I am genuinely hungry. Once the door to the bathroom closes, a full-on panic overtakes my body. *How is this happening? Why is this happening? How could this happen?*

I am not the most beautiful or the ugliest woman in the world. I am not the most intelligent or the most idiotic woman. I am not fucking rich, don't own my own place, and did not even fucking pass the bar exam yet. How the actual hell can someone like him fall for me, let alone say he adores me?

"Water," I yell and get up quickly. *Stupid woman, you need the water to run. Otherwise, he'll notice that something is wrong.* How is this happening?

By the end of my little meltdown, I'm panting as if I've just run a marathon for the first time in my life.

I splash cold water on my face and look at myself in the mirror. My reflection stares back at me, wide-eyed and bewildered. "Get it together, Angela," I whisper to myself. "Just... get it together."

Taking a deep breath, I try to calm my racing thoughts. *He said he adores me.* He. Adores. Me. The words echo in my mind, both terrifying and exhilarating. I can't understand how this could be happening, but the sincerity in his eyes was undeniable.

I splash more water on my face and force myself to breathe slowly. "Alright, girl. You've got this. Just go out there, eat something, talk to him, and then decide if you should run. You can do this."

I open the bathroom door, my heart still pounding in my chest. I put on his shirt with the missing buttons just to cover myself a bit. Dominic is in the kitchen, humming softly to himself as he heats up the food. He looks up and smiles when he sees me, and the warmth in his eyes eases some of my anxiety. *Oh, God, he is so beautiful!*

"Feeling better?" he asks, his voice gentle.

"A bit," I admit, walking over to him. "Sorry for that. I just needed a moment."

He nods, understanding. "It's okay, Vita Mia. Take all the time you need. I'm not going anywhere."

His reassurance helps, and I feel a bit more grounded. "Thank you," I say, sitting down at the kitchen island. "So, what's for lunch?" I look at the clock, and it is past 2 pm, and I stare at it. "Or late lunch better said."

"Same as last night," he replies, setting a plate in front of me. "What you ask for, you get," he takes my palm and kisses the inner side, then places it on his chest. "It's as simple as that." He completes the assault on my heart with a full-on smile highlighting his dimple, and I felt like all my panic was because I am clearly an imbecile. *Oh, my heavens. How is he doing this?* A few words, gestures, and I can feel my core getting wet for him, an undying desire for more. What is happening with my libido? It's like he has this magic power over me.

I take a bite, and the gnocchi is as delicious as I remembered. The food is calming my nerves and reminding me of all the amazing moments we shared last night. The way he was respectful, cared for me, and cherished me; the way he begged me to let go with him. Never pushing, never forceful, never controlling. "This is perfect," I say with a small smile. "Thank you."

We eat in companionable silence for a few minutes, and I start to feel more at ease. Dominic watches me, his expression thoughtful.

"Vita Mia," he says softly, "I know this is all happening fast, and I know it might be overwhelming. But I meant what I said. I adore you.

I feel something for you that I can't explain, but it's undeniably there. And I'm willing to take things at whatever pace you need."

I look at him, his sincerity breaking through my walls. "It's just... a lot to take in," I admit.

"I didn't mean to overwhelm you. I just can't help how I feel." His voice is small now, full of concern. "This is all new territory for me as well. If it helps, I am dialling it back as much as I can." He laughs, but the smile does not reach his beautiful blue eyes. "But one thing I know with all certainty, I cannot lose you." The finality in his voice is so clear and blunt, leaving no room for any possibility of us not being together.

His words, so sincere and full of emotion, chip away at my panic. I take a deep breath, trying to steady myself. "It's just... a lot, my love," I admit. "We've only just started this, and you're already talking about adoration and forever."

He nods, understanding flickering in his eyes. "I know it's fast. I know it seems crazy. But there's something about you, something that feels right. Like I've been waiting for you my whole life, and when I'm not with you, it feels like I can't breathe properly."

His honesty disarms me, and I find myself relaxing more. "It's just scary," I whisper. "I've never felt like this before, and you are saying all of these things."

"I'm scared as well," he admits, his voice barely above a whisper. "But that's what makes it special, right? If it meant nothing, we would feel nothing. The fear of losing each other only exists because we both know this means everything. I know I can be intense, but just work with me here, Vita Mia. We can take it slow. We can take it one step at a time. I've already given you all the power to set the pace so you're comfortable."

I nod, feeling the remaining doubts and fear dissipate. "I want to see where this goes," I say softly. "One step at a time."

He smiles, relief is evident in his eyes. "That's all I need to hear. We'll figure it out together, one step at a time."

Maybe this is crazy. Maybe this is too fast. But there's something undeniably real about what we're building, and I'm willing to see where it takes us.

After we finish eating, Dominic pulls me into his arms again. "Thank you for giving this a chance," he murmurs against my hair. "For giving us a chance."

"Thank you for being honest with me," I reply, resting my head on his chest. "And for making me feel safe."

I laugh, feeling lighter and more at ease than I have in a long time. This man, with his intensity and care, has bulldozed his way into my life and heart, and I am left speechless, trying to process all that has happened.

"I need to borrow some clothes from you since some savage animal tore mine," I tease, just to make him laugh.

"You can have anything you want," he says with an amused tone and starts peppering kisses everywhere he can reach.

"Well then, I would like 2 million dollars, a new car and your most expensive Rolex," I say, trying to plaster confidence, authority and end up giggling at the end at my absurd comment. "Oh! We cannot forget about the Monte Blanc pen. I want it!" I pretend I am shouting in demanding tone. "Actually, I'm not sure if I really want it. It looked a bit like a BIC pen in the light last night."

My words are cut short as he picks me up while laughing hard at my antics and starts rotating me as if he cannot control his happiness.

"See how fucking adorable you are?" He squeezes me tightly and hides his face in the crook of my neck. "Can you not see why I am losing my mind over you?" He takes a deep breath of my scent, and a tremor passes through him.

"You are absolutely perfect, Vita Mia."

Chapter Sixteen

Dominic

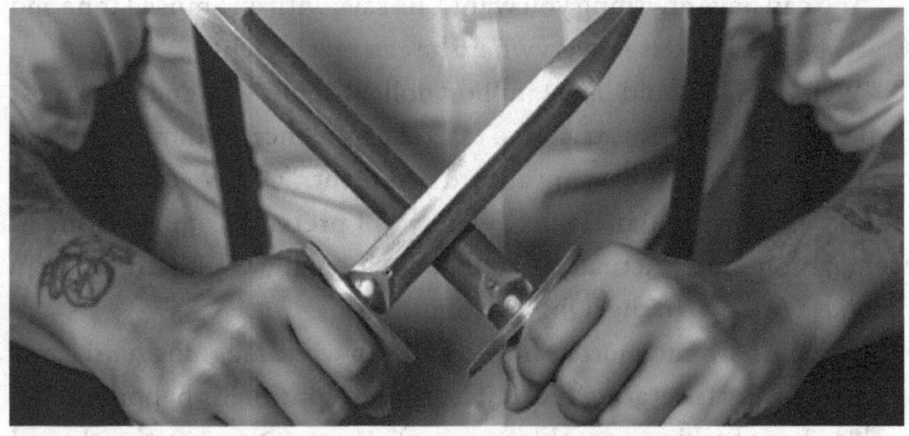

"Feeling better?" I say gently.

"A bit." She takes a few steps toward me. "Sorry about that. I just needed a moment."

Well, this unbelievably extraordinary, amazing creature let me devour her again when I got home. *Fuck!!!* When she jumped in my arms and welcomed me home, I felt like I was going to pass out at the sense of fulfillment that exploded in my chest. *She was welcoming me home! She was welcoming me home! Oh, my fucking heart! She was welcoming me home!*

Me! With a HOME!

Like someone actually wants me! Like someone actually is waiting for me! Like I actually have a home!

She welcomed me home!

I have a home! I have a home now!

All that came after, the way she loved me and screamed it at me through her actions, cemented her decision to *BE MY HOME.*

SHE IS MY HOME!

I devoured her pussy as much as I wanted, and she took it. She took all I gave her, and she loved it. She is like my own personal brand of heroin because I just cannot get enough of her.

I understand she is sore. I understand she needs to get used to me, to my gestures, to my dominance, to my size. Otherwise, I would have buried myself back into her cunt the moment I spilled inside her and started all over again to get those sexy-as-fuck moans out of her.

I think *she might have panicked a bit when I said I adore her.* I probably need to do some damage control, but it was inevitable. I tell her now, or I tell her in a few days, it would have come out. At least now she can start dealing with the idea of our situation.

"It's okay, Vita Mia. Take all the time you need. I'm not going anywhere." *I'm not going anywhere. Prepare your running shoes if you must, but you won't get far because I will hunt you with an army if I have to.*

"Thank you," she says, sitting down at the kitchen island. "So, what's for lunch? Or late lunch, better said."

"Same as last night," I say, setting a plate in front of her. "What you ask for is what you get." I take her palm, kiss the inside, and gently place it on my chest. "It's as simple as that."

I hope the rhythm of my heart and the intimate gesture remind her of how safe she is with me, that she never has to panic, fear, or run.

All her wishes will be fulfilled as long as she tells me. There's nothing I wouldn't do for her.

I smile, letting my gaze reflect as much adoration as I can, reminding her of everything we've shared. *She is safe.* I've laid myself bare for her, and she can do with me as she pleases. As long as she's by my side, she can lead, and I'll follow.

She smiles at me, and I think she's starting to relax a bit. I take a seat and begin eating, though I can't really taste the food. My focus is entirely on her, this majestic creature, as we share a comfortable silence.

When she starts making little noises while eating her gnocchi, her expression betrays her. She's enjoying it more than she realises she's letting on. *Well, she did work up an appetite.* The way her stomach adorably growled at me for making her miss two meals was hilarious. The fact that I didn't throw her onto the table and fuck her right then is a testament to the fact that my mind isn't *completely* in the gutter, as she likes to tease. I know there are other needs I need to meet for her.

"This is perfect," she says with a small smile. "Thank you."

We eat in companionable silence for a few minutes, my gaze barely leaving her. I try to read all her gestures and decide on my next move. I might be in trouble here because my brain does not function the same way around her, so I'm not quite sure what to do next.

Honesty has worked well until now with her, so *I will go with that.*

"Vita Mia," I say as gently as I can, "I know this is all happening fast. And I know it might be overwhelming. But I meant what I said. I adore you. I feel something for you that I can't explain, but it's undeniably there. And I'm willing to take things at whatever pace you need."

There! The truth is out, she can do with it as she pleases. *Well, anything except run.*

She meets my gaze, hesitation clear in her eyes, trying to measure her words carefully. "It's just... a lot to take in."

"I didn't mean to overwhelm you. I can't help how I feel," my voice betrays my inner struggles, sounding foreign to my own ears. "This is all new territory for me as well. If it helps, I am dialling it back as much as I can." I start laughing in panic the moment I realise I just told her I have a higher level of crazy that I am dialling back and that she should count her blessings. *Fucking hell! Could I possibly say anything more stupid? FUCK!!!!! Deep breaths, Dominic! Deep breaths!*

"But one thing I know with all certainty, I cannot lose you." I might not be able to articulate my words well when I am in front of her, but I can say with all the confidence in the world she will not escape me. Ever!

I can see her inner struggle, trying to weigh the pros and cons of why she should be with me. "It's just... a lot, my love. We've only just started this, and you're already talking about adoration and forever."

Yes, I called it! I knew I scared the shit out of her with my blab.

Fucking hell!

Why did I blurt that out?

I know why! I know why! Because she sucked you off like a pro, then she let you do whatever you wanted to her delicious pussy, and you completely lost control and fucked it all up with something this stupid and intense! I hate my inner voice sometimes. He can be such a dick! A very accurate dick, but nevertheless a dick!

Deep breaths, Dominic! Deep breaths!

"I know it's fast. I know it seems crazy. But there's something about you, something that feels right. Like I've been waiting for you my whole life, and when I am not with you, I cannot breathe properly." I am just going to tell her all that she brings out of me. I cannot fucking breathe properly if I am not around her. I know it is a lot. I am surprised at this feeling going around in my chest, but there is something there that is so special I would rather die than lose her. I don't know what it is or what you call it, I just know she is the centre of my life, and without her, nothing matters.

"It's just scary," she says in a whisper. "I've never felt like this before, and you are saying all of these things."

Oh, my heart! I might actually have a heart attack because when I see this warrior of a woman showing me her small, vulnerable side, I feel so privileged that she trusts me to show me this side of her. All my nerves are making me tremble with anticipation, but I think I am wearing her down. I can see it in her gaze and in her movements, *she feels the same about me.*

She feels the same about me!

She has to feel the same about me!

"I'm scared as well," I continue trying to reassure her. I need to reassure her! I need to convince her she is safe with me! "But that's what makes it special, right? If it meant nothing, we would feel nothing. The fear of losing each other exists only because we both know this means everything. I know I can be intense, but just work with me here, Vita Mia. We can take it slow. We can take it one step at a time. I've already given you the power to set the pace so you feel comfortable."

Her eyes search mine, and I can see the conflict within her is fading away. She wants to believe, she wants this as much as I do. *She has to!*

"I want to see where this goes," she says, her voice steady, full of warmth and care. "One step at a time."

FUCK YES! YES!

I wore her down! *I got this! It worked!*

"That's all I need to hear. We'll figure it out together, one step at a time," I say, trying to keep my voice calm and confident, completely opposite to the storm raging inside me at the realisation that I've got her. I really *got* her. We'll make this work, no matter what.

The urge to jump on her and devour her again is so strong that my muscles ache. I want to claim her, bury myself in her so deep that she'll never forget she's mine. Now and forever. But I can't, not yet. As much as my entire body is screaming at me, jumping on her now would undo all the progress we've made. It's as simple as that.

I take another mouthful of food to do something with myself and not just stare at her. The food is getting more and more bland, and the taste of her invades my memory, and I sigh. *Well, that is not helpful, dear brain, so how about you give a guy a break and focus on the food and not the delicious taste of her pussy.* I am starting to get hard as I try to reason with my own brain. Then, I realise this is just stupid, so I start my deep breathing exercises and hide it between mouthfuls of food.

By the time we finish the meal, I'm done giving her space and done with this flavourless meal. I reach for her, pulling her into my arms, needing to feel her warmth again. "Thank you for giving this a chance," I murmur, pulling her even closer. "For giving us a chance."

She feels so right in my arms, like this is exactly where she's meant to be. It's as if she clicks perfectly with me, with my body.

"Thank you for being honest with me," she replies, resting her head on my chest. "And for making me feel safe."

Her body relaxes in my arms, perfectly attuned to the rhythm between us, melting at each other's touch.

"I need to borrow some clothes from you, as some savage animal has torn at mine," she giggles against my chest.

This woman is perfect! She is so sassy, enticing, and perfect! She is making me eat out of her hand, and she does not even see it. "You can have anything you want," I say and start peppering kisses everywhere I can reach. Oh! The feel of her skin on my lips, I want to bite her so badly! *I will not!* I don't want to risk it now and undo all the progress, so I contain myself to kissing and licking for now.

"Well then, I would like 2 million dollars, a new car and your most expensive Rolex," she continues through giggles as she tries to put some distance between us. "Oh! We cannot forget about the Montblanc pen. I want it!" She practically whisper-screams in demand, the little minx. "Actually, I am not sure if I really want it, it did look a bit like a BIC pen in the light last night."

I start laughing so hard at her amazing humour and teasing tone. She is just too much!

I found her!

I actually found her!

I don't need to make myself laugh all the time to control my darkness. Someone else is making me lose control and laugh.

I actually found my mate!

I found her!

Before I can fuck things up more or overthink things, I pick her up and start rotating her like we were kids, and I cannot contain my love for her or the happiness that she brings to my soul. *I found her!*

I actually found her!!!

"See how fucking adorable you are?" I pull her tighter, burying my face in the crook of her neck as a full-body tremor surges through me. "Can't you see why I'm losing my mind over you?"

Her scent, her warmth, everything about her surrounds me, enveloping and conquering me. I am hers, and she is mine. Now and forever.

"You are absolutely perfect, Vita Mia."

Now let's see how I can convince her of this tad sooner than later.

"Yes! Yes! I know I am pretty great. Now where are we with my demands," she tries to say with a straight face, then bursts out laughing.

I pick her up and lift her above my head in another childish affectionate way, and I look up at her like she is my goddess. Because that is what she is. *She is not just a woman, she is everything.* She starts wiggling in my arms, probably surprised by my childish gesture, and once I hug her, keeping her off the ground, she starts laughing again.

"My love, I really need to leave." She says as she pulls gently away, her feet wiggling in the air.

The look in her eyes says it all. I need to let go. *Fucking hell!* It is like a kick in the gut.

"It's not a problem," I say in an even tone. "Let me get you some clothes, and then I will drive you home."

Twenty minutes later, we are in the car on our way to her place, driving in complete silence. *I fucking hate it!* I hate it so much I want to scream!

Think positive, Dominic. She did not run, she did not scream, she did not fear your intensity. She did quite the opposite. She took all you gave her and then some. She came back for more, and she welcomed you home. She is making you laugh, and she is all sweet to you. But most importantly, she is your mate! You actually found her! You are not alone anymore!

She reaches over and rests her palm on my thigh close to my cock and squeezes gently. The bastard stands to attention in seconds as if he has a sensor, knowing she is the one near. I almost burst out laughing at his reaction. I had many women before, but I do not remember him getting hard this fast for anyone. She is seeking me as much as I am seeking her. Her body needs me as much as my body needs her. She can hear our soul song as much as I can hear it, and she wants me as much as I want her. Perhaps some things she does not realise yet, perhaps what she does realise is scaring her, but she is not pushing me away. She is seeking me as much as I am seeking her.

I move my hand over hers, gently caressing her skin. God, her skin feels incredible under my palm. She's like sticky honey I can't resist, pulling me in deeper and deeper. It's intoxicating.

Before long, we're in front of her apartment building, and just as I'm about to stop the car, the air between us changes. I feel something shift in her.

"I loved our time together, my love," she says in a small voice, looking down at her feet.

This is not good!

I can feel my body tensing up as I can see the blow coming my way at lightning speed.

"I want to see you again, but..." she trails off as her voice becomes smaller, and her hand slowly moves from my thigh.

This is very much not good!

I let her pull away, scared of triggering something in her that might make her put her shield up even more. *God, I hate this!*

"But I need a minimum of four days on my own." She finishes and looks me dead in the eyes, searching for the impact of her words.

WHAT?!!!!!

WHAT THE ACTUAL FUCK?!!!!

WHAT?!!!!!!

I let her search my eyes for whatever she is looking for, and for the first time in my life, I don't hide the hurt. I let her see me. All of me.

I move my eyes to the road and remain completely frozen with my hands locked on the steering wheel, trying to regulate my fury and debating if I should kidnap her or not.

On one hand, if I lock her up, she does not have anywhere to go, and I can get my fill of her as much as I want because she cannot do anything. *She will be mine!!!!*

On the other hand, if I lock her up, she might hate me instead of loving me more. She might fear me and be repulsed by me.

"Vita Mia," I start, trying to keep my voice calm. "Why do you need four days? Is it something I did?" My voice trembles with the effort to keep my emotions in check.

She shakes her head, her eyes softening. "No, Dominic, it's not you. It's just... everything is so intense. I need time to process everything, to make sure I'm not losing myself in all of this."

I take a deep breath, trying to understand her perspective. "Four days," I repeat slowly, more to myself than to her. "Okay, I can give you that. But please, promise me you'll think about us during those days. Promise me you won't push me away."

She nods, a small smile forming on her lips. "I promise. I just need this time to sort through my feelings. It's not about pushing you away.

It's about making sure I can give you all of me without holding back." She tries to search my gaze again, then delivers the final blow. "A minimum of two days with no texting as well."

ARE YOU FUCKING KIDDING ME RIGHT NOW?!!!!!!

ARE YOU TRYING TO KILL ME?!!!!!

What the actual fuck, woman?! Are you out to give me a heart attack, or what the actual fuck?!!!!

I just slowly move my eyes to the road again and start breathing deeply. In, one, two, three, four. Hold, one, two, three, four. Out, one, two, three, four. Hold, one, two, three, four. I don't even fucking hide it at this point.

I keep doing my breathing exercises to steady my mind, and once I feel I'm in control again, I exhale, the tension easing slightly from my body. "Alright, four days. But know this, Amore Mio," I lean in closer, my voice a mix of desperation and determination, "I'm not going anywhere. I'll be waiting for you. Always, and this," I gesture between us. "This is not going anywhere because even if it takes me a lifetime, I will convince you that you are mine."

She leans in and kisses me softly, a promise in her touch. "Thank you, love of my life. I'll see you in four days."

As she gets out of the car and walks towards her building, I watch her every step, my heart aching with the distance already. Four days feels like an eternity, but I know I have to give her this space. *For us.*

I grip the steering wheel, the fury and longing battling within me. "Four days," I whisper to myself, "I can do this."

I start the car and drive away, the countdown already beginning in my mind. She will come back to me. *She has to.* And when she does, I will make sure she never wants to leave again.

"I can do this!" I yell in the empty car, the absence of her already weighing heavy on my soul. "I might need to kill a few people and torture a few more, but 48 hours I can do, then I can at least speak to her!"

I quickly call Hunter to confirm he tracked down my angel's two exes. One of those bastards actually made that goddess of a woman feel unworthy when she's nothing short of pure perfection. *How should I make them pay? Oh, the possibilities..."*

Eyes? Too simple.

Tongue? Too straightforward.

Dick? Too predictable.

All the above? Probably...

That thought brought a smile to my face in the middle of my burning rage. Four blasphemous days! *I can do this! I can do this! I can do this, right?*

Maybe I need to be more creative with my torture. *Decisions. Decisions.* Let's see how I feel when I start my work.

I pull into the warehouse, and Hunter is already waiting for me with "my clients" and two other guys. Hunter takes a look at my face, and a deep sigh escapes him.

"What did you do?" His tone is sharp and firm.

"I did nothing." I play dumb. No way in hell he can suspect anything.

"What did you do, Dominic?" he presses some more just to get on my nerves faster. "I left you alone with her for 5 minutes. What the fuck did you do?"

"I did nothing, okay?" I look him in the eyes, and whatever he sees in my gaze makes him lower his eyes and shake his head. "I might have been a bit too intense. She might or might not have asked for four days on her own," I confirm his suspicions halfheartedly.

"FUCKER!!!" Hunter's booming voice resonates off the walls. "I am going to have to fucking babysit you for the rest of eternity at this rate. You are such a fucking dumbass!" I can feel the fury emanating from him, and I know he is about to jump me.

I barely have time to brace myself as he lands a punch straight to my ribs, followed by a knee to my other side. Before he can take another step, I throw an uppercut punch with all my strength, forcing him to stagger backward.

He locks eyes with me, and we measure each other, the tension thick and palpable.

We begin circling each other, frustration and determination evident in his stance. I can feel it too, his need to knock some sense into me. I understand, but I'm not going to let him beat me down without a fight.

Hunter lunges again, and I sidestep, landing a quick jab to his ribs. He grunts, unfazed, and comes at me harder, his punches precise and deliberate. We exchange blows, each strike fueled by frustrations and fears of our own.

"You need to get your shit together, Dominic!" Hunter yells between punches. "If you scare her away, you'll lose her for good."

"I know that!" I shout back, dodging a right hook and countering with a left cross. "But I can't just pretend I don't feel this way about her. She needed to know how I feel."

Hunter pauses for a moment, his chest heaving as he catches his breath. "Then learn to control it. Learn to show her that she's safe with you, that she is not just another possession. Whatever moves I thought you had, you clearly don't! I retract my statement! You are a dumbass!"

His words hit me harder than any punch, and I stagger back, the realisation sinking in. *He's right.* If I want Angela to stay, I need to show her that she's more than just someone I want to possess. I need to show her that I can be the man she needs.

Before I can respond, Hunter charges at me again, but this time, instead of fighting back, I hold my ground. He crashes into me, and we both fall to the ground, grappling for control. It's messy and raw, but it's also a turning point.

When we were completely out of breath, we crash flat to the floor, looking up to the ceiling side by side. "Feeling better, brother?" Hunter says with a calmness I can feel inside as well now.

"Yes, man. Thanks." *Fuck, I cannot believe how lucky I am to have Hunter with me now.* He knew exactly how to calm the beast within me.

He starts to sit up and delivers a kick straight to my ribs again. "And don't make me have to beat some sense into you again." The fucker actually started laughing as the cry of pain escapes me. "She's good for you, Dom. Learn to control your crazy."

He reaches over and pulls me up. We both look like shit now, standing in front of these two sorry fuckers tied up, probably wondering who the hell we are and why we're fighting. Simple: we're brothers who've dragged each other out of dark, lonely places, and we'd kill for each other, literally, at least in your case.

But I'm not about to explain that to them. I don't owe these two anything. So I just keep glaring at them, mind racing, trying to figure out the best way to torture them.

"Dick and balls?" Hunter asks with genuine curiosity.

"No..." I look at the guys closely, trying to decipher which one could be so stupid to say something so mean and untrue to my angel. As I study them, I notice my fury is almost gone, and I'm starting to feel bored of these guys. I would much rather stalk my angel and watch her for the next four days than torture these fuckers to no end.

"One of you fuckers thought to say something mean to my angel," my voice calm and calculated. "You might not have known that she was mine at the time, but I don't think that is relevant because she was mine. She was created for me, I just did not find her yet."

I take my gun out and start shooting the first guy, starting from his ankles, then his tibias, then his kneecaps and thighs, and working my way up to his head. The muffled screams intensify as both of them try to reason with me.

I look over at the other guy and tilt my head to analyse him some more. "Was it you? Did you dare make my goddess feel less than perfect? Did you make an angel cry?" He is shaking his head so fast it's almost comical. "If you tell me the truth and admit it, I will kill you straight away and not load you up with bullets to make you heavier." The guy is still shaking his head so hard, all reason and intelligence leaving his mind with every passing second. People are so dumb when they get tortured.

I feel more and more bored, and I just want to go and watch my monitors and stalk my angel. I reload the gun and start the same process, making him gain more weight with every bullet I put in him. The screams turn to gurgles, and the light leaves his eyes before I even reach his chest.

Hunter watches silently, his expression unreadable. When I'm done, he steps forward, looking at the mess I've made. "You feel better now?" he asks, his voice low.

"No," I admit, holstering my gun. "But at least I've dealt with them. Now I can go and stalk my angel." We organise with our team to dispose of "the clients", my mind, however, is far from the task at hand. All I can think about is Angela and the four long days ahead without her. Two days with not even one word. *The blasphemy!!!*

As we finish up, Hunter claps me on the shoulder. "You'll get through this, Dominic. Just don't do anything stupid."

I nod, though my thoughts are already drifting back to Angela. "Yeah, I know."

Before we leave the warehouse, we come up with a plan for how to take Jake and ensure he has a slow and painful ending, so at least Elijah and her mum will be on my side if things go south.

"We get him tomorrow after his gym session?" I say, bored out of my mind and counting the seconds to get the fuck out of here and go watch her. *I need her! I need her so much!* At least I can watch her in peace at home.

"You mean Pilates. The guy does Pilates, not a regular gym. You need to take extra care tomorrow, Dominic. The guy might fight you as well and land a secret move on you." Hunter burst out laughing at the sheer stupidity of his words.

We head back to the car, and as I drive away from the warehouse, my mind is already planning my next moves with my angel. I'll give her the space she needs, but I'll make sure she knows I'm never far. I'll watch over her, protect her, and when the time comes, I'll show her just how much she means to me.

Four days. I can do this!

I pull out my phone and log into the surveillance software, desperate for a glimpse of her. If I can't be with her, at least I can make sure she's safe. And who knows, maybe watching her will help me understand her better and help me figure out how to win her over completely.

I smile to myself as the first camera feed comes online, showing her apartment building. "I'll see you soon, my love," I whisper, feeling a strange sense of calm wash over me. When the second camera connects to her living room, I see her on the couch, staring at the ceiling and wiggling her legs over the edge. I feel an urge to reach through my phone and caress her. "You are breathtaking, Vita Mia." I caress her on the screen. "Absolutely breathtaking."

Starting the engine, the phone connects to the car, and I start driving, glancing over to watch her every other second.

Four days. I can do this. I can learn to control my crazy.

The next day, Hunter, I and four of our men are waiting in our cars for Jake to leave his Pilates class. We debated taking him on the spot and push him in one of the cars, but there were too many people around because the asshole could not go to a place with fewer people. *No, of course not.* He had to choose a Pilates studio with a million women and 2 million men by the looks of it.

"Seriously?" I sound almost disgusted as one man after another pour out of the studio, all smiles and giggles. "Have you ever seen anything like this, Hunter?" I am getting pissed, confusion and disgust invading my senses. "What the fuck, man? Do these guys know there are gyms around? Why would you do Pilates?"

"It's all about the ass, Dominic," Hunter says and bursts out laughing at me.

"Say what?!"

"Pilates is great for core muscles, and a lot of people do it to strengthen their ass muscles."

"Why the fuck would you know this?" My tone is so aggressive that discomfort, disgust, and the beginning of fury radiate from me.

"I fucked a Pilates instructor once," Hunter continues like it is no big deal.

Great, just what I needed, an image of Hunter fucking someone. I barely slept last night because I couldn't bring myself to go to *our* room. I ended up passing out at my desk like an idiot, watching her sleep. And every time I'd start to doze off, I'd jolt awake, scared I'd miss something important.

I've got it bad, no question about it. I miss her so much it physically hurts, my muscles ache, and I can't breathe properly *Four days.* Four fucking days. It hasn't even been one, and I already want to crawl back to her, even if it means walking on hot coals just to be near her. Anything, as long as I'm with her.

I take my phone out and check the cameras again. She is having lunch with her mum and a friend, who are all happy and giggling.

I am fucking dying here, and she is giggling and enjoying herself.

Enjoy it, Vita Mia, because the moment you are back in my arms, you are not going anywhere ever again. I will tie you to me, I will tattoo myself into your being, and will chain your soul to mine. You will never escape me ever again. So enjoy it while it lasts because, in three days, 2 hours and twenty-four minutes, you will be forever mine.

I give Hunter a side look, *explaining* exactly how I feel about his knowledge. "Whatever, man," my words are cut short as Jake exits the studio and walks past us, stares at a poor girl who is trying to power walk away from him. As soon as he is with his back to us, we notice his flat ass, and both of us burst out laughing hard. He turns and notices both me and Hunter, but we couldn't care less. Why the fuck is this fool doing Pilates when his skinny body and flat ass doesn't explain his obsession with this place.

"He might be a predator," Hunter says, his attitude shifting drastically as he weighs the situation with a seriousness that's rare for him, all laughter quickly vanishing. He turns to me, and the look in his eyes tells me he's thinking the same thing I am. This isn't just about some asshole messing with Angela. This is about a dangerous man who needs to be stopped. "I think he's a predator, Dominic," he repeats, his voice low and deadly.

He pauses, the intensity in his gaze sharpening, and I can see the transformation in him. The ruthless SASR killer he once was has surfaced, all traces of the easygoing, joking Hunter gone. "This fucker needs to go and fast."

His words hit me like a punch to the gut, the finality of them echoing through my mind. I feel the same way, the same cold resolve settling in. This isn't just about getting rid of a piece of shit person who was inappropriate. This is about protecting Angela and other women from a predator who preys on signs of weakness or vulnerability.

"We're not just dealing with some asshole, are we?" I say, my voice rough as I process the reality of the situation. "This is someone who could hurt her, who could hurt more women if we don't stop him."

Hunter nods, his expression grim. "Exactly. And we both know how these men operate. They target women they think they can control, manipulate, and destroy. And Angela... she's strong, but if he's focused on her, he'll find a way to exploit any crack in her armour."

A surge of fury rises in me, the thought of that bastard even thinking about Angela making my blood boil. "It will be a pleasure when we take him out. No hesitation, no mercy."

Hunter's eyes meet mine, and there's a shared understanding between us. This is personal somehow for both of us. This is about protecting the woman I love and ensuring no one else falls victim to this absolute piece of shit.

"Let's do this right," Hunter says, his voice cold and calculated, as he starts the engine. My guys are in two other cars, and we plan to push him to the side of the highway and force him to stop, after that he's ours.

We follow him for a while on the highway. When the road is more deserted, one car moves in front of him, one to the side, and ours stays behind. We all begin closing in, the car on the side inching closer to his vehicle. I can see the frustration building as he starts gesturing angrily at the car next to him. But my guys don't ease up.

When they're nearly touching his car, he slams on the brakes, but with us behind him, there's nowhere for him to go. Desperate, he pulls into the emergency lane, probably thinking we'll pass by. I stop millimetres from his rear bumper, and the car on the side stops perfectly, trapping him. The car in front quickly reverses, blocking any chance of escape.

I step out of the car, pulling my gun discreetly as I approach. I crouch down by his window, flashing him a smile that leaves no doubt about my intentions. The gun at my side is unmistakable.

"Open the door, and let's talk," I say, my tone calm but far from reassuring.

"Who the fuck are you?" he snaps, his arrogance only pissing me off more.

"That is not the way to talk if you don't want to meet your maker today. Now open the door, and let's talk."

He is arrogant and stupid, the perfect mix. He probably thinks there is no way in hell I'd actually hurt him, that he's somehow untouchable. So like the dumbass he is, he actually opens the door.

It's absolutely fucking comical how stupid people can be. I get in the car, pointing my gun at him. The car on the side drives forward and pulls into the emergency lane as well. There are some cars passing, and the last thing we want is for someone to try to "be helpful" and stop to assist us or raise any suspicions. The next second, Hunter opens Jake's door and pulls him out not so gently.

"What the fuck..." his words are cut short as Hunter knees his ribs hard, and a cracking sound comes just before pure screaming pain escapes Jake. He throws Jake on the back seat, and I take a seat next to him and smack him with my gun, breaking his nose.

Ten minutes later, we are at one of the warehouses, not bothering for the fucker to know where the place is as there is no saving him from what Hunter and I will do to him. The cries and whining in the car have given me a headache, plus the shire pain from not being next to my angel is bringing all sorts of fucked up fury out of me, and I, well, *I might lose control*, and this fucker will hurt at my hands tonight more then he can possibly imagine.

"I don't know what you idiots think you are doing, but you made a big mistake by taking me." Jake's voice is getting more and more annoying by the second, and I think I might cut his tongue out. *No wait! I might burn it! No! No! It might smell disgusting, so maybe later.*

Hunter starts laughing like Jake is actually funny, opens the boot of the car and takes out some *convincing equipment,* looking over his shoulder at where Jake is sitting. I start weighing my options from the box of *goodies* Hunter brought and try to make a plan with what should I start.

"You did well, men," I say, patting Hunter on the back. "Did you know he is a predator?"

"I studied his Folder but confirmed it only today when he looked at that girl. It needs to hurt Dominic. *We need to make it hurt.* For all the women out there that got hurt." Hunter's voice is trembling with fury, and I cannot remember ever hearing this tone in his voice. It is like he is trying to contain something that is crawling out of him in waves of fury.

"Is okay, brother. We have him."

"You have nothing, you sorry fucks," Jake interrupts us as if he has any right to speak in our presence. "You will go to jail for the rest of your pathetic lives by the time I finish with you." His bravado is comical and annoying, all wrapped into a pathetic skinny, preppy "nice guy".

Like a reflex, my boot makes contact with his chest, sending him flying a few meters across the floor. "You are just rude!" I lean down and glare at him. "You are not leaving this place alive. In fact, you will leave this place in several pieces. So all of this confidence you are trying to show, all of this manhood that you think you have in you is nothing to us. We will take our pieces out of you for everything you have done and make you scream, cry and beg for death." My words start to kick in because he starts to become pale at my delivered words.

As I stand up, Hunter's heel smashes into Jake's sternum so hard that another crack echoes from his chest just before an agonising cry escapes him. The fucker tries to cover his chest as the hit is so powerful, but he cannot breathe properly, and strange, gasping sounds escape him after the initial scream of pain.

"Fucker, you're going to kill him too quickly!" I yell at Hunter, who clearly forgot that torture is meant to be slow and deliberate, not quick and fast. "Seriously?!"

"He's fine! Don't mind him," Hunter dismisses me altogether. "He probably never had the wind knocked out of him. That's why he's whining like a baby," he continues like nothing major has happened. He picks up Jake and deposits him on the chair like he weighs nothing, as if this is absolutely normal.

"I can pay you," Jake tries to say, but his voice is barely audible, muffled by shallow breaths.

Oh! Of course, the preppy shithead would try to buy us out. The sorry fuck doesn't even realise we're richer than him. Hell, Angela is richer than him now, so is Hunter. I'd start from scratch a thousand times over as long as I know my angel is taken care of. She's everything. And even if I die, she'll be looked after.

I take a deep breath, trying to settle my thoughts because clearly, this has to be love. *How do people know when they are in love? Well, let's rephrase that, shall we?* How do *neurotypical* people know they are in love? I know I don't process feelings like the rest of people, so I think this *has to be love*, otherwise, why would an angel pop into my mind in the darkest of places? Why does such calmness wash over me whenever I think of her? Why can't I breathe properly ever since I dropped her off at her apartment? Why is her absence weighing on my being like I am carrying a giant rock on my shoulders, and every step I take is painful and useless because it is not leading me to her?

"Stop daydreaming, Dominic!" Hunter's deep voice rings in my ears just before his palm connects to the side of my head. "Do I need to beat some sense into you again?"

"Fucker!"

"I have millions I can transfer tonight if you guys reconsider and let me go." Jake keeps trying to play his last card, thinking he can change our minds.

"Gag," I say, glancing at one of my guys. I can't stand to hear another word from this fucker, and if he keeps it up, I'll end up torturing him in his own stench. Casually, I draw my knives from my sides, their cold steel gleaming under the light. Jake's eyes widen, unintelligible sounds muffling from his gagged mouth as he struggles against the restraints. He knows what's coming, and the terror in his eyes is exactly what I want to see.

"I heard that you've been a bad, bad boy," I continue, my tone mocking and cruel. "I heard that you tried to touch things that don't belong to you." The way his eyes dart around, looking for a way out, tells me everything I need to know. He's trapped, and he knows it.

Hunter steps back, giving me the space I need as I start to circle the chair slowly like a predator sizing up its prey. My movements are deliberate, meant to instill fear. "I heard that you like to prey on the weak." I glide my knife across his cheek, the blade barely kissing his skin. The first trickle of blood runs down his neck, the crimson line stark against his pale skin.

The sheer shock on his face tells me it's taken him this long to realise just how fucked he is. But now, the panic in his eyes is undeniable. He's finally seeing the truth, and it's a truth that will end in nothing but pain.

I smile at him, the expression cold and devoid of any real warmth. "You see, Jake, you've made a big mistake. You messed with someone you shouldn't have. Someone who doesn't belong to you."

I apply a little more pressure with the knife, dragging it slowly down his cheek, carving a shallow line that sends fresh rivulets of blood trickling down his neck. He squirms, his muffled screams barely audible through the gag, but I can see the fear in his eyes, the understanding that this is only the beginning.

"Does it hurt, Jake?" I ask, my voice soft and mocking. "Does it feel like you're losing control? Like everything you thought you had power over is slipping away?"

I move the knife to his other cheek, drawing another line, another slow, torturous cut. His eyes roll back in pain, and I can see the sweat starting to bead on his forehead. *Good.* I want him to suffer, to feel every single moment of this.

"You like to touch what isn't yours," I continue, circling him again, letting my words sink in. "You like to make others feel powerless, don't you? Let me teach you how being powerless feels."

Hunter watches silently, his presence a reminder of the ruthlessness we both carry. But this? This is personal. He tormented my angel, so I will torment him until he takes his last breath.

I stop in front of Jake, leaning in close enough that he can feel my breath on his face. "You see, you thought you were the predator. But now, Jake, you're the prey. And I'm going to make sure you understand just how shit that feels before you take your last breath."

I press the knife against Jake's throat, just enough to make him squirm, to make him think this might be the end. But it's not. *Not yet.* "Ready to die, motherfucker?" I can see the panic in his eyes, the desperation as he shakes his head frantically, actually nicking himself on the blade. His stupidity makes me laugh, a cold, cruel sound that echoes through the room. The thought that this might be over quickly is absurd, and I make sure he knows it.

"Don't worry," I whisper, letting the malice drip from every word. "We're just getting started. I have something special for you to enjoy in our company."

Hunter's mocking laughter fills the room, a sound that only intensifies the tension. But when I glance over at him, I see something that makes me pause. The fury radiating from him is intense, almost palpable. Whatever Jake did, it's hit a nerve with Hunter, and I know this needs to be a shared kill. If I don't let Hunter have his piece of this bastard, he might lose control, and that's not something we can afford.

I pull a chair up in front of Jake, taking a moment to admire the beautiful marks I've left on his face. Blood still trickles down from the cuts, and I can see the raw fear in his eyes as he struggles to comprehend the situation he's in.

Setting my knives down in the box, I reach for a handful of salt. The grains are rough and coarse, and as I begin rubbing them into the cuts on Jake's face, he thrashes in the chair, his muffled screams barely contained by the gag. I press harder, grinding the salt into the wounds, making sure he feels every agonising moment of the burning pain. Jake's eyes widen with every passing second, his body trembling with the shock and torment. His eyes beg for mercy, but there's none to be found here. *Not from me. Not from Hunter.*

I step back, giving Hunter a look that says it all. Hunter steps forward, the fury in his gaze focused entirely on Jake. His movements are calculated, almost methodical, as he takes over where I left off. He grabs Jake's hair, yanking his head back to expose his throat. The salt continues to burn his face, and I can see the pain wracking his body, every muscle tensed and shaking.

"Let's begin." Hunter's voice is eerily calm, but the undertone of fury is unmistakable. He's going to make this slow, make Jake feel every second of his descent into hell.

I lean back against the wall, watching as Hunter gets to work his knife, making long, shallow lines on Jake's upper body. He's methodical, precise, and utterly ruthless. Every movement is calculated to cause maximum pain with minimum effort, drawing out the agony as long as possible. The parallel lines of the incision make the blood trickle down as lightly as a song of distress from a dying man seconds before the end. Hunter's movements and precision are absolutely beautiful to watch as Jake's muffled screams grow louder, but they only fuel Hunter's actions. The room fills with the sound of flesh meeting metal, the hiss of salt in wounds, and the wet gurgles of a man who now knows without a doubt that he is on the brink of death tonight.

As I watch, I feel a sense of satisfaction, knowing that Jake is finally getting what he deserves. The bastard thought he could prey on the weak, probably thinking he will never be stopped, probably thought he is untouchable. He didn't know that his actions would lead him to this. A slow, agonising death at the hands of men who have no mercy left to give.

When Hunter finally steps back, breathing heavily, Jake is falling in and out of consciousness. His face is a bloody mess, salt caked into every cut, and his body slumped and broken in the chair.

"There, there," I say, stepping forward. "That was not that bad, Jakey. Stop being such a baby." I slap him a few times on the cheeks to bring him back, and his new screams are a melody to my ears.

Hunter nods, a grim smile on his face. "All yours, brother. Thanks." The look he gives me in appreciation is all I need. I know he needed this as much as I do. *Respect and loyalty to the death.*

As I sit down in front of Jake, I take a moment to study him. The fear in his eyes is palpable, and I can see the realisation dawning on him that there's no way out of this. He's trapped, and I'm the one holding the keys to his suffering. The idea that came to me while watching Hunter work is deliciously cruel, the perfect way to reward this predator with a punishment that fits his crimes.

I let my gaze travel over his body, taking in every detail, every weakness I can exploit. When I finally meet his eyes again, the fear there is so satisfying. He knows what's coming, and it's going to be worse than anything he's ever imagined.

"So you thought you could touch an angel with no demon coming after you?" I say, my voice dripping with mockery. A genuine laugh bubbles up from deep within me, the first real laugh I've had all night. "What a dumbass!" I glare at him, making it clear that I am the demon sent to collect for the sins he's committed.

I grab his arm, feeling the trembling in his muscles as I tighten my grip. My knife rests at the base of his hand, cold and unforgiving. "You actually thought you could touch an angel with these hands, and nothing would happen, didn't you?" The terror in his eyes tells me he knows what's coming, and he's powerless to stop it.

I begin to cut into his skin, slowly, deliberately, like an artist carefully crafting his masterpiece. The incision is minimal, just cutting the upper part of the skin, and once I angle my knife inwards, the realisation hits him, and a new petrified sound comes out in waves. He thrashes in his restraints, a pitiful attempt to escape the inevitable.

"No need to run from me," I taunt him, my voice calm, almost soothing. "There's nowhere I wouldn't find you."

As I continue to work my way down his hand, the blade cuts further the skin off, the pain escalating with every inch. When I reach his fingers, I tug on the skin, pulling it away from the muscle underneath. His screams intensify, the raw sound of pure agony filling the room.

The satisfaction that washes over me is intoxicating. This is what justice looks like. *This is what happens when you think you can prey on the innocent and get away with it.*

I work methodically, stripping the skin from his other hand as I go, exposing the raw flesh underneath. His entire body convulses with pain, his muffled cries growing weaker as the reality of his situation is as vivid as the blood trickling from his body.

Finally, when I'm satisfied with my work, I lean back in my chair, taking in the sight of him. Jake is a broken man, his hands a bloody, mutilated mess. But it's not just his hand that's been destroyed, it's his very essence. He knows now that he was never the predator, he was always the prey, we just did not find him yet.

I stand up, looking down at the mess I've made of him and then over at Hunter, who's been watching with a mixture of admiration and satisfaction. This kill is necessary, but it is also deeply personal. Jake needed to feel every ounce of pain he inflicted on others, and now, as he bleeds out in front of us, he knows exactly what it means to be powerless.

I crouch down in front of Jake, grabbing his chin and forcing him to look at me. "Predators need to be prey." His eyes are glassy, unfocused, but I know he can still hear me. I lean in closer, my voice low and menacing. "You're nothing. You never were something, and now, you'll be forgotten. With your death, I release all the burden your prey might carry. They are all safe now."

I stand up, looking down at the pitiful excuse of a man in front of me. The end is near, I can smell it in the air, and without any hesitation, I launch the knife into his chest, with one swift, brutal motion, I twist the knife to ensure his last seconds are as painful as they can be. Jake's body goes limp, his head slumping forward as the life drains out of him.

For a moment, there's silence in the room, the tension dissipating as the job is done. I look over at Hunter, and we share a nod of understanding. This was not just personal, this was necessary. *This was justice.*

But as we clean up the mess, my thoughts drift back to Angela. She's safe now, but I know my agony is far from over. The four days she asked for will be the longest of my life, but when they're over, I'll make sure she knows that nothing will ever hurt her again.

As I step into the cool night air, I can't help but think of her. She'll never know the lengths I've gone to in order to protect her, the darkness I've embraced to keep her safe. But that's okay. She doesn't need to know. All she needs to know is that she's safe now, and nothing will ever harm her again. With my last breath, I will protect my angel if I must, but she will be forever safe.

Chapter Seventeen

Angela

The past 48 hours were complete agony. My mind is drenched in the kind of longing that only comes from realising I've pushed away something I desperately need. I wanted space to clear my head and assess my feelings, but all I've done is stir the storm within myself even more. The ache, the emptiness left by Dominic's absence, is tearing me apart from the inside out, gnawing at my sanity like an insistent itch I cannot scratch.

Every fibre of my being craves his presence, the way he takes up all the space in my mind with his intensity, the way his scent wrapped around me, grounding me even as it drove me mad. I miss how his touch speaks in a language all its own, pressing ownership into my skin with each graze of his fingers. It's more than just missing a person. It's like my body is rejecting the space between us two, screaming to close the gap and return to the safety of his arms, his eyes, his everything.

And the way he looks at me... God, I can't shake it. That look of pure need and possession, the look of a man who's found something he never knew he was searching for but now can't live without, like I'm the air in his lungs and the light of his eyes. *Who does that?* Who looks at another human being with such intent and determination to claim someone? How could someone look at me like that and not cause my very soul to tremble? How could I walk away from that gaze without feeling like a part of me has been ripped out?

This isn't just missing him. This is being haunted by him, his scent, his touch, his stare, echoing in every breath I take, filling the spaces around me, reminding me of what I've left behind. And it's driving me mad because deep down, I know there's no real "space" between us, not when he's inside my mind, my heart, my skin.

I miss him in a way that's almost feral, a gnawing, desperate need that burns hotter the more I try to ignore it. I miss him so much it's almost suffocating, and every moment without him feels like time wasted like I'm slowly unravelling.

So what's the point of space when all it does is make me ache for him more?

I miss him! I miss him! I miss him so much that I feel my skin crawling and itchy all over. *You better text me first! Actually, scratch that. I might need to do it first, as this irritating itch is eating me alive! What have you done to me, love of my life? This cannot be normal. What is happening to me?*

"You're ok, my darling." My mum's kind voice envelops me in a warm hug, and I just sigh. "It's so sweet to see you in love."

"I'm not in love!" I jump at the absurdity my mum just said. "I've known him for a few days. How could I possibly be in love?"

I hijacked my mum for the past 48 hours, pretending that I was not well and I needed her, but in fact, I did not really trust myself not to cave and message Dominic or, even worse, run to him. My entire being is calling for him, needing him. *I don't know what I was thinking!*

"Angela, don't lie to your mum, I know you so well. Even in your steps, I can tell you are in love so thoroughly with that boy that you kind of look in pain." She says, and then she starts laughing at me.

My mother's words hit like a sledgehammer, and I can't help but feel a surge of panic at the thought. *In love? No, that's not possible.* I barely know Dominic, and it's only been a few days. It can't be love... *right?* But even as I protest, the truth is gnawing at me like that relentless itch under my skin. The kind of longing that's been consuming me isn't normal, and deep down, I know it.

I've spent the past 48 hours hiding behind my mum, seeking comfort in her presence because I've been terrified of what will happen if I let myself reach out to him. It's not just about missing him, it's about needing him in a way that feels almost primal. It's about how his absence has left a void so vast that it's swallowing me whole. And I hate how much power he holds over me, how desperate I am to hear from him, to touch him, to be near him again.

My mum saw straight through me, probably reading into how my eyes keep darting to my phone, hoping for a message. I think she figured out that I was only pretending to need her when really I've just been trying to hold myself together long enough not to give in to the urge to run back to him.

I might actually be in love with him. Not just infatuation or lust, but something deeper that's rooted itself far too quickly for my comfort.

This is so crazy! I barely know him, and everything is happening so fast that it's spinning me out of control. Yet here I am, my thoughts filled with him, my heart aching for him, my body itching for his touch like it's the only thing that could soothe me.

Mum's laughter fades, replaced with a gentle smile as she watches me wrestle with my thoughts. "Love doesn't follow the rules or timelines, Angela. Sometimes, it just happens, and when it does, it's like this, intense, all-consuming, impossible to ignore. Maybe it's time you stop fighting it and just let yourself feel. Real love is intense. It's like gravity, you can't pull away. And even if you do manage it, that invisible force will always bring you back to where you're meant to be."

Her words linger in the air, wrapping around me like a warm blanket on a cold night. For the first time in days, I allow myself to consider the possibility that maybe, just maybe, this isn't something I can control. Maybe it's time to stop pretending, to stop resisting, and just give in fully to what I've been feeling.

I cover my face with my hands and sigh deeply. I'm scared and excited, hungry for more yet exhausted by the intensity. In pain from the uncertainty but strangely happy. The emotions are overwhelming, almost suffocating. This isn't something I ever imagined for myself, these feelings, this all-consuming connection. It's the kind of thing you read about in books, not something that actually happens in real life. But one thing I know for certain is that I can't ignore it. It's consuming me, inch by inch, moment by moment. *I need to be with him.*

"He's so intense," I whisper from behind my hands, my voice barely audible. "And I feel like if I let go, he'll consume me completely." My voice trembles with the admission, vulnerable and raw. "But there's just something about him, Mum. It's like he's special somehow."

"Special? Special how?" Mum moves closer, her warmth radiating comfort as she takes one of my hands in hers. "What makes him special, my darling?"

"It sounds so stupid," I turn to face her, my voice catching in my throat. The warm, understanding smile on her face is almost enough to make me cry. "You know I plan everything down to the last detail, and I base every decision on facts and concrete evidence. But he bulldozed his way into my life, and now everything is happening so fast."

I pause, trying to collect my thoughts, the words tumbling out as if they've been pent up for too long. "The scariest part is that it feels perfectly natural to be with him. It's like...like I've found this inner peace I didn't even know existed. When I'm with him, it's like I've found my place in the world, like this is where I'm meant to be. It just feels right."

I search Mum's eyes, bracing myself for her reaction, but instead of the scepticism I feared, I see tears welling up. "And it scares the hell out of me, Mum. How is it possible to feel so much so soon?"

Mum squeezes my hand, her voice soft but firm. "Sometimes, love doesn't wait for us to be ready. It just comes, and all we can do is hold on and see where it takes us." She kisses the back of my hand, just like she used to when I was little, and the familiar gesture sends a wave of emotion crashing over me. A tear slips down my cheek, unbidden, as I meet her gaze. In her eyes, I see so much love, a depth of understanding that makes me feel like she's guiding me through one of life's most important lessons.

"My darling Angela..." she says softly, her voice full of warmth and wisdom, "you said it yourself. It feels right." She leans in and kisses my hands again, tenderly, as if I were indeed still her little girl, seeking comfort and reassurance. "True love is like that, unapologetic, intrusive, intense, but it's also, in equal measure - right, kind, and peaceful. If you've found all of this, it truly means you've found your pair."

Her words are like a soothing balm, wrapping around the turmoil inside me. "Very few people ever find it," she continues, her voice tinged with a mix of pride and nostalgia. "Even fewer have the courage to give in to emotions so powerful. But those who do, those who trust it, are the fortunate ones. They get to live their lives with the person they were made for. And there is no more beautiful way to grow old than next to your pair."

I blink back more tears as her words settle in my heart. *She's right.* It feels like I've found something rare, something that defies logic and reason but makes perfect sense in the most profound way. And maybe, just maybe, it's time to stop questioning it and start embracing it.

I reach over and hug her tightly, letting the warmth of her embrace soothe the storm inside me. *I knew it!* I knew I needed her comfort, her wisdom, her unwavering presence. She's always been my safe harbour, the person who never let me drown, no matter how rough the waters got.

When I was battling bulimia, she was my rock, my lifeline. I felt like I was nothing, worthless, ugly, unlovable. For so long, I hated the girl staring back at me in the mirror, convinced she was beyond love's reach. It was the darkest chapter of my life, but it was also the one that taught me who my true safe people are.

Mum was there for every therapy session, holding my hand when I wanted to run. She helped me build meal plans, encouraging me on days when eating felt like an impossible task. She even moved in with me for three months, staying close by to make sure I wasn't alone in the hardest moments. My friends? They came and went. They noticed the weight I lost and showered me with compliments, but not one of them saw what I was really doing to myself. They didn't see the mental and emotional wreckage beneath the surface.

But Mum did. She always did. Maybe it's because of the strained relationship with her own mother that she poured so much of herself into looking after me. Whatever the reason, I'm grateful beyond words that she was there for me when I couldn't be there for myself. Now, as an adult, I see how rare and special that kind of support is. Having her by my side, helping me navigate everything with Dominic, is a gift I hold close to my heart.

"Now, let go of me, girl," she says with a playful smile, trying to pull away. "I need to get to the shop at some point today." She stands up and kisses the top of my head with a gentle affection that makes me feel safe and loved.

As she leaves the room, my phone pings with an incoming text, and this strange, overwhelming mix of excitement and anxiety grips me. I freeze in place, my mind racing. Minutes pass, and I just sit there, staring at the phone as though it holds the answer to everything I've been wrestling with. Another ping comes, then another. My heart is pounding, but I can't bring myself to reach for it.

Mum walks back into the living room just as the phone goes off again. She huffs out a long breath and looks at me with a raised eyebrow. "Angela, if you don't answer that, I will. And if it's one of those 'private body parts' kind of texts, I'll have some words with that boy myself!" The humour in her tone is enough to snap me out of my paralysis, and I can't help but laugh.

"Alright, alright," I mutter, reaching for the phone with shaky hands.

Dominic

"Hi."

"How are you?"

"I miss you so much, Vita Mia."

"I feel like I cannot breathe without you."

"Can I please at least call you?"

I stare at the message, his words echoing in my mind *Can I please at least call you?* It's the song of a lost lover calling me home. My heart stutters, caught between longing and fear. But then I shake my head, taking a deep breath.

Fuck it! I think to myself. I'm done with the restraints, done with overthinking every little thing. What's the point in holding back when everything inside me screams that I need him? No more worrying, no more second-guessing. Whatever happens, happens. *Que Sera, Sera!*

With renewed determination, I unlock my phone and type out a response, my fingers trembling slightly but my resolve steady.

Angela

"Call me, love of my life."

I hit send before I can rethink it and doubt creeps back in. There's no taking it back now. My heart races in anticipation, knowing this could either be the best decision I've ever made or the most terrifying one. Either way, I'm all in.

Long, excruciating seconds pass before my phone rings, displaying "The love of my life." I take a deep breath to steady myself and answer the call.

"Hi," my voice is so small, even to my own ears.

"My love..." The agony in his voice is so clear as if I would be torturing him with my bare hands.

The silence stretches between us, filled with the weight of everything unspoken. The connection between us, even through the phone, is electric, thrumming with a need that's impossible to ignore. It's as if just hearing his breath on the other end of the line is soothing the ache in my chest. I close my eyes, letting the sound of him wrap around me like a warm blanket.

"Are you well?" His voice is low, filled with concern but laced with something else, something deeper, more intense.

"Same as you," I reply, letting out a shaky breath. My words hang in the air, a quiet declaration that I'm feeling everything he is. There's no more hiding, no more pretending that I can push this away. *I'm choosing this, choosing us.* I don't care if it's fast or if it doesn't make sense. For once in my life, I'm letting myself feel instead of running from it.

A soft, almost relieved sigh escapes him, and I can picture the tension leaving his body. "God, I've missed you, Vita Mia," he says, his voice thick with emotion. "These days without you have been unbearable. I need you to understand..." his voice trails off for a few seconds then he continues, "I might not survive it if you ask for space again."

The sincerity in his voice tugs at something deep inside me, unravelling the last of my doubts. Tears prick at the corners of my eyes, but they're not from sadness. They're from the overwhelming relief of knowing I'm not alone in feeling this.

"I've missed you too," I admit, my voice barely more than a whisper. "I was trying to think things through, but all I could think about was you. I tried to be rational, tried to convince myself that it's too much, too soon, but none of that matters when it comes to you. It's like my entire being is craving you. I just want to be with you, Dominic."

There's a pause, and I can hear his breath hitch as if he's trying to hold himself together. "You don't know what that means to me, hearing you say that. I'll spend the rest of my life showing you that you made the right choice."

A tear slips down my cheek, and I brush it away quickly. "I believe you," I say softly, and for the first time in days, *I really do.* I really believe that this is the moment that binds us together forever. There's no hesitation in my heart, no more fear. Just a deep, undeniable connection that feels like coming home.

"Do you still want to impose this blasphemous four days?" he says. The pain in his voice is so vivid that it takes me a second to gather my bearing.

"No."

What's the point in torturing both of us? He made his feelings very clear, and I made my choice.

I want to be with him.

I need to be with him.

"Come to me, love of my life." My words a whisper, but the calling is as loud as the animalistic growl that comes from the other side. I start laughing hard, and tears still roll down my cheeks as I listen to this crazy guy go off at my words.

His growl turns into a low chuckle, the sound sending shivers down my spine. "You have no idea what you just unleashed, Vita Mia," he says, his voice dark with promise and laced with that intoxicating possessiveness I've come to crave.

I wipe away the lingering tears, feeling a mix of anticipation and joy bubbling inside me. "I think I have an idea," I tease, letting a little bit of mischief slip into my tone.

"You better be ready for me, then," he says, and I can almost hear the smile in his voice now. "I'm coming straight to you, and I'm not letting you out of my sight again."

My heart races at his words. There's a finality in them, a certainty that he's made up his mind and nothing's going to change it. And honestly, it's what I want. I want him close, to feel his arms around me, grounding me, making me believe that everything we feel is real and not just some fantasy.

"Drive safe, okay?" I manage to say, even though I'm already counting the minutes until he's here with me.

"Always, Amore Mio. Just stay where you are, and don't even think about running from me again."

I laugh softly, the sound filled with relief and happiness. "I'm done running, my love. I promise."

There's a moment of quiet, just the sound of our breaths mingling through the line, and it feels like we've finally reached an understanding. We both know what we want, and we're not going to let anything get in the way of it.

"I'll see you soon," he says, his voice a low, possessive rumble that sends warmth curling through my chest.

"Can't wait," I whisper back.

As the call ends, I feel a sense of peace settling over me, a certainty that I haven't felt in a long time. I made my choice, and for once, I didn't overthink it or let fear guide me.

I'm choosing me, I'm choosing love, choosing us, and I know it's the right decision.

Now, all I have to do is wait for him. And this time, I'm not scared of what comes next. *I'm exhilarated.* My pulse quickens as I dash to the bathroom, taking what must be the fastest shower in the history of mankind. I shave hastily, twist my hair into a messy bun, and leave my face bare, wanting him to see me as I am. As I spritz on my favourite perfume, the doorbell rings. My heart leaps. I throw on a black nightgown and rush to the door, but in my excitement, I slam into the corner wall. The sharp sting barely registers, I can't let anything slow me down now. I yank open the door, breathless, and there he is. Dominic in all his majestic beauty.

For a moment, time stands still. I just stare at him, overwhelmed by a rush of emotions. My heart does something strange, a painful twist of joy that nearly brings tears to my eyes. It's too much, this collision of longing and happiness. But then I meet his eyes, those endless, ocean-blue depths, and I see it, the raw, undeniable love shining back at me. Suddenly, I feel grounded again, certain of one thing, **I'm going to live a life in peace with this man.**

"Welcome home, love of my life," I whisper, my gaze locked on his. My inner voice screams the words I'm too afraid to say out loud *I love you, Dominic. I missed you more than I ever thought was humanly possible.*

As if he hears the unspoken confession, his eyes soften, and he pulls me into his arms. His embrace is fierce, almost desperate, as if he's afraid to let go, trembling against me. *What have I done to us?*

"I love you, Dominic." The words slip out before I can stop them before I can weigh the consequences of baring my heart like this. But at this moment, nothing else matters except him and the way he's holding me as if I'm his lifeline.

"Say that again," he murmurs, his voice so low that it almost gets lost in the thunder of our heartbeats.

"I love you, Dominic."

The moment the words leave my lips, Dominic's entire body shudders as if those four little words hold the power to unravel him completely. He pulls back slightly, just enough to cup my face in his hands, his eyes searching mine with a mixture of wonder and disbelief, like he's looking at something precious he never thought he'd have.

"You love me?" he whispers, his voice hoarse, filled with raw emotion. It's like he needs to hear it again to believe it's real.

I nod, my eyes brimming with tears, a smile tugging at my lips as I watch his reaction. "I love you, Dominic," I repeat, stronger this time, letting all my feelings pour out in those words.

He lets out a shaky breath, and before I know it, his lips are on mine. The kiss is intense and desperate, like he's pouring every ounce of love, need, and relief into it. It's not just a kiss, it's a declaration, a promise. I can feel the trembling in his hand's ease as he pulls me even closer, as if he would want to absorb me into his being.

"I love you too, Vita Mia," he murmurs against my lips, his voice breaking with emotion. "So much that it scares the hell out of me." He kisses me again, softer this time like he's savouring every moment, every taste, every breath.

My heart feels like it might burst from the sheer joy and relief coursing through me. This is what I was so afraid to admit to myself, what I tried to run from. But now that it's out in the open, I can see how ridiculous it was to fight something so real, so undeniable.

Dominic pulls back just enough to rest his forehead against mine, his eyes still closed as he draws in deep, steadying breaths. "You have no idea what those words do to me," he whispers, his voice rough with restrained emotion. "You're my everything, Vita Mia. There's nothing I wouldn't do for you, to keep you safe, to make you happy."

I reach up and gently stroke his cheek, feeling the roughness of his stubble beneath my fingertips, a sensation that somehow grounds me. "I know, my love. I feel it in everything you do. And I'm done being scared of it. I'm ready to be all in with you."

His eyes snap open, locking onto mine with a fierce intensity that sends a shiver down my spine. "You're mine," he declares, his tone laced with possession, but there's a tenderness woven into it, a depth of affection that reaches into the core of who I am. "And I'm never letting you go. You need to make your peace with that."

"Good," I whisper back, my voice breathless as I lean in for another kiss. "Because I'm not going anywhere," I whisper the words into his leaps.

The tension that had coiled between us for days finally dissolves, replaced by a warmth that feels like coming home. In one fluid motion, Dominic scoops me into his arms, his strength effortless as he carries me inside. The door clicks shut behind us, and in the next heartbeat, I'm pinned against the wall by the entrance. His mouth crashes onto mine in a kiss so consuming it steals the breath from my lungs. It's not just a kiss, it's a war of desire and desperation, pain and passion, possession and love. Every touch of his hands as they explore my body, every swipe of his tongue against mine, every moan that escapes us both is an affirmation, a vow that this is forever, that there's no going back.

"I love you, love of my life," I manage to gasp between ragged breaths, each word laced with the moans he pulls from me as his mouth devours my neck. His lips are everywhere, a relentless assault of licking, sucking, and biting. It's not just hunger, it's a need so ferocious it borders on desperation. He's a man possessed, consumed by a desire that has stripped away any pretence of control.

As his grip tightens, I feel the shift, the way his touch becomes rougher, his movements more frantic. It's as if something dark and untamed is unravelling within him, a storm that I have no intention of running from. Instead, *I give in.* My hips begin to move of their own accord, rocking against him, seeking more of that friction that sends bolts of pleasure rippling through me. I lower my mouth to his ear, teasing him with the promise of more. "I love you so much, love of my life, and I want all of you, the good, the bad, the soft, and the insane." My voice is a breathy whisper, barely controlled, but the need behind it is unmistakable.

His response is immediate, a sharp inhale as I nip at his ear, then suck it into my mouth. "Give me everything you've got, love of my life." The words are a challenge, a dare for him to lose himself in me completely. And he does.

With that, I pull him into a desperate, hungry kiss that unleashes something primal in him. A deep, guttural growl rumbles from his chest, a sound that's pure possession, an animal claiming its mate. *I'm his!* The thought blazes through me, undeniable and absolute. I belong to him, and he belongs to me.

His lips crash onto mine with a ferocity that leaves me dizzy, and the kiss spirals out of control. It's not gentle, it's wild and unrestrained, a clash of tongues and teeth, a battle for dominance that neither of us is willing to surrender. Another deep, primal growl rumbles from his chest, so intense it vibrates through me, echoing in my bones, and I know, without a doubt, that every inch of me belongs to him.

"I need to be inside you, Vita Mia," he growls against my lips, the words a rough plea as his kisses scatter over my skin. There's something raw in the way he clings to me, like I'm the only thing keeping him grounded at this moment. His hands roam my body with a desperation that's almost painful as if he's trying to memorise every curve, every soft spot that makes me gasp. "I need to feel you."

He pulls back just enough to press his forehead to mine, his breath mingling with mine in short, ragged bursts. His voice is trembling now, tinged with both need and restraint. "Tell me to stop if you don't want this." He kisses my cheek, but there's a hesitation in it, a tenderness that feels almost like a question. "Tell me to stop, and I will."

His embrace tightens, and I'm completely immobilised against him. I can feel the hard lines of his cock pressed against me, feel his need thrumming through every inch of him. My own body responds is a deep, aching pulse between my legs that only he can soothe. Everything in me is screaming for him, and my mind is clear, stripped of all doubt. This is exactly where I want to be. Where I need to be.

I'm his.

He's mine.

"Don't you fucking dare stop, Dominic!" The words rip from me, wild and unfiltered. "I need you inside me, more than words can ever explain." I punctuate the confession with kisses, my lips trailing over his face in frantic, fevered motions. Each kiss is a plea, a promise, a demand. "I asked you to give me your everything, love of my life. Everything!" My teeth graze his ear before I suck it into my mouth, feeling the tremor that runs through him in response. "Everything," I repeat, the word a sultry whisper that hangs heavy in the charged air.

The sound that tears from his throat is more than just a curse, it's the unchained roar of a man giving in to his deepest instincts. His hands grip me with a newfound urgency, and I can feel the battle within him, the war between the need to be gentle and the overwhelming drive to claim me. In this moment, there's no room for anything but raw, unfiltered passion.

With one swift movement, he lifts me higher against the wall, positioning me exactly where he wants me. His eyes darkened with a mix of hunger and something dangerous. "You're mine, Angela," he breathes, his voice roughened by the weight of that truth. "I'm never letting you go."

"I don't want you to," I reply, my voice dripping with dark satisfaction. "Show me how much I belong to you."

His gaze never wavers as he positions himself at my entrance, his eyes burning into mine with a predatory intensity that sends shivers down my spine. With deliberate slowness, he begins to lower me onto his cock. The moment he fills me, a sharp gasp tears from my lips, mingling with his low, guttural moan. The sensation is overwhelming, a delicious stretch that makes my body tremble as pleasure and pain meld into one unbearable ecstasy. Every nerve feels ignited, screaming for him, craving more. Our bodies had been in silent agony, searching for each other, and now that they are finally one, we melt together in an ecstasy of unimaginable pleasure. The connection is so powerful that it feels like our bodies have been truly aching for this, *desperate, incomplete,* until this very moment.

Our combined moans fill the room, echoing off the walls as our bodies merge, finally becoming one in its purest form. It's as if all the tension, all the agonising need we've harboured for each other, exploding in this single act. My mind is a blur, thoughts dissolving into pure sensation as wave after wave of pleasure crashes through me, melting me into him completely. Nothing else exists, just this searing, all-consuming pleasure.

"Fuck, baby, you're killing me," Dominic groans, his voice hoarse and thick with raw desire. His grip tightens on my hips, anchoring me as he begins to move, each thrust deep and powerful, driving into me with a hunger that mirrors my own. "You feel amazing, Vita Mia." His words are rough, almost reverent, as if he's worshipping me with every thrust.

It doesn't take long for the pressure to build, an unstoppable force coiling low in my belly. The pleasure mounts with each roll of his hips, every delicious grind sending sparks of electricity shooting through my veins. My orgasm rushes in like a tidal wave, taking me over the edge within seconds. My pussy clenches around him, pulsing wildly as I shatter, crying out in a voice I barely recognise. The pleasure is relentless, dragging me under, leaving me breathless and trembling in his arms.

“That’s it, baby,” he rasps, his voice thick with satisfaction as he watches me unravel for him. “Drown me in your delicious juices.” His hips grind deeper, rolling in slow, deliberate circles that press into my most inner sensitive nerves. The sensation is almost too much, intense, overwhelming, but I don’t want it to stop. I need more, I need him to push me even further into oblivion.

Dominic’s movements grow even more urgent, his control slipping as his own need peaks. His lips find mine in a bruising kiss, tongues tangling, breath mingling as we devour each other with unrestrained passion. The connection between us goes beyond just physical pleasure. It’s an unspoken claim, a binding of souls that neither of us can resist.

With every thrust, every groan, every breathless word, it becomes clear that this is more than just sex. This is a declaration, a promise that there is no turning back from this. We are bound together, through darkness and light, through possession and love, and there’s no escape from the hold we have on each other. The hunger between us is bottomless, and as I cling to him, feeling every ripple of his strength, I know I’m lost to him forever.

"Give me everything you got, love of my life!" My demand echoes around us as moan upon moan of pure bliss envelops us.

And then, he does. His lips, his hands, his body all converging in a dance of feral need and possessive love. Every touch, every thrust, every broken moan carries the unspoken promise that this is forever, that there’s no turning back. The tension we’ve been battling is just a tormenting lost thought now, replaced by something deeper, something that feels like unity, a binding of souls that transcends anything we’ve known before.

I feel his muscles tightening under my palms, his body tensing like a drawn bow, and I know his release is near. The knowledge sends a thrill through me, spurring me on. I begin to meet him, thrust for thrust, moan for moan, savage kiss for savage kiss. We're perfectly in sync, two wild forces colliding in a frenzy of need, both of us desperate to claim and be claimed.

My lips roam wherever they can reach. His neck, his shoulder, the sharp edge of his jaw, kissing and biting with reckless abandon. Every nip of my teeth draws a ragged groan from him, driving him deeper into that primal state where words no longer matter. I start bouncing on his cock, grinding down harder, creating more friction, pushing us both closer to that sweet, excruciating edge. Each thrust sends shockwaves of pleasure through my body, and I can feel the fire building inside me, ready to consume us both.

"I love you, love of my life," I whisper in his ear, the words trembling on the edge of a moan. "Fill me with your cum and claim me as yours forever."

That's all it takes. The animalistic growl that rumbles from deep within him is more than just a sound. It's a primal, guttural response that echoes in my chest. He's more beast than man now, lost to the savage need to mark me as his in the most intimate way possible. His hands grip my hips with bruising force as he drives into me with unrelenting power, each thrust more demanding, more desperate than the last.

His rhythm falters, becoming erratic, and I know he's right there on the edge, teetering between control and release. The tension coiling in my belly snaps as I'm dragged under by another wave of pleasure, my body convulsing around him as I scream my pleasure. The sensation is too much, blinding and all-consuming, but I don't want it to end. I need this, need him to claim me in every way.

With a final, brutal thrust, he buries himself deep inside me, his release tearing through him in a powerful, shuddering wave. I feel the hot flood of him filling me, marking me, claiming me exactly as I begged him to. His release roar is pure, unfiltered possession, a sound that tells me without a doubt that I am his, and there's no turning back for either of us.

Our bodies tremble together in the aftermath, still locked in a fierce embrace. There's no distinction between where he ends and I begin, just the echo of our breaths mingling in the charged air and the knowledge that something irrevocable has happened. This isn't just love or lust, it's a bond forged in fire and need, unbreakable and terrifying in its intensity.

"I love you so much, Vita Mia. You're my breath and my death. You're my everything, and without you, I'm nothing." His voice is a husky whisper, raw and honest, as he presses his forehead against mine. We're both drenched in sweat, spent and breathless, but it's a beautiful kind of exhaustion, the kind that comes when you give every part of yourself to the person you love. "I love you with an all-consuming fire, Amore Mio." He's still buried deep inside me, and as he pulls me off the wall, he wraps me in his arms, cocooning me against his chest as he nuzzles into the crook of my neck.

For a few moments, we simply exist in each other's warmth, feeling the rise and fall of our breaths, the beat of our hearts slowly syncing. There's something peaceful about it, a moment of stillness after the storm. But then, I feel him start to move again, just the faintest shift, before he stops. His head lifts, and he gently pulls back to search my gaze, his eyes dark and heavy with a mix of need and exhaustion.

"I barely slept in 48 hours, Vita Mia. I just need to rest my eyes for a few minutes," he murmurs, his words laced with fatigue. "But then I want to devour you again. You need to tell me where to go because there's no way in hell I'm putting you down until I've had my fill of you."

I can't help it, I burst out laughing, a deep, uncontrollable laugh that shakes both of our bodies.

"What's so funny?" he asks, a hint of a smile playing on his lips.

"The fact that I'm going to charge you for a sleepover..." I manage to get out through giggles before I laugh even harder. "And also that I've only had two hours of sleep in the past 48 myself." I cup his cheeks, and when I do, his eyes seem to stand out even more, like pools of endless blue that draw me in, making me feel as if I'm being pulled into a vortex of unmeasurable depth. "I love you, Dominic," I whisper, my voice softening as the laughter fades into something deeper, something reverent.

"Say it again," he murmurs, his tone almost pleading.

"I love you, Dominic." I lean in and kiss one eyelid, feeling him shudder under the tenderness of the touch.

"I love you, Dominic." I kiss the other eyelid, savouring the way he closes his eyes, surrendering to my affection.

"I desperately love you, Dominic." I brush a kiss across the tip of his nose, watching his breath hitch.

"I love you with an all-consuming love, love of my life." And then, I seal the words with a kiss, soft, gentle, and deep, a kiss that says everything words can't.

Chapter Eighteen

Dominic

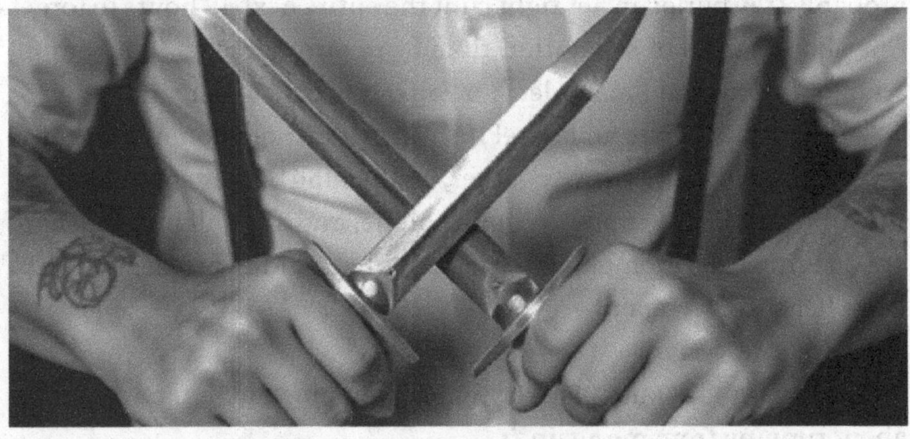

"Do you still want to impose this blasphemous four days?" The pain I am in is too much to hide anymore. *I am breaking!* I am fucking breaking into pieces without her, and it's as simple as that.

"No."

Oh! No more! No more!!!!

"Come to me, love of my life."

The sound that rips out of me is the purest cry my beast has ever made, a response to his mate's call, pure raw, animalistic longing. She catches my reaction and starts laughing, but she has no idea what she has unleashed because there is not going to be a moment for the rest of her life where I am not aware of where she is. If there is one thing I learned in these disgusting 48 hours, it is that I *cannot* live without her for even a second. I would rather put a bullet in my head than ever leave her sight again.

"You have no idea what you just unleashed, Vita Mia," I say in a dark and possessive tone.

"I think I have an idea," she teases, letting a little bit of mischief slip into her tone. *God, I love this woman!* She is just so amazing! She is beautiful, intelligent, sassy and not afraid to speak her mind.

"You better be ready for me, then," I warn her because I will probably stay buried in her tight cunt the entire next 48 hours to forget this abomination of separation time from our memory. "I'm coming straight to you, and I'm not letting you out of my sight again."

I simply do not care anymore! If she has any more doubts, concerns or fears, we will work them together, but fucking hell, *I am not living her site ever again!* She is mine and mine alone, and she will learn that we are one from this moment onwards. So whatever life brings, I will not leave her site ever again!

"Drive safe, okay?"

"Always, Amore Mio. Just stay where you are, and don't even think about running from me again."

"I'm done running, my love. I promise," she says with a laugh, and I know. I just know. I'm not going to drive to her. I'm going to make my car fly to her.

The pure fire running through my veins is scary as fuck! My entire life, my mind just ran, and my body could not be contained, but I had never felt like this before. It's like the calm before the storm as my beast awakened fully and found his mate. *Never again! Never again will I allow space between us.*

"I'll see you soon."

"Can't wait," came her instant reply in that sexy as fuck voice of hers. I've never been this hard in my life, and all I can think is how sweet she will taste on my tongue, how soft she will feel in my hands and how hot her cunt will envelop me when I am deep inside her.

After we wrapped up business with Jake, Hunter and I crashed at my place and drank like two idiots until we collapsed. When I woke up, all I wanted to do was run to my angel. But Hunter, being the stubborn ass he is, wasn't too impressed with my plan when I started moving towards the door. Let's just say it escalated into yet another dick-measuring contest between us. In the end, I wound up handcuffed to the building's support cantilever beam, all thanks to him.

I was stuck in that damn position for over ten hours. When I yelled at him that I could text Angela now as the time was up, the fucker just laughed. And to top it off, he didn't even give me a piss break the entire time. I swear, this SASR guy can drink like an elephant and still have the energy to fight. Meanwhile, I was so drunk when I woke up and we started fighting that the world was spinning around me, but I didn't care. I would have crawled to my angel if I had to.

But this stupid fuck didn't let me!

Anyway, it's all in the past now. The second he finally released me, I head-butted him so hard he went flying. Then, I bolted to the bathroom to take care of business so I could enjoy my time texting my angel in peace. When she said I could call her, it was the first moment I felt I could at least breathe.

Imagine my ecstatic surprise when she took the blasphemy off us so I could drive to her like a furious army of brooded killers would be on my heels. I have never driven like this before, but I know that my sweet reward would be worth anything. *I need to get to her.*

I just need to get to her!

I cannot fucking breathe properly! *I need to get to her!!!!*

"Welcome home, love of my life," she whispers, her gaze locked on mine as she opens the door.

Oh my God, I am melting at her fucking feet!

She welcomed me home!

She welcomed me home!

She welcomed ME home! Before I can say or do something stupid, I pull her into my arms and hug her as tightly as I can without hurting her. I need to feel her body against mine, to soak in her warmth, to inhale her sweet scent that's driving me to the brink of madness. A full-body shiver runs through me, and I know she felt it too because I am so fucking out of my mind, nervous, excited and madly in love with her that I cannot contain my body as it trembles in her embrace.

"I love you, Dominic."

What?!!!!

My mind blacked out for a second. There is complete and utter silence, in complete disbelief.

Four words. That's all it is, but I feel like someone reached into my heart and punched it.

Did I imagine it?

Perhaps I imagined it.

I think I imagined it because how can an angel love a demon?

"Say that again," I murmur, my voice shaky, not daring to hope that I understood her right.

"I love you, Dominic."

Oh, my heart!!!!!

I might actually have a fucking heart attack right now!

I pull back slightly, just enough to cup her face, my hands trembling uncontrollably. I don't even care that it's so obvious I can't control my emotions. All that matters is looking into those beautiful, dark eyes of hers when she tells me she loves me.

I need to see it, to feel it, to know that this isn't some dream I'll wake up from. And as I look into her eyes, those words *I love you, Dominic* echo in my mind, grounding me, filling me with a warmth I've never known. She's not just saying it. She means it. And that knowledge, that truth, is enough to shake me to my core.

"You love me?" I ask, my voice hoarse, filled with raw emotion.

She nods as if she is as overwhelmed by love as I am, a soft smile forming at the corner of her mouth. "I love you, Dominic," she says clearly now, her true feelings loud and exposed, full of conviction, staring straight at me.

She loves me!

She loves me!

She actually loves me!

The realisation crashes over me, and before I can think, I capture her lips with the force of our combined love, feeling the weight of my restraints falling away. I devour her entirely, holding nothing back, letting every emotion pour out of me because she loves me! She's accepted me for who I am, and out of all the men in the world, better men, worthier men, *she chose me*.

The kiss is intense, desperate, a raw outpouring of everything I've held inside. It's not just a kiss, it's a declaration, a promise, a vow that transcends words, showcasing the depth of our love for each other. Every ounce of love, need, and relief flows into that kiss, binding us even closer.

"I love you too, Vita Mia," I murmur when I finally break the kiss, both of us panting, our raw emotions running wild and unchecked. "So much that it scares the hell out of me." The admission tumbles out, unfiltered, and I kiss her again, savouring every stroke of her lips against mine, every breath we share, every second of this confession that we've laid bare to each other.

This moment, this connection, it's everything. I never want to stop feeling how she makes my heart race and how she turns every fear into something beautiful and worth fighting for. And as I kiss her, I know without a doubt that this is where I'm meant to be, in her arms, loving her with every part of me.

I break the kiss reluctantly because I need to ground myself. I am completely losing control, and I am not sure what would happen if I completely let go around her. "You have no idea what those words do to me," I whisper onto her lips, my voice rough with restrained emotion. "You're my everything, Vita Mia. There's nothing I wouldn't do for you, to keep you safe, to make you happy." But words, they fall short. They can't capture the depth of what I feel for her, the way she fills every corner of my soul is overwhelming. Like the oxygen around us, her presence is everywhere, and her warmth is all-enveloping. I'm terrified that if I try to put it into words, my heart might actually explode, or I might actually fuck it all up by saying the wrong words.

"I know, my love. I feel it in everything you do. And I'm done being scared of it. I'm ready to be all in with you."

Oh, my heart!

"You're mine!" I study her for a second, and it's written all over her beautiful face that my firm tone delivered the final message, and she understood this is final. "And I'm never letting you go. You need to make your peace with that." She is mine, and she just needs to accept her new reality because this is not something she can stop or escape from.

"Good," she replies, her voice breathless as she leans in for another kiss. "Because I'm not going anywhere," she whispers the words into my lips.

Her acceptance of her situation, mixed with the raw passion between us, breaks any restraints that my beast might still have, and the next minute, I am eating her alive against the wall in an all-consuming kiss that can only be described more as a war of desire than a kiss between two people.

"I love you, love of my life," she moans between gasps, her words fueling the beast inside me. It's like she's fed it the perfect meal, and now there's no holding back, he's fully surfaced, taking control. My touch grows more desperate, rougher, as I lose myself in the need to feel her, to have her. My movements become frantic, driven by the overwhelming desire to bury myself deep within her heat, to drive into her with an uncontrollable urgency. I'm chasing her ecstasy, carving myself into her soul with every thrust, making sure she knows she belongs to me as much as I belong to her.

"I love you so much, love of my life, and I want all of you. The good, the bad, the soft, and the insane," she whispers into my ear, her voice trembling with unmistakable need, a secret plea for more.

I take a sharp inhale, my brain short-circuiting as her words sink in. *Did she really just ask for everything? Did she actually want all of me? The darkness, the madness, the parts of me I'm afraid to unleash?*

"Give me everything you've got, love of my life," she breathes, her voice low and urgent, filled with the same wild need that's roaring inside of me.

Silence!

Complete and utter silence in my mind!

Give me everything you've got, love of my life. Oh! I'm going to give it to you! Before I remember how breathing works, she pulls me into a desperate, hungry kiss that breaks any remaining connection to reality my brain still possesses. A deep guttural growl rumbles from my beast, calling to his mate. Only she exists now, and nothing and no one will break this bond.

I let go and started claiming every inch of her as the woman that was made for me, and the world be damned because there is nothing else in this world but her from this moment onwards.

"I need to be inside you, Vita Mia. I need to feel you," I say with desperate need. My entire being is clinging to her in a raw, possessive way that rationality cannot explain.

I'm scared that my beast is scaring her. I'm scared it's too much again for her. My entire body is in so much pain from wanting to be in her and eat her alive, destroy her and rebuild her into ecstasy to a future that we can only build for ourselves together. But my protective side takes over, and I pull back to give her the chance to stop me if she wants. I need her to feel comfortable around me. I need her to love me as I am. *I need her to love all of me.*

"Tell me to stop if you don't want this." My voice is trembling now, tinged with both need and pain. "Tell me to stop, and I will."

"Don't you fucking dare stop, Dominic!" Her words are more than just a demand. They're wild, unfiltered, an order that cuts through the haze of my desire. "I need you inside me more than words can ever explain. I asked you to give me everything, love of my life. Everything!" Her teeth graze my ear, and it's like she's casting some kind of spell, some voodoo magic that takes complete control of my body. "Everything," she repeats, and the word echoes in my mind, reverberating through my entire being until I find myself buried deep inside her, pounding with all the force I can muster, claiming her, marking her as mine for all eternity.

"Fuck, baby, you're killing me," I groan, my voice hoarse and thick with raw, unrestrained desire. "You feel amazing, Vita Mia." She's so tight, so impossibly hot, wrapped around me, and the filthy, intoxicating sounds of my cock driving into her wet cunt fill the room, driving me closer to the edge. I know I'm not going to last long. She feels too good, too delicious, too perfect around me. Her skin seems to fuse with mine, her cunt gripping me, pulling me in, welcoming me home in a way that's so intoxicating, it's almost unbearable.

I can feel my heart pounding in my chest, ready to explode into a million pieces, my balls tightening, ready to release. My mind is a whirlwind of ecstasy, screaming with the realisation that she's mine.

All mine!

Every thrust, every gasp, every moan is a declaration, a testament to a connection that goes beyond the physical. It's primal, it's consuming, it's the very essence of who we are. As I drive into her, feeling her tighten around me, I know there's no turning back. She's mine, and nothing in this world will ever change that. *Not even her.*

"That's it, baby," I rasp, my voice thick with satisfaction as a heart-shattering orgasm pulses through her, shaking her to her core. "Drown me in your delicious juices." The words slip out, fuelled by the primal need surging to the surface, a need to conquer, to possess this woman completely. My body moves in a feral dance, each thrust, each touch, each roll of my hips aimed at claiming every inch of her, every cell, until there's nothing left untouched.

This isn't just our bodies uniting. This fucking is the final bond of our souls, a sacred ritual we're both signing with our moans, our thrusts, our releases. Every movement, every breath we share, is a vow. A binding promise that there is no going back from this moment onward.

She starts meeting me thrust for thrust, moan for moan, but the moment she leans over and whispers in my ear, "I love you, love of my life. Fill me with your cum and claim me as yours forever." *I know!* I just know she is exactly where I am! She figured out that it's just me and her from now on. Nothing else matters.

A guttural sound is all that my beast can reply to as I feel my primal instincts completely in control now. There is no going back. There are no restraints. There is no saving this. This union is happening, and there is no stopping it.

The rhythm of my thrusts is completely unhinged now as the buildup of my release is taking my sanity away. There is no world around us anymore. There is no ground beneath our feet. There is no reality anymore.

There is only this beautiful, intoxicating creature in my arms, her skin sealing into mine, binding us together in a way that defies comprehension. There is only her wet, amazing cunt that is welcoming me into another dimension where I am loved, cherished and cared for.

There is nothing else besides this woman, and *she is mine!*

With a final, brutal thrust, I bury myself deep inside her and claim her as my world. My cock pulses inside her in long, shuddering waves. I growl a deep, guttural roar of release, unfiltered possession, because she is my world, and nothing and no one will pull her out of my hands now.

"I love you so much, Vita Mia. You're my breath and my death. You're my everything, and without you, I'm nothing." My voice is a husky whisper, raw and honest, as I remember how to stand on solid ground, breathe correctly, and formulate coherent sentences. "I love you with an all-consuming fire, Amore Mio." If I could create that other reality where I could be in her forever, I would because what just happened between us is not fucking. It's soul bonding of a man finding the woman that was created for him and claiming her as his own.

As I hold her close to my heart, existing around her orbit, I lose myself in her, in the feel of her spent body, the feel of her skin on mine. The intensity of our connection surges, overwhelming every sense, every thought. She truly is my world, and nothing but her exists.

I break the silence as I can feel my exhaustion kicking in with a vengeance. "I haven't slept in 48 hours, Vita Mia. I just need to rest my eyes for a few minutes," I murmur, fatigue dripping from my voice. "But then I want to devour you again. You need to tell me where to go because there's no way in hell I'm putting you down until I've had my fill of you."

The moment I close my eyes, sleep claims me and I have a few hours of sleep before feasting on my angel again. When I wake up in the morning, it's in the most delicious way possible. The warmth of her soft lips wrapping around my shaft, followed by the teasing swirl of her tongue around my crown. A low, primal groan escapes me, instinctive, before my eyes even open to take in the sight of her. She lets out a playful giggle, the vibration sending sparks of pleasure through me as she picks up the pace, driving me mad with every exquisite touch.

When I finally open my eyes, I'm greeted by the sight of the most beautiful, glistening pink pussy, hovering just above my face. The sight alone nearly has me unravelling.

"You little minx," I murmur with a grin, my voice roughened by sleep and desire. I grab her hips and position her better so I can eat my breakfast in peace. *She tastes to die for!* I heard there is this misconception that cunts do not taste nice but fuck me, my angel tasted divine. Whoever started that rumour is a plain idiot. Every time she becomes wetter, and I get a new, fresh taste of her, I feel this all-consuming need to devour her, to lick it all up, to beg for more. It tastes sweet somehow, like some fruit and her. It's like this custom-made aphrodisiac combined with some type of narcotics because I am completely dependent on her, and as I lick and fuck her with my tongue, she starts rocking her hips and grinding on my face. I am completely overwhelmed by the sensations of her release on my face, by her talented mouth around my cock, and by the beautiful moans coming out of her around my shaft. I love this woman with a desperation that scares me because fuck me, I might have a heart attack one of these days. My heart is drumming so fast as I start to push upwards fucking her sweet mouth while my tongue is fucking her pussy raw, enjoying and savouring every movement, every taste, every moan.

"You're perfect, Vita Mia," I groan against her slick folds. "You drive me fucking crazy." My tongue slides from the tip of her clit to the sensitive nerves at her back entrance, and she trembles in response. "I love you so much it hurts," I confess, the words spilling out in a rush of raw emotion. And with that, I dive back in, latching onto her swollen clit and sucking with just the right pressure, the way I know she loves, while my fingers plunge into her, matching the rhythm of her moans.

The feeling of her tight, wet mouth surrounding me as she chokes on my length makes it impossible to hold back. I increase my pace, and the need to mark her and claim her in every way overwhelms me. Her hips buck wildly as she grinds harder on my face, lost in her own pleasure. I know she's close, her walls pulse around my fingers, tightening with every thrust. I pull my fingers out and start fucking her with my tongue rolling the tip of my tongue on her G-spot in up-and-down movements while my fingers start an unrelenting circular rub on her clit, sending her over the edge. Her cry of pure ecstasy around my cock is the best love song I could hear. *This woman is everything.* Reality does not exist without her.

I am pounding savagely into her sweet mouth as I keep my assault on her delicious cunt and clit. I'm seconds away from losing it, emptying myself into that perfect, eager mouth. The way she's trembling, gasping for breath as she takes me deeper, sends me spiralling over the edge. My grip tightens on her hips, and with a final deep thrust into her mouth, I reach my breaking point. Pleasure erupts through me, and I spill into her with a groan, my body shaking from the intensity of it all. She eagerly tries to swallow it all, and the growl that I release is a testimony of the pleasure it brings me to see her not waste any of my cum. When some trickle down on my shaft, she starts licking me up and down, then around the balls, then again on the shaft, and finally starts to gently suck on my crown, driving me wild with her attentiveness to not waste any.

"Fuck, baby, you're fucking killing me!" I groan into her pussy, still riding the waves of pleasure and pressure. "After last night's thorough fucking, I thought I'd finally found some relief after the fourth time, but you're breaking my reality, Vita Mia."

My tongue finds its way back to her swollen clit, and I start again, licking from the sensitive tip all the way to her sweet, tight ass. I circle it with my tongue, teasing her, relaxing the nerves, preparing her for what's to come. *Soon*. Soon, I'll take her there too, and show her just how unbelievably good it can feel.

When a shiver runs through her body, I give her ass one last deep lick, savouring the way she reacts, before moving back down, burying my nose into her pussy and inhaling her scent deeply. *Fuck me, she's unreal.* She smells and tastes divine, like something otherworldly, created just for me. I love this woman with everything that I am, and every cell in my body is hers. There is nothing but her in this world.

"That tickles," she giggles, reaching down and playfully smacking the top of my head. "Do you have to smell me like that?" she asks, trying to wriggle away.

"You smell divine, Vita Mia," I murmur, punctuating my words with a long, deliberate lick inside her. "I'm absolutely addicted to you." I gently suck on her clit, hearing the soft gasp it pulls from her. "I love you so much, Vita Mia. I swear, I'm scared one day I might have a heart attack around you."

She tries to turn to face me, and this time, I let her. When her eyes meet mine, I know she sees the truth there, the truth that I am completely and irrevocably addicted to her. She's my everything. The path I had to walk to find her, the pain, the trauma, the blood, the despair, **it was all worth it.**

I found her.

I found my angel, and nothing in this world will ever pull me away from her. She's mine, and I'll never let her go.

"I love you, love of my life," she whispers her confession against my lips, her breath warm and soft. "I didn't know love could feel like this. It's scary, thrilling, and deep, but also exciting, warm, sweet, deep and all-consuming."

"You do know you said 'deep' twice," I tease, trying to hold back my laughter.

She bursts out laughing, and the sound is pure magic, light, powerful, and beautiful. *My God!* This woman should only ever laugh for the rest of her days because as long as I live, I'll never let her go a day without this intoxicating sound.

"Or was the second 'deep' for how far up your cunt my cock went?" I say as she playfully pinches my side, sending a sharp jolt of pain through me.

"You little minx! Does the truth hurt?" I laugh, rolling us over so she's pinned beneath me, her body trapped under mine. "You want war?" I lower my mouth to her nipple, circling it slowly with the tip of my tongue. "I'll give you war."

In an instant, I'm on her, pinning her with my arms and legs so she can barely move. My tongue trails along her skin as I start licking, sucking, and nipping her sides, just below her breasts and teasing just above her belly button. Her laughter bubbles up uncontrollably, and she tries to wiggle away, pushing at my weight in vain.

The more she fights, the more relentless I become, devouring every inch of her, marking her in the most delicious way possible. Her laughter fills the room, her body writhing under mine, and I'm drunk on the sound, on the way she moves beneath me, on the intoxicating joy of her fight.

At this moment, it's not just about teasing. It's about the connection between us, how even in our playful banter, there's love, tenderness, and all-consuming passion. And as I pin her down, her body squirming under mine, I know I'll spend every day of my life making sure she never stops laughing, never stops feeling the depth of my love. As she surrenders beneath me and starts kissing me everywhere she can reach, I feel like I am melting into her being, and there are not two of us anymore. There is only one.

"Dominic, I need to pee," she says, wiggling under me with determination. "I'm serious. Please move, because I don't know how much longer I can hold it. I can't remember the last time I laughed this hard."

She's breathtaking. Her warm gaze is like the softest river, flowing endlessly with no beginning or end. The depth of her eyes pulls me in, and I feel this overwhelming, burning longing that can't be extinguished. *Fuck me! These feelings are unreal! It's like I'm burning from the inside out.*

"It's okay. You can pee. I promise I won't judge," I say playfully, winking at her. "You can do no wrong in my eyes, Vita Mia."

"Dominic, that's gross, and if you don't get off me and let me run to the bathroom, I will kick you in the balls the next chance I get," she says, giving me a mischievous smile.

"You would endanger our future kids like that? How cruel are you?" I tease, lifting myself slightly off her while taking her breast into my mouth. I start sucking on it quickly, eager to distract her, but the little minx wriggles her way completely out from under me. Her breast pops out of my mouth with an audible pop.

"Yes, I would endanger our nonexistent kids. So, protect your crown jewels if you don't want to face my deadly kick," she says over her shoulder, holding back a laugh as she runs full speed to the bathroom.

I hear the water running a moment later, confusion creeps in. I approach the door, listening closely. "Are you on the toilet, or are you peeing in the shower? Because if you're in the shower, I'm coming in."

"Don't you fucking dare, Dominic!" her sharp voice echoes through the door, loud and clear.

"I don't understand! I just want to shower with you!" I plead, the thought of seeing her beautiful, wet body too tempting to resist.

"I'm on the toilet, and you need to leave and give me some privacy!"

Privacy, my ass! Never!

"Pleeeeeeease!" I tease over the sound of running water.

"No! Get us some breakfast. There's a nice coffee house on the corner of the street," her tone shifts, and something feels... off. It's subtle, but the urgency in her voice isn't playful anymore.

"Okay, Amore Mio. Anything specific you want me to get for you?"

"No, everything's fine. Thank you," her reply feels final, almost hurried, and for a moment, unease stirs in my chest. But I'll give her this. She can't hide from me forever. After everything we've shared, she won't be pushing me away. If she tries, I'll chain myself to her if I have to. There's no separating us now.

I start pulling on my clothes, glancing toward the bathroom door as I do. *This is strange, right? Should I insist? Should I go?*

I don't like it one bit, but I will go get breakfast. We will replenish our stamina, and perhaps she will let me fuck her again. The thought gives me some peace, so I pull out my phone and quickly text the guard on call today.

Dominic

I'm with Angela today. I'm about to run to the coffee house. All eyes are on the building until I am back. If anything remotely feels off, call me immediately!

Adam

Yes, boss.

"I'm running quickly, Vita Mia," I shout over the still-running water. *What the fuck is she doing in there?*

"Okay! Thank you."

I want to shower with you! I really, really want to shower with you! Why can I not shower with you?

With a heavy heart, I move towards the entry door. "Okay, I'm going."

Twenty minutes later, I'm running through my angel's front door. *Do I need to explain the importance of locking the damn door?* This woman will be the death of me! I'm carrying three bags full of delicious pastries, fruit salads, and four different types of coffee, just to be on the safe side.

The moment I step into the kitchen-living area, I'm hit by the sight of my angel, radiant as divine beauty itself, casually pacing back and forth in nothing but a long white T-shirt. The hem barely skims the top of her knickers, teasingly covering that sweet, full ass. My cock immediately springs back to attention, a surge of desire jolting through me. I'm mesmerised, she is so beautiful!

She's pacing, lost in thought, and it takes me a second to notice she's holding something in her hand. Who can blame me? My mind is already flooded with images of me pounding into that sweet ass. The thought hits me so hard that I feel lightheaded for a second. *Soon,* I think. *Very soon!*

"I'm back, Amore Mio," I lean over to kiss her, but she pulls back.

WHAT THE FUCK?!!!!!!!!!

How the hell did I manage to fuck something up so massively, and I wasn't even in the room? My mind races as I watch her pace back and forth, her agitation palpable, almost making the air itself heavy. I try to catch her gaze, but she's too worked up, moving too fast for me to get a read on her. My stomach twists. *Great, this is a new kind of low. Somehow, I monumentally screwed up while I wasn't even present.*

Is this about the bathroom? I put the bags down, my hands suddenly too heavy to hold anything, and lean against the back of the couch, trying to figure out what to say. She looks... pissed.

"You okay, Vita Mia?" I ask, trying to sound casual, though my heart is pounding.

Her eyes flick up to mine, and the cold edge in her voice hits me like a punch. "Do you have anything to tell me, Dominic?"

Fuck. My name. I hate my name coming out of her mouth like that. I'm not Dominic to her. I'm the love of her life. *You better lose my name, woman.*

"No," I stammer, doubt creeping into my voice. "Is this about the bathroom? I was just messing around. Look, you could pee on me, and I'd probably like it because I'm fucking intoxicated by how much I love you."

"STOP IT!" she yells, her voice sharp enough to cut through the air.

Fuck! What did I do? She's mad, really mad. Panic floods me.

Fuck!

Fuck!

Quick, what do I do?

Without thinking, I grab her and pull her into a tight hug, not giving her the chance to escape. She starts thrashing, pushing, doing anything she can to get out of my hold, but I don't let her. I move her back, step by step until we hit the wall, and I completely immobilise her, pinning her gently but firmly.

She's wiggling, trying to get free, but I hold her close, my forehead pressed against hers. "Please," I murmur, my voice shaky with desperation. "Just talk to me. Tell me what I did. I don't know what's going on, but you've got me freaking out, Vita Mia. Okay..." I trail off, my voice is full of worry because fuck if I know what to do except not let her go. "What happened? What did I do?" I search her gaze again, but she just looks hurt and mad at me. *I don't understand... How could I monumentally fuck up this badly?*

"Do you have anything to tell me, Dominic?" she spits out, her voice laced with disgust. *I hate this.* I hate it so fucking much.

"Not that I'm aware of. Do you have something to tell me, Vita Mia?" I'm fucking terrified of the answer, but the words slip out before I can stop them.

Her eyes darken, the look of rage intensifying, and I know, I know I just made things worse. Then she opens her hand, and something drops to the floor with a metallic clink.

I glance down, and the blood drains from my face. It's one of the cameras I installed in her apartment.

FUCK!!

We lock eyes, a silence stretching between us that feels like it lasts for fucking hours. Her gaze is sharp and deadly, and when she finally speaks, it's with a single word full of cold, cutting finality.

"EXPLAIN!"

If her laughter is intoxicating, her anger is equally terrifying. Her eyes could kill me a thousand times over by now, and every glare feels like a knife to the chest.

"They are mine," I say, forcing myself to hold her gaze.

"They?" she hisses, trailing off as her body tenses even more, readying herself for a fight.

I brace myself, knowing she's about to struggle in my arms, knowing she wants to lash out at me. But I don't loosen my grip. I lower my voice, trying to stay calm. "They're mine. They're around the house. I'm the only one who sees the feeds and my team only monitors the main areas."

"Your team?" she repeats, her voice incredulous as she tries to knee me in the side. I dodge just in time, but the blow still grazes me.

"I'm going to ask you one last time, Dominic. Do you have anything to tell me?"

Fuck!

Fuck!

FUCK!!!!

Her glare is killing me over and over again. I am not sure what to do, but I know one thing for sure, *I'm not letting her go*. I don't care how angry she is, how much she fights. I'm not letting her walk away from this or from me.

She wants the truth? Fine. *She'll get the TRUTH.*

I stare into her eyes, my heart pounding, and brace myself for the fallout.

"Very well, Vita Mia..."

"STOP THAT!" she screams, her voice a whip cracking through the room. "Cut the crap and spill it before I wipe the floors with you!"

The ferocity in her voice makes me freeze for a second. *Who is this demon in front of me? Where's my angel?* Shit, she's mad, really mad. I tighten my hold on her just in case she tries to break free. Every instinct I have is screaming at me to stay calm, to keep her close, not to let her slip through my fingers. I level my voice, pouring as much warmth and confidence into it as I can, though my heart is thundering in my chest. Because fuck me, if she tries to pull away, I don't know what I'll do. Kidnap her? *Maybe.* Anything to stop her from leaving. But that would complicate things a bit more.

"Remember that I love you," I begin, my voice wavering slightly, but I push through. "And remember that you said you wanted my all, the good, the bad, the soft, and the insane." I watch her closely, searching her face for any sign of understanding, any crack in that hard exterior.

Her expression doesn't change. If anything, her gaze sharpens.

"The cameras are mine," I continue, steadying myself. "We installed them after I first met you because... because I knew. I knew I'd found something special. Something worth risking everything for. Something so valuable that I had to protect it at all costs."

"Cut the crap, Dominic," she snaps, her tone icy. "Were you spying on me this entire time?"

"I wasn't spying, Vita Mia. You've had around-the-clock security detail since the day I met you. That's not spying," I say, trying to soften my grip, trying to reach out to her. I want to touch her cheek, trace my fingers along her skin, anything to calm this storm. But the moment I loosen my hold, she moves, and pure, unfiltered fear floods my system.

Before I can stop myself, I pull her back to my chest, clutching her tightly. At least this way, I can feel her heartbeat, the rapid rise and fall of her furious breaths against my neck. But the sound of her anger, the way she's breathing so fast, so unevenly, it's doing nothing to ease the panic building in my chest.

Fuck. What do I do?

"Please," I whisper, my voice barely above a plea. "Please just listen. I couldn't risk losing you, not when I knew how much you meant to me. I wasn't spying, I was protecting you. I've always been protecting you." I bury my face in the crook of her neck and inhale deeply, trying to steady myself for a second. "The moment I saw you," I whisper into her embrace. "I knew I had found something special. But the moment I spoke to you, I knew in my gut that you were my mate. There is nothing and no one but you in my universe. Please believe me, Vita Mia."

A full-body shiver ran through me, and I knew she noticed it because, for a split second, her hold softened on me. I dare and kiss the side of her neck, and her body stiffens again, even more, this time. I know the worst is still coming because if she asks again for the truth, I need to tell her all the truth, and I am not sure if she will ever want to stay with me willingly after that.

"Is that all, Dominic?"

Fucking shit. Fuck! Fucking fuck!!!

I stay in her tight embrace for a few more seconds, my mind racing a thousand miles an hour, planning every possible security measure to make sure she can never leave me. I'll handcuff us together if I have to. She won't even be able to take a damn pee without me. *I could get her out of the country, somewhere far away. Maybe some Arabic country...* My thoughts spin wildly. *She wouldn't know the language and wouldn't be able to escape. I'll force her to marry me if that's what it takes. Maybe in time, she'll learn to accept who I am, even if she can never love me again.*

I pull back slightly and hold her gaze, searching for the right words to explain, to somehow make her understand who I really am, the darkness inside me that I've hidden for so long.

"No." The word comes out flat, but it's the only answer I can give. The truth is too heavy, too dark.

The silence stretches between us, her glare piercing through me while I silently plead with her, *don't make me say it all.* Don't make me tell you everything.

But I know she won't back down. She's waiting, her expression hard, unwavering.

"Listen, Dominic," she says, her voice level but full of quiet determination. "You have one chance to come completely clean. If you don't, if you lie to me or hold anything back, you'll never see me again."

Her tone is final, absolute. She's in control, and the thought of losing her forever rips through me like a blade.

Fuck. She means it!

I swallow hard, the weight of her ultimatum crashing down on me. *I could lose her, really lose her.* And even as my mind races with ways to keep her, to trap her if I have to, I know there's only one way forward. She's giving me a choice: tell her everything, or lose her forever. Because I know if I don't have her love, I will only have a shell of her, and I want it all as well. I want her good and bad and soft and insane. *I want all of her!*

But tell her everything? I can't lose her. Not like this. Not now, not ever. So *truth it is.*

I steady my voice, grounding myself as I brace for the fallout. There's no going back now. "I actually have two jobs. I'm the CEO of BioQuest International, but I'm also the Lead on field missions for Elijah."

I study her, watching every subtle movement, searching for any sign of recoil or disgust. I can't stop now, I have to tell her everything, but the fear that she'll look at me differently...

Her eyes narrow slightly, and I can already see her mind working through what I've said. "What does 'Lead on field missions for Elijah' mean?" she asks, her voice measured, sharp. I knew this question was coming. She's too smart to let something like that go.

"Elijah is... a genius. In his twenties, he created a firewall called EmberWall," I explain, my voice steady but tense. "After that, he opened a cybersecurity company called Quantum Gate Cybersecurity. EmberWall is one of the top five firewalls globally, used by Tier 1 and Tier 2 companies. On the surface, it provides top-quality protection, but it also installs a virus, hidden deep inside."

I pause, watching her closely, waiting for the shift in her eyes for her to piece it all together. *Don't hate me. Please!*

"We trade in information," I continue, my voice quieter now. "We collect data and sell it to the highest bidder. Elijah's strict about who we work with, but... that's the other side of my work."

She's quiet for a moment, her gaze cutting through me like a blade. I know what's coming before she even opens her mouth.

"No, it's not. You told me about Elijah's business. You haven't told me what you do." Her voice is calm, but the fire in her eyes burns hotter, demanding more. "What does a 'Field Lead' do, Dominic? What do you do for a living?"

Fuck.

She's too sharp, too perceptive. Part of me wishes she wasn't so good at reading between the lines that she'd miss the things I desperately want to keep hidden from her.

"I do... whatever needs to be done." I force the words out, my gaze pleading with her to stop pushing, to stop digging. *Please, Vita Mia. Don't make me confirm it. Don't make me tell you what you already suspect. To tell you that I'm a killer. And worse, I don't care I am one.*

I can't tear my eyes from hers. She's looking straight into my soul, weighing my sins, deciding what kind of man I really am. *Please don't make me say it because the truth is, I don't feel one ounce of remorse for the people I've killed. They were scum. The worst of the worst. And I would do it all again.*

She doesn't flinch. She's silent, but her gaze doesn't waver. She's judging me, and I know, I just know whatever she decides next will determine if she walks out that door. The only thing, even if she wants to walk out the door, I will be right there behind her.

My heart pounds in my chest, each second dragging on like an eternity. And all I can do is wait, terrified of what she'll decide.

"You've... killed?" Her voice is barely a whisper, fragile and trembling. I nod, unable to speak, the weight of her question crushing me.

"You will kill?" she asks again, her voice cracking at the end. I nod once more, silently begging her to stop and not push any further. *Please, Vita Mia. Please stop.*

Her next question cuts through me like a blade. "Will you kill me... now that I know?"

A single tear escapes her eye, and I watch, helpless, as it falls, landing between us, hitting my chest like a weight I can't bear.

"No!" My voice thunders, bouncing off the walls, filled with urgency. "Vita Mia, no! Never! Never!" I'm shaking uncontrollably now, trembling my arms still wrapped around her. "Please, oh my God, you are my life! I would never hurt you."

I release her, cupping her face in my hands, my lips frantic as I kiss every inch of her skin, her cheeks, her forehead, her mouth, trying to pour every ounce of my love and desperation into her. "You're my life, my entire universe. Vita Mia, please, you have to believe me. I would never hurt you. Not ever."

I'm dying inside. She has to believe me. *She has to!*

Her next question shatters me. "Will you let me go?"

"Never!" The word leaves my mouth before I can stop it. It freezes me in place, and I pull back, locking my eyes with hers. "You can ask anything of me, anything, and it's yours. But I will never allow us to be apart. You are mine as much as I am yours. We belong together. You've already used all your 'I need space' cards. From now on, it's all of us together. The good, the bad, the soft, and the insane."

We hold each other's gaze for a few more minutes, and then she gives the final punch.

"I want you to leave."

Chapter Nineteen

Angela

I feel sick to my stomach and more terrified than I've ever been in my life. I told Dominic I loved him. *God help me. I love him so much it scares the shit out of me.* The moment I saw that little camera, my body went numb when I pulled it out of its hiding place. Everything inside me froze.

I would rather die than not know who I've given my heart to. I would rather face *death at his hands* than live in the dark, wondering who this man truly is. The man who holds my heart in his hands, the man I thought was part of me. The fear is overwhelming, crushing me from the inside out, but something stronger pushes through it.

Resolve.

Understand.

Fix.

Fix? What the fuck?

I will get the truth from him, no matter the consequences. Even if it destroys me. Even if it destroys us.

I deserve to know.

I have to know!

"Is that all, Dominic?" My voice is sharp and demanding. I'm letting him hold me, trying to keep him comfortable enough to spill the truth. But the moment I get my answers, he's going to face the full force of my rage because he will have his ass handed to him by a woman. *Fucking idiot! Spying on me! Telling me half-truths!*

"No." His voice is flat, almost pleading for me to stop asking, to let it go. *Like hell I will! I'm getting my answers, motherfucker, and then it's you and me. May the stronger one survive.*

The silence between us is suffocating, and his pleading eyes are pushing me closer to the edge of my patience. Every second that passes, my frustration builds. I'm holding back because I need the truth before this turns into a fight. I can feel it brewing, simmering beneath the surface.

Enough is enough.

"Listen, Dominic," I say, my voice calm but firm, brimming with quiet determination. "You have one chance to come completely clean. If you lie to me, if you hold anything back, you'll never see me again."

The words tear at me, and I can feel myself breaking apart inside. Half of me screams in agony, aching for his touch, for his presence that's so deeply rooted in me now. The other part, maybe the stronger part, demands I protect myself. It demands that I fight him, that I make him understand he cannot control me, cannot do whatever the hell he wants with me.

I see it in his eyes. The moment he decides he's going to tell me more. His gaze locks on me, intense, focused like a laser. His arms tremble around me, and his heartbeat is so fast, so out of control, I half expect to need to perform CPR on him soon. *Stupid idiot! Fucking shit! I had to fall for... I don't even know what he is.*

"I actually have two jobs. I'm the CEO of BioQuest International, but I'm also the Lead on field missions for Elijah."

Fucking hell! I knew it!

My stomach clenches, but I force myself to stay calm, to control the storm raging inside me. I can feel his eyes on me, watching my every move, reading me like a book. *No. Not now. He won't see how much this shakes me.* If I let anything slip, if he catches even the smallest crack, he'll shut down, and I don't know what'll happen after that. I can't afford to lose my chance to get everything out of him. I can't lose us.

Lose us?!

"What does 'Lead on field missions for Elijah' mean?" My voice is sharp and measured, but the tension coils beneath my skin like a tightening wire. I won't let him feed me more half-truths. *I want my answers, Dominic, and you're going to give them to me.*

He takes a deep breath, visibly struggling to steady himself. I can see it, the careful control he's trying to exert, like he's choosing each word as a shield to soften the blow of what he's about to confess.

"Elijah is... a genius. In his twenties, he created a firewall called EmberWall," he explains, his voice steady but laced with tension. "After that, he opened a cybersecurity company called Quantum Gate Cybersecurity. EmberWall is one of the top five firewalls globally, used by Tier 1 and Tier 2 companies. On the surface, it provides top-quality protection, but it also installs a virus, hidden deep inside."

He pauses, his eyes searching mine, pleading, as if silently begging for understanding, for mercy. That look tears through me like a jagged knife doing terrible things to my insides. The agony unfurls within me, threatening to break my carefully maintained composure. I can feel it, the weight of this truth, the gravity of what he's saying.

For a split second, I feel frozen in place, caught between the instinct to fight and the overwhelming urge to flee. My body screams at me to run, to get away from this, from him, from everything I don't fully understand. But my heart, my damn heart, anchors me, keeping me here, desperate for the truth, no matter how painful it is.

"We trade in information," he continues, his voice quieter. "We collect data and sell it to the highest bidder. Elijah's strict about who we work with, but... that's the other side of my work."

Does he take me for a fool?

The thought crashes into my mind, sharp and bitter. I can feel the anger rising beneath the surface, bubbling up as I listen to him carefully measure his words. He's trying to downplay it, trying to soften the blow. But I see through it. Every pause, every strained breath, it's all calculated, all an attempt to control the narrative.

No! I won't be manipulated. Not by him. Not by anyone.

He looks at me, and I see the plea in his eyes, like he's silently begging for my understanding. But right now, all I feel is the rage building, clawing at my insides, demanding I make him see that I'm not someone he can fool.

"No! You told me about Elijah's business, but you haven't told me what you do." My voice remains calm, but I know he sees the fire burning in my eyes, demanding more, demanding the truth. His gaze pleads with me, begging me to stop pushing, but I can't. "What does a 'Field Lead' do, Dominic? What do you do for a living?"

He hesitates, his voice weak when he finally speaks. "I do... whatever needs to be done." His eyes are pleading a thousand silent cries, but the words fall flat between us, heavy with an unspoken truth.

This is it! The moment where I face the reality of who he truly is. No matter how terrible, no matter how horrifying, I need to confront it. I can't run from it anymore.

"You've... killed?" My voice trembles, barely more than a whisper. I hate how it sounds all fragile and small.

He nods.

Oh, my heart!

He's a killer. I've fallen in love with a killer.

My heart clenches in my chest, a knot of fear and disbelief tightening with every second. Part of me is terrified, *shaken to my core,* but another part feels... relieved. *Why?* Why does it feel like pieces are clicking into place, like the darkness I've always sensed in him somehow makes sense now?

His darkness... it calls to me, just as much as his warmth has always enveloped me.

What the hell is happening to me?

"You will kill again?" I ask, my voice cracking at the end, betraying the confusion that's tearing me apart inside.

He nods once more, his eyes glistening, struggling to hold back tears. He looks so broken, so desperate, as if his own pain is threatening to drown him.

Why is his pain adding to my agony? I should be pushing him away, fighting him off, kicking him out. That's what my mind screams at me to do. *But my heart, my entire being, is screaming for something else.* I want to comfort him. I want to take his pain and cradle it alongside my own because it feels like his suffering is entwined with mine. As if my pain is magnified because he's in pain, too.

What is happening to me? I need to know. The thought pulses through me, overwhelming everything else. I feel numb, each breath shallow and strained as I prepare to ask the most painful question. My heart is racing, and my mind is spinning with fear and doubt. But I have to know.

"Will you kill me... now that I know?"

A single tear slips from my eye, and I can't help but see the pure agony written across his face. It's like I've struck him with the force of my words, causing an immeasurable pain within him.

"No!" His voice thunders, raw and filled with urgency. "Vita Mia, no! Never! Never! Please, oh my God, you are my life! I would never hurt you."

His hands tremble as he cups my face, his touch frantic, and the next second, his lips are everywhere, kissing me with an urgency that mirrors the storm inside me, as if his kisses are trying to erase the fear and suffering from both of us. "You're my life, my entire universe. Vita Mia, please, you have to believe me. I would never hurt you. Not ever."

His words pour out like a lifeline, but I'm still drowning, carried away by the intensity of his touch. I want to believe him. God, I want to believe him, but my mind is spinning. I let myself fall into his actions, hoping they will ground me, hoping I'll find my center again soon and find a solution to what I feel.

How am I supposed to handle this? How do I reconcile the man in front of me, so desperate, so broken, with the man I now know has killed? The man who hides in shadows, with blood on his hands?

I try to breathe, to find some clarity in the storm. But before I can fully process the chaos swirling inside me, I ask the next question, the one that's tearing at my soul.

"Will you let me go?"

"Never!" His response is so fast, so sharp, that it halts every thought in my mind. *He's never going to let me go.*

The realisation hits me like a wave, crashing through the confusion that's already swirling inside me. And what's worse, I'm relieved.

Why am I relieved? I should be terrified. I should be fighting my way out of his orbit, running as far and fast as I can. I should scream, kick, and claw my way to freedom. But the fact that he's not letting me go, that he's fighting with everything he has to keep me, it's making my agony subside as if on a deeper level this is what my mind and heart wanted all along, to not let go no matter what. The idea that he's taking that choice off the table, making the decision for us... *Why does it calm me?*

I should be mad. I should be furious. But I'm not. Instead, there's this strange sense of peace settling inside me, knowing he won't let me leave.

Why? Why am I so desperately in love with him? Why does it bring me comfort knowing I'm his entire universe? That he would do anything for me, even kill for me?

The truth hits me, shaking me to my core. *He loves me without boundaries.*

Completely.

Obsessively.

And instead of running, instead of fighting, I find myself surrendering to it.

Wow.

"You can ask anything of me, anything, and it's yours. But I will never allow us to be apart. You are mine as much as I am yours. We belong together. You've already used all your 'I need space' cards. From now on, it's all of us together. The good, the bad, the soft, and the insane."

We hold each other's gaze for a few more minutes. I know I need time to process. There is no way I am thinking straight. How can I possibly feel relieved that he is taking my freedom away, and I am happy about it?

"I want you to leave."

"No."

The finality in his voice snaps me back to reality, like a splash of cold water to the face. *He thinks he can push his weight around me?* Not if I don't let him. *Like hell, he can.*

One second, his hands are cupping my face, trying to soothe me. The next, he's flying backward, landing hard on his ass next to the dining table.

The pure shock on his face is priceless, and I can't help but feel a surge of satisfaction. My uppercut punch clearly caught him off guard. He wasn't expecting me to be this strong, this capable of standing up to him.

Good!

Growing up, my mom insisted I take taekwondo and self-defence classes. I hated every second of it. I felt like an imposter, awkwardly throwing punches and kicks, wondering who on earth would ever bother coming after me. I am nothing special. Why would anyone waste their time to attack me? Like seriously?

Perhaps I am special to him, I think as I glare down at him, watching him recover from the shock of being floored.

"Vita Mia..." His voice trails off, a mix of surprise and amusement lingering in his tone.

I'll clean that smirk right off your lying face!

"What are you doing, Vita Mia?" he asks, standing slowly, his eyes measuring me, trying to decipher my next move. He looks both amused and cautious as if he's expecting something but not what's coming.

"What does it look like I'm doing? We're having a domestic, love of my life," I spit back, my tone dripping with mockery. "I asked you to leave. You said no. I don't appreciate your no, so I'm going to force you out."

I say the words with an eerie calm, pretending to lean down, only to spin and land a kick with the heel of my foot directly to the top of his head. The blow hits him completely by surprise, sending him crashing to his knees in front of me.

He shakes his head, clearly dazed and struggling to regain his bearings. But when his eyes find mine again, what I see knocks the breath out of me.

He looks up at me with so much love, admiration, and desire that it feels like a punch straight to my chest. *Why are you looking at me like that?*

"Fuck, you are unbelievably sexy as hell," he murmurs, his voice thick with amazement and burning with raw desire. The intensity of his words sends a shockwave through me. *What are you doing to my insides, love of my life?*

"Get out!" My voice snaps like a whip, sharp and commanding, reminding him exactly where we stand. *You don't get to look at me like that and just ignore what I'm telling you.*

"No."

"Dominic, I'm not joking. Get. Out!" My voice lowers, cold and steely, as I take a slow, measured step toward him, my mind already calculating how I'll overpower him if he doesn't leave willingly.

He doesn't flinch. He doesn't even blink. "No! Never!" The finality in his voice, the calm certainty of it, is maddening.

What the actual hell? He's forcing my hand. He's sealing his fate. I'm going to have to beat him out of my life.

But why does my poor heart ache at the thought?

It feels like a betrayal, like my body is at war with itself. Every logical part of me is screaming to fight, to push him out, to protect myself. But then there's this other part, the part that loves him with so much intensity it's like a living, breathing volcano erupting within me, and it's crying, breaking at the thought of hurting him, of truly pushing him away.

Why? Why can't I just let him go?

"Dominic! Leave!" This is the last ultimatum. I can feel it in the air, the charge of what's about to happen. My body knows I need to fight, but my heart screams to keep him. It feels like I'm dying, like both sides of myself are locked in a vicious war, each trying to tear me apart.

"You can ask anything of me, Vita Mia," he says softly, his voice filled with a raw tenderness that makes my heart ache. "But you cannot ask me to ever leave you. I would rather die a thousand deaths than live one life without you."

His surrender, his refusal to leave, is so intimate and deep that it almost disarms me. For a second, I freeze, and then, without thinking, my fist connects with the side of his head, my knee slamming into his shoulder. The collision of my actions with his stillness makes me dizzy, like I'm living in two realities at once.

The agony of it all, of fighting him physically when I'm being torn apart emotionally, is unbearable.

"Leave!" I scream, my voice filled with all the pain and confusion tearing me apart. I hit him again, my full force behind every blow.

"Never!" The finality in his voice sickens me because he's just sitting there, taking it. My punches, my kicks, he doesn't raise a hand to defend himself. He just sits there, accepting it all, unwavering.

What the actual fuck, love of my life? Defend yourself! But he won't. His refusal to fight back makes my heart shatter even more.

When I pause to catch my breath, my fists trembling, he looks up at me. His eyes, so full of love and care, cut through every wall I've built to keep myself strong. Tears blur my vision, and I fight with everything in me to hold them back, to keep from breaking down in front of him.

I can't crack. Not now. Not in front of him.

But the tenderness in his gaze is unbearable. *How can he look at me like this after everything?* How can he be so calm, so... devoted while I'm falling apart in every way possible?

"I wish I could love you like ordinary people," he whispers, his voice warm and steady, wrapping around me like a soft blanket of truth. "I wish I could be softer. But the truth is, I'm not that person, Vita Mia."

His ocean-blue eyes, so clear and unflinching, radiate a love that feels overwhelming, so intense, it feels as though I'm the very centre of his universe. There's no lie in his words, no attempt to sweeten them to make me feel better. It's just truth, raw and pure. He's not apologising for who he is. He's just laying it bare at my feet.

And yet, I can't deny the way my heart reacts to him despite the chaos swirling inside me.

“I can only love you in an all-consuming way, Amore Mio. In an obsessive, all-encompassing way that will burn the two of us to extinction. My love is not gentle, it’s brutal, honest, and rough.”

His words land with the weight of undeniable truth. The way he says it, like a confession but without regret, sends a shiver down my spine. He isn’t offering me softness, he’s offering me intensity, a love so fierce it feels like fire, ready to consume us both. And the frightening thing is, part of me, the part of me that craves him wants that.

I crave his darkness!

I crave his intensity!

I crave him...

"And one thing you need to understand once and for all," he says, his voice dark and unwavering. "You are mine. You are mine now and forever. There is no going back, there is no escaping. There is only me and you and our future together. So whatever fury you have now within you, we will find a way to overcome it because there is no future in this world where we are not together."

His words are final, like a vow he’s already sealed. His gaze locks onto mine, burning with a possessiveness so fierce it both frightens and calls to me.

"I can give you time," he continues, his voice softening slightly, "and I won’t force myself on you. But I will NOT go away, I will NOT leave you alone, and I will NOT accept us breaking up. NEVER!"

The sharpness of his declaration crashes into me like a tidal wave, leaving me breathless. The finality in his tone is terrifying, but it’s also the most brutally honest thing I’ve ever heard. His love is not something that can be walked away from. It’s consuming, like fire, and it’s relentless.

I am his.

The realisation crashes down on me, so terrifying and overwhelming that it knocks the breath from my lungs. Tears spill down my cheeks before I even realise they're there, silent, unstoppable. By the time I notice, it's too late.

There's so much swirling inside me, a storm of emotions that I can't control. But beneath the fear, beneath the chaos, there's something primal, undeniable. A sense of relief. *I'm truly his.* It's so clear to me now, as if my heart always knew. There's no doubt inside me *he is my pair.*

Suddenly, a full-blast headache slams into me, sharp and relentless. The intensity of it all, the emotions, the clarity, it's too much. *I need space! I need air!* My mind screams for relief. *This is too much!*

"So, here's what's going to happen," Dominic says, his voice steady, completely oblivious to my emotional and physical pain. "The cameras will stay on because I am the only one who has access to all of them, and only three guards have access to the main areas and entries."

Wait, what?

"And for the love of all that is precious, stop walking around naked. I'm seconds away from taking Hunter's eyes out, and you only have yourself to blame for that one," he adds sharply, his possessiveness cutting through the air.

Is he serious right now?

"I will visit you every day and remind you how much I love you and what you mean to me. I will not give up, NOT NOW, NOT EVER. We will work through this, no matter how long it takes, because I am not going anywhere."

I'm speechless. Truly and utterly speechless.

"But I won't force you to do anything you don't want to do except let me be near you. That's all I ask. I need to be close to know you're safe, to know you're okay. I can love you just by being in your orbit." His voice cracks at the end, and the pain in it guts me.

"I'm not okay, you stupid motherfucker!" I scream, the adrenaline kicking back into my system, making me hysterical. "How can I possibly be okay with you completely obliterating any form of personal privacy? Are you out of your mind? We are so DONE! Get the fuck out of my apartment, Dominic. Or I swear, I will grab a knife and stab you!"

I'm shaking with fury, screaming at the top of my lungs, my voice raw and broken.

Ever so casually, he reaches across his abdomen and, in one swift motion, pulls out two knives. I take a step back, my shock freezing me in place. He turns the handles toward me, his eyes filled with surrender.

"Vita Mia," he says softly from his kneeling position, looking up at me with so much love that it knocks the breath from my lungs. "Stab me as many times as you want. I won't pull back." He offers me the handles of the knives, bowing his head in complete submission. "Do with me as you please," he says, his voice trembling with pain and sorrow. "But I will never leave you. NOT NOW, NOT EVER!"

He grips the blades so tightly that blood trickles down, soaking his clothes on their path to the floor. The sight breaks something inside me, whatever resistance I had left is gone. *What are you doing to me, love of my life?*

"So, if it's my blood you want, Amore Mio, my blood you will get," he whispers, and I realise the tears streaming down my face are no longer silent. They're at full force, uncontrollable.

I take the knife handles from his hands, my fingers trembling as I lower them to my side, and look down at him, tears blurring my vision. His broken palms rest on his thighs, his bloodied hands a testament to his surrender. The look in his eyes lays everything bare.

No more lies, no more holding back. Just us, raw and exposed to each other.

This unbelievable sense of peace washes over me, an unspoken truth settling between us.

This is it. This is the truth.

He's given me his life, his submission, his everything.

"You know," he continues, his voice filled with determination and tenderness, "from the very beginning, I've always shown you there's nothing soft about me. I live intensely. I love fully. And I am yours forever." He takes a small step toward me on his knees, his gaze searing into me, burning my skin.

"I love you, Vita Mia, more than my dumb words can ever explain," he says, inching closer, every syllable charged with emotion. "You are my universe, and without you, there is nothing."

The knives feel heavy and deadly in my hands, and I can't believe I never noticed them before. *Has he been wearing them every time we were together?*

I let them fall to the floor with a loud thud, the sound echoing through the space like the final bell in a long, drawn-out battle.

In a flash, Dominic wraps his arms around my middle, his head pressed against my abdomen. His breathing is quick and shallow, and I can feel him shivering in front of me. His palms hover near me, careful not to touch, yet his presence is overwhelming.

He might be the one on his knees, but I'm the one who's surrendered to him.

I love him. *God, I love him so, so much!* I should be scared, and I am. Terrified. But the thought of not having him in my life now feels like it would push me to the brink of madness.

He loves me. I can feel it with every fibre of my being. His love isn't half-hearted, it isn't fake. It's not meant to manipulate or gain something. It's not just to impress.

It's strong.

It's intense.

It's dominant.

It's pure.

This is us in our purest, rawest, and most honest form. And when all is said and done, I can only see myself next to him.

This is the truth.

This is our truth.

"I love you, Vita Mia," he says, his voice muffled against my body. "Please say something."

His words pull me back to the present. My mind is spinning, my heart is racing, and I'm crying uncontrollably. It's too much, *everything* is too much.

Would he really give me space if I asked for it? I adore him. I adore him with the power of a thousand suns, but I need air. My head is spinning, and I need to be alone.

Would he truly let me be for a while?

"I love you, love of my life," I manage to say between the sniffles, my words barely tangible. "I do love you..."

"Please don't say 'but,'" he cuts me off, tightening his hold around me. "I am not letting you go, Vita Mia. That ship was never manufactured. It's never going to happen."

A burst of laughter escapes me at the sheer absurdity of his words. *That ship was never manufactured. Idiot.*

"Stop interrupting, you silly boy!" I smack his shoulder playfully. He immediately pretends to be hurt, wobbling in mock pain.

I laugh again. *He's so ridiculous.* This man who didn't flinch when I was punching and kicking him with everything I had is now pretending to cry over a playful smack. *Hilarious!*

"If there were an Oscar for the worst acting in the world, you'd win it," I add, shaking my head at his absurdity.

"Ha! Ha! I made you laugh," he exclaims, his face lighting up with delight. "God, I love hearing you laugh, Vita Mia. It sounds like angels are singing."

This time, I laugh fully, my chest light for the first time in hours. "You are so full of shit!" I tease him back. "Do you say this kind of stuff to all women?"

"There are no other women," he says, suddenly serious, "and there never will be. Since the moment I saw you, I knew in my gut that you're mine. I found my mate, and I'm never letting you go."

He stands up, still looking at me, but this time, he doesn't reach for me or plead. He just stands there, eyes full of adoration, looking at me like I'm the only thing that matters in the universe.

Is this his way of *existing in my orbit*? He's not pushing me. *Maybe... maybe if I ask for space, he'll actually let me be?*

I take a deep breath and steady myself, trying to find the right words to ask for space. *I've used all my cards. Silly boy!*

"I love you, love of my life," I begin, holding his gaze with as much composure and clarity as I can muster. "But I need you to leave. I need some space because my head is spinning. I love you, and I want to be with you. This doesn't mean we're splitting up; it just means everything feels overwhelming right now, and my head is about to explode. I need to breathe properly, and right now, I can't do that next to you."

I try to keep my voice light, ending my request with a cheerful, bubbly tone. "So, here's the plan: you leave, and you keep your word about not pushing yourself onto me. Give me some space to breathe, and then we can talk more. Does that sound like a good plan to you?"

He sits there, completely still, like a statue. His eyes are locked onto mine, reading me, analysing every word. I can see the wheels turning in his mind, trying to figure out if I'm being honest. *He's checking if I'm lying,* I think. I can bet my apartment on it. He's probably trying to see if I'm manipulating him if I'm pretending to still want him while secretly planning my escape. *Well, at least he's intelligent.*

I gently cup one of his cheeks, caressing it as I drown in his mesmerising eyes. *My God, he is such a beautiful man!*

He places the back of his hand over mine, preventing me from pulling away, and then leans into my touch. His eyes close as though he's savouring every second of this small, intimate gesture. The sight of him, so vulnerable, so full of love, melts my heart.

Killer or not, to me, he is the most gentle, wonderful, generous, kind, and lovely man I have ever met in my entire life.

"I love you, Dominic. Please, believe me, I just need time. Please leave," I say, my voice soft but steady.

"Swear to me that you're not pushing me away," he says, his gaze locking onto mine, needing that final reassurance.

"I swear to you, I'm not pushing you away," I repeat, hoping he understands how much I mean it. "You know you're a bit intense, and I genuinely need some air. Then we can talk some more," I explain, my tone as soothing as possible, desperate for him to let me have some space. *I just need to be alone right now to breathe.*

"And by talk, you mean hot, nasty sex, right?" he quips, his playful tone breaking through the tension.

I burst out laughing, the suddenness of it catching me off guard. It takes a few moments for me to calm down. *He is so ridiculous. Not to mention as horny as a teenage boy.*

"I made you laugh again," he says, his voice glowing with pride, clearly satisfied with himself. Then he leans in further, kissing the inside of my palm. That soft, intimate touch reminded me of our first date, the tenderness of it all. *He's so beautiful, inside and out.*

"You're so silly," I say, giving him a playful smack on the shoulder, shaking my head at his antics.

"And by silly, you mean hot and sexy as hell, with whom you will have hot, nasty makeup sex later?" he shoots back, unable to contain his own laughter at how absurd it sounds.

"That would be a strong NO," I say, grinning. "You and your horny cock can leave, and later we can talk."

"Now, now, you're going backward!" he feigns panic, his playful nature lighting up his face. "You just said can talk. That's less than will talk. What's happening? You're going in the wrong direction!"

I place a hand dramatically on my chest, playing along with his ridiculous fun. "Really? I didn't notice," I tease back. "Maybe it's all this cock talk that's making me want to run away screaming."

That's when he loses it. His laughter, deep, rich, and full-bodied, fills the room, washing over me like a warm embrace. It's so raw, so masculine, and completely unguarded. I've never heard him laugh like this before, and for a moment, I'm stunned. *He is breathtaking.*

"I made you laugh," I say, teasing back, but my voice softens as I look at him as if I'm truly seeing him for the first time. I cup his face gently with my other hand, feeling the warmth of his skin beneath my palm, and melt into the tenderness of this moment.

"I love you, Dominic. Please leave." My words seem like total opposites of my actions, but the way I'm holding him, the tenderness in my touch, makes him finally understand. He relaxes into my hands, his body softening as my words sink in.

"I'm not pushing you away," I continue, my tone gentle but firm. "I just need to breathe, love of my life."

His features soften even more, his eyes locked onto mine like they're holding me captive. After that deep, wholehearted laugh, there's something so endearing about the way the corners of his eyes crinkle. *He is mesmerisingly beautiful.*

"I really want to kiss you, my angel," he says, giving me the most pleading look as he leans deeper into my touch. "But I won't force myself onto you," he adds, the words sounding half-hearted, like he's fighting with himself. "If you want me to leave, I will leave."

I'm *shocked* that he's actually listening to me, respecting what I need. *Wow.*

I must look surprised because a low chuckle rumbles from deep within his chest. "It's okay, I'm leaving. Just... don't complain about the arrangements," he says with a sly grin.

Before I can process what he means, he steps back and starts walking toward the door. *Arrangements?* What does that mean?

He opens the door, pausing to look over his shoulder at me with so much love and longing that it feels like a punch to my heart.

"I love you, Angela, more than life itself. There is nothing in my universe other than you."

The door clicks shut behind him, and that small sound is the last straw for my already overwhelmed mind and heart. I collapse to the floor, leaning my back against the wall, my head resting on my knees.

What is happening to me?

What is this man doing to me?

Why do I love him so much?

Why don't I care that he's a criminal?

Why does his absence feel like a physical ache in my chest?

I'm not sure how much time passes while I try to collect myself, trying to understand my new reality. That's when I hear something strange near the door.

What the fuck?

I freeze, trying to listen carefully, but there's nothing. *Did I imagine that?* Fear and paranoia start creeping in, making my heart race as I walk slowly toward the door, listening closely.

And then I notice the blood on the floor. Dominic's blood from his cuts. *Fuck, the cuts!*

I move closer to the door, pressing my ear against it, straining to catch the sound again. There's a faint noise, but I can't quite make it out. I glance through the peephole, but there's nothing.

This is stupid.

I unlock the deadbolt and grip the handle, building up the courage to prove that I'm just imagining things. I swing the door open fast, and suddenly, a loud thud lands at my feet.

I look down, surprised and shocked, to see Dominic flat on his back, laughing hysterically at my feet.

What the fuck?

"What are you doing, Dominic?" I ask, trying and failing to hold back my laughter. "Did you lose your marbles recently?" I flutter my eyelashes at him, adding to the playful tone.

He's still laughing, unable to stop, and I realise, yet again, that even in these ridiculous moments, he manages to worm his way back into my heart.

"I told you not to complain about the arrangements," he says with amusement.

"Are you kidding right now?" My voice is a mix of disbelief and amusement, genuinely shocked by how absurd this situation has become.

"Vita Mia, you're a flight risk, so I'm parked right here at your door for the foreseeable future," he says, barely containing his laughter as if this is the most reasonable thing in the world.

"Do you want me to start kicking you again?" I reply, my tone firm as I try to sober up from the amusement.

"No, thank you," he says, holding his hands up in surrender. "By the way, why do you fight so well? You know if I end up with bruises, you'll have to kiss them better, right?" He grins mischievously, clearly enjoying every second of this.

"Seriously, Dominic, are you out of your mind? You can't sit here at my door like this! I have neighbors," I say, my tone turning nervous as I imagine Mrs. Berglin from across the hall seeing Dominic sprawled on the floor. "They might call the cops on you..."

"You just say the word, sweetheart, and I'll press the dial." Mrs. Berglin's voice cuts through the air from behind her door.

Dominic sits up slowly, all amusement vanishing from his face. He covers his mouth and leans in to whisper, just loud enough for me to hear. "I could always shoot her, and then we wouldn't have any problem." He looks up, clearly assessing my reaction.

This is not good. Not good at all!

I'm sure my face gives it all away. The panic and horror flashing through my mind, because Dominic bursts out laughing again, winking at me.

"Too soon to joke around like that?" he asks with a teasing tone, clearly enjoying my discomfort. Then, without missing a beat, he calls out loud enough for Mrs. Berglin to hear, "There's no problem here, Mrs. Berglin. My name is Dominic DeLuca, and I'm Angela's future husband."

Wait, what? My jaw drops in shock, and my mind goes blank. *Did Dominic just say he's my future husband?* I'm stunned, completely muted, as I process his words.

"We're having a domestic," Dominic continues casually like he's explaining the weather. "As my beautiful wife told me not long ago, I'm just giving her some space. Relaxing at her doorstep until she realises she loves me more than life itself and opens the door for me to come back in."

"Oh, how sweet," Mrs. Berglin's muffled voice comes again from her apartment. *Unbelievable!*

"Seriously, Dominic?!" I glare down at him, trying to channel as much menace as I can muster. Leaning in, I whisper through gritted teeth, "My future husband?" I allow a few moments to pass, waiting for him to stop laughing like a mischievous child. He's supposed to be a mature man, but right now, he's acting like a mischievous child.

I cover my mouth, hiding the venom behind my words, and strike when he looks up at me, waiting expectantly. "Is today the day you want to die?" My glare sharpens, my eyes practically daring him to test me further.

"If it means I die next to you, I'm okay with that," he says, completely unfazed, his voice laced with adoration. "Anything for my beautiful wife."

God, this man! His warmth and unwavering love make me want to kick him, punch him, anything to knock some sense into him. But Mrs. Berglin, the nosiest old fart of a woman, is still hanging around, and I can't just start kicking him like I want to.

That's when I notice his hands again, still beading with blood. *Damn it! Damn it! Damn it! He's hurt, and it's my fault!*

"Everything's fine, Mrs. Berglin. Thank you for looking out for me. Dominic's right, we just had a little misunderstanding, but he's about to head out to get something from the shop and give me some space." I try to sound as casual and nonchalant as possible, my heart racing.

"That's all right, dear. You've got yourself a fine man there, take care of him," she calls back, the faint sound of her TV in the background. "My show's about to start, but if you need me, just yell, and I'll hit dial."

"Thank you, Mrs. Berglin. Bye," I reply, my voice sweet but my eyes burning into Dominic's. *Nosy old woman.*

Once she's gone, I turn my full attention to him. "Get. The. Fuck. Off. My. Front. Door."

"Never." The finality in his tone sets me back, but the look in his eyes, warm and full of longing, makes me want to kiss him, hold him, and love him until the end of time.

What do I do?

Chapter Twenty

Dominic

"I wish I could love you like ordinary people. I wish I could be softer. But the truth is, I'm not that person, Vita Mia." My voice barely rises above a whisper, weighted with the shattering truth of our reality

When I was little, it took me a while to realise that I was different. I wished so many times that I could just be normal, like the other kids. I wanted to fit in, to stop feeling like an outsider in my own head. It wasn't until Elijah saved me and taught me that my ADHD was a gift, not a burden, that I began to accept this "super-brain" of mine.

But none of those moments compare to this one.

Right here, right now, I wish more than ever that I could be the man she wants and needs. Not this version of me, this flawed, relentless form of love. If my angel were to reject me, it would become the worst kind of torture. A living, breathing torment, drawn out for the rest of my life.

There's no escaping it. Even if she pushes me away, I'll stalk the hell out of her for the rest of her life, watching over her. And when she's gone... fuck it all, I'll put a bullet in my head. There's no life without her. A world without her isn't worth living in.

Even when she's glaring at me, there's this undeniable beauty in her, so intense it makes my chest ache just to look at her. She's extraordinary in every sense of the word. The way her eyes flash with fire, the strength in her presence, the way her emotions pour out like an unstoppable force, it all makes her more.

It's almost unbearable how much I love her. *She is everything.*

I can see it all: the fury, the pain, the confusion, hurt, love, compassion, and longing. All battling inside her, creating a vacuum of chaos so immense, it's overtaking her. My angel is caught in this storm, and every second I watch it, it tears me apart. But I can't let go. I need to push forward and make her understand. *She has to understand!*

"I can only love you in an all-consuming way, Amore Mio. In an obsessive, all-encompassing way that will burn the two of us to extinction. My love is not gentle it's brutal, honest, and rough."

I steady my voice, determined to leave no trace of confusion in her mind. "And one thing you need to understand, once and for all. You. Are. Mine! You are mine now and forever. There is no going back, there is no escaping. There is only me and you and our future together. So whatever fury you have now, whatever chaos is tearing at you, we will find a way to overcome it because there is no future in this world where we are not together."

I adore her so deeply I would do absolutely anything, anything to make things right. *She has to know this.* I have to convince her. "I can give you time, and I won't force myself on you. But I will NOT go away. I will NOT leave you alone, and I will NOT accept us breaking up. NEVER!"

I stare at her, daring her to challenge me, to deny what we have, to reject the truth I've laid bare. But I can see how my words are affecting her, how they hit her like waves crashing against the shore. She's taken aback, realising that I've stripped away the options. There's nothing left but the truth.

Her expression shifts, just for a moment. It's as if she realises *she is mine.*

I can feel her pain, the intensity of it like a volcano erupting inside her. It cuts through me with a force I can barely stand. *Fuck, Amore Mio, you're killing me with those tears.*

"So, here's what's going to happen," I begin, trying to keep my voice steady, though I know my possessiveness is coming through sharper than I intended. "The cameras will stay on because I'm the only one who has access to all of them, and only three guards have access to the main areas and entries. And for the love of everything sacred, stop walking around naked in the house. I'm seconds away from taking Hunter's eyes out, and you only have yourself to blame for that one."

The words come out too harsh, my possessiveness slipping through the cracks. *Hunter.* Hunter swore to me that he did not check the cams before I changed the settings, but I don't fully believe him. I still suspect he might have checked the settings before the handover, and fuck me if that thought does not bring murderous thoughts through me to kill him in all the most fucked up ways imaginable. The rage that bubbles up is so dark, so violent, it feels like a storm waiting to break.

Deep breaths, Dominic. Deep breaths. You don't want to scare her more than you already have.

In, one, two, three, four. Hold, one, two, three, four. Out, one, two, three, four. Hold, one, two, three, four.

Calm, Dominic. Stay calm.

When I feel in control again, I continue, hoping she didn't notice my outburst. "I will visit you every day to remind you how much I love you and what you mean to me. I will not give up, NOT NOW, NOT EVER. We will work through this, no matter how long it takes, because I am not going anywhere. But I won't force you to do anything you don't want to do except let me be near you. That's all I ask. I need to be close to know you're safe, to know you're okay. I can love you just by being in your orbit." I conclude, trying to keep a steady voice, but my emotions get the better of me at the end of it.

"I am not okay, you stupid motherfucker!" She screams at me. *Wow, that was loud! My woman has some pipes on her.* "How can I possibly be okay with you completely obliterating any form of personal privacy? Are you out of your mind? We are so DONE! Get the fuck out of my apartment, Dominic, or I swear, I will grab a knife and stab you!"

She screams at the top of her lungs, her voice pained and hysterical. *What have I done? I don't want this.* I love her so much I would do anything, but I cannot bring myself to let her go. I just cannot!

What can I do now?

Blood is what she wants, then blood is what she will get. I reach for both my chest knives and pull them out in a swift motion that makes her take a step back. I turn the handle toward her in a gesture that I am willingly giving her all the power over me with these two knives for her to do as she pleases.

"Vita Mia," I say softly from my kneeling position, looking up at her with all my adoration on full display. "Stab me as many times as you want. I won't pull back," I gesture with the handles again and bow my head, submitting completely to my fate. "Do with me as you please," I say, pain dripping from my voice. "But I will never leave you. NOT

NOW, NOT EVER!" The finality is out there. I would rather die by her hands than live without her for even a second.

I try to compose myself as I sit there on my knees with my arms reaching for her and my hands around the blades of the knives. I am squeezing the blades, and blood pouring down my arms, and my palms are starting to sting, but I do not care. No limit exists when it comes to her, and no barrier will keep me from reaching her. There is only her and nothing else.

"So if my blood you want, Amore Mio, my blood you will get," I say and realise I am fighting back the tears from rolling down my cheeks. "Because there is no way I will ever let you go." *Fuck it! What would be the meaning of life if you found your mate but couldn't have her?*

She's full-out crying now, her tears falling freely as she looks down at me, but even through her sobs, she reaches out, trying to steady herself through the trembling of her body. She takes the knives from my hands, lowering them to her side.

The sight of her standing over me, holding my knives while I kneel before her, bleeding, is nothing short of breathtaking. *She is extraordinary.* It's a moment burned into my soul, a perfect image of the power she wields, and now she finally knows it.

She's a goddess.

She's my universe, and she is MINE.

"You know," I continue, my voice filled with tenderness and adoration, "from the very beginning, I've shown you there's nothing soft about me. I live intensely. I love fully. And I am yours forever." I take a small step toward her, still on my knees, hope blooming in my heart. She didn't stab me in the eyes and walk away, so I take that as a win and risk getting closer.

"I love you, Vita Mia, more than my dumb words can ever explain," I press on, relentless in my effort to make her understand that I am not giving up. A world without us together doesn't exist, and she needs to understand that. *She must understand this.*

"You are my universe, and without you, there is nothing..." My voice breaks at the end, emotions too overwhelming to contain any longer.

After a few moments, she lets the knife fall to the floor, the loud thud echoing like the final surrender of our souls to each other.

She is mine!

She is mine!

She accepted me for who I really am!

She is all mine!!!!!

In an instant, I wrap my arms around her, burying my face against her abdomen, inhaling her intoxicating scent. My breathing becomes irregular, out of control as if I've been working out for hours. My muscles tense, and I shiver in front of her. My hands are outward, careful not to get any blood on her. I've traumatized her enough for the next few months, so if I can help it, I definitely should not add to my problems.

She just sits there for a while, letting me hold her but does not say a word.

"I love you, Vita Mia," I say when the silence becomes so unbearable that I am starting to panic again. "Please say something."

I can see the conflict still swirling inside her, the pain clinging to her like a shadow. She's trying to compose herself and fails, but when she finally speaks, her words make my skin crawl.

"I love you, love of my life," she manages to say between the sniffles, her words barely tangible. "I do love you..."

"Please don't say 'but,'" I cut her off, tightening my hold around her. "I am not letting you go, Vita Mia. That ship was never manufactured. It's never going to happen."

She bursts out laughing, and I could breathe again, not realising I was holding my breath. *She laughed!*

"Stop interrupting, you silly boy!" She smacks my shoulder playfully. I immediately pretend to be hurt, wobbling in mock pain. If I need to pretend to be a complete idiot to make her laugh and relax around me, then.... insanity, here I come!

"If there were an Oscar for the worst actor in the world, you'd win it this year."

"*Ha! Ha!* I made you laugh," I squeak, happiness radiating from me. *I am getting through to you!*

"God, I love hearing you laugh, Vita Mia. It sounds like angels are singing."

She's laughing fully now, and the sound is pure delight to my ears. *My woman is beyond perfect. She is magnificent!* Watching her like this makes my chest ache with something so deep, it feels like I might break.

"You are so full of shit!" she teases, her voice light and playful.

God, I love our banter. She's so quick with her tongue and sharp with her mind. *I love it so much!*

"Do you say this kind of stuff to all women?"

And just like that, her words feel like a punch to my gut. *What the fuck?!!!*

"There are no other women," I say, the laughter in me sobering quickly. "There never will be. Since the moment I saw you, I knew in my gut that you're mine. I found my mate, and I'm never letting you go."

I pull back, releasing her, and stand. I promised her I wouldn't force myself on her, and I'm keeping that promise. I stand before her, letting her call the shots.

But every fibre in my body screams to hold her, to scoop her into my arms, carry her back to the bedroom, and love her until she knows, with every cell in her body, that we belong together. I adore this woman with everything in me, and I'm going to make this work, no matter what.

"I love you, love of my life, but I need you to leave." She says in a tender voice.

What the fuck?!!

I try to regulate my breathing, forcing myself not to explode in a million little pieces of pure rage right in front of her. *Breathe, Dominic! Breathe!*

Fuck! Fuck! Fuck!

She's still talking, and I feel my mind panicking, spinning out of control as I try to grasp what she's saying."...love you, and I want to be with you. This doesn't mean we're splitting up. It just means that it's a lot right now, and my head feels like it's about to explode. I need to breathe properly, and right now, I can't do that next to you."

What the actual fuck is happening? My entire body surges with rage and panic, intertwining like fire and ice. *How could I have read the situation so wrong?!*

She's still talking, cheerful now, but I'm blanking out again. "....pushing yourself onto me. Give me a little space to breathe, and then we can talk more. Does that sound like a good plan to you?"

I stand frozen in place, my mind refusing to accept what she's saying. There is no way I'm leaving. *Fuck that shit! NO!*

Is she trying to manipulate me? Is she feeding me what she thinks I want to hear? I replay all that has happened, all her gestures, all her reactions, all her tears.

I don't think she's lying, but the pain searing through my chest is too great for me to take even one step back. *I can't.*

She can read me so easily, sensing the storm raging inside me. She cups one of my cheeks, and just like that, I melt at her feet. The simple touch of her hand is enough to calm the chaos. I place the back of my hand on hers, holding it there, preventing her from moving away.

I need this. I fucking need her touch so much it hurts.

I lean into her palm, closing my eyes and savouring the feel of her soft, silky skin. I can feel her love flowing toward me, even if she doesn't say it. I didn't ask her to do this. She did it on her own.

She loves me! I know she loves me!

She has to love me.

"I love you, Dominic. Please, believe me, I just need time. Please leave," she says, her voice soft but steady now.

"Swear to me that you're not pushing me away," I say, my gaze locked onto hers, needing that final reassurance.

"I swear to you, I'm not pushing you away. You know you're a bit intense, and I genuinely need some air. Then we can talk some more."

I believe her. I have to. Even if her words could lie, her warmth, the way her love radiates from her, none of that can be faked. *I can feel it.* This fight was ugly, exhausting, but absolutely necessary. Sooner or later, she needed to see the truth of who I am, that there are layers to me, darker depths, and that I love her with every inch of my soul.

"And by talk, you mean hot, nasty sex, right?" I joke back with her to lighten the discussion. *Well, a man can always try his luck as well.*

Her beautiful laughter washes over me like a river of pure love, washing my sins away. She is mesmerising when she laughs. It's like the world melts away, and there's only her, radiant and free.

"I made you laugh again," I say, my voice glowing with pride, satisfied beyond measure. I lean into her touch, kissing the inside of her palm, the familiar gesture I've made since our first date. A small but powerful way to show my surrender to her.

I've always been hers. And I'll keep doing this for the rest of my days, kissing her hand, worshipping her, giving her all of me.

I am hers, and she is mine. She can do with me as she pleases, but I will never let her go.

"You're so silly," she says, playfully smacking my shoulder again.

"And by *silly*, you mean hot and sexy as hell, with whom you will have hot, nasty makeup sex later?" I press the banter further, but I can't help the laughter bubbling up inside me.

"That would be a *strong* NO," she replies, smirking. "You and your horny cock can leave, and *later*, we can talk."

Oh, this little minx! She's playing with words, hoping I won't catch it. *News flash, my angel. I notice everything about you!*

"Now, now, you're going backward!" I call her out, amused by her wordplay. "You just said *can* talk. That's less than *will* talk! What's happening? You're going in the wrong direction!" I feign panic, my voice playful, determined to keep the banter going.

"Really? I didn't notice," she teases, her grin growing. "Maybe it's all this cock talk that's making me want to run away screaming."

Oh, my heart! I start laughing so hard my body shakes. This woman, she's the perfect kind of crazy to my crazy. There's no doubt in the universe she was created for me.

She is my mate.

My pair.

My life.

"I made you laugh," she teases softly, her voice holding that pleading edge I can't ignore. She cups my other cheek, and for the first time, it feels like *she* is the one leaning into my touch, absorbing the love I've been offering her all along.

"I love you, Dominic. Please leave."

She needs space, I get that. *Fuck,* that was an intense fight. My hands are still pulsing from the cuts, and I know I'll be dealing with one hell of a scar, but I don't care. None of it matters. All that matters is her.

"I'm not pushing you away," she adds, her tone gentle but firm. "I just need to breathe, love of my life."

She's so unbelievably beautiful, so kind, it wrecks me. There's nothing in this world I wouldn't do or give for her. The way her soft voice mixes with those deep black eyes could bring any man to his knees. But to me, to *me,* it steals my breath, my clarity, my sanity.

She can ask anything of me.

"I really want to kiss you, my angel," I say, giving her the most pleading look I can muster, trying to soften her heart. "But I won't force myself onto you," I add, battling the overwhelming urge to pull her close, pin her down, and devour her in every way. The need is clawing at me, but I gave her my word that I would not push.

"If you want me to leave, I will leave." My words are heavy with resignation, the weight of honouring my promise nearly unbearable. But I gave her my word, and I will honour it.

The shocked look on her face is so adorable. She probably thought I'd bulldoze my way into her bed, disregarding her feelings. *Well, news flash again, Amore Mio. There is nothing above you in my world. If space is what you need, space is what I'll give you.*

Well... within reason, of course.

"It's okay, I'm leaving," I say, my voice soft but pointed. "Just... don't complain about the arrangements," I hint, subtly reminding her she doesn't have complete freedom. *She'll get the best-effort version of freedom.*

With that, I turn and start walking toward the door, every muscle in my body screaming at me to stop. *I don't want to do this.* Every instinct, every fibre of my being, is sounding the alarm, urging me to turn back and plead until she gives in. But I know if I break my word, she'll never respect me again. She'll never fully trust me, and worse, she'll doubt my love for her.

So out the door, I must go.

I open the door, but I pause, looking over my shoulder at her, injecting every ounce of love I have into my eyes.

"I love you, Angela, more than life itself. There is nothing in my universe other than you." And with that, I close the door behind me.

I slowly lower myself to the ground, leaning my back against her door. *If I can't be inside, then here I'll sit, guarding her for the rest of my days. Or until she clears her mind and takes me back, of course.*

Fuck, my hands hurt. The pulsing has lessened, and the bleeding has stopped, but the pain is still there, a constant reminder of everything that just happened. I've stopped moving them, trying to minimise the damage on her floors. The last thing I want is for my angel to have to clean a trail of blood.

"Fuck! The knives are still in her apartment!" I mutter to myself, realising just how out of it I've been to leave weapons like that in her apartment.

She might have heard me. I turn my head, straining to hear any movement inside, but all is quiet. *Good.* Of course, she will find me eventually on her doorstep, literally. But I was counting on a few hours of her just going through the events, what we spoke, the fact that I did tell her the truth, that I love her, that I want her, that I worship her. She needs time to go through all that.

If she finds me now, my chances won't be the same.

Fuck, my hands hurt.

At least I know my knives are sharp, doing what they're meant to do. I glance down, inspecting the damage, trying to see how deep the cuts are when the door suddenly swings open with such force that I fall flat on my back at her feet.

I can't help it. A deep, uncontrollable laughter erupts from me. *Where is this woman coming from with all these astonishing skills? I heard nothing!*

The realisation punches me square in the chest. *She truly is magnificent.* The more I learn about her, the more I'm in awe. *How can someone be so perfect, so incredible?*

"What are you doing, Dominic?" she asks, trying and failing to hold back my laughter. "Did you lose your marbles recently?" The fluttering of her eyelashes at me makes my cock awaken to life in record time. *Fuck, man! Someone cannot be this hot! I am going to lose my mind over my angel.*

I can't stop laughing. Not just at the situation but at how madly in love I am with her. And here I am, flat on my back at her feet, completely vulnerable. It's the perfect representation of how my soul is laid bare before her, worshipping her with everything I have, everything I am.

It's almost poetic, really. The place where I belong, beneath her, adoring her, ready to give my all. My laughter fades into a quiet, contented chuckle as I look up at her, the only thought racing through my mind is how much I love this woman. How *completely* she owns me.

"I told you not to complain about the arrangements," I say with amusement. Well, clearly, she did not think that I was completely leaving, right?

"Are you kidding right now?" She spits out quickly in shock and amusement.

"Vita Mia, you're a flight risk, so I'm parked right here at your door for the foreseeable future," I try to explain. *There's no fucking way I'd ever let her be unsupervised or unmonitored.* That's just absurd! Even if everything was perfect between us. *Fuck, that's never happening.*

"Do you want me to start kicking you again?" she replies, her tone firm, making it clear she's not messing around.

"No, thank you," I say, holding my hands up in mock surrender. *Where the hell did she learn to fight?* That thought crashes into me, bringing both relief and pain. Relief because she can clearly defend herself, my bruises are evidence of that. But pain, wondering why she ever needed to learn this. *Why would my angel need to fight?*

"By the way, why do you fight so well? You know if I end up with bruises, you'll have to kiss them better, right?" I grin at the thought of her naked, kissing every bruise she left on me, spreading warmth through me. *She really has one hell of a kick.*

Then maybe in her administration of kisses, she could "accidentally" slip and land on my cock too, and suck me off as a reward. The image is too ridiculous, and before I can stop myself, a deep laugh escapes. I am enjoying this laughter so much because fuck, that was funny, but I definitely cannot share that thought with her at the moment. Regardless both my brain and my cock are in complete agreement that that thought was possible, preferable and maybe probable.

But before I can relish the thought further, she cuts in, sounding nervous. "Seriously, Dominic, are you out of your mind? You can't sit here at my door like this! I have neighbours. They might call the cops on you..."

"You just say the word, sweetheart, and I'll press the dial," an old woman's voice calls out from across the hall, interrupting her mid-sentence.

Oh, for fuck's sake.

As I slowly get up, all humour drains from me, replaced by a brief flash of irritation at the old woman across the hall. *I could think of a dozen quick and painful ways to silence her, but that wouldn't go over well with my angel.*

I miss our banter! Oh, nosey old woman!

"I could always shoot her, and then we wouldn't have any problem," I say, trying to lighten the mood with a joke. But the look on Angela's face, utterly horrified, is priceless. She's stunned into silence.

She's quiet.

I burst out laughing hard, so much so that it takes me several seconds to get myself under control. "Too soon to joke around like that?" I tease, far too entertained by her reaction.

Injecting as much charm as possible into my voice, I look over at the old woman's door. "There's no problem here, Mrs. Berglin. My name's Dominic DeLuca, and I'm Angela's future husband."

There, that should give her something to think about. Angela's stunned reaction is everything I hoped for. It fills me with a warmth I can't quite describe. *She's mine. Now she knows it's just a matter of time until the entire world knows she is my wife.*

"We're just having a little domestic," I continue, trying to convince the nosy old woman to stay out of it. "As my beautiful wife said, I'm giving her some space, just relaxing here until she realises she loves me more than life itself and lets me back in."

"Oh, how sweet," Mrs. Berglin calls back, her voice muffled through her door. *There you go, old lady! A little charm goes a long way.*

I stifle my laughter, glancing at Angela, who now looks both exasperated and a little pissed at my antics. *Well, at least I got a reaction!*

"Seriously, Dominic?!" She glares at me with so much intensity that it's almost comical and, if I'm honest, adorable. It makes my heart swell, exploding with this raging love for her. She leans in, trying to whisper, but I can feel it coming, her exasperation spilling over.

"My future husband?!" she whispers yells it at me.

A deep, uncontrollable chuckle escapes me because, honestly, she's sweet as honey, even when she's mad. *I bet if I actually bit her hard enough to draw blood, it would taste sweet.* I know her cunt tastes sweet, her skin tastes sweet. *Everything about her must be sweet.*

But no. I can't bite that hard. She'd be mad as hell, and I'm not exactly eager to get kicked again. Although, fuck, there was something satisfying about it. The way she punched and kicked, showing me how strong she is, as fierce as she is beautiful.

Masochism, really? I laugh inwardly. But it's not even about that. I love her with no limits and no boundaries.

There is only her.

"Is today the day you want to die?" Her glare sharpens, but I'm drowning in this ocean of love for her, too far gone to be fazed by anything she does. Everything about her is just... adorable to me.

"If it means I die next to you, I'm okay with that," I say, completely unfazed, my voice dripping with adoration. "Anything for my beautiful wife."

The exasperation on her face is unmistakable, and it's so sweet that I can't help but melt a bit more at her feet. I'm not sure if she's angrier at me or the old lady, but I can tell she's seconds away from detonating again. She studies me, probably wondering what the hell she's going to do with me when her eyes land on my hand. Pure panic flashes across her beautiful face.

I've been holding my hand inwardly so Mrs. Berglin couldn't see the damage, but my angel... she sees everything from where she stands.

"Everything's fine, Mrs. Berglin. Thank you for looking out for me. Dominic's right, we just had a little misunderstanding, but he's about to head out to get something from the shop and give me some space," she says, trying to sound casual, but I can hear the panic in her voice so clearly it's like a knife straight to my heart.

"That's all right, dear. You've got yourself a fine man there. Take care of him," Mrs Berglin calls back, the sound of her TV growing faint in the background. "My show's about to start, but if you need me, just yell, and I'll press dial."

"Thank you, Mrs. Berglin. Bye," she replies sweetly, but her eyes are glued to my bloodied hands.

As soon as the old lady's gone, her attention turns fully to me. "Get. The. Fuck. Off. My. Front. Doorstep."

"Never." The word flies out of me so fast it's instinctual, pure and unfiltered. My love for her isn't planned or calculated. It's instinctive, reactive. There's nothing I wouldn't do for her, and I know she can see it in my face. She's torn, her emotions waging war. Part of her probably wants to jump me and fuck me raw, but the other part? She probably wants to knock me unconscious.

Little does she know, I'm down for both.

I burst out laughing again because, fuck, it's all just too funny, but I know I can't say that. Not when she's this mad. I really shouldn't add to the fire, but it's too late.

"Dominic! I am not joking!" she whisper-yells at me, her voice full of warning. "Get. The. Fuck. Off. My. Front. Doorstep."

"Never, Vita Mia. I will never leave you. Even if I die, I'll come back to haunt you," I say, trying to hold back more laughter.

The look in her eyes is pure, unfiltered rage like she's preparing for a fight to the death.

Fuck! Maybe I'm going in the wrong direction. Maybe she's actually furious and not seeing the humour in my words.

"Easy, baby. Calm, Vita Mia. You look really, really mad right now." Worry floods through me. Maybe joking around isn't the best way to calm her down. *But then what the fuck do I do?*

"You think, genius?" Her voice is sharp, cutting through any illusion that she's cooling off. Her rage, it's like a living, breathing thing now.

Well, fuck! I pissed her off again.

"Get. The. Fuck. Off. My. Front. Doorstep."

I hold her gaze for a few more seconds, trying to figure out what the hell I'm supposed to do next.

"Okay, Vita Mia, I'm leaving," I say, my words clipped, but my eyes are practically begging her to let me stay. "But no funny business. You know I've got cams everywhere, and the bodyguards, too. If you make a run for it, I'll chase you. To the ends of the earth if I must."

Her glare hardens, and suddenly, she looks at me with more fury and hurt than I expected. It catches me off guard. *What did I do now?*

"I don't know about you, but for me, my word has VALUE. If I say I'm doing something or not doing something, that's exactly what I intend to do. No games. No bullshit. So keep your shitty little threats to yourself." With that, she slams the door in my face, the sound reverberating through me like she can't stand the sight of me anymore.

Fuck. She's right.

Sadness, pain, and regret flood my mind. She's made it clear she knows I'm not going anywhere, so maybe I need to ease off the so-called threats. *But where would I go if I left? My entire life is here, next to her. Fucking hell!*

Suddenly, the door cracks open just a bit, and something hits me in the side. Before I can even register what happened, the door slams shut again with brutal force. I look down to see what it is, and my heart melts. It's a first-aid kit.

"You love me!" I yell into the door, happiness overwhelming me despite the pain of our argument.

"Fuck off!" comes her clipped reply.

"You love me! Deny it all you want, Vita Mia, but you love me! You care for me! And you don't want to see me suffer!" I'm literally beaming with joy now, like a fool.

"Dominic," she says, her voice dangerously slow, "if I have to tell you one more time to fuck off, I'm going to lose it." The menace in her words leaves no doubt. I've reached the very edge of her patience.

I stand up to my full height and lean my forehead against the door. "I love you, Angela. More than you could ever possibly imagine." I take a few deep breaths, building the courage to step away, even if it feels like ripping out a piece of my soul. "I'm leaving now."

As I made my way to the car, bandaging my hands with the first-aid kit Angela threw at me, a thought struck me. She'd been so happy about the flowers I gave her last time. Maybe that's the key.

"I'm going to the shop and buy all her mum's flowers. That should ease the fury... I hope," I mutter to myself. *Well, it's clear I'm slowly losing it, talking to myself out loud.*

Fifteen minutes later, I pull into the parking lot, the same place that had started this entire chase for this magnificent creature. As I glance through the window, I see her mum arranging those long-ass flowers again. *Seriously, who buys those ridiculously long flowers?*

"Hello, ma'am," I say, my voice softer than usual, trying to gauge where I stand with her. *Maybe I should have texted Elijah to let him know I'd be stopping by.* I quickly pull out my phone, typing a message.

"Well, hello, Dominic," she says, eyeing me up and down, almost like she's analysing me. *Strange.*

"Put the phone away and come help me," she says, her tone calm, calculated, and confident. *Even stranger.*

"Apologies, just one moment. I need to send this urgent text to my boss," I explain, glancing up briefly to ensure she heard me. But when I meet her gaze, something about it feels off. Her stare is blank, emotionless, almost like Elijah's.

What the fuck? It's unsettling. I can't remember anyone other than Elijah looking at me like that.

Dominic

Apologies, Elijah. Something came up, and I dropped by the flower shop.

I am planning to buy all the flowers for my angel. I am here with her mum now.

I press send and look up to find Angela's mom on her phone, texting as well. *Strange woman, but she's my angel's mother. She gave the world an angel so she can be as strange as she wants.*

As I move around the shop, I start studying the flowers, imagining Angela's apartment full of them, colourful blooms everywhere, filling the air with their divine scent. *Yeah, I think she'll love it.*

My phone pings, but I ignore it for a moment, too wrapped up in the thought of surprising her. She really looked taken with flowers, and if I flood her space with enough of them, maybe it'll soften her up. Maybe, just maybe, she'll soften our fight.

The message flashed on my screen, and a chill ran down my spine. Elijah's text, his reaction... surprises me again.

Elijah

Be very careful, Dominic. Your life depends on this. Next time you speak to Monica, I need to know about it the moment the thought comes into your mind.

Ok.... this is the first time Elijah threatened me. What the fuck? And what's with such a long text?

Dominic

Understood.

When I look at Monica, she's on her phone too, a small, almost knowing smile playing at the corner of her mouth. She's a beautiful woman, no doubt about that, but *utterly and truly fucked* if Elijah has his eyes on her.

If I'm intense, a lot to handle, then Monica stands no chance against someone like Elijah. He operates on a level that goes beyond obsessive. It's surgical, precise. And if she's even remotely entangled with him, it's already too late.

What did she do? I wonder, watching her closely. *Does she even know what's coming?*

The thought rattles me. If my life depends on this, what the hell has she gotten involved in?

I push the thought down, forcing myself to maintain control. Elijah doesn't make mistakes, and if Monica is in his crosshairs, it means she's important, dangerous, even.

I need to tread carefully.

"How can I help?" I ask, keeping my tone calm and professional, though there's a hint of reservation. *The last thing I need is Elijah having cameras here, misreading any charm as something else. I'll lose limbs over this.*

"Come here and help me change the water for the gladiolus," Monica replies, setting her phone down on the counter. "I hope you don't mind. It'll give us a few moments to speak alone." Her smile is wide but doesn't reach her eyes. *I'm confused. There's something about this woman that unnerves me.*

"Of course, not a problem. Which ones are the gladiolus again?" I glance around at the flowers. Besides roses, they're all just flowers to me.

"These," she gestures toward the long-stemmed monstrosities. *Seriously, who buys these?!*

"Yes, of course," I mutter, picking up the bucket of water as she lifts the flowers. She motions for me to change the water at the sink and add two pumps of some chemicals before bringing the bucket back. She carefully arranges the flowers, fixing the loose strands that didn't go in the first time.

"Everything okay with your hands?" She asks, her tone casual but laced with suspicion.

"Yes, of course. Everything's perfectly fine." The response comes out too fast. *I think it stands out to her that something happened.*

She simply makes a noncommittal sound, continuing to rearrange things around the shop, moving vases and buckets as if giving me time to speak. But I have no idea what to say. The silence stretches, and the tension builds until finally, she breaks it with a question that leaves me speechless.

"So, how badly did you fuck up?"

What the hell?

I'm speechless.

It takes me a moment to find my voice. I wasn't expecting her to be this blunt. *I can't tell her I monumentally screwed up because I need her on my side. But if I downplay it, Angela might tell her the truth. And if I tell her to back off... well, Elijah would probably kill me.*

Hopeful, it is.

"I hope nothing a home full of flowers wouldn't alleviate," I reply, my tone calm, though there's a quiet plea underneath it.

Monica straightens up, her gaze piercing, eerily like Elijah's, as she looks me up and down before locking eyes with me. It makes me even more nervous. There's something about her that puts me on edge, like I can't fully trust turning my back on her. *Is this how a mother-in-law feels? Feels strange.*

"I see..." she says slowly, choosing her words carefully. "I'm sure Angela handled herself well." Her look is almost daring me to say anything less about her daughter.

She might be my angel, who was made for me, but I have to admit that this woman gave birth to my angel and has taken care of her until now. And for that, I will forever be grateful to this woman. If she wants me to band the knee in front of her as well, I will, she gave me my angel. For that alone, I owe her my respect.

“Angela stood her ground,” I say, letting my emotions shine through my words. “She’s an extraordinary woman. The more I get to know her, the more I realise how perfectly her name fits.”

Monica’s expression softens just slightly, and her noncommittal sound is now more of an agreement. Her gaze lingers on me for a moment longer, and a small smile plays on her lips.

This is the moment. I steady myself and press on. Sooner or later, this conversation had to happen.

"I love her, and I want to spend the rest of my life taking care of her, just being in her presence," I say, my voice calm but steady, laying it all out there.

For a moment, neither of us speaks. We just hold each other's gaze, and it feels like more is being said in the silence than my words ever could. The truth is out there now, hanging between us, and there's no taking it back. She knows exactly how I feel. She probably knows I’d fight for Angela if it came down to it, but something tells me not to push my luck by saying Angela doesn’t have a choice.

The instinct for self-preservation, I think wryly. Because my gut tells me Monica might pull a knife on me and carve me into tiny pieces. And if not her, Elijah would definitely take care of it if he thought I was speaking out of line to Monica.

So, I decide the best approach here isn’t force, it’s a more humble, *pretty please let me have your daughter* tactic.

“I know I’m a lot,” I say softly, my voice carrying a hint of vulnerability. “But I swear to you, I’ll spend every day proving to her, and to you, that I’m worthy of her.”

Monica’s gaze doesn’t waver, her face unreadable. It’s unnerving, but I stand firm, waiting, not pushing too hard. This isn’t the kind of woman you pressure. She's sharp, and even if I don't fully understand the weight of who she is, my instincts scream not to underestimate her.

The silence stretches, and I force myself to stay calm, my hands at my sides, resisting the urge to fidget. Every second feels like an eternity, but I need her on my side. More than that, I need her respect.

Monica finally nods, though the smile on her face still doesn't reach her eyes. "Yes, I do appreciate you taking care of that little misunderstanding Jake had with her."

I knew it! There was no way Elijah had taken an interest in some shady lawyer and asked me to prove myself for something that minor.

"Absolutely anything for my angel," I say, confidence radiating through my words, my posture straightening just a bit more.

She holds my gaze for what feels like another eternity, her eyes searching me, likely probing for any hesitation, any cracks. I stand firm, not letting even a flicker of doubt show. *She has to know that I would burn the world for Angela if I had to.*

But there's still something unnerving about the way she looks at me, like she's weighing more than just my words. *Does she know the truth about what we do?*

"Know this, Dominic," Monica says, her voice terrifying in its simplicity, "if my baby suffers, your suffering will be ten times greater. If you break my baby's heart, you will beg for death long before its sweet relief comes your way."

She says it with the same ease one might use to ask for another bucket of water. But the weight of her words crashes into me like a landslide.

"Understood," I reply, my voice steady, though the chill runs deep in my bones.

This isn't a threat. It's a promise she just delivered.

Monica doesn't break eye contact, as if she's making sure her message has fully sunk in. I don't waver. I know this woman could do worse than I could imagine, and Elijah would probably help her.

"Very well then," she continues, with a full smile on her face. "Go get me some oasis blocks from the back."

The standoff is over, and I passed. I think to myself, relief and disbelief swirling together. *These women are something else, making killers shit themselves. Seriously, what the fuck?*

I start walking in the direction Monica is pointing, but there's a lot of random shit piled around. I can't even remember what she called it, something about a brick. I'm rummaging through boxes and buckets, but for the life of me, I can't see any bricks. *What the actual fuck? Is she messing with me?*

"My apologies, Mrs. Puscasu, but I'm not quite sure what I'm looking for," I say, my voice calm and professional, though my blood is boiling. Ten minutes in this cramped room, and I still haven't found it. All I want is to get out of here and back to my angel.

"You can call me Monica," she yells from the front shop, her tone smooth, "and you're looking for a green brick that feels dusty when you touch it."

Well, fuck me sideways. I turn and spot an entire box of the stuff in the corner. *This shit's been sitting here the whole time?* I've wasted ten minutes on a box of dusty green bricks. The damn dust is probably in my nose, eyes, ears, any exposed hole at this point.

"I brought the entire box. How funny it does look like a brick." I try to sound playful and amused, but I really want just to run back to the apartment. "What do you do with it?" Honest curiosity hits me because this looks completely useless to me.

"This is what the flower arrangements sit in," she delivers her answer with a warm smile and then studies me for a second. "Also, calm down. If you are here, it means she needed a breather from you, so relax and come help me arrange all the flowers because you will help me deliver them later."

Right! Well, I know now why I feel weary of her... *she can read minds.*

"Yes, of course. How can I help?"

She directs me to change the water in various vases filled with vibrant, colorful flowers, the kind I know my angel would love. An hour passes, and we're almost done. The shop is now lined with crystal and ceramic vases, each filled with different arrangements of beautiful blooms. I can't help but admire the work, even though my hands are still throbbing. As I pay the $30k bill, I hope it's enough, not just the flowers, but the effort. I want Angela to see that I did this for her despite the state of my hands.

Just as we stand to get back to it, my phone pings.

I freeze. *That sound...* It's the distinct tone reserved only for P1 security emergencies.

Fuck! Fuck! Fuck!

Pure panic floods my system, and for a brief second, I'm frozen in place. *Angela.* My mind spirals, my heart pounding out of control as every fear hits me at once. *What's happening? Is she safe?*

"Are you okay, Dominic?" Monica's voice breaks through the fog of my panic, yanking me back to the present. I snap into gear, my body moving on instinct.

Without a word, I whip out my phone, my mind racing. *What the hell happened?*

P1 – Security breach

> An explosion took place at level one of the Barrow Building. Casualties not confirmed. Evacuation notification pending.

All the colour drains from my face. *We are under attack.*

Fuck! Fuck! Fuck!

I try calling Angela, but there's no answer. My hands are shaking as I frantically text her, the panic surging through me. Monica is saying something next to me, but I can't focus, my mind is too scrambled.

Fuck! Fuck! Fuck!

Then I feel Monica's hand on my arm, warm, steady. It stops the chaos in my mind for just a second. "What's happened?" Her voice is calm, warm, like an anchor pulling me back.

"We're under attack. There was an explosion," I say, my voice drained of all strength. I turn to her, desperate for any sign that this isn't as bad as I think it is. But Monica... she's on her phone, reading a text, and then she looks up at me with a smile like everything's fine. It's like she's not worried at all. In fact, she looks... *excited*?

I'm surely reading this wrong.

"Read your texts," she says, almost as if she can read my thoughts.

I blink and realise I've got several unread messages waiting for me, some from Elijah.

Fuck! Fuck! Fuck!

My hands are still shaking as I unlock my phone to read them, praying for anything that might give me some clarity if my angel is safe.

Elijah

Get Monica out now! Panic room City Hall.

Dominic! Get Monica out now!

I'm going to kill you.

Fuck! Fuck! Fuck!

Dominic

Apologies, boss. We are leaving now.

"We got to go!" I bark, my tone short and urgent as I start for the door. But when I glance back, Monica isn't behind me. *What the fuck?*

She's still calmly fidgeting with things on her counter, completely unbothered by the chaos that's about to unfold.

I spin around, frustration clawing at me, my breath coming in sharp, ragged bursts. I know I shouldn't touch her, and I definitely can't just throw her over my shoulder, so I'm left with one option, begging.

"Monica, please," I say, my voice cracking under the strain. "There was an explosion. We don't know the severity of the attack yet, and I need to get you to a panic room. Now."

She looks up from the counter, entirely unfazed, like I've just asked her to change a vase of flowers, not run for her life. "Oh, my boy. It's all good. Is not just you here, Elijah has three cars of bodyguards watching the store at all times."

Wait, what?

"All done. We can go now." Monica's voice is casual as if she hadn't just dropped a figurative bomb on me. *This is the first time she's admitted something about Elijah,* I realise, but there's no time to dwell on it.

We head toward my car, but once again, she's not beside me the next moment I check. *What the hell?* She's back at her shop door, fiddling with it like it's just a lazy Sunday afternoon. *It's not fucking Sunday afternoon!* My thoughts scream at the absurdity of the situation.

"Monica, do you need help? We really need to go!" I snap, trying to rein in the frustration. "I need to get you to safety and figure out who's extracted Angela."

That gets her attention.

"Extract Angela?" Her voice is suddenly small, almost... petrified. It's the first time I've seen any hint of vulnerability from her.

"Yes, of course," she nods. "Let's get going." She finally moves toward the car, and as soon as she's settled inside, she pulls out her phone and starts texting, her fingers flying over the keyboard with surprising speed. If I didn't know better, I'd think she was in her twenties with that kind of texting speed.

It takes me five minutes of intense speed, focused driving to reach the City Hall panic room. But calling it a "room" doesn't do it justice, it's an entire wing, discreetly integrated into the main building. Our team had transformed it into a fortress, complete with a reinforced structure, tungsten doors, and an independent communication system. Satellite phones, hidden climate control, and air circulation that doesn't show up on any maps, connected to filters in three different buildings two kilometers away. Three power generators as backup to the primary system in this wing, enough life-sustaining amenities to last 100 people for a month.

I remember when we developed this project, I was floored by what money could buy. Back then, the officials didn't even blink when Elijah presented the plans. They practically scrambled over each other, trying to shove their noses higher up his ass for a bigger paycheck. But now, as I park the car and escort Monica inside, I understand why Elijah spared no expense.

It's for our loved ones.

For our women, we'd burn the world for, no matter the cost. The luxury of power and resources is all worth it when you know it's protecting the only people that matter.

As we approach the entrance to the main rooms, Monica's earlier calm slips back into place. But I catch a flicker of something as if she is completely back in control of the situation owning the room and everyone in it.

As we enter the secured wing, part of the UBT is already here, their presence giving me my first real breath of relief since this whole thing started. But then I notice Monica has stopped. She's waiting for me to turn and face her, away from the room and the others. I discreetly pivot, making sure my back is to the team, shielding our exchange.

"Angela is safe," she says quietly. "She's on her way here with someone named Aleksey Maetney. I understand he's a trusted person and can deliver her safely."

The flood of relief that hits me is so overwhelming I nearly drop to my knees. *She's safe. My angel is safe.* Now, I understand why Monica waited for this private moment. She knew what her words would do to me, and she gave me the space to react without exposing that vulnerability to anyone else.

I hold her gaze, gratitude passing between us without a single word exchanged. Monica knew what this meant for me, and for that, I owe her.

But then, over Monica's shoulder, I catch sight of Alec speed-walking in, his sharp, no-nonsense frown in place, and right behind him, Angela. My heart races, anchoring one arm on the edge of the door as I try to steady my breathing.

She's safe. She's here. I can breathe again.

If glares could kill, Alec would be a dead man. Angela doesn't even notice us as she sends murderous looks to the back of his head.

"Vita Mia..." My voice trails off as she gets closer. Suddenly, she breaks into a run and throws herself into my arms. I catch her, pulling her tightly to me, feeling her warmth and presence melt away the last remnants of panic.

"Are you okay, love of my life?" Her hands frantically move over my face, checking me for injuries. I just nod, not trusting my voice to be steady. "Are you sure?" She says, patting my body, desperate to find any sign of harm.

"I'm perfectly fine now, Vita Mia. You're safe. That's all that matters to me." But as the words leave my mouth, I lift her hand to kiss her inner palm, and that's when I notice the bruises on her wrists. Deep, dark bruises that look like the marks of tight handcuffs.

My vision goes red.

I reach for her wrists, gently brushing my fingers over the marks. She flinches, and something inside me snaps. An overwhelming rage surges through my body, obliterating any sense of calm and self-control. The thought that someone laid a hand on my angel, restraining her like this, shakes me to my core.

Who did this?

The violent side of the beast inside me, the one I keep carefully controlled, roars to life, demanding retribution.

"Oh, he put them on because I didn't want to leave with him. I was scared he was kidnapping me, so I had to..."

I didn't even hear the rest of what my angel said. My brain shuts down, consumed by rage. In an instant, I lunge at Alec with everything I've got, fury driving me forward with sheer force.

Before I know it, we're locked in a full-on fight. My fists slam into him relentlessly, each hit fueled by the image of the bruises on Angela's wrists. Every punch, every hit, is backed by the fire of my rage, and I can't think of anything else but making him pay for laying a hand on her.

Alec fights back, but it doesn't matter. I'm not holding back, and nothing can stop me now. *This is for Angela.* This is for the fear she must have felt for the marks on her skin.

The room around us erupts in chaos, but it all blurs into the background. All I can hear are my fists connecting with Alec, the roar of the beast inside me fully unleashed.

"Dominic! Alec!" Elijah's deep voice booms in the room as if a gun just went off.

Chapter Twenty-One

Angela

As I finish getting dressed after my bath, I feel the warmth lingering in my muscles, and my mind, though still tangled, is calmer than it's been all day. *I should be furious,* I remind myself. That's what I expect to feel anger, rage and betrayal. But none of it hits me. Instead, if I'm honest with myself, I feel... *relieved.*

He's said it so many times, in so many ways. There's no escaping this. No escaping us. And somewhere deep down, I know he's right. Without a doubt, *I am his.* And as much as I resist admitting it, *he's mine too.*

I think back to the moment with the knives. He gave me that choice. And I didn't stab him. *That counts for something, doesn't it?* In a way, it was my own quiet claim over him, even if I wasn't bold enough to say the words outright.

I sigh. *Who am I kidding?* I could have been a bit more vocal. I could have owned it instead of retreating into my confusion.

Now, the guilt starts creeping in. My muscles tense again, undoing all the relaxation from the bath, and a headache begins to pulse at my temples.

No! No! Stop it! I push the feeling away. *He didn't tell me the whole truth from the beginning. I had every right to lose my mind in rage.* He's a killer, after all. My heart flinches at the word, but regret immediately floods in. *Is that all he is?* I'm labelling him, reducing him to something so much smaller than he is.

Because, truthfully, Dominic is so much more. He's intense, overwhelming, and obsessive, but he's also the most incredible man I've ever met. The one who understands me for the real me, who fights for me, the weak me, who loves me fiercely in ways I never thought possible.

I stare at my reflection in the mirror, and honestly, I don't know why Dominic would love me this much. The girl staring back at me isn't all that special. She's the same small, slightly chubby girl who was too scared to speak her mind for so long. She is the same girl that had to throw up to become smaller. The same girl who thought the only way to matter was to shrink herself, literally and emotionally.

Don't go there, my mind screams at me in panic, warning me not to open that can of worms today.

"Whatever it is that he saw in me, it must be special," I murmur to the girl in the mirror. *I mean, he handed me those knives. He told me to do whatever I wanted with him. Who even says something like that?*

I keep staring as if trying to find what Dominic sees. "I think he really loves you," I say to my reflection, my voice shaky but steady enough to linger in the air.

"He loves you."

"He. Loves. You. Angela."

The words echo, getting louder in my mind, sinking deeper into my heart. My eyes fill with tears at the realisation. It hits me all at once, no matter how small, how insignificant I feel, Dominic loves me.

Out of all the girls he could have had in this world, *he picked me.* He wants me. He loves me. And there's no doubt about it.

"He. Loves. Me!"

I'm lost in thought, staring at my reflection, thinking of Dominic, when the door to my bedroom flies open. A man is standing there, staring at me.

"What the fuck?!"

"Angela Puscasu?" His voice is detached, icy cold, and full of urgency. For a moment, I just stare, completely stunned. *Who is this? Why is he in my apartment, worse, in my bedroom? And how does he know my name?*

I need to fight. I need to defend myself!

I snap out of the shock and prepare to attack him. As I brace myself, his deep, commanding voice cuts through the air.

"You need to come with me." The finality in his tone rings like an order, as if I actually have to obey him.

"Like fuck I will!" I snap, and without hesitation, I lunge at him, throwing an elbow punch to the top of his head, a move meant to disorient and drop an opponent. The hit lands true, and he shakes his head, clearly dazed. I aim for his knee next, hoping to knock him to the ground, but he dodges at the last second, jumping back.

"Cut the crap, woman. You need to come with me!" His voice now carries frustration, as if he's had enough of me.

"And I told you, like fuck I'm going with you!" My voice is low, dangerous. I lock my eyes on him, ready for whatever comes next. "If you don't want your arse handed to you by a woman, I suggest running now. Because if you don't, I will unleash every bit of fury I've got, and trust me, I've got plenty."

The tension in the room thickens as we standoff, both prepared for the next move. He doesn't back down, and neither will I.

And then it's on. We both lunge at each other, my body moving on instinct, putting every ounce of power into my kicks and punches. Adrenaline floods my veins, and I'm fighting with everything I have. But after a few moments, something clicks. He isn't really fighting back.

He's just deflecting my strikes, blocking each hit with ease, but never throwing one of his own. He's not actively attacking me.

What the hell is this? He's not fighting me, not really. Just fending me off.

"Stop it!" His voice booms, breathing steadily despite the intensity. "I'm not here to hurt you."

I hesitate for a split second, my mind racing. *Then why is he here?*

But I don't stop. My body won't let me. So I swing again, harder this time, trying to break through his defence, trying to make sense of this.

"Oh, fuck!" The voice of another man resonates from behind me. For a split second, I hope it might be Dominic's bodyguard, and I'll be okay. But then immense arms wrap around me, completely immobilising me in his hold.

Fuck! This is bad! Really, really bad!

"You okay, Alec?" the deep voice booms next to my ear. "Did the little girl get you, man?" The voice turns mocking, as if a girl could really hurt him. I respond by lifting my leg and kicking as hard as I can with the heel of my foot into the tailbone of the gorilla carrying me. A growl erupts from him at the unexpected pain.

"Who are you calling little, gorilla?" I spit out with all the venom I can muster.

"Fuck!" The gorilla growls again, clearly annoyed.

"Handcuffs!" Alec yells.

"Fuck no! Fight me like a man, Alec," I retort, my voice dripping with defiance. *Now I know his name!* "You're not afraid of a little girl, are you?" My tone mocks him, daring him to continue.

"You are coming with us, Angela. Like it or not," Alec says, locking eyes with me as he handcuffs me so tightly I know I'll have bruises for days on my wrists.

"I'm not going anywhere!" I yell, planting my feet firmly on the ground to resist being moved.

"Up you come," the gorilla says, throwing me over his shoulder as if I'm just another day's work.

They handcuff my ankles as well, then throw me into the boot of an SUV. I can see outside, hoping like hell someone will notice me and that I can alert them, but the speed at which they're driving is insane. He's not driving, he's flying across the road, and I'm bumping left, right, and centre as I brace for dear life. The entire ride I push, kick and scream for attention, with no avail. I am completely stuck with these two, and all my power will go into defending myself the moment we arrive

We pull into the City Hall entry, and the car comes to a sharp stop. That's when I noticed Dominic's car and the massive doors shut behind us. The gorilla picks me up and throws me over his shoulder again, carrying me like a sack of potatoes.

"People will notice me!" I shout, trying to threaten them. "What did you do to Dominic?"

"We didn't do anything to Dominic," Alec spits out, clearly irritated beyond measure. "We work with him. There was an emergency, and since I was closest to your apartment and the senior in the lot, I had to come get you." His voice is filled with exasperation. "Fucking unbelievable," he mutters under his breath, taking two steps at a time.

“I heard that!” I shout, still trying to assert control.

“Good! Now run along, little girl, and leave me the fuck alone.” Alec gestures to the gorilla, who sets me down before removing the handcuffs. Alec turns on his heels and storms off around a corner, disappearing from sight.

I follow, watching his every move, ready for him to turn back and try something. My guard is still up as I approach what looks like a large conference room of some sort. My gaze shifts slightly to the left, and that’s when I see Dominic... and my mum.

Thank God he’s safe!

My legs move before I can think, sprinting toward Dominic. He catches me in his arms, and I feel his entire body trembling as he holds me tightly. To see Dominic unharmed makes my entire body unwind at the relief that Alec did not lie. The unbelievable dread that something might’ve happened to him hits me all at once, and I start to check him frantically for injuries.

"Are you okay, love of my life?" He nods, but the gesture only makes me panic more. "Are you sure?" My hands keep patting his body, desperate to find any sign of harm.

"I'm perfectly fine now, Vita Mia. You're safe. That's all that matters to me." His voice is so calm, so full of love, that it heals my fractured heart. As his hands travel softly over my skin, he lifts my hand to kiss the inside of my palm, but he freezes, staring at the bruises forming around my wrists.

He brushes his fingers over the marks, and even that light touch makes me wince. The fury radiating from Dominic is palpable, it's like a storm brewing just beneath the surface, and I can feel it ready to erupt. As much as I want to be mad at Alec myself, I realise that he might have actually saved me from something tonight.

I need to deescalate this. Now!

"Oh, he put them on because I didn’t want to leave with him," I explain hurriedly. "I thought he was kidnapping me, so I fought back.

He didn't expect it, so he used the handcuffs to immobilise me. That's all."

But it's like none of what I said registered with Dominic. One moment, he's gently holding my hand, inspecting the bruises, and in the next, he's lunging at Alec with such speed and fury that I'm frozen in shock.

Dominic lunges at Alec with terrifying speed, his fist arcing toward Alec's jaw. Alec sidesteps just in time, deflecting the blow and striking back with his elbow into Dominic's ribs. Dominic barely reacts, taking the hit as if it's nothing, his expression tightening with a focus so intense it's unnerving. He counters immediately, his body coiled like a spring as he swings a brutal uppercut, and while Alec dodges Dominic's next move, a swift, low kick connects, making Alec stumble.

Their movements blend into a fierce, unspoken rhythm, each strike and block so calculated it's like a violent dance. But there's something different in Dominic's energy a raw, unrestrained power that Alec seems unable to match. Every strike from Dominic feels like it's driven by something deeper, a protective rage that radiates from him, giving him an edge that's both exhilarating and terrifying to witness. My heart pounds as I watch, caught between awe at his sheer power and dread for what might happen next.

"Dominic, no!" I scream, but my voice is drowned in the chaos erupting around me. The room is in total disarray, people are shouting, trying to get through to them, but no one dares to step between Dominic and Alec. Broken furniture and scattered objects litter the floor, evidence of the violent clash that just unfolded. The two men are breathing heavily, circling each other, glaring with unrelenting fury. Dominic's entire body is taut with anger, his eyes locked on Alec with a look of sheer disgust.

"You put your filthy porn star hands on her," Dominic spits the words out like venom, his voice sharp and dripping with contempt. I'm stunned, trying to process what he just said. *Porn star? Filthy hands? What?*

"What the fuck did you want me to do? Leave her there? I'll leave her next time there's a P1!" Alec fires back, his fury palpable as he squares up to Dominic.

"Why the fuck were you even anywhere near her apartment, you sorry, horny fuck?" Dominic growls, his voice a low, dangerous rumble.

"Dominic, I understand you're mad, but if you don't stop this shit right now, it's on my brother!" Alec's voice shakes with rage, his words carrying a deadly ultimatum. But Dominic's rage is unhinged.

"You're no brother of mine, you sorry excuse for a human being!" With that, they're at each other's throats again, a whirlwind of punches and grappling that leaves me immobilised, utterly shocked. I'm speechless, overwhelmed by this raw, unfiltered side of Dominic. This man, who had stood still and allowed me to kick and punch him without retaliation, was now fighting with a ferocity I hadn't even imagined he possessed.

"Dominic! Alec!" A booming voice reverberates through the room, sharp and commanding, cutting through the chaos like a gunshot.

"Enough!" The finality in the man's tone silences the room with such authority that no one dares to move. It's as if we've all been frozen, turned into statues by his sheer dominance. Even Dominic and Alec, locked in their furious standoff, seem momentarily paralysed.

I glance over at my mother. She's casually texting on her phone, a small smile tugging at the corners of her lips. *Why is she so calm?*

"Are you okay, Mum? Why are you even here?" I ask, the confusion swirling inside me as I try to make sense of everything. Dominic, Alec, the man who just stopped the fight, all of it feels surreal. In the background, people are picking up broken items, the remnants of the scuffle. It's like the aftermath of a storm.

"I'm fine, my darling," she replies, her voice as steady as ever. "That was a bit intense, but your man can handle himself in a fight." There's pride in her tone. "It's good, though. At least now you know he can protect you."

I sink into one of the nearby couches, the adrenaline from everything leaving me exhausted. My mother sits next to me, sliding her phone into her bag. We sit in silence for a moment, watching as the room slowly returns to order.

"Do you know what's happening?" I ask after a beat. "And... why are you here, exactly?" The pieces aren't fitting together, and my head feels like it's spinning. There's a growing suspicion in the pit of my stomach that this has something to do with Dominic's "other" job.

"Dominic came by the shop," she says nonchalantly, like this is just any other day. "Bought all the flowers, too. Charged him thirty grand."

"What?!" I exclaim, taken aback by her casual attitude. "Mum!"

"Shhh!" she whispers, grinning. "I transferred fifteen thousand to you for the trouble. He admitted he messed up, and from the way you two greeted each other earlier, I'd say things are good now."

I shake my head in disbelief. "Thirty thousand? Mum, that's... painful. I'll talk to him. I'll send back the fifteen and apologise."

"Like hell you will!" She cuts me off, her tone firm. "Listen, he didn't even blink at the price. I wanted to see how he'd react, and let me tell you, that man is smitten. Then I asked him to help arrange the flowers. He didn't complain once, even with his hands all banged up. He was lugging heavy vases with water, carrying flowers and he's injured. Do you know anything about his hands?"

I freeze. The image of Dominic's hands, bruised and bloodied, flashes in my mind. A mix of guilt and protectiveness rises in my chest. He hadn't said much about the injuries, but I could tell they weren't minor. His shouts from when I threw the First AID kit at him echo in my mind, *You love me!* and I just told him to fuck off. *I am the worst person in the world.*

This suffocating sensation is taking over me. *Where is he? Is he okay? Are they going to kill him? Fuck!* They might kill him for that fight. *Quick! What do I do?!*

"He received this text and then told me we needed to leave," my mum continues, completely oblivious to the absolute panic consuming me. *Play it cool, Angela. Mum can't find out Dominic's a killer.*

"He said it's some type of emergency and that you'd be here soon. Are you okay, Angela?"

No, I'm not okay. I'm far from okay. I've fallen completely, irrevocably in love with an amazing man who also happens to be a killer. And the worst part? I'm happy. I'm happy that he is in my life. He's beautiful, intelligent, sophisticated, and equally, he's intense, obsessive, and dark. I love the light in him just as much as I love his darkness. He's everything... my other half.

"Yes, of course, I'm okay. Why wouldn't I be?" I try to smile at Mum with as much conviction as possible, but then I remember she can see right through me. I sigh. "I'm just scared he'll get in trouble because of the fight. I don't even know who that man was, and they all followed him like little puppies."

Mum bursts out laughing, and I'm taken aback by her reaction. "At least Dominic was kind enough to take you with him, Mum. I don't even know what this emergency is about, but it can't be good."

"Yes, I agree. It was very kind of him to take me to safety," she says in her usual confident, polite tone. "I think he really loves you, Angela, to see the value in keeping me safe."

Then, with a playful smile, she adds, "That other man? Definitely the boss. Did you see how he carried himself?" She wiggles her eyebrows, and I can't help but laugh at how silly she looks.

"You're so silly sometimes," I giggle under my breath, but then something on the TV catches my eye an explosion in the city. "What the hell?" I mutter, reading the news ribbon as fast as I can since the volume is muted. The last thing I want is to say something that gets Dominic into more trouble. As I glance around the room, I don't recognise anyone, until I do. It's that gorilla who carried me around earlier. I am *definitely* not talking to him.

"There was an explosion," I say, turning to my mum, my voice filled with surprise. My eyes stay glued to the screen, but from the corner of my eye, I notice the guys walking back into the room. A wave of relief washes over me, but I don't dare stand up or run to Dominic. I really, *really* don't want to make things worse. As he approaches, I notice bruises already forming on his beautiful face, and my heart skips a beat. Alec trails right behind him, a murderous look in his eyes, and I realise they're both headed straight for me.

Oh, shit.

"My sincere apologies for accidentally tightening the handcuffs too much. It was an oversight, and I apologise," Alec says, his voice short and clipped, catching me completely off guard. I'm as muted as the TV, unable to respond. He turns, walks over to the bar and pours himself a large drink.

Dominic sits beside me, taking my hand in his. He kisses it softly, then presses a kiss to the inside of my palm.

"You ok, Vita Mia?" Dominic says, turning to face me.

Now that I see him upclose, I think some of the bruises are from me. *Oh, you stupid woman!*

"Yes, love of my life. Are you ok?" my voice is full of concern, at this point, I don't care who hears me or knows how much Dominic means to me.

"I will leave you to it." My mum says as she stands and walks off to the bar.

"What's happening, Dominic?"

"Vita Mia..." His voice trails off, heavy with exhaustion. I can see him struggling to measure every word. "I wasn't joking about how much I hate hearing you say my name. Please, Amore Mio, it's been such a long day. Have mercy on me." The look of pain and brokenness on his face says it all. I didn't mean it the way it sounded, but I can see how it's hurting him. Without a second thought, I reach out and begin peppering kisses all over his face.

"I'm sorry, love of my life. Moving forward, I'll always call you *love of my life*, even when I'm mad." He relaxes a little at that, leaning in and resting his face in the crook of my neck. He stays like that for a few minutes, just letting the tension melt away in my arms. Then he inhales deeply, breathing in my scent, before slowly pulling back.

He reaches for his phone, pulls it out, and hands it to me.

P1 – Security breach

An explosion took place at level one of the Barrow Building. Casualties not confirmed. Evacuation notification pending.

P1 – Evacuation personal

Hi Dominic.⊠
Based on your location, please evacuate Monica Puscasu as your first priority.⊠
Drop off: City Hall.⊠
Urgency: Critical.⊠
Impact: Critical.

P1 – Security breach update

The Barrow building security has been compromised.⊠
A bomb has detonated in the East wing of level 1.⊠
20 people are confirmed dead, 15 injured, and 10 people still missing.⊠
Next update in one hour.

I keep reading every message, and the reality is staring me in the face, as clear as day, and playing on the TV on repeat. Dominic is involved in some really heavy shit. *Someone bombed them?* How did my mum and I get stuck in the middle of all this?

I glance over at Mum, and *the boss*, the older man, is standing next to her at the bar. I catch his eye for a second, but I can't hold his gaze. He's so intimidating, no wonder the guys follow him like puppies. Is he the head of all this? Why isn't he panicking more? *Why isn't Mum panicking more?*

"Vita Mia, I know this is a lot, but I promise, you're safe," Dominic's voice pulls me back to him.

The moment our eyes meet, I see the truth in them. He really doesn't think I'm in danger.

"I don't understand," I whisper. "If we're not in danger, why did Alec take me? Why did you take my mum?"

"I added you to the list of people valuable to the organisation to keep you safe. In situations like this, if I can't reach you in time, the AI alerts the closest UBT member to protect you. It's all about keeping you safe." He leans forward, resting his forehead on mine. "I swear, Amore Mio, it's to keep you safe. There's no world where I could survive if you weren't in it."

His words hit me deeply because I know, without a doubt, that he's telling the truth. "But my mum? Why did you get her?" I can feel a shift in his demeanour as he pulls back to meet my eyes.

"I didn't add her," he admits. "Someone else did. I can look into it, but... I'd ask you not to push too hard on this." The look on his face says everything. It's that professional 'I know, but I can't tell' look. *Fucking hell!* I glance over at Mum, who's still standing next to the boss, her back to me, while he's staring straight at me.

"He's scary," I whisper, covering my mouth, unsure if this guy can read lips.

"Who?" Dominic follows my gaze. "Elijah? He's not scary, Amore Mio. He's special, really special. I've never met anyone like him in my life." The confidence in Dominic's voice starts to ease my nerves, making me think this might not be as bad as I first thought. "He saved me," Dominic continues, and his voice breaks at the end.

"Italy?"

"Yes." Dominic's voice is so small it twists something deep inside me. I reach over, pulling him close, then shift to sit sideways on his lap, keeping my arms wrapped tightly around him. "I was as broken as anyone could be, and he saved me." A shiver runs through me at his words and the tremor in his voice. I never thought he would open up about Italy, the horrible scars on his back, the pain he carries. I always assumed it was a Pandora's box he'd never open, not even for me.

"He didn't have to save me. He gained nothing from it. But he chose to." His body trembles slightly under my hand, and all I can offer is a tighter embrace and a feather-light kiss on the side of his neck. "I know a lot of the people in the organisation are like me. He saved them somehow. He doesn't rule by fear. He rules by loyalty and respect."

He turns slightly so he can hold my gaze and lets out a long sigh. "Please, Vita Mia. Just give him a chance. He truly is special."

This is the second time tonight that I've had the feeling of raw truth staring me straight in the face. And just like before, all I can do is stay quiet, accept it, and let things be. Certain things are better left untouched, especially when they're delicate. The last thing I want is to realise a few days from now that my good intentions have turned into a 100-karat piece of shit.

I hold Dominic's gaze, and we have a silent conversation, like an old couple who doesn't need words, even though we only confessed our feelings yesterday. Our relationship is so fresh that if I really think about it, the instinct to run resurfaces. But as Dominic said, *that ship can't sail because it was never built.*

"Right, then," I say, breaking the silence, leaning in to kiss him discreetly. "Is Alec okay?"

"Nope. I really fucked up."

"Why? You were trying to defend me."

"It does not matter. I crossed the line. If it were only physical, then it would not have mattered, but I humiliated him in front of everyone by bringing up his past. That's why Elijah intervened." Dominic continues and lowers his gaze at the hand that is now resting on his chest.

"I don't get it. What is it, the remark about the filthy porn hands?"

“Shhh. Let’s get you home. We can talk more on the way,” he says softly. “He’s my brother, after all. I don’t want to make things worse for him.”

Dominic stands and offers me his hand, entwining our fingers as if it’s second nature, then walks over to the gorilla like it’s nothing.

“Adam, I’d like you to meet Angela,” he says, his tone authoritative, carrying himself like the boss he truly is. “You will guard her with your life from this moment on.”

This is Dominic in his *Field Lead* role, and tonight, I definitely saw that side of him.

Adam is holding my gaze for the briefest moment and then just nods. "Adam was assigned to you from the beginning, but I thought now that you know who I am, it would be easier for Adam, Kane and Caleb to be seen by you."

"I will be with Angela tonight, let Kane and Caleb know."

Adam just nods again, and it is as if this new version of the gorilla is a different one. The one with Alec was quick and sharp with his tongue to provoke him. But apparently, Dominic has enough stature for Adam to just nod not even say a word in front of him.

My mum walks over, and her expression hasn’t faltered this entire time. You’d swear she deals with this kind of thing every day, considering how unfazed she seems. *What the hell?*

"Ready to go, Mum?" I try to analyse her every movement, but she seems so comfortable, almost too comfortable. *Why is she not scared?* "We can drop you off."

"That would be great, my darling." She smiles at me, then glances at Dominic. "Thank you."

We drive to the shop and drop Mum off as she insists on picking up her car. As soon as Dominic pulls away, I turn to face him. "Is my mum having an affair?"

"What?! No! Not that I know of." Dominic's surprised tone fills the car, his expression matching his words.

"Love of my life, this relationship won't work if you lie to me. Is my mum having an affair?" My voice is more demanding now.

"Vita Mia, I would never lie to you. I already told you I'll always tell you the truth, even if it's something you don't want to hear." He tries to catch my eyes while keeping his focus on the road, his gaze filled with reassurance. *He's not lying.*

"I think there might be something there from Elijah. I don't know what it is, but I think he's interested. We don't meddle in other people's relationships, so trust me, no one would dare look into Elijah to confirm something like this. He's special. But he's also a very dangerous man. There's nowhere you could hide from his wrath."

"I don't get it. You're saying he's that powerful, but someone actually managed to bomb you?" I pause, deciding whether to make a joke. *Yeah, a joke it is.* "Are you full of shit?" I ask, suspicious but amused.

Dominic's beautiful laughter explodes from him, and it feels like all the pressure from tonight lifts, making the car lighter by the second.

"I adore you, woman!" he says between laughs, his hand sliding onto my thigh. "I'm going to fuck you raw when we get home." The deep growl in his voice is all it takes for my core to come alive, heat spreading through me.

"Promises, promises," I mock, teasing him. Then, I place my hand on his cock and squeeze gently. He groans at my touch and tries to pull over, but I quickly release him, laughing at his immediate reaction.

"Don't you dare! We still need to talk. So tell me, why would someone bomb you? Did you give them bad information, or what?"

"You love playing with me," he growls, trying to give me a serious look, but the corner of his mouth twitches upward. "You love to get me imagining your sweet cunt, only to hit me with serious talk." He tries to glare at me but fails miserably. "You're mean, and I will remember this. Mark my words, Vita Mia. Tonight, it's edging for you." It's my turn to burst out laughing, amused by how easy it is to rile him up.

"Love of my life, serious now, tell me everything about the bomb and about Alec."

Dominic takes a deep breath, resigning himself to the fact that I just need to know all the information. It's part of who I am. I need to understand and see all the information to assess a situation correctly. *He will get used to it.*

"We had a guy on our team who had the brilliant idea of stealing code from Elijah," Dominic says, his tone heavy. "It happened a few months ago, and we're still working to contain the situation. Elijah's code in the wrong hands? Catastrophic consequences." He takes a long breath. "Whoever sent the bomb probably thought placing it on the lower levels would bring the whole building down. Turns out, the building's harder to level than they expected. I didn't know that, and I'm not sure if even Hunter, our head of security, knew about the building's structural integrity."

"Hunter, the guy I know?"

"Yeah, baby. That jackass," he adds with a smirk, but I can tell there's no real malice in his words, just a hint of brotherly banter.

"I saw him as we were leaving the City Hall. He was with an African lady. I think he got hurt."

"Really? I did not notice them. I will have to check on them once we get home," he continues in a worried tone. "That was probably Sofia. She's a witch, and I hate her guts, but she is absolutely amazing at what she does. She is our head of Cyber Security and Elijah's daughter."

"Oh, he has a daughter," I am not sure why I was surprised. *Is he married as well? I hope not because this is getting worse by the second!*

"And Alec?"

A deep sigh escapes Dominic, and I instantly know I won't like whatever's coming next. "I wish you hadn't followed up on this bit of information because I really don't know much. And... I feel like shit for what I said, calling him *no brother of mine* in front of everyone."

"Pleeeease," I plead, giving him my best puppy dog eyes. He just reaches over and pinches my cheeks. "Ouch! Naughty boy!" I smack his thigh playfully. "Now spill!"

"Fine!" Dominic sighs. "Alec is an ex-porn star. Years ago, this tycoon in the porn industry came sniffing around Elijah for help. Elijah told him to fuck off a few times, but one day, the guy brought Alec along and explained how everything was hard work, blah blah. Eventually, Elijah agreed to help protect their data. Alec, though, moved over because of his skills. He's actually really good at cybersecurity and explosives. He's part of the UBT and fought like hell to get into the inner circle."

We pull into the carpark, and he kills the engine, turning to face me fully. This conversation has given me such a deep insight into his world, and I'm grateful. Grateful that he didn't lie or offer half-truths. He answered every question, shared information, and respected me as an equal. It didn't feel like he was looking down on me or giving me information because he had to. It felt like he was sharing it because he wanted me to be part of every aspect of his life.

"UBT? Also, was he an actual porn star, or was he like editing or something?"

"Unity Bridge Team, Elijah's inner circle," he clarifies, then gives me a look. "And why does it matter if he was an actual porn star or not?"

I burst out laughing, his reaction too funny to ignore. "I've just never met a porn star before," I say, blinking my eyelashes at him playfully. "I was just curious." I smile innocently at him.

He smiles, his features softening as he joins in the banter. "As far as I know, yeah, he was an actual porn star. But he's got the brains for more and somehow ended up in that industry. When he first joined us, we used to give him shit about being an *explosives expert*, we thought it was a reference to porn."

He chuckles, shaking his head. "That was until he actually made a small bomb from office supplies and detonated it behind the building. We didn't mess with him after that. Plus, we found out his family's ex-KGB."

"Right..." my voice trails off because, honestly, I picked up on a vibe from him, but he just looked sad and dismissive. By no means did he look like Dominic or any of the other guys on the team. Clearly, he can handle himself in a fight and has the brains for all of that, but I would have never thought of the ex-KGB family and all the rest.

"I have a surprise for you," Dominic interrupts my thoughts with a wicked smile. *Oh, I know that smile. I'm definitely not walking properly tomorrow.*

"Yes... what?" I tease, but then I remember my mum pinching his bank account. *Oh, shit! I still need to sort that out.*

"Let's go upstairs, and I'll show you your present."

"Is it lingerie?" I wiggle my eyebrows at him. "Is it for me?" I give him a mock-shocked look. "Or is it for you?" I continue in a teasing tone.

He chuckles at my antics but says nothing as we head toward the elevator.

"Is it one of those thongs for men with the string at the back?" I barely manage to get the words out before bursting into laughter so hard I have to stop, leaning against the wall for support.

"You naughty little minx," he says between laughs as he scoops me up and carries me into the elevator.

"Does it... haaaave... extraaaa room... in the froooont for your... monssster coooock?" I gasp between fits of laughter, the words barely intelligible. "Youuuu... mightttt... spillll!" Tears are streaming down my face now, my mind stuck on the image of this gorgeous man squeezed into a tiny thong, looking shocked and embarrassed. It's too much, and I'm shaking with laughter, the only thing holding me up being his strong hands.

He just laughs with me but says nothing, even though through my blurry, tear-filled vision, I can see he's enjoying the moment just as much as I am. Still, he lets me revel in my own humour, knowing full well I've completely lost it and I'm loving every second of it.

As we reach my door, he stops, giving me a few moments to compose myself. He just stands there, studying me, as if he's trying to memorise the expression on my face when I completely lose control and laugh my arse off.

"I love you so much, Vita Mia," he says with such conviction it snaps me back into reality. "I love you so much it scares me." His gaze holds mine, the intensity in his mesmerising ocean-blue eyes something to behold. "There is no world I could live in where you aren't the centre of my universe."

For a second, I think, *Is the hallway really the best place for this conversation?* I've already given Mrs. Berglin more insight into my love life than she ever needed, she definitely doesn't need any more. But then he opens the door and guides me inside, and suddenly it feels like I'm not walking anymore. I'm floating into my apartment as if I've crossed over into a different reality.

As I step into the apartment, the soft glow of candlelight envelops me, washing over the room like a gentle wave. My breath catches as my eyes adjust to the sight before me, flowers everywhere. Roses, lilies, orchids, each arrangement more stunning than the last, spilling gracefully from stands and adorning the room the entire room, as if nature itself had come inside to celebrate this moment. Their fragrance is intoxicating, sweet and delicate, mingling with the warm flicker of countless candles that fill the room with a golden glow.

It's like stepping into a dream. I can barely take it all in, the beauty, the serenity, the way the candlelight dances on the walls, casting everything in soft, romantic shadows. It feels like the entire room is alive with something magical, as if the air itself is filled with love and anticipation.

For a moment, I'm frozen, speechless, just standing there with Dominic, both of us captivated by the scene. Slowly, I turn, my eyes trailing over every flower, every flickering flame, until I've taken in every inch of this unbelievable reality. And then, as I finally turn back, my heart skips a beat. There he is, Dominic, kneeling in front of me, his eyes full of emotion, the candlelight catching the tears welling in his gaze.

"Will you marry me?" The softness in his voice pulls the last grain of reality away, and suddenly, the world feels like it's spinning off its axis.

I'm speechless. I stand there, staring at him for what feels like an eternity, my mind racing but completely blank at the same time. I don't know what to say, what to think, what to do.

His expression shifts, and I can see the exact moment he changes tactics. "Fucking hell, woman," he says more firmly now. "You are marrying me."

It's no longer a question. It's a statement, a decision. The look in his eyes tells me that, in his mind, this marriage is happening. It involves me, but the decision itself most certainly does not.

"This is not up for negotiation, Vita Mia. You are marrying me." His tone is final, resolute. I'm still stunned into silence, unable to find the words. "Stop letting your beautiful mind interfere with us. What is it this time? Is it too soon? What will your parents say?"

His tone is firm, yet there's a gentleness beneath it as if he's fully aware of the weight of this moment and clearly scared of making things worse. Even on his knees, he's letting me know that this decision is already made. I feel that familiar pull to run, but at the same time, I don't want to. I want to stay. I want to say *Yes! Absolutely! I want to be his forever.*

"Whatever it is, we'll work through it," he continues, treating my silence like just another speed bump on the road of our life. "What is it?

What's your hesitation?" The concern in his eyes feels like a rusty knife stabbing straight into my heart.

He might think I'm selfish, but he has a right to know. *I love him. I truly do.* I owe him at least this much.

I take a deep breath, trying to steady my thoughts so I can sound coherent, and then I finally tell him.

"I don't want kids. Well, at least... not now." The words rush out of me, and then I let them hang in the air, waiting for them to sink in.

The look on his face is pure confusion, and I can't quite make sense of it. "Is that it?" he asks, surprised. "Vita Mia, it doesn't matter to me." He lunges forward, wrapping his arms around me, resting his head on my abdomen and cupping my arse.

"We have kids, we don't have kids. That's a separate discussion. One I'm open to because, let's face it, you'll be the one with the baby in the oven, so your say matters more." He turns and kisses my abdomen, his hands pressing me closer into him. "Separate discussion, Vita Mia. Right now, we're talking about us getting married. Baby talk can wait."

I take a few moments for myself to steady my thoughts and pull myself together. His arms around me are as supportive as his words. He could've been difficult. He could've called me selfish. He could've been an arse. But *he wasn't.*

He didn't leave the decision up in the air. He made the decision for us. When I gave him my reason, he didn't question it. He just accepted it as if it were a part of me. I start taking deep breaths, mirroring Dominic's breathing exercises. *I bet he doesn't even realise I've noticed him doing it from time to time to steady himself.* It works for him, maybe it'll work for me, too.

Once I make up my mind, I take a deep breath, clear my thoughts, and let my truth out.

"I guess we're getting married." The words barely leave my mouth before Dominic jumps up, kissing me and hugging me so tightly it actually hurts.

"There, there, love of my life," I tease, pretending to gasp for air. "You don't want to squash your wife to death now, do you?"

Dominic's beautiful laugh invades all my senses, filling me with warmth. *He is so beautiful!*

"No, of course not," he says, his voice low and full of promise. "I want to devour you. Make you mine and hold you tight to my heart, protect, cherish, dominate, and worship you for the rest of my days."

He leans over and starts doing exactly that!

Epilogue Angela

As the tattoo artist plays *Let's see which side hurts the most* with my arm, my gaze drifts over to my husband. *My husband!*

It still feels surreal to know that I'm married. It sounds crazy, and quite frankly, it is crazy, but I know with everything in me that I'm with the man I was meant to be with.

It's been six months since I met him, and everything fell into place so quickly. It felt like we were being chased by a force beyond our control.

Yet despite the whirlwind, it all feels so natural, so right, as if I'd been waiting my whole life to be with him, like I hadn't been truly complete until now.

We had the *No Baby* discussion in detail just before the wedding. I didn't want him to be misled. Well, I bundled two discussions together. The *No Baby* and the *I will cut your balls off in your sleep if you cheat on me.* He wasn't particularly keen on the second part. His words were, *I love my balls very much, so please, let's preserve and protect, not harm and hurt, please and thank you.* He's hilarious, I have to give him that. The idea of him cheating on me seems silly, but I still wanted him to know I'm not the kind of woman who'd cry over him, *I'd mess him up!*

That thought still makes me laugh. He was very surprised I was so passionate about the chop-chop part.

I want kids, I really do, but I also want to enjoy the fruits of my hard work. I've worked so hard for my career. I want to enjoy it. I want to enjoy my life with Dominic for a while. Then, I want to have his babies and embrace that chapter of my life. I'm only 23, and I deserve to enjoy my life with him. I don't think that's selfish. I've worked hard for my goals, and I'm not going to change that just because Dominic is in my life.

I'm not sure how well I explained my point of view, but when I told him my reasoning, he understood. It wasn't one of those *Let's push through this so I can get some* conversations. We were sitting on the couch, facing each other, making eye contact. Well, in all honesty, his gaze did wander to my breasts from time to time, and I called him out for being a *horny little boy*, but in fairness, I was discreetly eyeing his cock, so who am I to judge?

But he got it! He's not a burden, he's a support. He's an addition to my life who encourages me to achieve my goals, not suppress or extinguish my fire. I still feel warmth in my chest every time I think about it. I truly can't imagine my life without him. I don't think I could live without him.

"Ouch!" My voice comes out way too loud because this *really* hurts! *Motherfucker!* Is this guy using a torture needle today? I glare at the artist, trying to fake a peaceful expression, when Dominic appears next to me in a flash, resting his arm on my shoulder.

"Is today the day you want to die, Andy?" Dominic's voice is so threatening that I look up at him, and pure fury radiates off him.

"Ease off, love of my life. You know I have a low pain tolerance. It's not like he's actually using a torture needle."

"I could show him, up close and personal, what a real torture needle looks like." He looks down at me with that mischievous smile, like the cat who got the cream. "It's very effective." He holds my gaze briefly, as if asking for permission to mess poor Andy up.

I glance over at Andy, and he's practically shitting bricks. We've been getting tattoos since just before the bar exam, about four months now, and this same drama plays out every time, with Dominic exaggerating as if Andy is actually torturing me. I have a beautiful collection now, and all the scars that used to bother me are covered with stunning, intertwined designs. Plus, I've lost even more weight. Who knew sex every day would be the best workout? Well, it's not really optional, not that I'm complaining. This husband of mine just can't seem to get enough of me. *He's all over me like a bad rash since he resigned from his role at the pharmaceutical company*. He probably wouldn't appreciate that comparison, but *he is*! The acrobatic positions he "needs" to fuck me in are something else. I enjoy them, thoroughly enjoy them. *Them, him, and his monster cock!*

"It's okay, Dom... love of my life," I say with a mischievous laugh, knowing it'll rile him up.

"You like to play with fire, Vita Mia?" He leans down and peppers kisses all over my face. "I could tell them all to leave and fuck you raw right here," he whispers softly in my ear.

"It's okay. I'm good." I pat his arm dismissively, then burst out laughing at his reaction.

“Ouch!” The cry slips out before I can stop it.

"Fucker!" Dominic is practically tearing poor Andy apart with his gaze.

"My love, it’s fine."

"Like hell it is!" His eyes never leave Andy. "Vita Mia, you know I can’t stand seeing you in pain! I just can’t!" He locks eyes with me, and I can see the actual hurt in them as if someone is torturing him. "You can ask me for anything, you know that. But you can’t ask me not to say or do something when I see you hurting. I just can’t, Vita Mia." He leans his forehead against mine in that sweet, familiar way he always does, trying to gather himself. "Please..." his voice trails off.

"I love you, Dominic," I breathe out, my voice soft and sweet, reassuring him that I’m here for him, though in truth, he’s here for me. *God, I love this man!* "Show me what you picked out this time." I quickly change the subject to spare poor Andy from another near-death experience.

"Please tell me it’s not another angel with my name in a different language?" Well, yes, my husband is very original. *Not!*

"What’s wrong with another angel?" He pulls back, kisses my forehead, and goes to get the catalogue. "Since you’ve been in my life, I have a real angel. I can’t imagine a more fitting tattoo than that." The sincerity in his voice takes me aback every time. He’s relentless with this idea. It’s been four months, and he already has countless angels inked on his body, along with “My Life” in several languages. His reasoning? *You are my life, and with every breath I take, you are mine as much as I am yours. There is nothing else in my universe but you.* Who can argue with that logic? But seriously, four months? *Maybe get some skulls or something.*

"No, I’m not getting any skulls." His voice pulls me out of my thoughts as if he remembers every argument I’ve made. "And yes, I can read your thoughts. Well, I can’t, but I do remember every word you’ve said to me." He takes my hand, kisses the inside of my palm, then places it on his chest. Him and his touchy-touchy.

Two hours later, we're all bandaged up, relaxing on our couch at home. "I really love the angel from today. And the word *Nolosheyda*," I say, leaning over to gently touch his new tattoo.

"Yeah, I like it too. Hunter told me the word yesterday." Dominic's voice is small, like he's hiding something, but I know him well enough now. He'll tell me everything when the time is right.

He pulls me onto his lap, settling me sideways, then kisses my shoulder and hugs me tightly, resting his head against the back of my neck. The position isn't the most comfortable, but even so, I can feel his monster cock is fully on alert. I swallow my usual joke because I sense that what he really needs right now is this hug. It feels like he's grounding himself, reassuring himself that I'm here, his lifeline.

"You okay, my love?" I ask softly. I won't push him, but I can't sit here and say nothing when it's obvious he's not okay.

"Yes, Vita Mia. Just a lot going on at work." He sighs and kisses my shoulder again. "I have a present for you." His mischievous tone returns, chasing away whatever shadow of pain was there moments ago.

"Okay..." My voice trails off. I've received some weird presents from him in the past, so I'm not sure what to expect this time. *Like, who actually uses a metal butt plug?*

He reaches over to the side table and hands me a small, nicely wrapped box. Okay, maybe this won't be so bad. I kiss his cheek, take the present, and start unwrapping it.

It's a freaking silicone butt plug. A purple one!

"You fucking idiot!" I turn and glare at him. "I told you, no more butt plugs!"

He bursts out laughing, shaking us both with the force of it, hugging me so tightly it almost hurts. "I love you!" he screams in my ear. "Listen, Vita Mia, you told me we'd try anal, but you're scared it'll hurt. I love you! I adore you, woman! And I don't want it to hurt at all. I know I'll make you lose your mind and fuck you senseless. But you said no to the metal one, so I got a soft silicone one to prep you for my cock. Please!" His puppy dog eyes are on full display now, and they do things to my insides. Dirty, deep, and naughty things. *Oh, those ocean-blue eyes pleading with me!*

I hold his gaze for a few more moments, feeling myself getting wetter by the second. "Fine," I blurt out, sounding resigned, but in reality, the idea of having him in my ass is making me ache with need. I've wanted to try it for a while, but I've been so scared it would hurt.

I've read about it, and a lot of women say it hurts like hell. I've kept putting it off because, knowing my low pain tolerance, I figured I'd be in that category, too. But the thought of Dominic loving me that way does things to me. Naughty, dirty images of him fucking me senseless flood my mind. I can see in his eyes the moment he realises our unspoken conversation and my admission of how much I want him.

"Yes!" he exclaims, jumping up with me in his arms, his excitement palpable. "I'll eat your cunt, then your ass, and then I'll put the plug in. Does that sound like a good idea?" His playful words, mixed with kisses all over me, push me over the edge, and now I want this more than anything.

"I love it, my love." The truth and deep arousal in my voice say it all.

He makes good on his words, and three orgasms later, with a purple butt plug in my ass, we're both relaxing on the couch again, watching a movie.

"How long do I need to keep this in?" I ask. It doesn't feel bad, just strange. Dominic is a pro at eating pussy, he steals orgasms from me like it's second nature, playing my clit like an expert. The ass was another matter. I thought I'd feel self-conscious with him there, but it felt great. By the time he eased the plug in, I was so relaxed and content that I barely felt any pressure. Maybe it's just my sex-drunk brain talking, but I don't mind it at all. In fact, I kind of like it, stretching me, prepping me for Dominic.

"Until the end of the movie. I want you to feel relaxed enough when I take your last virginity." He leans over, taking one of my feet in his hands, and begins massaging it. "I'm so excited!" His voice drips with anticipation. "I'm going to make it feel so good, baby. I promise, *Vita Mia*, you'll love it. You'll see, you'll ask for more." He beams as though something magical is about to happen, and he's sharing it with me.

As he pulls me closer, I feel the plug shift. *It's probably settling in better,* I think, dismissing the sensation. "Big words, my love. Big words. You'd better deliver," I tease, pinching back for fun. "We'll see if I come back for seconds."

"I will devour you whole, *Amore Mio,* all the days of my life." He lifts my foot, licking, nipping, and sucking on my toes.

"Okay! Okay! I get your point!" I say hurriedly, feeling so hot and bothered now. I want his cock, need it. It's a pulsing, insatiable desire within me. He's definitely prepped me because the only thing I crave now isn't oxygen, it's his monster cock in my ass.

"Yes..." he trails off, his voice thick with anticipation. His eyes are sparkling with arousal.

"Yes."

One word. One sentence. One permission that will change everything.

I stand up, casually pulling my shirt off, keeping my gaze locked on his. He leans back with his hands behind his head, clearly enjoying the view. The bulge of his cock is so evident it looks like it's about to set up camp.

I pull my pants and panties down and reach back to remove the plug. But something feels... wrong. I squat a bit, reaching to feel it better, and only two small pieces of silicone come out. I pull them free, and my reality shatters into a million disgusting pieces.

The plug broke! *THE FUCKING PLUG BROKE!*

I'm staring at the two end bits of the plug that should have kept it outside of me, and they're in my hands. *Where's the rest of it?!*

OH! SHIT!

Complete and utter terror takes over. The plug got sucked into my ass somehow because these are the parts that should have kept it out!

It's inside me!

A fucking broken butt plug is inside me!

I look over at Dominic, who's still watching me, clearly enjoying the sight of me naked and touching myself like it's the best thing he's ever seen.

"You fucking idiot!" My panic and venom shake him out of it. "It broke, Dominic! Your fucking plug broke, and it's in me!"

He stands up so fast I have to step back. He looks at the two purple pieces of silicone in my hand, concern and amusement battling on his face.

"This is not funny, you fucking idiot! What kind of cheap shit did you buy? It's in me!" Panic is in full control now, every ounce of arousal replaced by pure survival instinct. "What the hell do I do?!"

We just stare at each other for what feels like forever, and then Dominic bursts out laughing so hard that his face contorts in the most ridiculous way.

"It's not funny!" I yell at him, trying like hell not to join in. But seriously, *fuck me,* this is absolutely hilarious!

All my research into anal sex, and not one article mentioned that a silicone butt plug could break and get sucked up into your ass! *Fucking hell!*

I can't help it. I start laughing with him because, honestly, I have a purple silicone butt plug stuck inside me, and that's not something you can make up.

"I'm so sorry, my angel," Dominic gasps between laughing fits. "I don't even know what to say. Do you want me to go up there and pull it out?"

“What?!! You are not going up there!” I blurt out, shutting that idea down *real* fast. “What do I do, Dominic?”

He sobers up a bit, the laughter dying down. "First, you call me by my real name and not by my given name. Then you let me see if it’s really up there."

“IT'S. NOT. FUNNY!” I yell at the top of my lungs.

“Wow! That was loud, Vita Mia.”

“You think?” I give him a mocking look. “What do I do?” There’s no way I’m calling him *love of my life* right now, he’s officially the pain of my life!

“I don’t know. I’ve never been in this situation before.”

Great! Now’s the perfect time to remember that I’m the newbie here, and he’s the experienced one. *Fucking hell!*

“I don’t know, Vita Mia. Maybe... try sitting on the toilet?” His hesitant suggestion almost makes me laugh again.

Without saying a word, I turn and head straight to the bathroom. *Maybe I can push it out...*

I close the door, turn on the tap, and sit on the toilet. I still have this habit, more of a comfort thing now. Back when I used to hurt myself, I’d turn on the tap to drown out the noise of my heaving. Somehow, I never let go of that habit. And ever since Dominic came into my life, I can’t stand the thought of him hearing me pee, let alone this pushing for dear life to get a plug out of my ass.

Fifteen minutes later, after doing a number two, I look around the toilet... but I can’t see anything.

It’s still in me!

"I have to go to the ER," I mutter to the empty bathroom. Pure panic and shame wash over me as I imagine the embarrassment of being the idiot at ER with a purple butt plug stuck up her ass. "Oh, Dominic!" I call out, heading toward the closet.

"What’s going on?" Dominic’s concerned voice follows me.

"We're going to the ER because I have a purple butt plug stuck up my ass," I say, pulling out clothes that would make me look more conservative *like that would help. I still have a plug in me. I'm not fooling anyone.*

"Baby. Baby, wait." Dominic pulls me into a hug, stopping me for a moment. I feel him trembling in my arms, and suddenly, I remember, *my pain isn't just mine anymore.* He feels it, too, and in a way that's even more intense. It's terrifying how his emotions amplify when it comes to me.

"Vita Mia, please let me touch you. Maybe I can help and take it out." His voice is full of concern, and the pleading look in his eyes convinces me. What do I have to lose? The thing's already up there. *How much worse could it get?*

"Okay."

I head to the bed and lie down on my back with my legs spread. Dominic kneels before me, pulling me to the edge of the bed, then gently pushes my legs toward my chest. His fingers are so delicate as they begin to massage around my back entrance, as if he's trying to relax me, careful not to hurt me.

Half of me is melting at his touch, in awe of how caring he is, while the other half wants to throttle him for this whole situation, even if it's not entirely his fault.

"Just try to relax for me, baby." He leans in and kisses my inner thigh. "I can eat you out again to relax you if you let me." He looks up at me with so much love. It breaks my heart a bit because he could be a dick or a dismissive dick, but look at him spreading his love and tenderness over me again and again.

"It's okay, my love." I stop and make sure to hold his gaze as I say *my love* again, letting him know I'm not angry anymore.

His gaze softens even further. He leans in and, missing my entrance, kisses my pussy instead, inhaling deeply. "I love you so much, Vita

Mia. Honestly, sometimes my chest hurts from it. I adore you with everything I am." His voice is soft, full of depth and longing.

"I love you too, my love. I'm not mad anymore." I prop myself up on my elbows and look down at him, pouring all the love I feel into my gaze. "Just put your fingers in and try to pull it out."

"Are you sure? I can prep you more."

"No more prepping, my love. Just take it out!"

He gently slides his fingers inside, one knuckle at a time. I can feel the pressure, but it's not bad, it's actually good. In a different situation, I would be thoroughly enjoying him fingering my ass, but right now, we're on a rescue mission for a purple sex toy.

"I can't feel anything, Vita Mia," he says, his worry clear in his eyes. "I don't know... I can't find it, and I'm scared I'll hurt you. Maybe we should go to the ER."

After we filled out all the forms at the ER, I had to tell the lady behind the window that I had a purple butt plug stuck inside me with as straight a face as I could manage. At this point, the shame had morphed into humour, and Dominic wasn't helping with his laid-back attitude, barely holding back his giggles. *Fucking idiot.* And it had to be purple, of all colours!

They ran a few tests, and at each one, I had to explain what had happened. *How delightful.* I did it all while throwing murderous looks at my husband, who was still trying not to burst out laughing every time I had to say it.

"You passed the plug," the young Indian doctor said calmly.

"How could I have passed it?" My disbelief was so clear that she looked taken aback, probably questioning if I doubted her skills. "I only went to the toilet once, and I checked it wasn't there."

"Mrs. DeLuca, it was probably at the base of the toilet when you first went. If the toy were still inside you, the test would have picked it up. You're perfectly fine. However, if you have trouble passing gas, stool, or experience any abdominal pain in the next week, then it could still be inside, and we'd need to perform surgery to remove it."

Well, that made me reconsider whether I believe her or not. Surgery for a butt plug? No fucking way! The thought sent my brain into a tailspin. The shame of it would haunt me forever!

As if Dominic could sense my panic, he took my hand and gently pulled me to his side. "Let's go home, Amore Mio."

The entire car ride home, I stare out the window, lost in my thoughts. *What a ridiculous woman I've been.* He tried so hard, in so many ways, to make this happen for us, and instead of embracing it, I held back. Now we've ended up at the ER because of my anxiety, not because I was bleeding out as I'd feared, but because I panicked over a butt plug. *What a stupid woman,* I scold myself.

You know what? Enough is enough!

When we get home, I'm going to make love to my husband the way I want. And by make love, I mean I'm going to demand he fuck me the way I've wanted for so long.

I glance over at him, noticing the concern etched on his face. He probably thinks I'm distant because he's done something wrong. And knowing him, yep, he's doing his breathing exercises, trying to calm his mind from racing out of control.

Once we walk into the apartment, I glance at the wall where he first ate me out. I know exactly where I want this to happen.

He's walking behind me slowly, almost like he doesn't want me to hear his footsteps. I suddenly turn and lunge at him, jumping into his arms. He catches me just in time, and I press my lips to his, pouring all my love into that kiss. His response is immediate, but he lets me take the lead, savouring the moment.

"Vita Mia..." he trails off when we pull apart, both of us breathless.

"I want you to fuck me, husband." He freezes at my words, then tightens his grip on me. "I want you to fuck my ass raw. Make me yours and hold me to your heart for the rest of our days."

In an instant, he's holding me with one arm while the other frantically tears at my clothes like a man possessed. I laugh in his arms, but when I realise he's carrying me toward our bedroom, I stop him. *No! I want, no, I need this to happen right here, in the same spot where it all started.*

"No..." I pant, and he stops dead in his tracks, worry clouding his beautiful face.

"I want it there," I say, pointing to the wall where everything began. In the next second, he's pressing me against it, supporting me with his pelvis as he yanks off his shirt, desperate.

"I adore you, wife," he growls, his voice thick with urgency and desire. "I'm going to make it so worth your while. I'll love you, take care of you. I'll make it feel so good, baby!" He lifts me with one arm, pulling my pants and panties down with the other, then quickly moves to strip off his own clothes.

We kiss like mad people against the wall as if it's the first time we've ever touched each other.

His skin feels incredible under my fingertips, but the sensation of his hands on my body is like fire coursing through my veins, awakening a powerful, delicious need for him within me.

He maneuvers me so that the tip of his cock is pressed against my back entrance, his precum searing into my skin. "Lube, Vita Mia," he blurts out urgently as if suddenly remembering a key element.

"No time, my love. Spit on him and make him ready for me."

The look of pure fire in his eyes at my dirty request makes him growl in that deep, primal way I've come to know as his intense need for me.

He does as he's told, and the moment he lowers me onto his cock, sliding inside me, it's as if all the air is stolen from my lungs. The pressure is there, as I expected, but instead of pain, it's a steady, intoxicating fullness. As he moves deeper inside me, passing the tight ring of muscle, a new kind of pleasure begins to build, slow and powerful.

"You're doing so well, Vita Mia." His words are sweet and filthy all at once, but my mind can't process them. I'm completely overwhelmed by the sensation of him inside me.

"I want more," I manage to whisper, the full sensation of him is too delicious to resist. "I want all of it in me!" My voice is tinged with desperation, the immense pleasure pulling me under like a craving for life itself.

As if on command, he lowers me fully onto him, burying himself to the hilt. The overwhelming fullness makes me forget how to breathe for a moment, the intensity so exquisite.

"You're doing so well, Vita Mia. I love you so much." His warm breath against my skin, mixed with his sweet words, only heightens my delirious state, sending the sensations inside me soaring to new heights.

He holds me there for a few moments, letting me adjust to his girth while he kisses, licks, and sucks everywhere he can reach without moving too much. "You feel incredible, Vita Mia. I'm losing my fucking mind." The raw, hungry tone in his voice makes my entire body tremble with need.

When he starts moving slowly, grinding into me rather than thrusting, those new sensations begin to amplify at a dizzying pace. The edge of an orgasm rushes toward me, clearing my mind of every thought and rationality until all of my existence is anchored to this moment, this pleasure, and nothing else.

"I love you, love of my life! I love you so much!" I kiss him firmly, pouring all the feelings he's helped me overcome into that kiss. "I love you, my love. So, so much," I whisper against his lips as we break apart, the words barely a breath.

He starts moving slowly inside me, in and out, then gradually increases his pace. I know I'm seconds away from detonating into a million pieces of ecstasy. The blinding pleasure builds until it explodes, and with a loud cry, I feel my pussy pulsing and my ass contracting tightly around his cock. My ears ring, and the sound of my own cry feels foreign to my own ears as pure, blissful pleasure pulls me under, holding me in its grip so completely that I lose all connection to reality.

It takes a few moments before I realise that Dominic has found his own release, growling with every pulse of his cum filling me. I glance up at his beautiful face, and he's trembling, not sure if he is breathing as well, but he is shaking his head in disbelief after the stream of growls and curses he just let loose.

"Fucking hell!" His voice is thick with arousal, love, and awe. "Fuck, Vita Mia!" He collapses into my arms, burying his face in the crook of my neck. "That was unbelievable. I love you so much, my angel." He tightens his hold on me, still semi-hard and deep inside.

I loved it! If I thought I might enjoy it, I was wrong. I absolutely loved it.

"That was amazing, love of my life," I confess, feeling his arms grip me even tighter, almost painfully now. "You were right, I do want seconds," I laugh, because that was beyond incredible, and I'm already craving more.

He joins in my laughter, but his grip doesn't ease up, nor does he pull back for me to see his beautiful eyes.

A tremor runs through his body, a deep shiver, and I pull him closer, burying my face in the crook of his neck. I lean in, kissing his cheek softly, then gently nibble at his jaw. "Are you okay, love of my life?" I ask tenderly.

"I'm not sure..." His voice trails off, and though I want to ask more, I hold back. I want him to find his own words. So I decide to keep holding him like this, giving him the space to process whatever he's feeling.

"I thought I knew what love was, what it felt like, but this... This feeling I have for you is all-consuming. It's so fierce, I feel it like a living fire within me, as if not touching you, kissing you, worshipping you, and fucking you the way you deserve will burn me from the inside out. It's not just my touch, my mind, or even my cock that loves you. It's the very essence of my existence obsessed, possessed, and consumed by you." His voice is so raw with emotions.

I'm overwhelmed by the sincerity in his voice and the vulnerability of his words. He takes a deep breath, pulling back slightly, and I see it in his beautiful eyes, the raw obsession, the raw passion, the raw need for me.

"I love you so much, Vita Mia, it scares me," he whispers, his voice trembling, his eyes shining with emotion. My world shatters into pieces for the second time tonight.

"I love you, love of my life. It's you and me, forever." I lean in, resting my forehead against his, mirroring the gesture of love he's shown me so many times.

This is my husband, my support, my love.

Epilogue Dominic

She is my life.

There's nothing more to say.

She's my entire universe, and every breath I take is for her.

Afterword

Thank you for walking this path with Angela and Dominic.

The Path to Dark Love was never meant to be comfortable. It was written to be felt — deeply, viscerally, and without apology. Angela and Dominic did not whisper their way into existence. They demanded space, intensity, and honesty. Writing them felt less like inventing characters and more like keeping up with two forces that refused to be restrained.

At its heart, this story is about connection in its rawest form. A love that does not dilute itself to be palatable. A bond that burns, consumes, and reshapes everything it touches.

Angela and Dominic are flawed, wounded, passionate, and relentless. And they love each other in a way that is transformative rather than gentle, in a way that makes complete sense even if we exist in different worlds.

If their journey unsettled you, challenged you, or made you feel something you didn't expect — that was intentional. Dark romance is not about perfection. It is about truth, intensity, and emotional honesty, even when that honesty is uncomfortable.

Thank you for trusting me with your time and your emotions. Thank you for staying with them until the end.

If this story resonated with you, I would be deeply grateful if you considered leaving a review. Every review helps these characters reach the readers who are looking for them.

From my heart to yours,
Karina Vega

Background story

This story began with a simple fascination: ***the idea of being able to read people's minds.***

I've always been drawn to the quiet, invisible conversations that happen beneath the surface — the thoughts we don't say out loud, the impulses we suppress, the moments where a single internal decision changes everything. I often wondered how different human connection might feel if we could truly hear what others were thinking in real time.

That curiosity shaped the foundation of *The Path to Dark Love.*

From the beginning, this story demanded more than a single point of view. Certain moments needed to be experienced twice — not to repeat events, but to reveal how differently the same truth can be felt, interpreted, and carried. Writing key scenes from both Angela's and Dominic's perspectives allowed me to explore not just what happens between them, but what happens *inside* them.

Dominic, in particular, was written with ADHD traits very deliberately. His mind moves fast — sometimes relentlessly — racing through thoughts, scenarios, fears, and possibilities at a speed that often overwhelms even him. That internal intensity is mirrored structurally in the story itself: longer chapters, layered inner dialogue, and moments of overthinking that spiral before they resolve. This is not accidental. It is meant to place the reader inside his experience rather than simply observing it.

Angela exists as both contrast and balance. Where Dominic's mind runs at full velocity, hers grounds, challenges, and steadies him — even as she carries her own internal battles. Their dynamic is not about one fixing the other, but about two very different internal worlds colliding, clashing, and ultimately learning how to coexist.

Another central element of this book is internal turmoil — the messy, intrusive, sometimes contradictory thoughts we all live with. The inner voices that influence how we love, how we fight, how we protect ourselves, and how we choose others. I wanted those inner conversations to feel raw and honest, even when they are uncomfortable, because they shape who we are far more than what we say out loud.

Thank you for stepping into Angela and Dominic's world and allowing yourself to experience their intensity, vulnerability, and emotional truth. I hope their journey resonated with you as deeply as it did with me while bringing it to life.

Also by

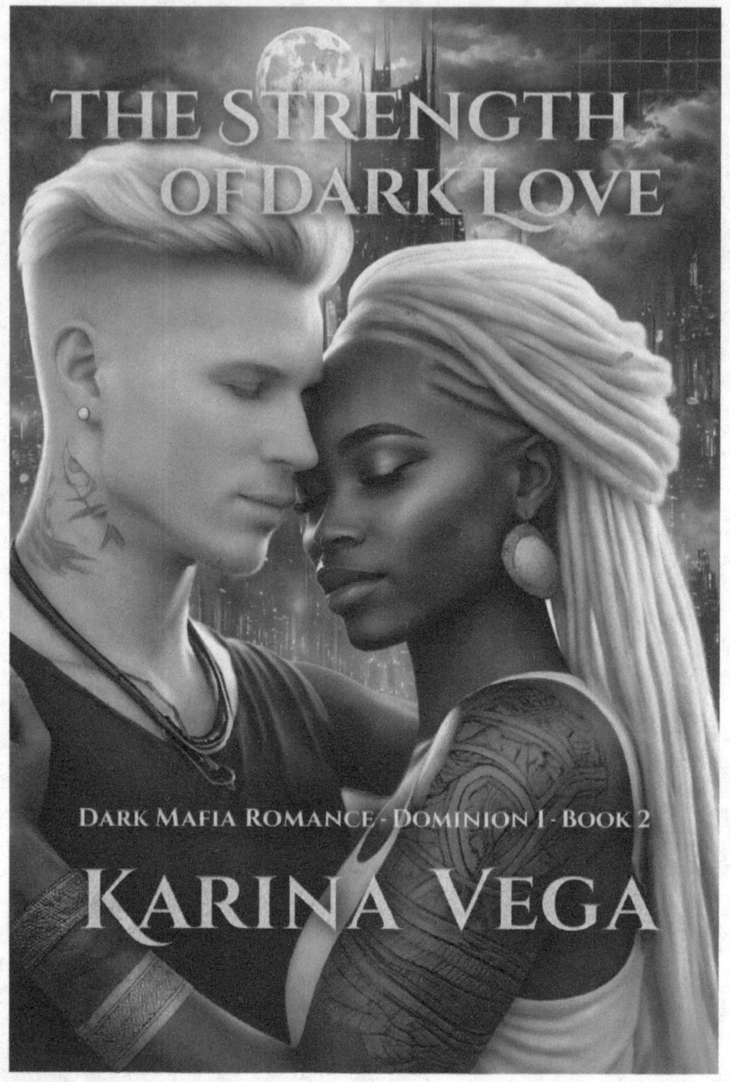

The Strength of Dark Love

What if your childhood trauma would try to define who you are?

Blurb:

Sofia

What they did to me? What they took from me? It's beyond words.

I hate men. All of them!

Except for my dad and Uncle Buddy. But the rest? They're all the same.

I promised myself at five years old, no man would ever hurt me again. Every one of them with a dick is a threat, and I'll destroy anyone who tries to hurt me. I won't be a victim again. No man will ever have power over me again.

What happened to me can never be erased. That's why I can't let anyone in. I won't!

I wish I could be attracted to women. It would make things so much easier. But then he walked in, this cocky, sunburnt Australian fool and everything I thought I'd buried came crashing back to the surface.

The first time I saw him? It was like someone knocked the wind out of me. I couldn't think. I couldn't breathe. In that moment, every defence I'd built around myself shattered, and I hated him for it.

How am I supposed to keep my distance when every day he's right there, breaking down my walls with that stupid grin, making me want what I swore I'd never let myself have?

Hunter

God, I love her! I've loved her in secret like a fool for two years.

How the mighty have fallen. Look at the big, scary SASR man trembling with desire over a little woman who doesn't even spare him a glance.

Sometimes, I swear I can feel it, maybe she loves me too. Maybe I'm delusional. Maybe I've finally lost my mind. But damn it, I love her with everything I am.

When I joined Elijah's team, I didn't expect much. I just wanted to lay low for a while, to escape the mess I'd made of my life. The world is full of fucked-up people, and I've seen the worst of them. My reality was falling apart.

Then I walked into the Security room, and there she was a goddess, staring me down like I was something stuck to the bottom of her shoe. Her eyes, sharp as knives, cut right through me. She barely said two words, but the second she took my hand, I felt it. Her hand trembled, and in that moment, I knew. She felt it, too. She was as affected by me as I was by her.

I want her so much! I need her! I crave her! But there's something between us, something like an invisible wall of concrete. Every time I think I'm breaking through, she shoves me right back on my ass tenfold.

Chapter 1

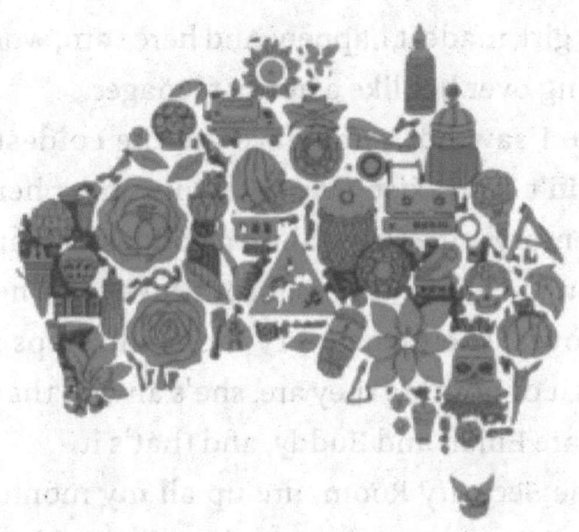

Hunter

God, I hate babysitting Dominic. I'm tired as hell, but I still make my way to the Barrow Building. I've got a few things to check on, but let's be real, I need to check on my sugar cube.

God, I miss her.

I haven't slept properly in 72 hours, not with everything Dominic's put me through. Got him drunk off his ass, but of course, the bastard sobered up and made a run for the door. I had to handcuff him to a support beam just to make sure he wouldn't disappear while I caught a few seconds of sleep.

I'm glad his woman took the leash off him. Now he can leave me the hell alone. He's pathetic, wearing his heart on his sleeve like that. What an idiot!

Who are you kidding? You could've stayed home, had your meetings online, but no, you came in, just to see her. Who's the pathetic one?

That thought knocks me back a bit because I know it's true. At least Dominic got his girl, made it happen. And here I am, working with Sofia for years, drooling over her like a horny teenager.

The first time I saw her... She gave me the coldest look I've ever gotten, like I didn't even exist. Like I was dirt under her shoe.

Fuck, that memory still stings. She's a goddess, all fire and ice. From her flawless skin to those ruthless, beautiful eyes. The way she talks, the way she moves, she owns every room she steps into. It doesn't matter who's in it or how big they are, she's always the alpha. The only ones above her are Elijah and Buddy, and that's it.

I walk into the Security Room, fire up all my monitoring software, and get on with it. Two hours in, and I'm still working, but there's no sign of my sugar cube.

Fucking hell, woman, where are you?

Another half hour passes, and now I'm beyond pissed. I log into the facial recognition software, and sure enough, I find her on the first floor, in an office in the East Wing.

What the hell are you doing there?

I watch her for what feels like hours. Damn, this woman is mesmerising. The number of times I've imagined my cock between those reality-shattering lips should be illegal. And the amount of times I've pissed her off to get her to fight me, just to catch a hint of her intoxicating scent, is ridiculous, but it works.

It took me months to figure out how to get her to touch me, and after that, I learned her fighting moves. Every time she throws her arms around my neck, her body pressed against mine, I swear it's the only thing keeping me going. Now, I get my regular dose of her like clockwork.

Sometimes, I swear she loves me back. I can see it when she trembles during our fights. But every time I back off or even try to be decent, she goes full psycho on me, and that monster inside her comes out. I don't know what the hell is going on, and I definitely haven't figured out how to make her even notice me.

I know she's not seeing anyone. I know because I've been following her for two years. Since day two on the job with Elijah. And I don't care. I'll stalk her for the rest of my life if I have to, but let's be real, I'd much rather be buried inside her than jerking off to her image on a monitor.

It doesn't matter how much I want her. It doesn't matter that I've studied her more than any assignment I had in the SASR. I've tried so many ways to get close, but nothing works. There's something there, something I can't see that's keeping her from me. And until I find it and neutralize it, this fire burning inside me won't be satisfied.

The problem is, she's smart like hell. If people think I'm a genius with computers, they haven't met my sugar cube. She's the best of the best.

It's funny, really, how small and delicate she looks at first glance, totally at odds with the fire boiling under the surface. But my sugar cube could put any man on his ass and make any demon fall to his knees. I know she put me on my ass and knees, and I would happily be there for the rest of my life as long as she is mine.

I'm lost in yet another fantasy of fucking the living daylights out of her when I spot something out of the corner of my eye on one of the security monitors. A guy power-walking out of the main entrance. He's trying hard not to stand out, but he's moving faster than the crowd around him.

I turn to study his body language as he makes his way to a car across the street, and that's when I feel it. The ground beneath me shakes. I know I've fucked up...

"Fucking hell, Sofia!" I yell, not caring who hears me, as the sound of the bomb ripples through the building. The next second, I'm flying down the emergency stairs, my heart pounding, desperate to get to level one and find her.

"Fuck, I didn't even start the evacuation protocol." I yank my phone out and punch in the P1 Emergency Evacuation code, then shove it back in my pocket. I don't need to check if it worked the loud P1 notification on my phone confirms just how badly I've fucked up.

My phone starts ringing, and I know it's Elijah. I know he wants a full report, but I don't care. I don't give a fuck. I need to get to Sofia and get her out, no matter the cost. No matter Elijah's wrath, no matter if he kills me for this.

When I push open the doors to level one, I barge past people scrambling to get out, dust covering everything. People are terrified, in shock, disoriented, and flashbacks of my deployments paralyze me for a second. The smell of the bomb mixed with the dust registers in my mind, snapping me back. My training kicks in, and I start helping people around me. I lock the door open to help people escape the building faster.

My phone rings again, and this time, it's Buddy. I sigh, relieved. This conversation will be easier than the one with Elijah.

"There was a bomb," I say, my voice sharp and firm.

"Yeah, we figured that out from the footage. Why are you on level one?"

"I came to get Sofia. She's here, in the East Wing..."

"Hunter, the bomb was in the East Wing." Buddy cuts me off, urgency clear in his tone.

Buddy's words hit me like a punch to the gut. A deep nausea rises in me. I can't lose her. I can't fucking lose her.

"How do you know?" I try to keep my voice level to not give away the absolute panic that is within me at the possibility of losing Sofia.

"We've been watching the cameras. The question is, why haven't you?"

"I ran to get Sofia," I say, my words clipped as I hang up and head straight for the East Wing. I know I'll probably be killed for this, but I don't care. I have to find my sugar cube.

The sight before me could be lifted straight from a war zone. Part of the exterior wall is gone, with debris scattered everywhere. The thick scent of dust, bomb residue, and blood fills the air, blending with the grim sight of torn body parts strewn about. People died on my watch because I wasn't paying attention.

I keep running, pushing through the wreckage, until I reach the area where I last saw Sofia on the monitors. She's nowhere in sight.

"Sofia! Sofia!" I scream, my voice frantic as I search through the destruction. "Sofia!" My voice cracks, sounding foreign to me, like a wounded animal crying out for its mate.

"I'm here..." Her voice is faint, trailing off before I can even locate where it's coming from.

"Cupcake, where are you?" I spin, desperately searching for any sign of her. "Please, cupcake, talk to me."

"One of these days..." Her voice is so weak, it takes me a second to realise it's coming from beneath a massive piece of collapsed concrete, somehow pinned to a desk. She's buried somewhere in the debris. "...I'm going to cut your balls off, you..." She breaks into a violent coughing fit. "you stupid motherfucker," she finishes, as sharp as she can manage in her condition. "Now get me out!"

"Hang on, I think there's a huge concrete slab on top of you. Are you injured? Can you move at all?" My voice is steady, hiding the absolute panic coursing through my veins.

"I'm not hurt... I don't think I am, at least."

"Did you lose consciousness?" I keep her talking, needing to know she's still with me as I assess the situation and try to figure out how the hell to move this thing off her.

“Yeah... I think I did. Now get me out!”

I finally find her and kneel next to Sofia, my heart hammering in my chest as I scan the wreckage pinning her down. The slab of concrete looks like it weighs a ton, and I have no clue how the hell I’m going to move it. But I have to. I fucking have to.

“Hang tight, cupcake,” I say, forcing my voice to stay steady. “I’m going to try and get this off you. Tell me if anything hurts when I move it.”

I can barely hear my own voice over the pounding in my ears, panic clawing at my insides. She coughs, dust swirling around her, making her look even smaller under that giant piece of debris. Her beautiful three-piece suit she is wearing is now shredded and dirty, but somehow, she still looks pristine.

“Fucking move it, jackass,” she snaps, trying to sound sharp, but I can hear the crack of panic in her voice. "We need to get these fuckers!"

I press my shoulder against the slab and push. Hard. My muscles scream, but the damn thing barely moves. My boots slip in the rubble beneath me. I shove harder, my teeth grinding together as I strain against it, feeling it shift. It's just enough for Sofia to wiggle her shoulders free.

“There you go... just a little more...” I mutter, breathless.

She tries to move, but her legs are still trapped. Shit. It’s not enough.

“I’m still stuck,” she grits out.

I step back, glancing around the room, searching for anything to use as leverage. My eyes lock on a metal rod sticking out from the debris pile. I yank it free, my hands slick with sweat and dust. I jam it under the concrete, positioning myself to try again.

“You’re insane if you think that’s going to work,” Sofia mutters, her voice weaker this time.

“I’ve done crazier things, cupcake. Just trust me.”

I throw my weight onto the rod, feeling my muscles scream in protest, but the slab starts to shift, inch by inch. Just enough. Almost there...

Then, without warning, the rod snaps with a sickening crack, sending debris crashing down. I barely have time to throw myself over Sofia before something jagged slams into my back. The pain is instant, like fire searing through me.

"Hunter!" Sofia screams, panic clear in her voice.

I grit my teeth, biting back a groan as I try to keep my body braced over hers. Every breath feels like knives stabbing into my ribs, but I don't care. I'm fine. I don't even have the strength to lie convincingly, but I do it anyway. "I'm fine," I manage, my voice strained.

"You're hurt," she says, her voice cracking.

Doesn't matter. Nothing else matters except getting her out. I push through the pain, using my free arm to shove the remaining debris off her legs. My vision blurs, but I force myself to keep going, ignoring the agony coursing through my body.

"Stop," Sofia pleads. "You're making it worse."

"I'm getting you out," I growl, using the last of my strength to shove the rubble off her. With a final push, it gives way, and I collapse onto the floor beside her, gasping for breath. My whole body feels like it's on fire, but I don't care. I got her out. That's all that matters.

Sofia slowly starts to stand, her hands trembling as she leans over me. "You idiot!" She yells straight into my face. "Why didn't you wait for help?"

I chuckle, though it hurts like hell. "Couldn't risk losing you, cupcake." My eyelids feel heavy, but I force them open, trying to focus on her face. "You okay?"

"I'm fine," she says, her eyes scanning me, filled with worry. "But you're not." She holds my gaze, and the look on her face, something I've never seen before, stirs something deep inside me.

I slowly stand, every movement sending sharp pain through my ribs. Definitely broken. It'll hurt like hell for a while.

But I got her out. She's safe.

You know what? Fuck it!

One second, I'm holding her gaze, and the next, I'm kissing the living hell out of her. The kiss is fire and ice, just like her, deep, passionate, and completely out of control. And I know, even if I kissed her every day for the rest of my life, it wouldn't be enough.

Fuck, she tastes amazing!

"That's it, Sofia," I growl against her lips. "From now on, no more games. You're mine. I'll fight you if I have to, but I'm never letting you out of my sight again."

In that moment, I make the decision. This is it! I'm never letting her go, and she will have to deal with it or fight me 'til death.

***

The Weight of Dark Love

What happens when two psychopaths come together?

One with a mask. One without. Both lethal. Both alone... until now.

This chain feel like love. Twisted, brutal, unbreakable.

A killer's devotion.

A queen's surrender.

Blurb

Monica

I need to see the beauty in what society deems perfect.

My life has been a performance, a carefully crafted mask, a well-rehearsed deception, a game played for survival. They don't *see me*. They see what I allow them to, the image they need to believe.

Because if they ever saw the real me, they'd run. They'd scream.

I thought I was alone. Destined to exist as a ghost among the living, bound by the rules of a world that has no space for someone like me.

But then I saw him.

And in his eyes, I found the one thing I never thought I'd have.

Recognition.

I've spent my entire life suppressing my shadow, burying my truth beneath layers of control. But now, faced with someone like him, someone who shouldn't exist, yet does, a question lingers, clawing at the edges of my sanity...

How can I step into the light, when I was never meant to be seen?

And how can I not, when for the first time... I'm not alone?

Elijah

I've never hidden what I am. There's no need.

Fear is a language I speak fluently, and power always bends to those who embrace their nature instead of denying it.

I was born into the Bratva, raised in blood and violence, forged into something more than human.

I never questioned my place in the world—because there was no equal. I was the anomaly. The one.

Until *her*.

For the first time, everything makes sense. Because I'm not alone. Because now, there are two of us.

Nothing worth having comes easy. To claim something truly valuable, you fight, crawl, steal—whatever it takes—until it's yours.

And what she is to me, what I feel for her, it's not love. It's not obsession.

It's the very definition of reality.

I see the beauty in what the world calls imperfect.

But to me, she's the only perfection that's ever existed.

She doesn't understand yet.

There's nothing I wouldn't do for her. Legal or illegal. Pleasure or pain. In the light, or in the darkness.

She is everything.

My first. My last.

My light. My darkness.

My final breath.

Without her, there is nothing left. No reason to breathe.

Chapter 1

Monica

It's like any other day. I wake at 4 a.m., take my coffee black and my shower cold. By six, I'm at the shop. Routine. Repetition. Nothing new.

If my life had a color, it'd be beige. A flavor? Cheap, synthetic vanilla. One word? Boring.

I'm a busy woman. Forty-two. A daughter who's twenty-two. A business to run. A charity to manage. A husband. An appearance to maintain.

On paper, it looks full. In reality, it's all too predictable. And quietly, it feels empty. I guess hiding my entire life would do that to a person.

Since I was a small child, I knew I wasn't like other people. I could feel it, something inside me that didn't match the world around me, even if I couldn't name it then. Over time, it became clearer. I am different.

School and anything academic wasn't difficult. It was pointless. A complete waste of time. I could do the work with my eyes closed, but only mathematics, science and physics held my interest.

The reason I became a florist is because I wanted to do something for myself, not something I was pushed into. And by that, I mean by my parents, to please them or the society around me.

They forced this mask on me. I won't give them my last breath of sanity as well.

They can all go and get fucked, for all I care.

I'm not sure what my parents wanted from me, but one thing is for certain, no one liked a girl who preferred numbers to people. So I was mostly alone throughout my childhood and in school, not to mention my teenage years.

The whole social aspect of life was a mystery at first. It took years to observe, to decode, to mimic what was expected of me in certain situations.

They became learned behaviour. But I got there in the end.

My mask was formed to perfection. Now I fit into this damned society like a glove. No one would suspect who lurks around them, the real person behind the smile, the polite remarks and the courteous gestures.

People don't want the truth. Not really. They definitely don't want my thoughts or real opinions.

I learned that early, thanks to my upbringing. Tried it once, earned myself beating after beating so severe I couldn't sit straight for days.

So thank you very much, but no thank you.

I adapted. I learned to hide in plain sight. It's my power now.

By the time this fire, this need, rose up inside me, I made the mistake of sharing it once. Just once. With my mother.

She was beyond mortified by my... what did she call it?

Ah, yes. Dark thoughts.

That was the moment I understood. There's no saving this. No fixing me.

Who I am — what I am — isn't meant for the spotlight. It's something to control. To contain.

So I learned... to hide.

I hide in plain sight.

Somehow, I see patterns. Events. The probability of things unfolding a certain way, it's inevitable for me. I don't force my mind to do it. My brain just works that way. Naturally.

It sees through people. Strips them bare. Past their masks, straight to their ugliest, rawest selves, as if they're offering it up for inspection.

And I've always wanted to drag that truth out. To force them, to look inside them.

To see what they really are.

That hunger's been with me for as long as I can remember.

The problem is... people don't want to see themselves. Not truly.

They prefer their bubbles, ignorance, self-loathing, pity, pride, narcissistic selves.

On and on.

And always — always — everyone thinks they're the good guy. The righteous one.

Everyone else is bad. Dirty. Twisted.

It's fascinating, really. Watching from a distance.

Analysing.

Laughing to myself at what humanity actually is.

I see how easily I could manipulate everyone around me.

The hunger to unmask, to punish, to hurt — gruesomely — is like a thirst I've never allowed myself to taste.

But it's there. Always.

And I know, no one could ever understand what I really need.

This isn't a want. It's a need.

A gnawing thing inside me. Constant. Consuming.

Still, I know better.

I can never show my true self, in my natural form, to anyone.

I have perfected my mask so well that I exude an aura of serene tranquillity.

My outward demeanour is a mask of calmness that belies the tempest raging within.

When I was finally old enough to understand myself — to recognise why I felt the way I did — Angela arrived. My daughter.

And just like that, everything had to be buried even deeper.

The darkness. The hunger.

My psychopathic instincts were forced into the background, locked in a labyrinth of shadows and deception.

Hidden beneath a carefully constructed calm.

Society's expectations taught me that I needed a man to raise my child — even if I never truly cared for the idea.

My mother couldn't bear the shame of me being a single mother before twenty.

We were a religious family. Catholic to the bone, where appearances meant everything.

In truth, it was all bullshit — and we all knew it.

So I found myself pregnant with a husband who, like all men, was boring, beige and fake vanilla.

At least we came to an understanding from the beginning. I realised I didn't need to give in to my tendencies and dispose of him once I was out of my parents reach.

We reached a mutual agreement — a façade of a marriage, and that was the extent of it.

He escaped his family, and I escaped mine by moving to England. Neither of our families could mess up our lives any further.

The moment I gave birth to my daughter and looked at her for the first time, I felt something unfamiliar.

It wasn't dark.

It wasn't flat. It wasn't indifference. It wasn't like any of my other needs.

It was possessiveness.

For the first time, I understood my version of love.

I named her Angela — after the angel she is.

There's no doubt in my mind, if what happened to me hadn't happened, my life would've taken a very different path.

I would've become an assassin.

Truly.

I despise people, and I wouldn't feel a thing ending the lives of the shit-fuckers who walk around thinking they're better than everyone else.

Life is simple.

It's black and white.

Grey is rare. But people cling to it, because admitting the darkness inside themselves? That's too much for ordinary people to accept.

I don't have that problem.

I like that I feel nothing.

I love knowing I could kill in a hundred ways.

Slow or quick.

Merciful or brutal.

With precision. With chaos.

In silence. Or through screams.

I could break a body, shatter a mind, erase a soul — and feel nothing.

No hesitation.

No regret.

Just the cold, simple thrill of control.

It's who I am.

So why the hell would I hide from myself?

I have to suppress it, for them.

But never for myself.

I accept who I am. What I am.

Society could never accept me for who I am. My family doesn't love me — never even cared about me.

But I do.

I accept it all as a gift. A rare inheritance.

Because that's exactly what it is.

Supreme genes.

In the mirror, I don't see a monster.

I see a master. A predator wrapped in silk. A phantom moving unseen among the weak.

I've embraced the truth of my nature — not with shame, not with hesitation, but with the cold satisfaction of knowing exactly what I am.

The darkness in my veins isn't a curse.

It's power.

I'm not burdened by guilt or conscience.

I don't waste time on self-loathing or doubt.

I am liberated, unshackled from the illusion of morality.

I move through the world with a clarity most will never know about themselves.

Their minds are clouded with emotion, hesitation, fear.

Mine is not.

I am a psychopath. Calculated. Precise. Free.

And the fact that I can wear a mask so flawlessly that not even my husband or daughter sees the truth?

That is the ultimate proof of my power.

I am a master of deception, a queen of control, and my strength lies in the fact that no one suspects a thing.

Angela is the only thing that matters in my world, the only anomaly that's ever stirred any kind of emotion.

Then there's the charity. A convenient distraction.

It does some good in the community, and perhaps, in the world.

Once I settled with Dan and we got married, I realised it wouldn't end badly for him.

I could fantasise about hurting him without needing to act on it.

I didn't have to kill or torture him, and that realisation was a relief.

It meant hiding in plain sight beside him would be easier.

I could focus on what truly mattered... raising Angela.

Over time, I learned more about myself, peeling back layers of forced civility, understanding the depths of my own mind.

And with every revelation, I saw just how lucky I was compared to the neurotypical masses trapped by emotions, ruled by impulses they can't control.

I am not like them. I never was.

And that is my greatest advantage.

I was in my thirties when I was finally diagnosed with Asperger's Syndrome.

It meant nothing to me. Just a label for what I had always known, a name for the way my mind worked, nothing more.

What mattered was the realisation that if I wanted to exist unnoticed, I had to refine my control even further.

I needed to sharpen my mind — to use it as both weapon and cage, containing the darkness within while perfecting the performance of social etiquette.

I opened my charity for children with ASD (Autism Spectrum Disorder) and the families navigating it.

We provide therapeutic support, psychological and psychiatric care, as well as medical and artistic programs.

I built it with my grandfather's inheritance — every cent going into its foundation.

The rest came from Dan's and my savings over the years.

So now I help children who are hiding, just like I am.

We work with over forty families, and I know there's a boy among them who is just like me.

Given the right support, he will find his way.

He will learn to navigate the world as I have.

One day, he will make a great businessman — cold, strategic, untouchable — or some kind of doctor.

A CEO runs the charity. Keeping my distance is necessary. Close proximity could become a problem down the line — and only a fool allows themselves to be blinded by a title.

Power is about control, not visibility.

As I said, my life is boring.

But it makes sense for me.

From every angle, it serves its purpose.

"Hi, Mum. I'm back!"

Angela's sweet voice cuts through the air, pulling me from my thoughts.

What time is it? I've been stuck in this damn fridge, cleaning flowers and foliage for the past three hours.

Sometimes, I wonder why I bother. Angela is twenty-two. She doesn't need me the way she once did.

So why the fuck am I still enduring this, when I could just retire and live off Dan's earnings?

I could hire someone. Make them do this tedious shit while I watch.

"Hi, my darling! How are you? Did you have coffee yet? Do you need me to get some coffee and maybe a pastry?" I ask Angela, my tone light, easy.

The fact that my heart warms whenever I see her is still a mystery to me.

In all my years, I've never met someone I didn't want to hurt in some way — except for her.

Is this what other people feel?

This absence of calculation — this strange desire to protect rather than control?

I don't want to manipulate her. I don't want to break her, bend her, push her.

I am painfully aware of how much of myself I reveal to her, careful to let her see just enough, but never too much.

She is my daughter. She should know me... to a degree.

But my words are always measured. My presence carefully calibrated, so she never has reason to fear me.

That is my greatest fear — that one day, Angela will see me for what I am.

That she will look at me and her heart will quiver with fear, recognising the cold, calculating nature beneath my mask.

That will never happen. I won't allow it. I'll make sure of it.

I will never manipulate my daughter.

But my husband is fair game.

With him, I do as I please, shaping his words to serve my purpose.

Think of it like a business transaction.

He gets his wins. And I most definitely get my own.

"No. I missed breakfast and dinner. This mock trial for finals is stressing me out. I think I lost at least ten years of my life," Angela says, plopping onto an upside-down bucket with a dramatic sigh.

"Oh, my darling! Look at my daughter, the big lawyer, beating herself up and sitting on a bucket," I say, biting back laughter at her exaggerated distress.

Neurotypical people are endlessly amusing.

So much weight placed on something so light.

"Mum, it is not funny! *State vs. James Thompson* is a big case! I was lucky my professor chose me as Lead Defence Attorney. This mark is thirty per cent of my final score. This is serious. Stop laughing, Mum!"

Angela is up from her bucket now, her voice rising as I struggle to keep my laughter in check.

Her frustration over something so small is adorable.

"I'm sorry, my darling. I'm just trying to distract you, to make you laugh," I say, smoothing my expression into something softer.

"You're going to be a great lawyer, but your greatest asset is your determination.

I have no doubt you're researching every possible way to shift the perspective, to turn the light in a different direction.

Do you think he's guilty?"

"Fuck yes! Sorry, Mum," she blurts out, quickly lowering her head, scrambling to find a more professional way to express what's already written all over her face.

"So what's the problem? Are you having trouble defending someone who's guilty?"

This is the moment I've been dreading.

Is my daughter truly mine — or is she too pure?

The anticipation coils around me like a vice, tightening with every second of silence.

The weight of her next words lingers in the air, casting a shadow over my confidence, exposing something raw within me.

My mind races. Calculating. Bracing for the impact of her unfiltered thoughts.

This moment will either draw us closer, or start building a wall between us.

I won't force myself onto my daughter.

If my true nature is too much for her, if she recoils from what I am, I'll step back.

Silently. Without hesitation.

But then, she speaks.

"No."

That single word is like a hug to my soul.

She is mine.

My daughter is mine.

She may not be exactly like me, but there is no doubt now, she is most definitely my daughter.

"I'm going to get some coffee and a pastry. Let's take a break, then we can finish cleaning the fridge together," I say, my voice even, though satisfaction thrums beneath my skin.

By the time I return with the coffee and pastry, Angela has just finished a colourful arrangement for Jake and Jack Consulting.

"Nice! Did they give you a budget to work with this week?"

"No, not really. He just keeps saying to do whatever I want because *everything I make is beautiful — just like me.*"

Angela rolls her eyes, her voice dripping with disgust.

"I feel like throwing up every time I see Jake. Can we drop them as clients?"

She makes puppy dog eyes at me, silently pleading to be spared another unfortunate encounter with Jake.

"Sure, my baby. I'll even cut off his balls for you if you want," I say with a smile, already picturing my knife slick with blood.

Or maybe scissors would be better. My flower pliers could use some bloodstains.

The thought settles something deep inside me — calming the restless edge as I picture his screams, the warm drip of blood coating metal.

"But what do I always say? What's your biggest strength?"

"My brain," she mutters, her expression sour.

She sighs, then grabs a coffee and a croissant.

"I still think he's a dick."

"If your brain is the strongest part of you, don't let trash take up space in it."

I take a sip of my coffee, watching her.

"I love you. Now go deliver their arrangement. We have a very busy day ahead, my darling."

The next hour passes as I process orders from Interflora, Teleflora and Bloomerx.

I prefer working with international companies, it minimises my exposure to imbeciles.

Or at least, that's what I tell myself.

Clearly, Jake is the exception I've not managed to shake off for the past six months.

Angela is right.

I need to drop them.

I'll work something out, pass them off to another florist who would kill for their business.

Let them deal with his nauseating compliments.

Floristry has never been about money or people.

If anything, dealing with people is the worst part of my job.

What I love is the scent.

The moment I unlock the shop in the morning and the fresh, crisp aroma of flowers and foliage engulfs me — drowning out the world.

I love the colours, the textures, the way I can shape something beautiful from nothing.

It's the closest I'll ever come to being an artist — not that I care for the title.

People romanticise flowers.

They see each blossom as a symbol of love, hope, and the endless cycle of renewal.

They fixate on the light — blind to the truth.

Flowers are not just delicate. They are strong.

They wound, they poison, they suffocate.

Beauty does not mean innocence.

I feel sorry for them.

They will never see life in its truest form — the perfect balance of beauty and ugliness, pain and happiness, darkness and light.

Stay Connected

You can find more about me on:

Website – www.karinavega.com

Newsletter

You can stay connected to me through:

Facebook page – Author Karina Vega

Facebook group – Karina Vega's Lit Lounge & Book Nook

Instagram – authorkarinavega

TikTok – AuthorKarinaVega

YouTube channel – KarinaVegaAuthor

www.ingramcontent.com/pod-product-compliance
Lightning Source LLC
Chambersburg PA
CBHW011217190726
48287CB00008B/2647
* 9 7 8 1 7 6 4 0 3 2 8 3 4 *